LIZ CARLYLE

POCKET BOOKS
New York London Toronto Sydney

This book is a work of fiction. Names, characters, places and incidents are products of the author's imagination or are used fictitiously. Any resemblance to actual events or locales or persons, living or dead, is entirely coincidental.

An *Original* Publication of POCKET BOOKS

POCKET BOOKS, a division of Simon & Schuster Inc.
1230 Avenue of the Americas, New York, NY 10020

ISBN-13: 978-0-671-03826-7
ISBN-10: 0-671-03826-5

First Pocket Books printing May 2000

10 9 8 7 6 5 4 3

Manufactured in the United States of America

To my most distinguished & learned colleagues
the ladies & gentlemen
of
The Romance Journal
who have propped me up
with faith and cheer
lo these many years.

Prologue

The golden Axe falls in Brook Street

At the advanced age of seven-and-fifty, Henry Rowland, the sixth Marquis of Mercer, was still a fine figure of a man. His broad shoulders bespoke power, his hooked nose revealed arrogance, and his tightly clenched fist showed an implacable resolve. But above all things, his lordship's appearance proclaimed wealth, for the marquessate of Mercer was an exceedingly rich one. Had there been any doubt—and among the two men present there was none—the issue might easily have been settled by a sweeping glance at Mercer's dinner attire, which gave every impression of having been sewn to his skin.

His lordship was a big man, too, standing—under normal circumstances—just under six feet, with a trim waist and calves that were still long and muscled. Dr. Greaves let his gaze slide down those legs, and ended by studying Mercer's perfectly shod feet. As with everything else his lordship wore, the shoes were the best Bond Street had to offer, with soles that were barely scuffed. Dr. Greaves could plainly see that, given his unusual vantage point.

"Indeed! Fine figure of a man," proclaimed the doctor in a solemn, carrying voice. Then, casting a furtive glance at the weeping woman in the adjoining sitting room, he poked out a tentative toe and gave Mercer a hearty shove with the tip of his boot.

As he had been throughout the whole of his life, his lordship was unyielding.

"Bloody rigor mortis setting in," grumbled the plump, elderly doctor. "Dead at least two hours, I daresay."

"Good God, Greaves," hissed the magistrate at his elbow. "Devil take you and your bad back! Get down on that damned carpet and do something!"

The doctor quirked a thick gray eyebrow. "And what, pray, would you have me do, Mr. Lyons? Lord Mercer is quite dead, you may be sure."

"Blister it, Greaves! I want him examined properly," the magistrate retorted, dropping to his knees on the carpet and striving to look solicitous. For the fourth time in an hour, Lyons felt for a pulse and found nothing. "Just be *sure,*" he insisted, glancing up from the floor. "Be *unerringly* sure that Mercer has been sent on to his great reward by natural causes, or the Home Office will make certain that I see mine sooner than I'd be pleased to!"

With a heaving grunt, Greaves lumbered down onto his knees on the floor of Lord Mercer's opulent bedchamber and began a routine examination of the well-dressed corpse. His heavy but confident hands flew, lifting this, prodding that, and checking his lordship's body for any indication of the cause of death. Nothing. Just as he had expected.

"Heart failure," he grunted, shifting his weight to rise.

"Be certain," the magistrate cautioned again, his voice a lethal whisper. "Other than a recent bilious complaint, Mercer was in perfect health."

"Do you say so?" Greaves scowled. "He bloody well isn't now, is he?"

Lyons sat back on his haunches and let his shoulders sag. *Murder in Mayfair.* He could hear the patter of avaricious street hawkers as they peddled their headlines up and down. Wearily, he sighed. "Look here, Greaves. According to the valet, his lordship suffered only minor complaints. Not a bit of him gone to fat. No excessive use of alcohol or tobacco."

"Excessive whoring mayhap," muttered the doctor, his tone barely audible.

"*What?*"

With a grim smile, Greaves looked up. "There was a New Year's Eve dinner here last night, did you not say? By chance, was the indefatigable Mrs. Lanier in attendance? Perhaps the poor devil finally fucked himself to death."

"Lord, you are disgusting, Greaves! Besides, he's on the floor."

The doctor shrugged in the way of men who have lived long and seen much. "Mercer was not known to be overly discerning with regard to who, when, or where."

"Look," said Lyons, exasperated. "All I know is, according to the valet, there was one hell of a row downstairs last night—and loud enough for the watchman to hear when he passed by at eleven. And plenty of other witnesses, too. *Wellborn* witnesses, if you take my meaning." He jerked his head toward the young couple seated together inside the sitting room, their heads leaned companionably together. "Care to hazard a guess as to what it might have been about?"

"Have you any proof?" asked Greaves, his attention suddenly engaged.

"Not precisely," Lyons hedged. "Though I cannot help but wonder why Lord Delacourt is already here, consoling the grieving widow. The arrogant bastard showed up not five minutes after I did, behaving as though he already owned the place. Which I daresay he now has every hope of doing!"

"Do not be ridiculous, Lyons," argued the doctor. "This house and everything in it now belongs to a nine-year-old child. Lord Stuart Rowland is the new Marquis of Mercer."

"*Hmph!*" said Lyons, his gaze fixed upon the sitting

room sofa. The lovely Lady Mercer chose just that moment to sob, loudly and deeply, as if her very life had ended. She then fell into Lord Delacourt's embrace, her perfect nose pressed into his elegant lapel. "Just look at that, Greaves! For whom is this little charade enacted, eh? All of society knows she hated her husband."

"Perhaps not without reason," said the doctor softly. With a strong tug, he rolled the body over onto its side to check for some sort of exit wound. Not that one could expect any, when there was no entry wound. There was no wound of any sort. No blood. Not even so much as a good conk on the sconce from the force of his fall. Apparently, the marquis's head was as hard as his heart had reputedly been.

"No wound, is there?"

Greaves shook his head. "None. Tell me, who else knows of this?" He let Mercer flop back gracelessly.

"I cannot say," answered Lyons. "All of the household, certainly. According to the chambermaid, she came up at half past three to stir the fire, believing her master to be downstairs. A bit of a suspicious tale, that. In any event, she set off the hue and cry, and someone snared the watchman just as he was going off duty."

Greaves pulled down Mercer's lower lip and studied the color of his gums. "Hmm," he said. "And then what did the watchman do? Touch anything? Move anything?"

Lyons looked at him in exasperation. "Good God, Greaves! The man was going *off duty*. What do you think he did? He dropped this muddle into the lap of the constable, who in turn sent for me. And here I am. Doing about as much good as either of those lack-wits would have done, I daresay."

With his broad thumb, Greaves rolled back first one,

and then the other eyelid, to study the pupils of the corpse, trying without much success to bestir a bit of sympathy. Still, the man was dead, and one could hardly ignore the fact. But Greaves could not see into the sitting room. He jerked his head in that direction. "Look, Lyons—what is Lady Mercer doing now?"

Lyons flicked an anxious glance through the half-open doorway and snorted. "Still hanging upon Lord Delacourt's every word, so far as I can see. The blackguard still has hold of her hands. Both of them."

"Then shut the door and let me examine the body further," whispered the doctor, deftly stripping away Mercer's cravat. "Pray God you are wrong, Lyons, but perhaps there is something more to this. There is an odd color about him which I cannot like. Mercer was the devil himself, may God rest his soul. Nonetheless, if it isn't his heart, I suppose we must know the truth."

"You may rest assured that everyone else will know it," complained the magistrate bitterly, getting up to close the door which led into Lady Mercer's sitting room. "I hold my job by patronage, and I damned well mean to keep it. And even as we dawdle here, some scullery maid or bootboy is already halfway to the *Times* with this nasty tale."

"Yes, yes!" grumbled Greaves. "A little grisly excitement for the masses."

"I don't give a damn about the masses, Greaves. It is the Home Secretary who concerns me. He'll have my head on a pike when he hears that a peer may have been murdered in my parish, and we do not know by whom, nor even how." Lyons crossed the carpet toward Greaves, pausing briefly by his lordship's cluttered dressing table. "Blast it, Mercer died of something, and I should prefer to know what it was before every rag in town gets hold of the news!"

"As should I, Mr. Lyons," murmured the doctor, absently scratching his balding pate. "As should I." When the magistrate made no further answer, Greaves crooked his head upward to look at him, noting as he did so the empty wineglass Lyons now held deftly between two fingers.

The magistrate held the glass aloft and stared through the ruby dregs, then hesitantly poked his nose into the mouth of the glass, inhaling deeply.

"What have you there?" grumbled the doctor, curiosity warring with irritation.

Lyons merely sniffed again, then squinted at the bowl, studying it intently. "Damned if I know, Greaves," he muttered uneasily, his starkly intense gaze suddenly catching and holding the doctor's. "Damned if I know."

1

A brave Officer is tactically Deployed

London's spring weather was at its most seasonable, which merely meant it was both wet and chilly, when Captain Cole Amherst rolled up the collar on his heavy greatcoat and stepped out of his modest bachelor establishment in Red Lion Street. Mindful of having lived through worse, Amherst glanced up and down the busy lane, then stepped boldly down to join the rumbling wheels and spewing water as carts and carriages sped past. The air was thick with street smells; damp soot, warm horse manure, and the pervasive odor of too many people.

A few feet along, the footpath narrowed, and a man in a long drab coat pushed past Cole, his head bent to the rain, his hat sodden. Skillfully, Cole stepped over the ditch, which gurgled with filthy water, and was almost caught in the spray of a passing hackney coach. Jumping back onto the path, Cole briefly considered hailing the vehicle, then stubbornly reconsidered. Instead, he pulled his hat brim low, then set a brisk, westerly pace along the cobbled footpath, ignoring the blaze of pain in the newly knit bone of his left thigh.

The long walk to Mayfair, he resolved, would do him nothing but good. The rain did not let up, but it was less than two miles to Mount Street, and just a few short yards beyond lay the towering brick townhouse to which he had been so regally summoned. It often seemed to Amherst that he had been summoned just so—without regard to his preference or schedule—on a hundred other such occasions over the last twenty-odd years. But one thing had changed. He now came only out of familial duty, not faint-hearted dread.

"Good evening, Captain," said the young footman who greeted him at the door. "A fit night for neither man nor beast, is it, sir?"

"Evening, Findley." Cole grinned, tossed the young man his sodden hat, then slid out of his coat. "Speaking of beasts, kindly tell my uncle that I await his pleasure."

The desk inside Lord James Rowland's study was as wide as ever, its glossy surface stretching from his vast belly and rolling forward, seemingly into infinity. This effect was particularly disconcerting when one was a child and compelled to look at a great many things in life from a different angle.

Cole remembered it well, for he had spent a goodly portion of his youth staring across that desk while awaiting some moralizing lecture, or the assignment of some petty task his uncle wished to have done. It had been difficult to refuse James, when Cole knew that his uncle had been under no obligation to foster his wife's orphaned nephew, and had done so only to allay her tears.

But Cole was no longer a child, and had long ago put away his childish things, along with most of his hopes and his dreams. The ingenuous boy who had passed the first eleven years of his life in a quiet Cambridgeshire vicarage was no more. Even the callow youth his aunt and uncle had helped raise was long dead. And now, Cole could barely remember the gentleman and scholar that the youth had eventually become. There were few memories, Cole had found, which were worth clinging to.

Now, at the age of four-and-thirty, Cole was just a soldier. He liked the simplicity of it, liked being able to see clearly his path through life. There were no instructors, no vicars, no uncles to be pleased. Now, he served only the officers above him and took care of those few soldiers below whom fate had entrusted into his care. What few hard lessons the rigors of military training had failed to teach him, the cruelty of battle had inculcated. Cole felt as if his naïveté had been tempered in the fires of hell and had come out as something much stronger. Pragmatism, perhaps?

But the war was over. Now that he had returned to England, Cole opened his uncle's rather dictatorial messages only when it suited him to do so, presented himself in Mount Street if he had the time, and appeased the old man if it pleased him to. Although in truth his uncle was not an old man—he merely chose to behave like one. What was he now? Perhaps five-and-fifty? It was hard to be certain, for like well-aged firewood, James Rowland had long ago been seasoned—but by presupposed duty, supreme haughtiness, and moral superiority rather than wind and weather.

Abruptly, as if determined to throw off the insult of age, Lord James Rowland leapt from his desk and began to pace. He stopped briefly, just long enough to seize a paper from his desk and shove it into Cole's hands. "Damn it, Cole! Just look at that, if you please! How dare she? I ask you, how *dare* she?"

"Who, my lord?" murmured Cole, quickly scanning the advertisement. His eyes caught on a few words. *Established household . . . Mayfair . . . seeks highly educated tutor . . . two young gentlemen, aged nine and seven . . . philosophy, Greek, mathematics . . .*

Lord James drew up behind him and thrust a jabbing finger over Cole's shoulder. "My Scottish whore of a sister-in-law, that is who!" He tapped at the paper, very nearly ripping it from Cole's grasp. "That—that *murderess* thinks to subvert my authority. She has returned from her flight to Scotland—she and that insolent cicisbeo of hers—and now has had the audacity to dismiss every good English servant in that house." The jabbing finger shot toward the north end of town.

"Uncle, I hardly think 'murderess' is a fair desc—"

James cut him off, slamming his palm onto the desktop and sending a quill sailing, unnoticed, into the floor. "She has cast off good family retainers like an old coat—turned them off with nothing, belike—then fetched down two carriageloads of her own servants! Hauled them all the way from the Highlands like so many sheep, mind you! And fixed them in Brook Street as if she owns the bloody place! And now—look here!"

Cole lifted his brows in mild curiosity. "What?"

James jabbed at the paper again. "*She* means to employ a tutor, and deny me my right to see that his young lordship is properly educated. Upon my word, Cole, I'll not have it! The titular head of this family must be suitably schooled. And it cannot be done without my advice and concurrence, for I am the trustee and guardian of both those children."

Cole swallowed back a wave of bile at his uncle's words. So it was a "proper education" that James sought for his wards. Did he, perhaps, wish to see the young lords ensconced as lowly Collegers, as Cole himself had been? Was that still James's preferred method of fulfilling his family duty? To cart sheltered boys off to the cold beds and sparse tables of Eton, where they might subsist on scholarship, and survive by their fists?

Cole trembled with anger at the prospect. But it was none of his business. He had survived it. And so would they. "I take it we are discussing Lady Mercer?" he dryly replied, bending over to retrieve his uncle's quill.

"Bloody well right we are," answered Lord James, his voice stern. "And that is why I have called you here, Cole. I require your assistance."

His assistance? Oh no. He would not back a bird in this mess of a cockfight. He wanted nothing to do with the Rowland family. The young Marquis of Mercer meant nothing to him. Cole was merely related to the family by marriage, a fact his cousin Edmund Rowland had always been quick to point out, since it was crucial that the dynasty keep their lessers in their proper places. *Well, fine!* Then why must he suffer through an account of the machinations of Lady Mercer?

Her husband's suspicious death had nothing to do with Captain Cole Amherst. Lord Mercer's lovely young widow might be Lucrezia Borgia for all he knew—or cared. Certainly many people held her in about that much esteem. And while they had liked her late husband even less, in death there was always veneration, no matter how wicked or deceitful the deceased had been in life. Yes, Lady Mercer's life was probably a living hell, but Cole needed to know nothing further of it.

"I am afraid, my lord, that I can be of no help to you," Cole said coolly. "I do not know the lady, and one cannot presume to advise—"

"Quite right!" interjected his uncle sharply. "I need no advice! I daresay I know my duty to the orphans of this family, sir. You, above all people, ought to know that perfectly well."

Duty. Orphan. Such ugly, dreary words, and yet they summed up the whole of his uncle's commitment to him. He could almost see young Lord Mercer and his brother being locked up in the Long Chamber of Eton now. Cole bit back a hasty retort. "With all due respect, uncle, these children are hardly orphans. Their mother yet lives, and shares guardianship with you, I believe?"

"Yes," Lord James hissed. "Though what Mercer meant by appointing us jointly defies all logic! That woman—of all people!"

Inwardly, Cole had to laugh. He rather suspected that Lord Mercer had known better than to circumvent his wife's parental authority altogether. From what Cole had heard, her ladyship was capable of flying in the face of any authority or command. Indeed, the woman whom half the *ton* referred to as the Sorceress of Strathclyde was reputedly capable of anything. Had the provisions of her dead husband's will displeased her, she would simply have set her pack of slavering solicitors at James's throat.

But quite probably the lady would have lost, for despite her own Scottish title and her status as the dowager marchioness, the patriarch supremacy of English law died a hard, slow death. But from all that Cole had heard, Lady Mercer—or Lady Kildermore as she would otherwise have been called—had seemingly forgotten St. Peter's admonition about women being the weaker vessel and having a meek and quiet spirit.

At that recollection, grief stabbed Cole, piercing his armor to remind him of Rachel. How different the two women must have been. Unlike Lady Mercer, Cole's wife had been the embodiment of all the Bible's teachings. Was that not a part of why he had married her?

At the time, she had seemed the perfect wife for a religious scholar, for a man destined to enter the church, as his father before him had done. Yes, like Uncle James, Rachel had known her duty quite thoroughly. Perhaps it was that very devotion to duty, Rachel's own meek and quiet spirit, which had been the end of her. Or perhaps it had simply been Cole's callous disregard for her welfare.

Shifting uneasily in his mahogany armchair, Cole shook off the memories of his dead wife. It should have been harder to do. What he had done should have haunted him, but most of the memories were so deeply buried that he was not sure if it did. He forced his attention to return to his uncle, who was still pacing across the red and gold carpet, and ranting to the rafters.

Suddenly, Lord James wheeled on him, standing to one side of the desk, his feet set stubbornly apart. One fist now clutched the advertisement. "You remain on half-pay?" The question was blunt.

Cole inclined his head slightly. "At present," he acknowledged.

"And what then?"

"When my leg is fully healed, I will rotate to garrison duty." Cole shot his uncle a wry smile. "By autumn, I'll be posted to Afghanistan. Malta or the Indies if I am among the more fortunate."

Lord James resumed his pacing for a time. At last, he spoke again. "Good. Then we have a little time."

"I beg your pardon?"

But Lord James did not respond. Instead, he seemed to collapse into his desk chair, looking suddenly pale and drawn. He cleared his throat sonorously. "Look here, Cole—it is like this. I simply cannot bend her to my will." He said it quietly, as if it shamed him to confess such a failing. "I have done my damnedest. Lady Mercer will not even receive me. Not unless I insist upon consulting her in regard to the children, and then her solicitors must be present. Can you imagine such audacity?"

Cole felt a grin tug at his mouth. "Shocking, my lord," he managed to reply.

As if pleased by his nephew's sympathy, James nodded, then continued. "She has spent the months since my brother's murder hiding out at Kildermore Castle, a cold, godforsaken place hanging off a cliff over the Firth of Clyde. I was powerless—indeed, our legal system is apparently powerless—to stop her. Curse her impudence! She poisons her own husband, and it would seem she has gotten away with it. Nothing can be proven. Not only is she an adulteress, she is a murderess, and now, she thinks to undermine my authority over her children!" James shook his head until his jaws flapped. "I tell you, Cole, I greatly resent it."

All you resent, thought Cole sardonically, *is that the awe-inspiring family title is not now yours.* But wisely, he held his tongue. Lord James reared back in his chair and rested his hands atop his paunch. "I simply must have someone inside that house, Cole," he muttered.

Briefly, Cole considered the point. He personally knew at least two hundred good soldiers who were without work since the war's end. Several had the makings of a good spy, but he was loath to pitch anyone into the viper's pit which passed for the Rowland family. "You require an investigator, do you not?" he mused. "To discover what happened to your brother?"

Quickly, his uncle shook his head. "No, no. Too late for that! What I require is someone to watch her. I *will* have my nephew, Cole. It is in young Lord Mercer's best interest, because his mother is unfit to raise him."

"Is she indeed?" asked Cole softly, his tone hinting at doubt.

James swore violently under his breath. "Why, she

drives men mad with lust!" he insisted. "Indeed, that besotted, brazen Delacourt practically lives under her roof now! And one has only to look at that younger boy to plainly see that he is no child of my brother's, though I suppose one cannot prove it."

"What, precisely, do you want, Uncle James?" asked Cole very softly.

"I want her every move watched with utmost care. I want her every indiscretion, her every temper tantrum, and indeed, her every movement documented." James pounded his fist upon the desk for emphasis. "And I want those boys properly educated, until such time as I can get them out of that house, and into this one. Or at minimum, enrolled in a decent school."

Cole felt a moment of concern on behalf of Lady Mercer, for James's ruthless determination was apparent. And had his uncle's concern been less personally motivated, Cole might have agreed with his assessment. From what little Cole knew of her ladyship, it was quite possible that she was not fit to parent her sons. Even he, a man who had no interest in the *beau monde,* had heard the whispered rumors of her lovers and of her husband's apparent murder.

Indeed, the tale about Lord Mercer's death was rather more than a rumor, for poison had been mentioned at the inquest. And her ladyship's rather obvious affection for David Branthwaite, Lord Delacourt, was the talk of the *ton.* Their relationship had begun long before Mercer's death and had continued unabated. Fleetingly, Cole felt sorry for the children, then just as quickly squashed that notion, too. *None of it was his concern.* No one had felt sorry for him when he had been left in similar straits—nor had he wished them to, he inwardly insisted.

Cole looked up at his uncle and spread open his hands in a gesture of helplessness. "I see your predicament, my lord. I wish I could be of some service, but this is clearly no matter for a military man."

"You misunderstand me, Cole. What I want is a tutor."

"A tutor?" Cole lifted his brows inquiringly.

"Good God, Cole!" James laid his palms flat upon the glossy desktop and leaned halfway across it. "How plain must I make my meaning? I want *you* to answer Lady Mercer's posting. I want *you* to apply to her in Brook Street. And who could be more qualified? You are a brilliant scholar."

Cole drew back in his chair. "Absolutely not."

"Cole, please understand. If you cannot do this for me, think of young Lord Mercer. He is left at the mercy of that—that *harridan*. The child is your cousin, for pity's sake."

"I am sorry to disabuse you, my lord—but neither of those children is any kin of mine."

Lord James's breath seized, as if he had been stabbed in the back. His dark eyes narrowed. "After all this family has done for you, Cole, you cannot know how those words wound me. These boys are mere babes. How can you be so selfish, when you have had the advantage of the best schools? Eton, Cambridge, King's College, for God's sake! Your academic achievements are nothing less than stellar. Moreover, you have a vast deal of experience in educating young men of good families."

"I am now a cavalry officer, sir. A return to teaching is utterly out of the question. I am no longer fit to be a companion to young men of good families. And more to the point, Lady Mercer would never agree."

"Cole, sometimes I despair of you, my boy! I truly do! You must not *tell* Lady Mercer who you are! It has been ten years or better since you met her—and in any case, I cannot imagine she would have troubled herself to remember *you*. Besides, war has aged and hardened you a bit."

Oblivious to the insults he had just leveled, James held out his hands as if the matter were settled, and only the details wanted ironing out. "We shall dissemble your credentials just enough to explain away your years in the army," he continued. "And of course, I shall make certain that your references can be verified—"

"It is out of the question, my lord," Cole interjected. He rose abruptly to his feet, pulling out his father's gold watch as he did so. "I regret that I must take leave of you, sir. I am engaged to dine at my club with Captain Madlow at half past."

James jerked his impressive girth from the chair and circled around the desk. "Cole, you owe me this. Far be it from me to remind you of all that I have done for you, but look at the facts—"

Cole threw up a hand to forestall his uncle. "The only fact which matters to me is that you propose to do something deceitful. I must assume that your usual good judgement has been exhausted by your concern for the children. Were it otherwise, I am persuaded you would never propose such a thing."

"Cole, Cole!" James let his face fall forward into his thick fingers. "Have you no gratitude?"

"Yes, my lord. I am exceedingly grateful. And yes, I do care about the innocence of children. God knows I lost my own innocence rather too soon. I am sorry that my—my *cousins* have lost their father under such unfortunate circumstances. But I do not choose to teach again, and I shan't be wheedled into misrepresenting who and what I am."

Suddenly, the door to his uncle's study drew open with

such force that the candles upon the desk very nearly guttered out.

"Upon my word, it is Cousin Cole!" said a deep, overly polished voice from the doorway. "What a delight." His cousin Edmund Rowland strolled casually toward the desk, his hand extended limply in greeting. "Father failed to mention your coming, dear boy. Are you to dine with us?"

Cole stared down his nose at his uncle's dandified son. "No, Edmund. I thank you, but I am otherwise engaged."

"Yes, well!" Edmund gave a neat little tug on his shirt cuffs. "I am sure you must be exceedingly busy, what with your . . . well, with whatever it is you military fellows do when there are no infidels in want of killing!" He laughed uproariously.

"Oh, shut up, Edmund," said James on a resigned sigh. "And sit down if you plan to stay. Cole and I are discussing what is to be done with Lady Mercer."

Edmund's thin, black brows flew up at that. "Oh, dear Cousin Jonet! Why, I know perfectly well what I should like to do with such a lively wench as she." He beamed insinuatingly, showing his perfect white teeth, then slid into the chair next to Cole.

James hissed aloud. "The children, you dolt! What is to be done with her children!"

"Why I hardly think I care, Father." Edmund turned a sarcastically inquiring glance upon his sire. "Indeed, I find the lot of them rather inconvenient. Do not you? Two small boys standing in the way of all that wealth and power? *Tsk, tsk!* Damned inconvenient—that is what my lady wife says." He looked at Cole, flicking his gaze up and down, then settled on Cole's red and gold regimentals. "Though what business it is of yours, Cousin, I cannot begin to imagine."

"Precisely my point," said Cole, trying to keep the muscle in his jaw from twitching. He stood, still half turned toward the door, and yet suddenly hesitant to leave. He wanted to leave, did he not? Setting aside his uncle's insulting request, Cole avoided being in the same room with Edmund whenever possible. Still, something in his cousin's snide tone held Cole's boots fast to the carpet. Just what it was, he could not say. Edmund was always malicious.

"I have asked Cole to go to Brook Street as tutor to Stuart and Robert," said James impatiently. "We are discussing the particulars."

Edmund barked with laughter. "Half-pay caught you a bit short, old boy? I would be better pleased to go to the devil myself. I can hardly envision your return to academia, but then, one must earn one's crust, and the war does indeed seem to have ended."

"I shall go to Brook Street tomorrow," said Cole abruptly, turning to hold his uncle's stunned gaze. It seemed as if the words were spoken by someone else, and yet they tumbled forth with perfect clarity. "I shall wait upon Lady Mercer at three, if that is convenient to her schedule. You will send word of my purpose in coming, and ask her permission for me to do so. You will explain to her my credentials—including my military service."

"I—yes, I suppose . . . ," answered James with uncharacteristic docility.

Cole crossed his arms over his chest. "Moreover, Uncle, it is your burden to persuade her to accept me, for I shall not bully her. Nor shall I lie. Nor shall I spy for you. Is that understood?"

"I—well, I do not know." James slid a beefy hand down his face. "I am gravely concerned . . . about the children."

Suddenly, Edmund leapt from his chair. "Why, what

nonsense! You cannot send him! Cole has no business in this! None whatsoever."

Cole ignored his cousin, focusing his full attention on his uncle's increasingly florid visage. "I shall see to the children, my lord. Rest assured that I shall have only their best interests at heart. That is your concern, is it not?"

He waited for his uncle's reluctant nod before continuing. "Should I observe anything which is inappropriate, unsafe, or unseemly, I will discuss it with both you and Lady Mercer at once."

"Discuss it with *her*?"

Cole would not be swayed. "That is only fair, do not you agree, since you hold joint guardianship?"

James scratched his jaw hesitantly. "Cole, I am not perfectly sure that will serve . . ."

Cole went to the door and laid his hand upon the brass handle. "I realize, my lord, that this is not quite what you wanted, and I am sorry for it. This is all I have to offer. Consider it until tomorrow morning, and if you can think of someone who can better do the job, I shall be all gratitude."

Cole was halfway down the steps in the pouring rain when he realized he had walked right past Findley, who had been holding his coat and hat. As if to remind him of his folly, a cold drop of water trickled off his hair and slithered behind the facing of his collar, sending a shiver down his spine.

Now, what the devil had he just done? And why? Cole turned around to run back up the steps, wondering if perhaps he had taken grapeshot to the head instead of the leg.

The sun had barely risen over Mayfair when an urgent knock sounded upon the door to Lady Mercer's private parlor, a small but elegantly appointed sitting room which connected her bedchamber to that of her late husband. For a moment, Lady Mercer did not respond, so engaged was she in staring over her writing desk and through the window into the quiet street below. Lightly, she laid a finger to her lips, then took up her quill once more. The knock came again, heavier this time.

Lady Mercer sighed deeply. Apparently, there would be no escape into solitude today. "Come in," she finally said, pushing back her chair and standing.

Her butler entered, wavered uncertainly in the door, then hastened forward, a small silver salver extended. "A message, milady," said Donaldson in his faint Scots accent. "I asked that the boy wait belowstairs, should y'wish tae send a reply."

Jonet Cameron Rowland, Marchioness of Mercer, Countess of Kildermore, Viscountess of Ledgewood and Baroness Carrow and Dunteith, inhaled sharply. "From whom?"

Donaldson watched her sympathetically. "I regret tae say 'tis Lord James again, milady."

Lady Mercer snatched the note from the salver. "You say his servant waits?" she asked darkly.

"Aye, but in the kitchens!" Donaldson threw up his hands, palms out. "Cook will'na let him from her sight, she swears it."

With a terse nod, Lady Mercer went to her desk and took up a heavy gold paperknife, delicately carved into the Celtic cross of her ancestors. With a flick of her wrist, her ladyship laid open the letter and held it across the palm of her hand as her eyes darted over it.

She was a willowy, delicately boned lady, with hair as black and slick as a raven's wing. In her girlhood, she had been considered a great beauty, but age and experience had stripped much of the vivacity from her face, leaving in its place an intense, almost cold, wariness. One could see it in the wide, expressive blue eyes, which were quick to narrow, and in her full, mobile mouth, which was more often than not drawn into implacable lines.

Lady Mercer's gaze was steady and certain, and capable of pinning a careless servant to the wall like the hurl of a corsair's blade. Moreover, her wit was as quick as her temper, and she did not suffer fools—gladly or otherwise. After two children and eight-and-twenty years, Lady Mercer still had a figure to turn a man's head, while her cutting expression could just as quickly snap it back again, should she wish it. With her patrician forehead, elegant cheekbones, and fair, flawless skin, she looked every inch the *Gāidhealach* aristocrat, and she was.

There were many who thought Lady Mercer proud, brash, and volatile, and of late, a few had callously added the term *cold-blooded* to her emotional repertoire. Whatever she was, she was much as life had made her, but by virtue of their many years of close companionship, Donaldson was also aware of a few things which were not commonly known of his mistress. That she could be generous to a fault and unfailingly devoted to those whom she trusted.

Woe betide her enemies, but those whom she loved, she loved deeply and faithfully. All of this despite a life that was very different from the one that she had wished for.

Donaldson stood stoically to one side, watching as the dull black bombazine of Lady Mercer's skirt began to tremble. At once, her eyes began to blink spasmodically and her knuckles went white. Across her hand, the letter began to quiver. Tension thrummed through the parlor like a gathering storm.

Prudently recollecting that one word—*volatile*—the butler narrowed one eye and drew back incrementally as her ladyship hissed like a cornered cat, seized up her inkhorn, and hurled it viciously against the hearthstone with a bloodcurdling scream.

"Roast in hell, you black-hearted bastard!" she exploded, dark ink splattering up the pale pink marble of the mantel.

"Milady!" Donaldson laid a gentle, steadying hand upon her trembling forearm. "God in heaven, what now?" Gently, he dragged her toward the small sofa near the fireplace and urged her down.

Lady Mercer sank onto the proffered seat and handed the letter to him. With eyes that were momentarily horrified, she looked up at him. "A *tutor*, Charlie," she whispered, her voice suddenly breaking. "He sends a tutor for my children! He shall force his way into this home by whatever means possible. What are we to do?"

Charles Donaldson went down onto one knee beside her and skimmed the letter. "I think . . . I *think*, milady, that we can fight this." The young Scotsman looked up to hold her troubled gaze. "Shall I send a footman tae fetch McFadden? Or one of the other solicitors?"

Lady Mercer swallowed. "I do not know," she admitted wearily. "I am sick to death of all this bickering! I advertised for a tutor, and heaven knows the boys need one. We cannot go on as we are, acting as if life as we knew it has ended."

"Aye, but sich a one would be a stranger tae us, Lady Jonet," he softly cautioned, reverting to her old name. "What d'we know of this man?"

"Nothing good," she answered grimly. "James is sending a snake into our midst. Depend upon it."

"Shall I have the footmen send him packing then,

milady?" inquired the butler. "It says he's tae come at three o'clock."

Lady Mercer grasped the letter in both hands, crushing it to her lap in obvious frustration. "No, don't send him away, Charlie." She rallied again, just as she always did, stiffening her spine and pulling back her narrow shoulders. Her deep voice returned to normal, with its hard edge and faint burr. "Undoubtedly he is nothing more than one of James's henchmen, and therefore only minimally qualified. Once I have met the fellow, perhaps I can unearth some shortcoming, and find a better candidate. Even James cannot argue with that."

"Verra good, milady." Smoothly, Donaldson stood. "You look a wee bit drained. May I send Miss Cameron to attend you?"

Her lips tightly compressed, Lady Mercer stood and shook her head. "No, I thank you. Cousin Ellen cannot understand me when I am blue-deviled. I'll do naught but distress her, and you know that as well as I."

"Aye, milady." Donaldson could not help but smile. "Ye might at that."

As was his custom, Cole rose at dawn to throw on his clothes and saddle his horse for a long morning ride. Shunning the more fashionable environs of town, he ignored Hyde Park and everything in between, riding north instead, up Gray's Inn Road and into the countryside. On this particular day, he pushed his horse hard for almost an hour, turning toward home only when the need for breakfast compelled him to do so.

Despite Cole's admittedly academic bent, he had always done his most serious thinking from the back of a horse. Today it was not working. Halfway through St. Pancras, with all of London now stirring about him, Cole still had no notion why he had agreed to his uncle's mad, self-serving scheme. What had he been thinking? Just what did he hope to achieve?

Oh, matters were a bit dull within the army just now, it was true. But there were things to do. His club in Albemarle Street, the two or three academic societies to which he still belonged, and an occasional trip to the War Office to chat up old friends. Reading his scientific journals, writing letters to inquire into the welfare of his former men, and every evening, a little drinking in the local public house, which was filled at night by an eclectic mix of actors, students, and poets, along with a great many men such as himself, old soldiers with too much time to spare.

Well—! The truth always slipped out in the end, did it not? The fact was, Cole was just dead bored with his life. After hobbling about Paris for three months, making minimal contributions to the peace effort, he had returned at last to London—how long ago? Seven months? He counted on his fingers. Yes, and damned dull months they had been, too.

His splintered thigh was solid once again, and the few shards of metal which were destined to work their way out had long since done so. Cole knew he was fortunate to have broken the bone in a fall from his horse, and that the grapeshot had been glancing and secondary. Better men than he had lost a leg to amputation. Almost a year later, only a few scars and the occasional ache remained.

And now, he no longer had any excuse to avoid going home. Home to Cambridgeshire. Home to Elmwood Manor, the estate he had not seen since leaving England before the war. As manor houses went, it was hardly a grand place. It appeared to be early Georgian, with two small but well-balanced wings, but from the rear gardens, one could see a goodly portion of the original Tudor structure. Long ago, perhaps in his great-great-grandfather's day, Elmwood had been a vicarage. Indeed, it was still referred to as such by the villagers, because for a hundred years or better, even after the house itself had been sold by the church, someone within the walls of Elmwood had served them as vicar of Saint Ann's. But no longer.

That was yet another of life's crossroads which Cole had managed to circumnavigate. For a time after leaving his position at Cambridge, he had acted as curate, with every good intention of stepping into the pulpit at some future date. But in the end, he had chosen muscular Christianity over the more pastoral sort, and had resolutely beaten his plowshare into a sword.

Cole still was not perfectly sure why he had done it. He knew only that he had felt driven to join the army; driven toward war by an emotion he could not name. Patriotism, he had called it at the time. Certainly, he had not done it for financial gain. His officer's commission had been expensive, and he had had a wife at home for whom to provide. And although Cole was far from being a rich man, his mother's marriage settlements had provided him a steady income upon his twenty-fifth birthday and his father had left him Elmwood Manor.

Elmwood consisted of a small home farm and five tenant properties, whose holders tilled the same land their fathers and grandfathers had before them. Since the war, Cole had taken the unheard-of step of leasing the whole of it, parceling the home acreage into fifths, and giving it over to his trusted tenants. The manor, for all practical purposes, now ran itself.

Three months past, unable to reconcile himself to the

thought of going home, he had sent along Moseby, his orderly, to look things over. All was well, according to Moseby's infrequent reports. Cole's plan to follow shortly thereafter had come to naught. And now, he had to admit to himself that he had no wish to return.

Cole spent the remainder of the morning at his club, taking a late, leisurely breakfast and debating with his cronies the state of the empire's residual military strength. But as always, Cole came away a little empty, finding himself unable to fully savor the morning despite the intellectual stimulation it afforded him. Such occasions merely served as a poignant reminder of those men who had been left in the ditches of Portugal. Good officers and valiant men who would never again argue field strategy, never again take up arms for their king.

Other men seemed to accept such things more readily, and Cole often suspected that his scholarly devotion to religion and philosophy had left him singularly unsuited for an officer's life—or at least unsuited to the aftermath of such a life.

Eventually, Cole returned to his rooms to catch up on correspondence, and then, with unerring care, he shaved and dressed for his meeting with Lady Mercer. He was half reluctant, and yet more than a little curious, to meet the lady once again after all these years. Although Cole was certain she would not remember him. No, she would not. Would she?

He presented himself in Brook Street, only to find that he had arrived a quarter hour early. Cautioning himself that it would not do to wait upon the marchioness betimes, Cole resolved to spend his excess energy in pacing further up the street, then turning the corner to stroll through the mews behind. Like any good military man, he reconnoitered the establishment from all angles as he went.

It was a typical Mayfair townhouse, though somewhat larger than most. Four rows of deep windows across the front, a service entrance below the ground floor, a narrow, well-shaded backyard with an elegant garden, and a row of fourth-floor servant's dormers in the rear. Opposite the yard lay the mews. The quarters could probably house two carriages and provide accommodations for another half dozen servants.

On this side of the alley, no one stirred. But in the back garden, a servant lingered, a huge, red-haired fellow, who was rather aimlessly hoeing about in a freshly turned flowerbed, seemingly unaware that he had just trod across a swath of spring daffodils. At Cole's approach, the man tensed and lifted his eyes to stare malevolently across the low fence at him. The message was clear. Cole touched his hat respectfully and moved on past the garden gate. Lady Mercer's servants, it would appear, were not the sociable sort.

"*Psst*, Stuart!" In a sunny shaft of dust motes, Lord Robert Rowland stood, tugging plaintively upon his elder brother's coattail, nearly yanking him off the crate on which he perched. Precariously balanced on his knees, Stuart, Lord Mercer, shook off his pesky young sibling, then stretched up to meet the high attic window, peering out over the dusty sill.

"Quit jerking, Robin!" he cautioned his brother, looking down from the crate over one shoulder. "If you make me fall, Nanna shall hear it, and we'll both be put to bed without supper!"

Standing on tiptoes, Robert pulled a pitiful face. "But what's that fellow in the mews doing now, Stuart? Let me up! Let me up! I want to see, too!"

Stuart turned back to the window. "He's just walking around the back." The boy grunted a little as he tried to scrub the grime from the glass with his coat sleeve.

"Hey, Stuart, d'you think he might be a spy?" asked Robert eagerly. "D'you reckon he's the fellow who poisoned Papa? Perhaps we could trap him and catch him, if he's the one."

Stuart looked down with a scowl. "Shut up, dolt! We're not to know about that! And this fellow in our mews is an army officer, I told you already. They just shoot the enemy. They don't have time to go about poisoning folks in their bedchambers."

But Robert was desperate for a little excitement. "Well, can you tell if he's spying on us? Maybe that's what he's up to?"

"He's snooping a bit, but he isn't spying!" reported Stuart from his perch. He leaned closer to the window. "Anyway, I don't think he's the fellow who's to come this afternoon. Not wearing those fancy regimentals."

"What regiment is he from?" asked Robert enthusiastically, trying harder to scrabble up beside his brother.

Stuart hesitated, and Robert knew why. The sighting and identification of all things military was a source of constant dissent between the boys. And despite his being the younger, Robert accounted himself more of an expert in the field. His collection of toy soldiers was vast, much loved, and intently studied.

"*Umm . . .* ," Stuart hesitated. "Life Guards."

At last, the smaller boy succeeded in scrambling up and squeezing into the dormer with his brother. He sighed sharply. "Oh, Stuart, you are an *ejit* and that's a fact! That fellow there is a *Royal Dragoon.*" Robert pronounced the words with the same awe one might reserve for the heavenly host.

"Is not," retorted Stuart, clearly affronted.

"Is too!" insisted the younger boy. "And that's what I call a proper coat, too! D'you see any cheap brass buttons stuck all over it? No. And the trousers, Stuart! They are not at all the same."

"Oh, it's Life Guards and I know it," insisted his lordship haughtily.

"Oh, Stuart! You are such a—a—" Lord Robert groped desperately for the new phrase he'd overheard in the stables yesterday afternoon. "A horse's *arse!*" he bellowed triumphantly.

"Am not!" answered Stuart. "And you are just a—a *dog turd.* A scrappy little dried-up dog turd."

"No, I'm not!" wailed Robert, outraged.

His brother narrowed his eyes. "Are too!"

"Horse's arse!"

"Dog turd!"

"Horse's arse!"

"Dog tur—*yowch!*"

Abruptly, a meaty fist reached out and dragged his most noble lordship rudely backward off his perch. "Aye, an' just what d'ye think yer aboot, my fine fellow?"

"Nanna!" cried the boys in unison.

"Doon't 'Nanna' me, my laddies," the plump old nurse said grimly, grabbing up Robert in the other hand and giving him a little shake. " 'Tis no good yer up to, plain enough. Now, doon the stairs, w'the both of you, and we'll see if there's tae be any supper."

2

After long years, How should I greet Thee?

Perhaps it would have eased Cole's mind had he known that his visit to the tall brick townhouse in Brook Street was as unwelcome an event from within as it was from without. But he did not know it, and as he laid his hand upon the cold brass knocker at precisely two minutes before the appointed hour, his faint curiosity began to give way to a grave sense of uncertainty, which was further heightened by the hollow echo of the knocker dropping onto the wood.

After a long moment, the door swung noiselessly open to reveal not one but a pair of ruddy-faced footmen, and not the tall, handsome sort of fellows that one would normally associate with the finer homes of London. The decidedly elegant gray and maroon livery aside, it appeared that the Marchioness of Mercer employed a couple of former pugilists as household servants.

"Aye, wot 'cher want?" grumbled the first, his language a dead giveaway. Apparently, Lady Mercer really didn't give a damn about who opened her fine front door. Strangely enough, Cole's assessment of the lady went up a notch.

With military precision, Cole whipped out his card. "Captain Amherst to see her ladyship," he announced, shifting his weight forward to step into the hall.

"Aye, 'old up just a bloomin' minute, gov'!" said the other, planting a handful of beefy fingertips in the middle of Cole's chest. The footman glanced to his right where his sparring partner stood, squinting at Cole's card. Together, they looked it over, silently mouthing the words. "Cap'n *Am*-Erst, eh?"

"Yes, and I believe I am expected," said Cole, striving to keep a straight face. "You might just drop that card onto a little tray, take it up to her ladyship, and put an end to your troubles."

"Oh, our *troubles,* is it?" The footman with the card flicked a rather suspicious look up at Cole. "An' just wot would yer be knowin' about 'em, sir?"

Cole glanced back and forth between them, more than a little confused. The second pugilist seized upon his hesitation. "No soldiers s'pected," he announced, moving as if to shut the door in Cole's face. "An' the 'ouse is still in mourning."

Cole should have been relieved by their refusal to admit him. In fact, at that very moment, had he possessed one grain of sense, he would have accounted himself the most fortunate of men, turned on his heel, walked right back down to Pall Mall, and gotten himself cheerfully drunk. Unfortunately, there was just enough muscular Christianity left in him to resent the affront to his dignity.

"I am expected," he insisted, in the tone of a man who was accustomed to seeing soldiers snap to his command. "I come at the behest of Lord James Rowland to wait upon Lady Mercer. Now if you would be so good as to take my card and go up those stairs with it, I am sure all will be revealed to you!"

Invoking James's name was a dreadful error. Eyes bulging, both men shifted their weight forward onto the balls of their feet, but Cole was saved from an almost certain death—or at least severe dental damage—by the sudden appearance of a tall young man in butler's garb.

"Why, here now!" he said in a light brogue. "What's all this trooble?"

"Gent 'ere says he's to see 'er lay'ship, Donaldson," answered the first footman a bit defensively. "I tole him she weren't receivin' but I reckon 'e finks 'e can stroll on in."

"Right," the second footman chimed in. "Claims ter be another o' that Lord James's chaps wot keeps coming 'round ter bother 'er la'yship."

Donaldson's eyes skimmed down Cole's length, mild surprise lighting his expressive blue eyes. "Gads!" he said softly. "Are *you* Amherst?"

Despite the fact that for the first eighteen years of her life Lady Mercer had been an innocent, provincial miss, she realized that she had become—out of necessity—a woman who was rather indurate and cold. At times, her very heart felt like a chunk of winter's ice that had been hacked from a frozen pond, packed in sawdust, then dropped into a deep, dark pit for storage. After a decade of such an existence, she was now rarely caught unprepared by anyone or anything, and certainly not by the vagaries of fate.

Nothing, however, could have prepared Jonet for the man who came striding down the hall toward her drawing room at five minutes past three on that fateful afternoon. She had expected a man to arrive, certainly. Someone who would look at least marginally like a tutor of young men, she had assumed. But from the very first, she had doubted that Lord James's lackey would be the usual impoverished Milquetoast of a fellow in a rumpled frock coat and a scraggly haircut.

Well—at least she had gotten that much right, Jonet weakly decided, watching her caller walk inexorably nearer. With a gait that was long and lean-hipped, Cole Amherst moved with his shoulders set rigidly back, his heavy boots echoing through the corridor. He wore the fine red coat of a

Dragoon's officer, turned back into facings of midnight blue, and covered in a shade of gold which perfectly matched his hair.

As he paused formally at attention in the frame of her doorway, the army captain looked more like a work of portraiture than a man of flesh and blood. As if the painter, in the way of some so-called artists, had looked at a normal man, then imbued him with all the artistic license reality might allow. Amherst's shoulders were just a little too broad, his jaw too elegantly chiseled, and his chin too deeply dimpled to belong to a mere mortal. And his mouth! Sinfully full, rich with promise and passion, Amherst's mouth was that of a profligate, yet Jonet was sure he was anything but.

He was tall, too. At least six feet, and most of it looked to be legs. Long, lean, very fine legs that seemingly went on forever. Or was it chest? Jonet swallowed hard again. Yes, there was a great deal of chest there as well. Her eyes skimmed up his length. Only a brow which was lightly furrowed and a nose which was a touch too aquiline saved Captain Amherst from what might have been ruinous beauty.

Jonet had told herself she would not stand when James's spy entered her drawing room. She had schooled herself to be as haughty and disdainful as her late and unlamented husband had unwittingly taught her to be. She was a lady, she tried to remind herself. Moreover, she was this man's superior. And yet, curiosity got the better of her. Jonet was out of her chair and halfway across the drawing room before Charles Donaldson finished announcing him.

"Captain Cole Amherst, my lady," he said, pulling shut the door with a hearty thump.

Jonet was not sure just how long she stood in the center

of the drawing room ogling the strapping, golden-haired officer. As she stared, Amherst swept out of a graceful, fluid bow, drawing back one of his very fine legs with an elegance befitting the Regent's court. His warm, golden gaze flicked up at her. "Lady Mercer?" Amherst's voice was rich, and it held a hint of dry humor. "I find myself at your service, ma'am."

His lightly mocking tone served to jerk Jonet back to cold reality. A purposeful rage swept over her like a brush fire. "Why, how droll you are, Captain," she coolly retorted, a hint of sarcasm in her voice. Deliberately, she turned her back on him and returned to her seat. "I somehow fancied you to be at my brother-in-law's service. Sit down."

Without looking at him, she pointed to the chair opposite her own. Then, feigning every possible indolence as she struggled to gather her wits, Jonet settled back into her seat, taking a moment to arrange each pleat in the dull black fabric of her skirt. However, when she lifted her eyes, she was stunned to see Captain Amherst still standing near her doorway, ramrod straight and impossibly large.

"May I take it from your almost total lack of manners, ma'am," he said very calmly, "that you are not amenable to my uncle's plan?"

Forgetting her vow to show him nothing but disdain, Jonet came out of her chair and stalked back across the length of the room. "Keep a civil tongue in your head, Captain Amherst," she snapped. "I dislike impudence above all things." Jonet fixed him with her most quelling look.

But her quelling look had obviously been wasted. Other than stubbornly setting his perfect mouth and chiseled jaw, the captain did not so much as twitch. "Then perhaps you might take it upon yourself to learn civility, ma'am," he smoothly returned.

Jonet knew then and there that she had badly underestimated James's strategy. She prayed to God this man—*this soldier*—could be either intimidated, charmed, or otherwise rendered ineffectual by some clever form of manipulation. Most men of Jonet's acquaintance certainly could, for they were a vain and transparent lot, but this situation already looked distinctly discouraging. Deliberately, Jonet narrowed her eyes. "I know nothing of your uncle, nor of any plan," she answered scornfully.

"I understood from my uncle, Lord James Rowland, that you were in need of an instructor for your children." His words were still soft, but clipped and demanding. "And I believed you to be wishful of my providing such assistance, madam, else I should never have wasted my time and yours by coming here."

Jonet merely looked at him, trying to assimilate his words. *His uncle?* This officer was no one she had ever seen before, of that she was certain. And cavalry officers did not tutor children.

Amherst. *Amherst?* Who the devil had James sent to vex her this time? Jonet's head began to pound. The bone-deep weariness which had plagued her for months now threatened to drag her down. Her knees nearly buckling, her hands unsteady, she fought for control and somehow found it.

"I have not the pleasure of understanding you, sir," she said, her voice faltering only a little. "Lord James did indeed write yesterday. He told me only that he was sending a tutor for my sons—and that is a most *diplomatic* interpretation of his message, I do assure you."

The light furrows deepened as his heavy brows drew together. "He said nothing further?" Amherst growled. He had the look of a man who might slide past the point of being dangerous were he to be pushed just a fraction too hard. Already, he was angry. He was whipcord lean, and his eyes were quick. Too quick.

Jonet had meant to show him immediately who was in command, but Amherst had hardly spoken a dozen words, and she had the sick, sinking sensation that the tables had already turned. There was something else, too. Something even more confusing. *Captain Amherst did not want to be here.* She was certain of it. Why, then, had he come? Uneasily, Jonet began to pace back and forth across the width of the room. Amherst remained stoically motionless. In the silence of the drawing room, the stiff swishing of her bombazine seemed over-loud and annoying. Suddenly, she whirled to face him, knowing that she must regain the upper hand—a task which, in the past had generally presented her little challenge.

"Did he say anything further?" Amherst repeated, gritting out the words.

"Nothing, sir!" she retorted, haughtily lifting her chin to stare at him. "Other than to say that you would call at three today. Moreover, you are no cousin of mine—" her gaze flicked up and down, "—and you are no tutor, to be sure. What game does Lord James Rowland play now? I insist you tell me just what spite the two of you are scheming."

She stood almost toe to toe with the cavalry officer now, yet sick with the terrible knowledge that the thing she held most dear might be at stake. If this man were as dangerous as she supposed, she simply could not allow herself to succumb to weakness, to fear, or to self-pity. And she certainly could not allow herself to be distracted from her purpose by his golden good looks. By sheer force of will, Jonet drew herself up to her full height. She was a tall woman, but Amherst still topped her by a head or better. He dropped his hypnotic eyes to hers and gave her a long, level stare. There was still nothing of awe or subservience in it.

"I did not come here, Lady Mercer, to permit my integrity to bear the brunt of your insults," he said coolly. "Nor will I take the razor's edge of your tongue. I have better things to do with my time."

At that very moment, however, something in the officer's eyes, in the turn of his face, sparked a sudden flash of memory so sharp and sweet she trembled at it. Then the name came rushing back on a wave of embarrassment. Oh, God! *Poor little Cole?* Could it be he, the orphaned cousin? And barely a relation at all, according to her late husband's callous definition. Well! He certainly was not anyone's poor little *anything* now. He was big, and he was threatening, and he hardly looked poor.

Jonet remembered having met Cole Amherst once or twice. She had some vague recollection of his having attended her wedding. Oh, yes—and he had been handsome then, too. But callow, and far less cynical. A smattering of impressions flashed through her mind; fair hair that was much too long, elegant hands, quaint clothing, and scholarly, gold-rimmed spectacles which slid insistently down his nose.

And she remembered something else as well. A gentle touch, a soothing voice, and his murmuring some remarkably sweet platitude into her ear at a time when she had so desperately needed it. There had been no mistaking his inherent warmth and kindness. And then, a fleeting kiss—firm, heated lips pressed to her brow—and he was gone from her life. The rest of that fearful day had been obscured by a cloud of apprehension. Nonetheless, those indistinct memories of Cousin Cole were warm, almost comforting, and not at all unpleasant.

It struck her as odd that it should be so. Her mind raced. Amherst was a cousin by marriage, a relation of James's wife, and not a Rowland at all. How fortunate for him. "Your pardon," she said stiffly. "I do seem to recall you now."

"I am inordinately relieved," he sarcastically replied.

She looked up at him then, preparing to lash out again. But she was not prepared for the hot stab of desire that knifed through her belly. Though the sweet memory lingered, the quaint, callow youth was gone, and the hard-eyed, cynical officer was back. Amherst lifted his golden eyes to hers and pinned her with another long, steady stare that told her she had no control over him whatsoever. That whatever he might once have been, she would never be able to intimidate him now. And yet, it was a look rich with promise; the knowing look of a man who was sure of himself, in a steadfast, unpretentious way.

But how fanciful such thoughts were! She was no green girl. She could not possibly lust after a man she scarcely remembered, and particularly not this one. It was the strain, no doubt, of the last four months. It was simply time for a different approach. "I am persuaded, Captain," she said, her voice surprisingly even, "that we should discuss this strange situation in which we find ourselves. Please, will you not sit down?"

The civility of her request seemed to placate Amherst, and he crossed the room to take the same seat she had previously ordered him toward. As he settled his long length into the delicate chair, Jonet noticed that he carried a thin leather folio in his left hand.

The captain waited until Jonet was seated before speaking. "Ma'am," he began, looking a trifle vexed, "I find I cannot account for the brevity of my uncle's letter to you. I had understood that he would inform you of my circumstances and background, and that the decision was to be yours. As you see by my attire, I have no real need of a position."

Jonet interrupted him. "And are you qualified to be a tutor, sir?" she asked skeptically.

Stiffly, Captain Amherst inclined his head. "I daresay some might consider me so. However, I expect to return to garrison duty shortly. I have reluctantly answered my uncle's summons, but since you seem to require assistance even less than I wish to give it, I see no need in prolonging this meeting."

"I . . . well, that is to say, I am not perfectly sure," she stammered, unaccountably flustered, and suddenly eager to stall for time. She licked her lips uncertainly. Really, what *was* James up to? "Perhaps," she said slowly, "you might enlighten me as to why your uncle feels you are qualified to teach my sons."

Jonet studied him intently, her curiosity fully engaged. Cole Amherst had the golden, glittery eyes of a tiger. At times, they seemed almost heavy with sleep, and then abruptly, they would flare to life. As if to further emphasize their beauty, he drew a pair of eyeglasses from his pocket and settled them onto his nose. Another shard of bittersweet recollection pierced her at the sight, and she remembered again the shy young man who had once shown her a small but unselfish act of kindness.

If he had hoped to make himself appear more studious, it was something of a failed effort. He simply looked more solemn. "Of course," he replied, flipping open his folio with an efficient snap. For a fleeting moment, Jonet found herself wondering if he disliked James as much as she. There was a dark, restrained undertone in his references to his uncle.

Deftly, Amherst flicked through the pages, cleared his throat, and began to read. "I was schooled at Eton for five years, ma'am, as a King's scholar. Thereafter, I matriculated to King's College, Cambridge, and began my divinity studies. Upon completion with honors, I became a fellow of the university, with the emphasis of my research centered upon a studied comparison of the *a priori* versus the empirical methods of philosophical theology."

He paused to pull out a single sheaf of paper, passing it to her with long, elegant fingers. "Here, my lady, are my references and the dates of my various degrees and positions. Moreover, prior to joining the university, I tutored extensively in the subjects of philosophy, mathematics, classical literature, as well as Latin and Greek. I also served for a time at Saint Ann's in Cambridgeshire as their cur—"

"Captain Amherst!" Jonet held up a staying hand and paused to collect her wits. *Good heavens, the man really was the scholar he had once appeared to be. She was truly doomed.* "It would appear that you are somewhat . . . overqualified for this position."

"Quite so," he answered simply.

Feeling woefully ignorant, Jonet rearranged her skirts once more, choosing her words with utmost care. "Though you are obviously very learned, sir, my sons are young, and require training in mathematics and literature and perhaps rudimentary Greek—all very basic things. And of course, they must learn to ride well. To dance a bit, and to—to, well, to play *cricket,* for heaven's sake! Have you any such *ordinary* experience?"

Something which might have been sarcasm tugged at his handsome mouth. "Forgive my impertinence, ma'am, but the British Army has managed to make a fair cavalry officer out of me, and so I can sit a horse with some skill.

And hefting all those weighty tomes in the library has not completely impaired my ability as a batsman."

"Oh!" said Jonet lightly, realizing too late that she had insulted his masculinity. What a joke that was. Delicately, she touched the tip of her index finger to her bottom lip. "And what of those dancing skills, Captain Amherst? Are you as physically talented in everything you undertake to perform?"

She wanted to bite back the words as soon as they left her mouth. Amherst's eyes narrowed perceptively. *Good God, what was wrong with her?* First she was an ill-mannered shrew, now she was acting like a vulgar flirt. The captain's poor opinion of her could not but be furthered by such contemptible behavior.

"Why, I must confess you have caught me out there, madam," Amherst said coldly. "With regard to indoor athletics, you'd be better *served* by hiring yourself a dancing master."

Jonet wanted to sink through the floor in mortification. Unfortunately, that was not an option available to her. There was nothing else for it but to brazen it through. She reminded herself yet again that there was too much at stake; that her first instinct—abject panic—was a luxury she could ill afford. Intimidation it would have to be.

Restlessly, she tapped her fingernail against the arm of her mahogany chair. She did not like the look of Captain Cole Amherst, her long-lost and should-have-stayed-lost cousin. Or rather, the problem was she liked the look of him all too well. He was something of a challenge, and Jonet had not felt challenged by anything in a very long time. Tormented, yes. Tortured, often. But that was hardly the same thing as an invigorating contest of wills or wits.

Moreover, it would be hard to justify throwing a man

with his credentials—not to mention his obstinacy—into the street. Not unless he wanted to go. *Did* he want to go? She rather thought he did. So why the devil was he here?

Jonet still felt the danger thrumming all about her, as she had now for months on end, but her almost unfailing instincts could not fix Amherst as the cause. Nonetheless, he had been sent by the very person who posed the greatest threat. The man who wanted above all things to see her hanged, and never mind the scandal.

She looked at Captain Amherst again and realized that beneath his masculine exterior, there was a powerful intellect. Jonet had not one whit of doubt as to the validity of his academic accomplishments. Even James would not be so witless as to send someone with trumped-up credentials to school her children. Briefly, she wondered if her brother-in-law had some sort of hold over Amherst, but the thought was just as quickly gone.

This man was razor sharp, while James was almost as obtuse as his now-dead brother had been. But the inescapable fact remained that James had somehow discovered her advertisement for a tutor, though she had done it discreetly and anonymously. Now, he had correctly concluded that she had been stalling for time and that she would never permit the children to go away to school. Not unless they were dragged out of Brook Street over her lifeless body. The thought made her stomach knot with panic.

And so it seemed there was to be a compromise, and the compromise apparently had a name. And gorgeous golden eyes. For if it were not Cole Amherst, it would likely be someone else of James's choosing. And eventually, she would be powerless to stop it. "Well, Captain," she said in an over-bright voice. "It seems we have arrived at *point non plus*, does it not?"

"You may have arrived, ma'am," he answered calmly, "and perhaps taken my uncle along for the ride. I, however, had no intention of going anywhere with either of you." He shifted his weight impatiently, as if he might rise from his seat. "Have we concluded our discussion, Lady Mercer?"

The set of his jaw was stubborn, even a little contemptuous. Perhaps, like everyone else, he believed he had the right to judge her. Jonet should have been accustomed to such prejudice, but in this particular man, it made her extraordinarily furious. "Pray tell me, Captain Amherst, just what did my dear brother-in-law tell you about me?"

Amherst slipped off his eyeglasses and delicately folded them up with hands that were surprisingly gentle. "Anything my uncle might have said would have no influence upon my judgement, Lady Mercer. I form my own opinions."

"Ah, and rather quickly, too, I surmise."

"Quite," he said, his tone clipped.

She gave him an intense, sidelong glance as she rose to cross the room. "And what are those opinions, sir? Will you share them with me?"

"I think not, ma'am." He carefully returned the eyeglasses to his pocket.

"Oh, but I believe I must insist," she replied, swishing toward him and pausing before his chair. She had the damnedest urge to torment him.

Cole Amherst looked her straight in the eyes. "And do you always get what you insist upon, Lady Mercer?"

Jonet paced back and forth for a moment, then turned to him again. Her hand simply itched to slap him for his arrogance. But that would not do. "You have been listening, I daresay, to the rumor mill, have you not?" she said in carefully measured tones. "You have no doubt heard things about me."

The captain's golden eyes dropped halfway closed, as if he were perfectly at ease. "If you insist upon airing such contemptible gossip, Lady Mercer, then yes, you do seem to have made something of a reputation for yourself." The husky drawl of his voice was suggestively smooth, like the finest cognac. It made one think of warm wool and wood smoke. And the scent of a man.

She should have been angry, but instead, Jonet found herself wondering what Captain Cole Amherst smelled like beneath his dashing regimentals. *Perhaps she should simply seduce him and find out.* Perhaps she could offer him something that James could not, and move their little game to an altogether different playing field.

She should have found such thoughts appalling, but she did not. Jonet ascribed that fact to sheer desperation, praying it was nothing more perilous—such as true attraction. But from the look of him, it would be no great sacrifice to seduce Cole Amherst, save for the fact that it would be another black mark on her soul. But Jonet was long past counting, when she had so much at stake.

She looked at him again and saw that his eyes were no longer heavy but keen and quietly watchful. It felt as though Amherst could see right through the wall of her charade and into her heart. Could he? Could he even, heaven forbid, sense the inexplicable attraction she felt for him? That capricious piquing of her desire, those shards of sweet memory, which had caught her unaware, then melted through her with a hungry need? Almost absently, Jonet gave herself a little shake. Dear heaven, she often felt alone, but when had she become so pathetically lonely?

"Lady Mercer?" Amherst's deep, smoky voice cut into her unease. "Believe it or not, some of us do not live a life of indolence. If I can be of service, might we get on with it?"

"Get—*get on* with it?" She dropped into her chair.

He nodded curtly. "Yes, if you please. And if you have no interest in my assistance, I must take myself home now, for I have other plans for the evening."

His mood increasingly sullen, Cole studied the woman seated across from him. He was beginning to think that for once in his narrow-minded life, his uncle had been even-handed in his judgement of another human being. Lady Mercer was something of a hellcat. She reminded him of a cat, too; long and sleek, with motions so sinuous they could not possibly have been bestowed by the Divine Creator. Indeed, it was entirely possible that she was the slut James had called her.

She obviously took pleasure in teasing and tormenting men. Certainly, she was tormenting him. Lady Mercer's pale, slender hand rested casually upon the arm of her chair, but the rhythmic motion of her fingertips as they caressed the leather, absently rubbing back and forth across the brass studwork, was wildly entrancing. It was a sensual, hypnotic, and very feline motion. Ruthlessly, Cole pulled his eyes from her hand, taking some measure of satisfaction in his ability to do so. Circumspectly, he took in the unrelieved black of her gown, which was plain to the point of severity and provided the perfect foil for her flawless ivory skin. From a single strand of jet beads, a cross hung suspended between breasts that were high and rounded.

Her hair was dressed in a fashion that perfectly suited her delicate face, yet the arrangement was unfashionably soft and loose, silently inviting a man to slide his fingers through it, to pull out all the pins and let it tumble to her waist. Cole swallowed hard and jerked himself back to reality. For pity's sake, there was really nothing all that extraordinary about the woman's hair. Indeed, she was dressed with all propriety. Four months into her widowhood, Lady Mercer's attire still gave every indication that she deeply mourned the loss of the man who, were the gossips to be believed, had been nothing but an inconvenience.

Cole found it strange that he now remembered every detail of how she had looked on her wedding day, which had occurred but a few short months before his own. Lady Jonet Cameron she had been at that time. Uncle James had insisted that the entire family be present at the auspicious occasion of the marquis's second nuptials. Even Cole, a distant relation, had not escaped his uncle's edict. And so he had reluctantly set aside his research, left his offices in Cambridge, and gone down to London for the festivities, only to spend the better part of the day hanging back from the crowd as best he could. And still, he remembered her.

At eighteen, Lady Jonet had been little more than a thin, almost frail girl, swathed in expensive wedding finery. Cole recalled with perfect clarity the profound sorrow he had felt for her, a lovely young woman he had not known at all. He had thought it a miracle that she had made it down the aisle of St. James's, so visible had been her trembling.

Later, when good taste had required that he offer the bride his congratulations, Cole remembered leaning near her in the crush of the wedding breakfast to whisper some inane compliment, and feeling her slender body shudder against him. He remembered, too, his own shiver of sensual awareness, and the heated shame which had followed. He had kissed her and moved on, leaving her trembling with fear, and himself with selfish lust. Oh, yes. He had never forgotten that strange sensation, though he had never felt it since.

At the time, he had been unable to imagine a worse fate for a sheltered Scottish miss than a marriage to the annoyingly superior Lord Mercer, who was more than twice his young bride's age. Apparently, he need not have worried. By all accounts, Lady Mercer had given as good as she had gotten. And she had been quick about it, too. After the wedding, Mercer had hidden his new wife away at his seat in Norfolk until Jonet had done her duty and given him the treasured heir his first wife had been unable to provide.

Immediately thereafter, his lordship had gone back to town, and Lady Mercer, so far as Cole could tell, had gone where she damned well pleased. And that had been, for the most part, home to Scotland, where she had catered to her sickly mother and conspired to make trouble with her wily fox of a father, or so Uncle James had often grumbled.

Cole had been a scholar. He had understood little—and cared even less—about the intricacies of noble marriages and the complexities of their titles, particularly the strange Scottish ones. He certainly had not understood that Lady Jonet was an heiress. His Uncle James had complained vehemently about the liberal settlements which the wily Kildermore had negotiated on his daughter's behalf, many of which became effective upon the birth of her first son.

And then, Lord Kildermore had died, and in James's definition, matters had gone from bad to worse. Jonet Rowland was a peer, with more titles hanging off her name than Cole had neckcloths, and apparently she was none too meek about it. James had made it plain that he found it disgraceful that his brother's wife should go about so boldly in society, making friends with whomever she pleased, and acting with such an unbecoming degree of independence.

Lord Mercer, it had seemed, had still had the whip hand on his wife. But just barely. The marquis had wed her no doubt thinking that the comely lass had not a clever thought in her pretty little head. Well, Mercer had been wrong on that score. Even at this moment, it was apparent to Cole that Lady Mercer was busy planning her next move. The smile she shone upon him was blindingly gracious, almost sweet. "You are hired," she announced flatly.

As Cole searched his rather extensive vocabulary for a more civil way of saying *No way in hell am I working for you,* Lady Mercer rose gracefully from her seat to ring the bell.

"As I am sure you are aware, the terms of your employment, as well as the salary, were set forth in my advertisement," she said briskly. "You shall have a half-day off per week, during which time you will no doubt wish to call upon your Uncle James." She then set her head at an angle and stood haughtily in her lusterless black, assessing him much as a bright-eyed raven might study an unsuspecting worm. "Mr. Donaldson will show you to your chambers, Captain Amherst," she said in a tone of finality. "Your things will be brought up as soon as may be."

Cole rose to his feet and stood in the center of her drawing room, his hands clasped very tightly behind his back. For reasons he barely understood, he bit back his tart refusal. When he spoke, he schooled his words to be crisp, almost brutally courteous. "Let us understand one another, Lady Mercer. I am not your servant. I do not require a salary. *If* I am to assist your children, I shall teach Monday through Friday, and the occasional half-day on Saturday. I have no things 'to be brought up.' I do not plan to take up residence here."

Jonet suppressed a gasp. Her anger chased fast after confusion, with unbridled lust hot on their heels. *Good heavens, this Captain Amherst was a hard man to understand.* She felt her already racing pulse ratchet up another notch. Terror had been her constant companion for so long she had almost grown accustomed to it. Now, in the space of five minutes, it seemed as if the rest of her emotions had been set loose like a pack of ill-trained hounds.

Only a severe twitch in Amherst's chiseled jaw belied his temper, but unless Jonet missed her guess, it was a fierce one indeed. It had never occurred to her that he might prefer to reside elsewhere, and Jonet knew that she ought to be inordinately relieved that he would not be sleeping under her roof. Instead, she was quite vexed. "My advertisement stipulated that the tutor would be expected to live in," she insisted, her voice a little more querulous than she intended.

Captain Amherst spoke again in his same carefully modulated tones. "With all respect, my lady, I have not come in answer to your advertisement. I have come at my uncle's behest. Moreover, I have come to teach, not to nursemaid."

"Oh, I daresay I know why James sent you here, Captain Amherst," she snapped, swishing across the room as boldly as she dared. "What I begin to wonder is whether you do."

Crossing her arms over her chest to keep her hands from visibly shaking, she turned her back to him and stared out the window. In her agitation, Jonet had given no thought to how rude such a gesture might appear. Amherst, however, seemed to have grasped it rather quickly. Almost at once, she was shocked to feel the heat of his hand high on her arm, burning through the fabric of her gown. She whipped around to face him, a cruel reprimand dying on her lips.

Amherst's face was so close she could see the insolent curve of his mouth and the shadow of a surprisingly dark beard beneath his skin. He was so tall she could feel the warmth of his breath stir across her forehead. Like a heavy shadow falling, the man loomed over her. Jonet could smell him now, his angry heat edged with nothing but clean male sweat and a hint of soap as he pressed his fingers into her upper arm. His hands were powerful, and a little rough.

A deep tremble ran through her, but whether it was outright fear or perverse lust, Jonet could not have said. One was as bad as the other. Amherst leaned another inch nearer. His lush, carnal mouth now looked tight and mean. "If I am as dangerous as you seem to believe, Lady Mercer," he said in a soft, lethal undertone, "perhaps you ought not turn your back whilst I'm in the room. Moreover, if your children require instruction in drawing room deportment—and from what I have seen, I daresay they may—then I shall cheerfully add it to their curriculum."

Jonet refused to back down. "Why, Captain," she softly retorted, staring straight into his eyes, "you are standing so close, one might imagine you are trying to seduce me." To her undying mortification, she realized that she burned to kiss that hard, uncompromising mouth until it softened and molded to her own. For a moment, Amherst's dark lashes lowered, and a hungry expression passed over his face.

Almost at once, his fingers dug ruthlessly into her skin. And then, he shoved her roughly away. "Make no mistake, madam," he growled, his eyes flashing sparks of gold. "When I try to seduce a woman, she is well aware of it. And I do it under my own roof. On my own time."

Before she could gasp at the insult, Amherst's powerful stride had carried him halfway across the room, and he had snatched up his leather folio in one of his long, capable hands.

"And just where do you think you are going?" Jonet asked with as much dignity as she could muster. She still stood by the window, rubbing her bruised arm.

Amherst turned from the door to glare at her. "To find your butler, ma'am, who seems a good deal more reasonable than you. If I am going to spend my time squabbling with children, I should prefer it to be those whom I am intended to teach."

At that very moment, however, the door swung inward to reveal Donaldson, a tea tray balanced neatly on one hand. A round-faced, elderly woman stood behind him in the hallway, tufts of white hair springing from beneath her starched white cap. The butler stared back and forth between them inquiringly.

"Oh, thank heaven you are here, Nanna!" Jonet said irritably, looking past Donaldson and his tray. "Take this *gentleman*—Captain Amherst—to the schoolroom, if you please. And stay near him at all times." Nails digging into her palms, Jonet narrowed her gaze as Amherst strode from the room. Obviously aware of the strain inside the drawing room, Donaldson pushed shut the door and looked at her expectantly.

Jonet jerked her head toward the closed door. "Charlie, send someone round to Bow Street with a message for Pearson," she ordered, trying to steady her voice. "I am persuaded that we must learn all there is to know about Captain Cole Amherst. I want to know where he is from. Where he has been. Where he gets his shirts starched. Where he sleeps, and—" she paused for a heartbeat—"with whom."

"Of course, milady. And for the nonce, shall I set a footman on him?"

Sharply, Jonet nodded. "An excellent notion! And one more thing, please. Send word to Lord Delacourt. Ask him to come early for dinner, if he may. As early as possible. Tell him . . . just tell him that I require his good advice most urgently."

3

In which Lady Mercer rallies her Troops

Still wildly invigorated by his heated encounter with Lady Mercer, Cole found himself alone in the hall with the woman known to him only as Nanna. As round as she was tall, the woman was attired in a gown of dark gray worsted with a crisp white over-smock. The look she shot him could hardly have been called welcoming. Indeed, her small, dark eyes seemed to glare resentfully out at him from the nest of wrinkles which formed her face.

Cole made a little bow and offered her his hand. "Good afternoon, Mrs.—?"

"Nanna," she said succinctly, fingers splayed stubbornly upon her wide hips.

"Very well then, Mrs. Nanna." He withdrew the proffered hand. "I suppose that would make me Captain Cole."

"Oh, you're a right smart one, aren't you?" She eyed him up and down.

Cole managed to smile. "I should hope, madam, that I am not entirely without intelligence, if I'm to tutor two young boys."

Nanna shot him another quelling look, shrugged, then turned with amazing agility toward the stairs. "Aye, well you'll be needin' a good deal more than wit, sir, if you're t'manage them two imps. Now, follow me, if there's to be no getting rid o'you." As she heaved her way up, she shook her head vigorously, and another iron gray curl sprung free. "Though what that Lord James is aboot a' sending you here, I'm sure I have no notion. Her ladyship is perfectly capable of seeing to those lads, and Lord James has no call to go poking his nose where it's nither wanted nor needed. Been nothing but trooble to her ladyship, he and his brother both."

Nanna's oratory droned on as they labored up the two flights of stairs. Twice the elderly woman paused to sigh deeply, but otherwise, her breath was spent in complaining until they reached the schoolroom door. Then she set her hands back on her hips, puffing mightily. "And anither thing, sir! These lads are hellions, and I dinna mind to tell you so. They're good boys, both, but too clever by half. And what's worse, they run wild, though they've been raised up proper enough." She drew another exasperated breath. "So I hope you and that fine Lord James know what you're aboot. Now, go in there and sit yourself doon 'til I can ferret out the wee rascals and make 'em presentable." On that parting comment, Nanna shoved open the schoolroom door and stalked away, her huge hips rolling laboriously beneath her gray skirts.

Cole entered the empty schoolroom, his footsteps echoing hollowly upon the bare wood floor. Once inside, he closed the door, then leaned back against it. Good Lord! Jonet Rowland had been worse than he had imagined, and she had shaken his control. Badly. For a long moment, he paused, eyes tightly closed, and turned his energy inward, seeking to quiet the outrage and hunger that had momentarily clouded his judgement. How unlike him it was to lose his temper so thoroughly. How disconcerting it was to lust after a woman he did not like. Devilish uncomfortable, too. And her behavior! Audacious was too mild a word. A lady would never have spoken such thoughts aloud, would never have referred so openly to tawdry gossip, and a lady most assuredly would not have moved through a room with such physical energy, dark eyes flashing and skirts swishing boldly.

He should have turned away from Lady Mercer the first time she tempted—no, *tormented*—him. Yes, he should simply have turned and walked out of her house. He still was not sure why he had not done precisely that. All he knew, and it was a fanciful thought indeed, was that something seemingly drew him to this place. And strangely enough, to her. Though in what way, and on what level, he could not say. But it was there, that vague sense of . . . of *urgency*. It nagged at him, creating hesitation where there should have been only swift certainty.

Eventually, Cole felt the tempest inside begin to ease, and he opened his eyes to see the late afternoon light spilling softly through the windows onto the wide oak planking of the floor. It was time to forget Jonet Rowland and her wicked, tempting ways and get on with the business at hand. He came away from the door and drifted aimlessly through the room, inhaling deeply the scent of dusty chalk and old bookbindings. They were familiar, somewhat soothing smells, which, by and large, brought back good memories. The latter half of his childhood had not been the happiest of times, but in the classroom, beneath the high ceilings and transom windows, Cole had finally found a sense of belonging after the death of his parents.

Casually, he hefted an atlas from its stand, balanced it over his palm, then began to aimlessly flip through it, seeing nothing. No—seeing the past. On the whole, he had despised Eton, it was true. He had hated the bleak living quarters, and despaired of the incessant shortages of warmth and food. The utter lack of supervision or compassion. And yet, he had survived. In part because of his sheer physical size. But mostly because his needs were simple. And because his mind was simple—not weak, but uncomplicated and ingenuous.

For as long as Cole could remember, he had never felt true enmity toward anyone or anything. Yes, he had despised much of what Eton *was*, but he could not remember ever having despised what it had *given* him, for it was only there, in the classrooms, that he had truly begun to excel. To develop the knowledge, the insight, and the self-confidence which had been lacking, and which would finally set him free. For a moment, Cole let the more satisfying memories wash away the bad as he paced the length of the room in silence.

It was not a large chamber, but it was well lit, spotlessly clean, and amply stocked. Bookshelves covered one wall, a sturdy desk stood in one corner, and a narrow worktable filled the center. A long, leather sofa stretched beneath a pair of deep, lightly draped windows, which overlooked the front of the house. Yes, under normal circumstances, this was a place where he might have found some measure of happiness. Where he might have immersed himself in the satisfaction of his work and enjoyed the tutelage of two young men who were no doubt ripe with the promise of youth.

But the circumstances which had brought him here were far from normal. He was not wanted. Lady Mercer had made that plain. She did not trust him, believing him to be loyal to his uncle, whom she clearly considered her adversary. Obviously, the idea that Cole might actually have come out of a sense of duty, that he might feel some sympathy for the plight of her fatherless children, had never crossed her egotistical mind. At first glance, she seemed everything the world accused her of being—arrogant, cold, conniving . . . and hauntingly beautiful, of course.

Good God, how the woman had flirted with him. Even Cole, in his self-confessed ignorance, could hardly have missed that fact. It had been her intent to unsettle him, to toy with him, like a cat with its prey. She had strolled languidly across the room, coming so close that Cole had been able to see every silken eyelash as she had swept them down across her ivory cheeks. She had stood so near that he had been able to inhale the exotic, spicy, almost masculine scent she wore. Deliberately, she had lifted her stormy blue eyes to his, then touched the tip of her tongue to that tiny, almost invisible mole at the corner of her mouth, her every move calculated to torture him.

Cole was very sure of her purpose because, to his undying shame, it had worked. Despite his contempt and mistrust, he had felt a stab of desire for her, and Cole reminded himself that it was not the first time the lady had had such a disquieting effect on his senses. But this time he believed her behavior had been willful, almost malicious. Jonet Rowland had deliberately challenged his every masculine instinct. And his traitorous body had reacted, just as she had probably known it would.

Gentlemanly deportment be damned. He had found himself shaking inside with a rage which was wholly unfamiliar to him. The woman had so incensed him that he had resorted to insulting her, more or less to save his own sanity. It had been all that he could do not to jerk her violently into his embrace and kiss her insolent mouth until she was weak in the knees. Ah, yes—that was what he had burned to do, but could he have accomplished it? It might take a great deal to weaken such a strong woman.

Cole was no angel, and he knew that some women found him attractive. Yet his monkish existence and military life left him so rarely in the company of females—and never one so dangerous—that he had scarce known what to do, while Lady Mercer knew precisely what she was about. It seemed to Cole that the woman raised sexual frustration to a form of torture that even the Spaniards would have admired.

Merely at the memory of it, his groin tightened and stirred, annoying him to no end, and making him ache with need. Clearly, he had now ventured well beyond his narrow range of social skills. Perhaps now that he was on military leave, he had no business in town. Perhaps it would have been better, after all, to have forced himself to return to Elmwood.

Lost in such thoughts, Cole walked to the window and pulled away the under-drapes to stare into the street below. It was quite late in the afternoon now, and those few carts and drays whose business brought them into the exalted environs of Mayfair had now slowed to a trickle. Suddenly, the door flew open, and Cole spun about to see an explosion of boys and dogs burst into the room.

The dogs, border collies by the look of them, seemed as large as the boys, and moved almost as quickly, their claws clacking back and forth on the wood floor like hail spattering a windowsill. In the doorway behind, Nanna stood, looking grim. Cole was beginning to believe her hands were permanently affixed to her hips.

The smaller of the two boys managed to squeeze between the prancing dogs and the table to stand just in front of Cole. He narrowed his eyes and studied Cole's regimentals. "Are you a Dragoon?" he boldly demanded. "I said you were, and Stuart says you ain't."

Cole glanced through the door toward Nanna. "Ma'am, if I might have a few moments alone with Lord Mercer and

Lord Robert? I do assure you that they will not get the best of me quite as quickly as you fear."

The elderly nurse crossed her arms. "I'm tae stay near, sir," she said in a warning tone. "I'll be just in the hall here."

The dogs lay down in a patch of sun beneath the table, and Cole returned his attention to the boys. "You must be Lord Robert Rowland," he said, bending down to the younger boy and putting out his hand. "I am Captain Amherst."

The boy reached up to pump Cole's hand enthusiastically. "Pleased-t'make-your-acquaintance," he said, rapidly running all the words together. He pointed perfunctorily at the dogs. "You can call me Robin. An' this is Scoundrel, and this here is Rogue. Are you a Dragoon, sir?"

Cole held up a staying hand and turned toward Stuart Rowland, the seventh Marquis of Mercer. He was a lanky, good-looking boy, a little solemn for his nine years, and with the unmistakable Rowland coloring. "And you must be Stuart, Lord Mercer?" he said.

"Yes, sir," said the boy, rather reluctantly taking his hand. "Good afternoon." Stuart quickly broke off the contact, leaving Cole to study him. The boy's hair was dark, his gaze somber and mistrustful behind eyes that were hazel and deep-set. He looked familiar, too, for Stuart's eyes were the very same that Cole had often seen staring back at him from the portraits which lined the corridors of Lord James's country house. At the moment, however, Stuart's gaze was shuttered, almost afraid.

"Well, that's that, then, isn't it?" said Lord Robert. He seemed cheerfully unaware of his elder brother's discomfort, or of Cole's burning curiosity. "Now, *are* you a Dragoon, sir? Stuart says you ain't. That you're Life Guards. But I said that he was wrong."

Cole turned his attention from Stuart and tried to frown disapprovingly at the younger boy's interruption. It was rather difficult, for the child was so charmingly impertinent, not to mention persistent. "*Aren't*, Robert," Cole corrected. "Please do not speak cant in the schoolroom. And yes, I am a Dragoon. But there is a possibility that I may become your tutor. For a few months, until something more permanent can be arranged."

"*Dragoons!*" Robert gave his brother a rather smug look. "Told you so! Told you so!" he taunted. At once, the room exploded and all hell seemed to break loose. Stuart's hand lashed out, whacking Robert soundly across the back of the skull. Robert went for Stuart's throat then, fists and elbows flying as he lunged. The dogs erupted from beneath the table, aimlessly growling and snarling as they darted through the room.

Stuart leapt backward, knocking over a chair. A pile of books went tumbling to the floor. Cole tried to grab them, but the bigger collie plowed between, scrabbling wildly across the floor in a valiant attempt to seek and destroy the enemy, whom he had yet to identify.

"Stop!" shouted Cole, finally battling back the fray long enough to push the boys apart. His voice must have carried its old level of command, for Scoundrel and Rogue bolted beneath the table to cower. The boys, however, seemed not to notice. They continued to ineffectually lash out at each other with feet and elbows.

"Gentlemen, let be!" Cole gave them both a swift shake and tore them further apart. "There will be no hitting. Military regulations do not permit it, nor do I."

Robert's eyes narrowed still further. He crossed his thin arms over his chest. "Then I'll—I'll just *bayonet* 'im. You can do that in the army, I know it for a fact, 'cause

Donaldson took a bayonet in his arse at Vittoria, and couldn't sit down for a week, and then they had to send 'im home, and Duncan had to put horse poultices on 'im for ever so—"

Cole smacked his hands palms down upon the table and leaned intently forward. "Sit down, gentlemen!" he bellowed. "There shall be no hitting. No bayoneting. No shooting. No knifing. No violence of any sort! Am I understood?"

"Yes, sir," muttered Robert, righting the chair, which had been knocked over, and settling into it.

Stuart shot his brother one last ugly glance. "Oh, all right," he reluctantly agreed, shoving in his shirttails with a suppressed violence.

"And don't say *arse*," added Cole for good measure, wondering even as he said it just what he had gotten his own arse into. Nanna, it seemed, had been right. Lady Mercer's children really did appear to be willful, undisciplined hellions. Blood would always tell, it seemed.

Robert squirmed in his seat, then brightened a bit. He was obviously the more blithe of the two boys, but even his ebullience could not hide the fact that he was just a little uneasy. "Anyway, sir, I knew you were a Dragoon when I saw you spying on us from the alley."

"Shut up, Robin!" snapped his elder brother. "Don't be bloody stupid!"

"I wasn't spying." Cole looked quickly from one to the other, wondering what lay behind their words. "And don't ever say *bloody* again, Stuart! Moreover, do not call your brother stupid. He is mistaken, that is all. I was merely strolling in the alley so that I would not arrive early for my meeting with your mother."

"But Duncan was worried you *might* be a spy," argued

Robert, obviously reluctant to let go of his notion. "I saw him watching you. He thought you were a suspicious character lurking about," he added, clearly parroting something he had heard.

Stuart darkened his scowl. "A 'suspicious character' does not walk up the alley in broad daylight, you lack-wit. A 'suspicious character' will just leap out of the dark and throttle you senseless. Or murder you when no one is looking—just like with Papa." His manner seemed on the surface merely scornful, until one realized that an element of some darker emotion lay behind it.

A sudden, oppressive chill settled over the room, and Cole felt the skin prickle up the back of his neck. Trying to ignore it, he turned his full attention to the younger boy. "Duncan? Is that the big, red-haired fellow in the back? Your gardener?"

"Ha! Fooled you," said Robert, his saucy grin returning. "Duncan's our head groom from Kildermore Castle. But now, he's to stand out back, and keep watch for—*ouch!*"

Stuart's blow made solid contact this time, his open palm smacking Robert soundly across the back of the sconce. "Jesus, Mary and Joseph, Robin! You've a mouth as big as a beer keg!"

Cole dropped his head into his hands, suppressing the urge to walk straight down to Whitehall and plead for a speedy dispatch to the Punjab. Even excessive heat and questionable rations had to be easier than this. At least in the army, Cole knew how to command his troops. "Please do not ever take our Savior's name in vain, Stuart," he managed to grumble from behind his splayed fingers.

How in heaven had he ever thought himself qualified for this job? It had been years since he had tutored, and even then he had taken one student at a time, and always older boys than these. It should have been a simple job, but it wasn't. It simply wasn't.

"Are you done being our tutor now, Captain Amherst?" Robert's question was soft this time, a little chagrined. Cole looked up to see a face that seemed to be the epitome of childhood innocence. Robert's eyes were wide, a startlingly vivid shade of green, and his dark auburn hair curled, almost pixie-fashion, about his ears. He could hardly have looked more unlike his brother.

"No, Robin," he said softly. "I'm afraid you'll not escape me quite that easily. Now, I wish to speak with your brother, and I do not want you to interrupt. I shall ask him some questions about his previous studies, and then I shall do the same with you. Is that understood?"

One foot thumping rhythmically against his chair leg, Robert snagged his lip and nodded. "Very well," said Cole, turning to face Stuart. His gaze was hooded, his expression stark but otherwise unreadable. Had the child been a few years older, Cole would have said that something besides his father's death weighed heavily upon his mind. But honestly, what could it be? Lord Mercer was only nine years old. Cole shrugged off the strange sensation and spent the next half hour trying to ascertain just where both boys stood in terms of academic development.

It was quite late by the time Cole concluded his interviews with Robert and Stuart. He had taken two pages of notes about their past studies, and completed a list of books and supplies that would be required to go forward. *If* he went forward, and he was not at all sure he should. But the niggling sense that something was very wrong with Lady Mercer's children continued to plague him.

When at last Cole quit the schoolroom, the house had fallen quiet. No doubt the servants were already belowstairs beginning their preparations for the evening. There would be dinner to cook, draperies to draw, and even in May, hearths to be swept and laid for the night. The upstairs hall beyond the schoolroom was empty, with no sign of either the nurse or the butler.

And what was the butler's name? Donaldson. A very familiar looking fellow. Indeed, he was apparently a former soldier, if Robert had been correct in his childish chattering. Had Donaldson's path perhaps crossed Cole's somewhere on the Continent? It was, he supposed, rather unlikely. And yet, Cole decided, making his way downstairs, there really was something about the fellow that sparked a sense of recognition.

It struck him as odd, too, that Donaldson was such a handsome fellow, and rather young to be a butler. What was it James had said? That Lady Mercer had dismissed all her servants and brought new ones down from Scotland? That story, perhaps, explained the erstwhile head groom who was now reposing as a slipshod gardener. Or did it? No, it just confused things all the more. The man really had seemed to be *watching* more than he had been *gardening*. He had been trampling a bed of young daffodils, for pity's sake.

Cole tried to shrug off the thought. It seemed that Lord Robert Rowland's fanciful ideas were contagious. Nonetheless, there was no denying the fact that the boy was bright beyond his seven years, and highly intelligent often meant wildly imaginative. The older boy, Stuart, Lord Mercer, was more introspective, harder to read. And yet he was definitely on edge, and the cause seemed to be something more than simple grief.

Cole had paid little attention to James's rantings before, but now his words took on a new significance. Why bring servants all the way from Scotland? And why hire two bully-boys right out of St. George's-in-the-East and rig them out as footmen? As Cole skimmed his hand lightly along the banister on his way down the next flight of stairs, another thought struck him.

He hit the landing and froze in his tracks. Why was young Lord Mercer so frightened? *Unease* was far too weak a word for what Cole had seen flash across Stuart's face. It really had been stark fear; a fear that had long ago gone beyond panic and become hopelessly familiar. He had seen it before, on the faces of young but stoic soldiers after a seemingly ceaseless battle. That, more than anything else Cole had seen today, began to chill him to the bone.

He remembered himself all too well at just that age, unexpectedly orphaned and scared out of his wits. It was a very difficult age at which to lose one's parents. And while it was true that Stuart had lost only his father, Cole harbored grave misgivings about the parent who was left to him.

In Cole's case, his Uncle James had not helped matters at all, shipping Cole straightaway to Eton and demanding Cole's undying gratitude, as if his wife's nephew was some sort of charity case. Cole had been halfway through his studies at King's College before he had realized that he was *not* a poor relation. That although he would never be a rich man, he was moderately wealthy, at least by the standards of rural gentry. Moreover, Cole had finally realized that he had the freedom to live a life which was independent of the Rowland family. And since that day, he had more or less done exactly that.

But young Stuart had nowhere to go. He had no one to look after his happiness and his well-being. No one except his guardians, James and Jonet. Small wonder, then, that the child was so troubled. Cole was troubled, too, because he realized one more thing. He realized that it would be very, very hard to go away and leave those frightened and fanciful children to the devices of two people whom he did not fully trust.

Sobered by that thought, Cole was halfway down the last flight of stairs when he heard the front knocker drop peremptorily. From his stance half a story above, he could see that Lady Mercer's ruffians were nowhere in sight. Instead, Donaldson slid from the shadows to open the door, and a startlingly handsome young man stepped into the corridor.

"Evening, Donaldson," said the gentleman briskly, giving the butler a blinding smile and handing him a fine, gold-knobbed walking stick.

"Good evening, your lordship," answered Donaldson as the man shrugged out of an elegant black greatcoat. "Lady Jonet awaits you in the book-room, I believe."

"Ah, fine and good!" said the man, briskly rubbing his hands together. "Is there cognac? Upon my word, it is unseasonably chilly to be so near to June, do you not think?"

Donaldson nodded. "Aye, sir. And I've set a bottle of your favorite on the sideboard by the door."

"Just so, Charlie! You are a prince among men. What would we do without—well, *hello*! Who's this?" The young man looked pointedly up at Cole just as he descended the last three steps.

Donaldson stepped back. "Lord Delacourt, have you met Lady Mercer's distant cousin, Captain Amherst?"

"Why, no, indeed," murmured Delacourt, drawing out that most vile of foppish accoutrements, the quizzing glass. "I have not had that pleasure."

The butler turned to Cole. "David Branthwaite, Viscount Delacourt."

Cole murmured a polite greeting, his eyes taking in every detail of the man whom his Uncle James had claimed was "practically living under Lady Mercer's roof." Apparently, his uncle had once again been correct in his assessment.

Moreover, there was no doubt whatsoever that Delacourt was a popinjay of the first order. Perhaps not an out-and-out dandy, for his clothing was just a little too subtle for that, but rich and arrogant nonetheless. He seemed utterly to ooze wealth and charm from his every pore, and Cole hated him on sight, a most unchristian sentiment. Delacourt was young, too, not more than six-and-twenty at most. Younger than Jonet Rowland. It really was shameful.

Abruptly, Cole all but clicked his heels, making a perfunctory bow. "Your servant, Delacourt."

"My *servant,* do you say?" said the young man archly, lifting the glass to sweep his brilliant green gaze down Cole's length. "It looks instead as if someone's called out the cavalry." He dropped the device abruptly and pinned Cole with a dark, assessing look that was in deep contrast to his superficial manners and appearance. "Do tell me, sir. How is it that we've never met? I rather fancied I knew all of Jonet's family."

Cole inclined his head stiffly. He had not missed Delacourt's deliberate use of Lady Mercer's given name. "I am a nephew by marriage to Lord James Rowland, her ladyship's brother-in-law," he said rigidly. "James has asked that I tutor her children, his wards, for a time."

A definite chill fell across the corridor at that remark. Delacourt's elegant brows went up a notch, and he pulled back incrementally. "Has he indeed?" he said coolly. "James is ever thoughtful, is he not? Now, if you will excuse me, Captain, I have come to wait upon her ladyship." And on that remark, he turned and strolled languidly down the hall, seeming perfectly at home.

At once, the door to the drawing room flew open and Lady Mercer stepped into the hall. She stood there, hands clasped before her like a little girl impatient for some long-awaited treat, watching Delacourt walk toward her. There was a sweet look of anticipation fixed on her face, and a hint of something else, too. Relief, perhaps? If she saw Cole, she gave no indication of it.

Abruptly, Donaldson handed Cole his hat and threw open the door. Cole fleetingly wondered if perhaps Delacourt and the butler had greased the front steps to ease his way down. It would be dark soon, and the air did indeed hold a bit of a chill. Cole settled his hat on his head, then set a brisk pace along Brook Street, feeling as if he had just escaped a world to which he could never belong, filled with people whom he could never understand.

But there were the children to think of, and he did understand them. He was worried. And what was worse, he did not fully comprehend why. His concern aside, however, Delacourt's animosity was too strong to have been misunderstood. There was something else, too, which could not have been misinterpreted. Something far more disconcerting. With his thick auburn hair and brilliant green eyes, Delacourt was the very image of young Robert Rowland. Just as James had hinted. Damn it all, he hated it when his uncle was right.

Indeed, Cole felt a sense of heated disappointment in Lady Mercer, followed fast by anger—even more heated—aimed at himself. What business was it of his whom the lady took to her bed? And when had he become so bloody self-righteous?

Cole was not precisely sure as to when he had made the decision to go north through Mayfair, and wind his way over to High Holborn, but he realized he had done so at about the same time he grasped the fact that he had missed Red Lion Street and was halfway up Holborn Hill. Vaguely, he looked about and jerked to a halt, but after the initial wave of confusion passed, he realized that he was really not as absentminded as he had feared. As so often was the case, Cole's feet had simply taken him where his heart needed to go.

He glanced to his right, where a pair of inebriated law students were picking a careful path along Shoe Lane. They were headed, he had no doubt, to The Mitre. Cole vaguely recognized them as pub regulars, and so he slowed his steady gait just long enough to pass a few amiable words of greeting. As soon as they had crossed the light traffic to the other side of the street, however, Cole spared them no further thought, his destination now certain.

He stepped off the street to see the soft lamps of Saint Andrew's cut into the falling dusk, casting a welcoming light into the graveled walk beyond. Cole approached the door, pushed it inward, and made his way toward the chancel. Smoothly, Cole slid into the second pew, dropped to the kneeler, and proceeded to do something he had neglected to do for far too long. He prayed. He prayed for guidance in choosing the right path toward helping Stuart and Robert Rowland. And he prayed to be delivered from the unthinkable temptation Jonet Rowland presented. But more importantly, and perhaps even more sincerely, Cole prayed for the same thing he always did. Absolution.

* * *

Other than the soft crackle and hiss of the newly lit fire, all was silence inside Jonet's drawing room. Despite the elegance of his dinner attire, Lord Delacourt sprawled gracelessly across her long rosewood couch, a well-shod foot dangling aimlessly off one end, the opposite elbow splayed over the side. With the hand that was not thus engaged in propping up his handsome face, Delacourt swirled a dram of brandy about in the bottom of an etched crystal goblet, his expression uncharacteristically grave.

Her eye discerning, Jonet studied him. He looked so mature tonight. Older even than his years might dictate, for Jonet knew that he was not yet five-and-twenty. Delacourt was to celebrate his birthday in another ten days, and Jonet had chosen his gift weeks ago.

They were close, too close for the strictures of society, yet she had long ago ceased to trouble herself over what the *ton* talked about behind their backs. Initially, even Henry had not cared—until the intensity of the gossip had become too much to bear. Certainly Jonet had not meant to bring harm or humiliation to anyone, but there were some things in life she simply would not surrender. Her relationship with Lord Delacourt was at the top of the list, second only to her children.

Delacourt cut a glamorous swath through the salons and ballrooms of London. Despite his youth, his effect on women was already becoming the stuff of which torrid rumor—if not outright legend—was made. Oh, Delacourt was brash, even occasionally arrogant, but that did not overly trouble Jonet. She let her eyes drift approvingly over his length. Before her mourning had begun, the young lord had made her a handsome, gracious escort. And at present, he was an affectionate companion who carefully hid his own pain behind a façade of cutting wit.

But the pain was nonetheless there, acute and real. The knowledge left Jonet reluctant to add to his troubles. But there was, simply put, no one else to whom she might turn for solace, and sharing her concerns about Cole Amherst—or at least *some* of her concerns—had already brought her a measure of peace.

Abruptly, Delacourt spun about to a fully seated position and sat his empty glass upon the table between them. "Blister it, Jonnie, if I've a clue as to what's best done," he said bluntly, running a hand through hair that was such a dark shade of auburn it appeared black in the candlelight. "It was well done to send for your Bow Street fellow, but what sort of hearsay he shall turn up on a man such as Amherst I cannot imagine."

"Captain Amherst's credentials are impressive," agreed Jonet, leaning forward to take up the brandy bottle from its salver. "I daresay he is all that he claims. I simply hope he isn't something more."

"He is very striking, m'dear," said Delacourt casually, his languid gaze on her hand as she filled his glass. "I hope that you do not fancy him."

Jonet narrowed her eyes. "I should slap you senseless, David, for suggesting such a thing."

With an arm that was long and graceful, David reached across the narrow table and slid one finger beneath her chin. "Go ahead, Jonet, if you dare. And you are a very daring woman."

With a heavy clunk, Jonet put down the bottle. "Do not be impudent, David! This is a serious business. These are my children. You know I'll run no risk where they are concerned."

The young man looked suddenly solemn, yet he shrugged his shoulders uncertainly beneath the fabric of his fine claret-colored coat. "What would you wish me to do, my dear? Have some Southwark sea dog slit his throat?" He gave a little shudder. "That is very vulgar, not to mention messy. But I will do it, if it pleases you."

"Rather tempting, but I think not, you vicious boy." Jonet gave him a sweet smile, then snapped her brows together as a troublesome thought recurred. "And another odd thing, David. Amherst refuses to live here. Have you any idea why? Surely James wants his spy within the house—at all times, not just during the day. I wonder he did not jump at such an opportunity."

David leaned across the table then and laid out his right hand, palm up. Reflexively, Jonet slid hers into it, and lightly, he squeezed it. "All of our jesting aside, Jonet, I shan't let him hurt you," he said softly. "You know that, do you not? I would never have let Henry hurt you, and I shan't let Amherst."

"Ugh!" answered Jonet. "Let us not talk of Henry. I vow his very presence haunts this house."

"Would you be better pleased to remove to my seat in Derbyshire? You are very welcome to it, you know." Instinctively, he stroked his thumb back and forth over the palm of her hand in a gesture that always soothed her. "Or perhaps we might return to Kildermore, where at least we can reside under the same roof without setting all of London ablaze with gossip."

Jonet lifted her eyes from their clasped hands and stared up at him. "We cannot hide, David," she said bleakly. "It was no safer at Kildermore than it was here. You know that. Please do not press me to leave again. I must remain fixed in London until I can discover just where the danger lies." She looked plaintively into his deep green eyes. "You understand that, do you not? That we can never be safe until I have put this matter fully to rest?"

David ran his free hand down his face, looking suddenly weary. "Yes, you are right. If we rid ourselves of Amherst, there will simply be another of James's schemes to replace him. Let him stay, I suppose. Whilst he is here, I shall make every excuse to be in and out of this house. I shall dine here whenever possible—*if* you will have me?" He paused for Jonet's sarcastic look, laughed lightly, then continued. "And your man from Bow Street can make it a point to have him watched should it become necessary."

Slowly, Jonet nodded and drew her hand from his. "Yes, Charlie has already set a footman on his heels," she answered, sliding back into her seat to gaze at him across the table. "Oh, David," she said a little despairingly, "I grow so tired of all this. Let us talk of more pleasant things." Abruptly, she got up from the sofa, crossed the room to a stout mahogany secretary, and pulled open the top drawer.

She returned to her chair, a tiny velvet box held in her outstretched hand. "I cannot wait, David. This is your birthday present. May I give it to you now?"

David pulled a hesitant face. "I hope, my dear," he said in a chiding tone, "that you have not been extravagant again this year. Last year's jeweled snuffbox must have cost a king's ransom."

Hand still outstretched, Jonet bit her lip and shook her head. "Have no fear," she finally said. "This one cost me nary a farthing." She dropped the velvet box into the palm of David's hand, sinking back into her chair as he flipped it open to stare at the ornately carved gold ring.

With a sharp intake of breath, David lifted it out and held it to the candlelight, turning it this way and that as he watched the gold gleam. Carefully, he slid it onto his right hand and studied the deeply etched crest for a long, expectant moment.

"My dear," he said at last, "where did you get this?" His voice was a little accusatory.

Jonet leaned forward and poured herself a drink, striking the rim of the goblet a little too hard. The chink of glass on crystal pierced the silence, and Jonet noticed that her hand was shaking ever so slightly. But indeed, she had not expected this to be easy.

"It is a family heirloom of the earldom of Kildermore, David," she said lightly. "The ring is very old, and legend says that it will bring its owner good luck and great fortune. I want you to have it."

"No, I cannot take this," said David, his voice unsteady. He replaced the ring and shoved the box away from him. "It is simply not done. People will talk." His gaze lifted to hold hers, his eyes questioning and intense, as if he searched her face for some hidden meaning.

"Nonsense," she retorted. "I want you to have it. I find I no longer care what people say about us. Put it in your vault where it will be safe. I certainly understand if you prefer not to wear it in public, but it would mean a great deal to me to know that you have it."

Jonet was saved from further argument by Donaldson, who arrived to call them in to dinner. Quickly, she snatched up the box and pressed it into his hand. "David—please? It is an outward token of my love and esteem for you. Come, can you not accept that?"

After another long moment, he mutely nodded and slipped the box into his pocket. Then, impulsively, Lord Delacourt slid his fingers into the soft hair at the nape of her neck and bent to kiss her lightly on the forehead.

Cole returned to Brook Street the following morning, his mind somewhat more settled. During the seemingly endless night, he had finally decided what to do. He was going to accept the post as tutor to Lord Mercer and his young brother. He did not fully understand *why* he had reached such a decision, but when he had weighed all the factors and made up his mind, his choice had brought him a measure of inner peace, and he had at last been able to sleep.

More surprising than that, however, was Cole's decision to accept Lady Mercer's edict that he live in her home on Brook Street. He hoped he was doing it for the right reasons. But in truth, he had already heard enough, and seen enough, to make him very ill at ease. Although he was far more trusting of James than was Lady Mercer, Cole, too, wondered about his uncle's true motivations. Moreover, he had thought a great deal about Stuart's reticence and apprehension. What could make a nine-year-old boy behave so strangely?

There were other signs, too, that all was not well at Mercer House. The footmen who quite obviously were not footmen, the gardener who did more watching than gardening. Edmund's snide remarks about finding Lady Mercer's children inconvenient had also continued to nag at him. But most disturbing of all was Lady Mercer's erratic behavior. Initially blinded by his own unfamiliar and unsettling emotions, Cole had failed to fully note the nuances in her demeanor. Upon further consideration, however, he conceded that she had at times appeared almost . . . *worried.* Perhaps that was too strong a word. Nonetheless, he suspected that some of what he had taken for anger might instead have been thinly veiled anxiety.

And so, in the end, Cole had accepted the fact that it was left to him to make certain that all was well. After all, he reminded himself, there were the children to consider.

He was admitted to Lady Mercer's house without incident by the two sturdy footmen, who were now surprisingly civil. The shorter of the two dutifully trotted off with Cole's card and returned a moment later to say that her ladyship was at work in the book-room, and would be pleased to see him there.

There was a comfortable sort of warmth within the book-room, which was long and narrow, yet inviting despite its size. With its high, elegant ceiling, and a bank of deep windows heavily draped in bottle green velvet, the room looked to be an oasis of masculine affability. The interior was warmed by a burnished oak floor, and softened by an Oriental carpet in time-worn shades of burgundy and brown. At the long end of the chamber stood a fine chimneypiece of pale green marble, topped by a high oak mantel. Cole could see that the hearth had long since been swept. The room was filled end to end with fine leather-bound books, and it possessed a simplicity of décor which Cole found tranquil and inviting.

Beyond any doubt, this was a man's room. And yet, Cole knew instinctively that it belonged to her. To the woman who sat sewing to one side of the hearth, the two silky border collies lounging at her feet. As he crossed the threshold, Cole remembered his words of yesterday and wished he had not spoken them. He wished he had not lost his temper with Lady Mercer, though he had no intention of apologizing for that which she had so deliberately goaded. He must have hesitated in the doorway for several moments after the footman announced him. She did not rise, but instead put her sewing aside and motioned him toward a chair.

"Good morning, Captain." Her voice was throaty, with a pleasing, almost masculine resonance. Despite its haughty edge, Cole felt lust stir inside his chest, and ruthlessly crushed it. Rogue, the younger collie, leapt up to sniff lazily at Cole's boots as he crossed the length of the room, but Scoundrel lay quietly upon the carpet, tucked beneath the chair at his mistress's heels.

"Lady Mercer?" Cole swallowed hard and reluctantly took the chair across from hers. It placed him a little nearer to her than he cared to be. "I believe I spoke precipitately yesterday."

"Indeed you did," she agreed with a regal tilt of her head. "And on any number of points. But to which of those precipitate remarks do you refer, Captain?" She shifted in her chair, sending the carved jet cross sliding seductively along the creamy flesh above her neckline. Her demeanor was still cool and detached, reminding Cole yet again that his duties here might be more difficult, and far more complex, than he had first believed.

"I refer, ma'am, to my refusal to take up residence here," he said calmly.

Her deep blue eyes flew open wide at that, and suddenly, Lady Mercer no longer looked detached. She looked agitated. Perhaps even apprehensive. Cole had no wish to frighten her. "If you have changed your mind, my lady, you need only say so. However, your sons . . . well, I am a little concerned, that is all."

"Concerned, sir? In what way?" Her voice was sharp with unease, and the elder dog sensed it. He came from beneath the chair and circled Jonet, sniffing at her hand until she touched him. Absently, she slicked a hand over his snowy head and the dog flopped down again.

Obviously awaiting an answer to her question, Jonet leaned forward, tightening the plain fabric of her mourning dress to reveal breasts that were high, full, and perfectly shaped. To his consternation, he discovered that he could not pull his gaze from her—from *her*. Even the swell of that exquisite bosom could not compete with the beauty and intensity of her face.

The woman had a way of focusing the whole of her attention on him. Boldly and purposefully, in a way that few women of Cole's acquaintance had the confidence to do. And yet, there was no hint of capriciousness in her. Like a watchful tigress, Lady Mercer's eyes were ever wary, and Cole was certain she would not hesitate to spring were it necessary. Such confidence was the mark of a good soldier. In selecting and assigning men, Cole had deliberately sought out those special few who had that same purposeful look, that utter lack of vacillation. At his next thought, he found himself compelled to suppress a bark of laughter. But dear God, it was so true! Lady Mercer would have made one hell of a warrior.

"Have I said something humorous, sir?" she asked pointedly. "I fancy you are laughing."

Cole was taken aback. "Why, I do not believe that I am, my lady."

"Have a care, sir," she cautioned, her tone mocking. "After all, I understand that I am called the 'Sorceress of Strathclyde.' I can see into the darkest corners of men's hearts."

Cole suppressed an impulsive grin. It felt strangely incongruous in her presence. "Then you shall see little enough humor in mine, Lady Mercer," he said lightly.

"Call me Jonet," she corrected abruptly. "And I beg to argue, sir. You are laughing inside, and it is all the same, you see. Now, I merely wish to know what it is you find so humorous. Come, will you not share your joke with me, *Cousin*?"

He did not miss the hint of sarcasm, but today he

merely wondered if something more serious lay behind it. "Very well, ma'am. It seems you have caught me out. I found myself thinking that you would have made a fine soldier. I have trained a few in my day, and I believe I know the necessary traits."

Lady Mercer set her head to one side again in that quizzical way of hers. "And those traits would be . . . ?"

Suddenly, Cole sobered. He looked at her and could see no reason not to answer. "A good soldier never hesitates when battle finally comes, ma'am," he responded, lightly resting one hand across his knee. "Perhaps he does not seek it. Indeed, he may even be filled with dread at the prospect, but he takes up the challenge boldly. It is a knack some men simply do not have."

"And few women?" she asked a little caustically. "I have often been accused of being overly bold, sir."

Cole nodded. "It was not ill-meant, your ladyship."

"You will call me Jonet," she said again.

"I think that unwise, ma'am. I am your children's tutor."

Lady Mercer drew her full lips into a stubborn line and stared into the depths of the book-room. "Captain, you have come to me ostensibly as a member of my late husband's family. You refuse to accept a salary—at least from *me*." She flicked a guarded look at him. "And if we are to reside in this house together under such circumstances, I daresay we ought to go on as we have begun."

"And that would be?"

"As *cousins*. Therefore, I am Jonet. And you are—*Cole*, is it not?"

"As you wish," he stiffly replied.

"Thank you," she said softly, then pulled her gaze from his and took up her sewing once more. With quick, precise motions, her needle began to dart in and out, then draw taut the thread, time and again. As with most of Jonet Rowland, her hands appeared superficially delicate, but Cole could sense the tremendous strength contained within them.

For a time, he was content to simply watch her, and she seemed equally content to let him do so. It was an unusual level of familiarity between two people who were so vastly different from one another; who did not even like one another, but who had quite obviously decided to bow to the dictates of civility and pretend. As if she felt his eyes upon her task, Lady Mercer's gaze caught his for a moment, and she smiled. "Satan finds some mischief for idle hands to do," she quoted, as if an explanation were expected. "Is that not what the Bible teaches?"

Cole shifted uncomfortably in his chair. "The Bible does caution us that sloth is an insidious vice, ma'am. But I believe those particular words belong to Mr. Watts."

"Indeed?" She looked at him a little strangely. "How astute you are, sir. And who is Mr. Watts?"

"A theologian, ma'am. And a writer of hymns."

"Ah, yes! I am persuaded you are right," she replied, drawing taut her final stitch. Then, with sharp white teeth, she bit her thread neatly in two and set down her work. "Now, do you mean to tell me, Cole, just what it is about my children which concerns you? I have, of course, my own worries."

Cole felt the heat of her steady blue eyes on his face. It was a good question, and yet he hesitated. He had seen her children, he had felt their vulnerability. But how could he explain it? How could he share with this woman things he had never shared with anyone—not even the one person with whom he should have shared all things? He had no wish to lay bare his own soul to Lady Mercer, a woman who, by some accounts, had none herself. Cole was not sure he believed that, but he simply could not bring himself to explain to her the truth; that he had once been afraid and fatherless, and that he would forever understand a child's sense of terror and loss. And as to his other concerns—the scent of danger, that prickling sensation which crept down his spine at odd moments—how could he account for what was mostly a soldier's instinct?

Only last night had he begun to lend words, and perhaps some small amount of logic, to those feelings himself. Good God, he would scare Lady Mercer out of her wits. Or she might simply accuse him of attempting to frighten her. Or she might think him mad. Perhaps he was. Where *was* the danger? To *whom* was it directed? He had no notion. Perhaps he was merely suffering from the residual stress of battle. It had been months, he suddenly realized, since he had slept well. And Lady Mercer certainly seemed to shake his sanity at odd moments. Absently, Cole pulled the eyeglasses from his face and began to rub hard at his left temple.

His head was beginning to ache again, and the new glasses had not helped at all. "Perhaps your sons are struggling with their father's death rather more than I had initially suspected, ma'am," he finally managed to utter. "And I hope you will take no offence when I say that your children are in need of more attention than I had first believed."

Lady Mercer nodded slowly, still looking past his shoulder. She had the look of a woman caught in the web of her own introspection. A woman who, just perhaps, had a few regrets after all. And what sort of regrets? Cole burned to know. In truth, he burned to know her better.

He did not like her, it was true. She was proud, distant,

and almost painfully beautiful to look upon. And it was entirely possible—entirely likely, in fact—that she had had a hand in her husband's death. But she was a fascinating woman just the same. Moreover, he was a philosopher, a student of human nature, was he not?

A very devoted student, too, it would seem. For at that very moment, Cole would have cut off his right hand to know what was in Jonet Rowland's hard, but very obviously melancholy, heart. Perplexingly, however, Lady Mercer neither asked for nor offered further explanation. Instead, her words seemed carefully chosen and hesitantly spoken.

"His late lordship had many failings, Captain," she said quietly. "But he *was* an adequate father. Perhaps not the sort I would have chosen for my children, had I any say in the matter. But Lord Mercer did care for his sons, and they loved him deeply. And they now suffer greatly from his loss."

Cole politely attempted to keep the cynicism from showing in his face, but apparently he failed. Lady Mercer fixed him with a long, assessing stare, as if taking his measure against some standard he did not understand. A ghost of what looked like regret drifted over her eyes, and abruptly, she shoved aside her sewing, jerked from her chair, and crossed to the window.

Cole felt tension draw tight in the air as he watched Lady Mercer pull back the draperies and stare out into the street. When at last she spoke, her voice was thick with emotion. "Did you imagine, Captain, that I was so unfeeling as not to know that? That I had failed to notice my children are hurting? If so, let me disabuse you of that notion. I do feel, and I do know it. And it is breaking my heart."

Cole could hear the catch in her throat; he could almost

see the unshed tears which threatened, and he felt deeply ashamed. He had risen from his seat and unwittingly crossed the room to join her by the window. Lightly, he laid his hand upon her shoulder. "I am sorry, ma'am. I did not mean to imply that—"

"I do not give a damn what you did or did not mean," she interjected harshly, spinning away from the window to stare up at him. Cole stood facing her now, but she jerked her eyes away, refusing to hold his gaze, as if she were ashamed of her own weakness. In the pale sunlight, Lady Mercer's face was wan, her eyes limpid, rapidly blinking. Inside the sheath of black, which she wore with such innate elegance, she seemed almost to tremble.

In the face of such profound emotion—grief, guilt, pain; he neither knew nor cared—Cole's gentlemanly instincts rose to the surface. Unfortunately, a few of his more libidinous ones came along with them. He was frustrated to realize how urgently he wished to draw her into his arms, to kiss away the tears that now spiked her long black lashes. She was dangerous. *Wicked.* And yet, in that moment, Cole ceased to care.

He stood very near to her now, near enough to draw in her exotic fragrance, made more potent by the heat of her emotion. The turn of her cheek and jaw was delicate, her face molded as if from the finest ivory porcelain. Cole wanted desperately to cradle it in his rough hands and kiss away the sadness. And almost as though the extremity were not his own, but someone else's, Cole watched as his right hand came up to do just that.

Gently, ever so lightly, he let his willful fingers slide around the curve of her face, delicately cupping it, and brushing his thumb tenderly across the satiny flesh beneath her eye, as if to wipe away the tears which had not yet fallen. To his shock, Lady Mercer's eyes dropped slowly shut, the damp, silky lashes fanning across her cheeks, and almost imperceptibly, she turned her face into the warmth of his hand, opening her mouth ever so slightly against the broad palm, and drawing in a deep, unsteady breath against his callused skin.

In that instant, it seemed to Cole as if the earth stopped spinning. Time froze, and in this one infinitesimal moment, no one else existed, save himself and this beautiful, darkly enigmatic woman. It was as if there were no higher purpose in his life, save comforting her, keeping her safe from the demons which so obviously threatened. But then slowly, without opening her eyes, Lady Mercer slid her left hand over his own, hesitated ever so briefly, and dragged his hand from her face. Almost ruthlessly, she pushed it away, and turned her back on him.

No longer able to see if her eyes were open or closed, Cole felt a heated sense of mortification sweep over him. Anger followed fast on its heels, directed both at himself, and inexplicably, at her. When she spoke, her words were flat, wholly without emotion of any sort. "I suggest, sir, that you save your sympathy for my children, whom I can assure you have every need of it. Do we understand one another?"

Strangely, the rebuff stung, as if it had come from an old friend rather than a distant acquaintance. Reluctant to examine that emotion too closely, Cole steeled his gaze and stared at her. "Perfectly, ma'am," he answered.

"Very well." She came away from the window, her shoulders set stiffly back, and returned to her chair, sitting down so rigidly that her spine never touched the upholstery. Cole watched her go, not knowing what further to do, and then followed. It was as if those few emotional moments had never existed. Clearly, that was what Lady

Mercer wished. With grim determination, Cole decided to oblige her. What the devil had come over him, anyway? Did she truly have an almost magical hold over men? It was often said of her. It seemed his hand had moved to touch her entirely of its own accord.

Suddenly, Cole's attention jerked back to the present. Lady Mercer was speaking, her voice cool, as if nothing untoward had occurred. "You may remove from your lodgings in Red Lion Street as soon as is convenient, sir, if that is still your wish. But understand me. The welfare of my children comes first in this house. You are to teach them well, and above all, to keep them safe. You will exercise no undue influence upon them"—her tone seemed to soften—"and you will discipline them as best you can without breaking their spirits."

"Their spirits, ma'am?"

"I would have you make race horses of them, sir, not dray horses," she answered a little more crisply. Then, Lady Mercer leaned forward and sighed. "But they are mischievous, and occasionally willful, it is true. Perhaps I have even spoilt them a bit these past few months, but I have been so very af—so very concerned. About their losing their father," she belatedly added.

Cole listened, not just to her words, but to the tone behind them, and heard nothing but the voice of a devoted mother who was sincerely concerned for her children. Just as she professed to be. But not at all as he had expected. Still, words were one thing, and actions quite another. It would not take long to ascertain just what sort of mother Lady Mercer really was. "They are lively boys, ma'am," he agreed with a stiff smile, "but they are quite bright. I promise I shan't resort to beating them."

Lady Mercer looked at him and lifted her shoulders a

little beneath the black fabric of her dress. "If you cannot manage them, there is no shame in it, sir. Simply come to me, and I will intervene. I do assure you that I *can* make them behave, for they know perfectly well that they cannot pull the wool over my eyes."

Cole smiled wryly at that. "No, ma'am. I expect few people can."

Looking surprised, Lady Mercer opened her mouth as if she might reply, then reconsidered it. After a moment, she returned to their earlier topic. "Regarding your removal from your apartments, Char—*Mr.* Donaldson—can send someone, should you wish him to."

Her words held a wealth of significance, but it took Cole a moment to understand the two very important things she had just confirmed: Lady Mercer and her butler were on very familiar terms. Indeed, Cole had already noted the knowing glances which passed between them. But the second realization gave him rather more pause. Cole had never told her where he lived.

The former was none of his business. Cole did not doubt that Jonet Rowland was more woman than Lord Delacourt could handle. Charles Donaldson was a strapping, good-looking fellow, and stranger things had happened amongst the *ton.* His Uncle James had called Lady Mercer an immoral whore, but on that fine point, his uncle's blue-blooded double standard became glaringly obvious. Lord Mercer's penchant for courtesans and widows had been no secret, and on more than one occasion, even the haughty James himself had been known to toss up the skirts of a half-willing parlor maid.

What was it to them or to Cole—or to anyone but God—if Lady Mercer chose to take her pleasures with a butler? Or chose to bed a vigorous and handsome young man like Delacourt? On moral grounds, Cole disapproved of such behavior, particularly when it was done with so little regard for discretion. Adultery flew in the face of all that he believed in. But was her sin any worse than theirs? And what right had any of them to pass judgement on another's transgression? Cole was hardly a candidate for sainthood. Indeed, it was all he could do to keep his own lust at bay. Ruthlessly, he forced away all thought of his employer's proclivity for mortal sin—and his rather vivid imaginings of what she might look like in the midst of it.

Further, he decided to ask Lady Mercer nothing about her knowledge of his address. That little fact bore further thought. Indeed it did.

"I believe I shall keep my rooms, ma'am," he finally explained. "As it happens, I have a great many personal possessions, primarily books, which I arranged to have sent down from—er—by my orderly. I daresay they would be an inconvenience."

"Not at all," she smoothly replied. "There is a small suite on the third floor which you may take if it pleases you. It contains a bedchamber with a dressing room, and a sitting room in which you may receive personal guests, should you wish to."

"You are most accommodating, ma'am," he demurred, "but I do not entertain. My leisure hours are generally spent at my club, or in the various organizations to which I belong."

Lady Mercer's eyes narrowed in a rather feline fashion. "To which club do you belong? And to what sort of organizations?" Her questions were sharp, and brooked no opposition.

Cole hesitated, more unwilling than ever to reveal anything of himself to this woman. Perhaps Jonet Rowland really did have the Scottish gift. Perhaps she really could see into his heart. How appalling. How fanciful. "Nothing very grand, ma'am," he hedged.

"I wish to know the habits of the man who is to educate my children," she insisted.

"The United Service Club and the MCC," he reluctantly answered. "I also belong to the London Society of Theologians, and the Philosophos Society."

Lady Mercer's delicate black brows flew up in amazement. "Are you really something of a theologian, then? How quaint!"

Cole had the distinct feeling that her mild condescension was meant to place a distance between them. To set him, perhaps, in his place. He felt his temper spike. " 'Quaint' is not a word normally applied to the subject, ma'am."

If she noticed his ire, she gave no sign of it. "And the *Philosophos* Society, did you say?" She gave a humorless smile. "I understand my late husband was a member of the Society of Philistines himself—or was it the Philanderers? I can never quite remember."

Lady Mercer looked up at him with a perfectly straight face, and suddenly, Cole wanted to burst out laughing. She really was the most perplexing woman. The scholarly moralist inside him knew that he should have been appalled by her jest, not to mention her apparently total lack of contrition. A moment ago, he had been angry, and now, he could find little of that emotion inside himself. He felt confused and uncharacteristically unsteady. With a bemused expression, Lady Mercer reached into her sewing basket and tugged out another bit of fabric. Cole looked at it in some amazement, his senses reeling again.

Bloody hell. *The Marchioness of Mercer was darning*

stockings? Her children's, by the look of them. How out of character it seemed. But what was her character? What manner of woman was she, really? In truth, Cole suddenly realized, he knew so little. He did not like her, he reminded himself. No, he did not. But he could not help but admire her at times. Forcing away those thoughts, Cole flipped open his folio and began to talk of lesson plans.

4

The Captain encamps behind Enemy lines

An hour later, Jonet watched in silence as Cole Amherst left the book-room, his backbone rigid, his gait smooth and soldierly. Good Lord, she was relieved to see him go. Absently, she slicked her hand back and forth over Scoundrel's silky head. Jonet felt inordinately stupid for having surrendered to her fears; for letting her knees almost buckle beneath her from the grief and the anger. For having believed, even for a moment, that it was safe to take comfort from Captain Cole Amherst.

Instinctively, however, she had yearned to do precisely that. Just why, she could not say. Perhaps it was the uniform? That perfect, ramrod straight posture? Or his incredibly wide-set shoulders? Lightly, Jonet laughed at her foolishness. Yes, Amherst certainly looked to be the sort of man a weak woman might lean on. But she was not weak. It was a luxury she could ill afford.

Thank heaven she had quickly set matters aright between them. Jonet knew how to drive to an inch; men or horses, it made no difference. Both were carefully honed skills, and neither suitable for the faint of heart. From a young age, she had learned when to push them forward, and at precisely what point one should hold them back. And how to show them who held the reins. Now, both talents had become almost instinctive. And in her world, both were survival skills. Jonet snagged her lip and bit a little too hard, wincing at the pain. Only with Cole Amherst did her control seem to slip. How very rare that was. She almost never let a man get the upper hand on her.

But all was not lost. Indeed, there was some small element of promise. Amherst's visit had been relatively short, yet in that time, they had managed not only to reach an uneasy truce but they had also formulated a lesson plan for Stuart and Robert that should carry them successfully through the following three months. In his quiet but insistent way, Amherst had given her a list of items he required for the schoolroom. Her eyes fell upon it, taking in the neatly lined columns and small, precise letters. The man seemed entirely serious about his business. In fact, Amherst had obviously given the needs of her children a great deal of thought. And amazingly, he had included her in his planning without her having demanded he do so.

There was something else she found very odd, too. Cox, one of the new footmen whom Charlie had handpicked from amongst his regimental cronies, had followed Amherst home the previous night. Amherst had not gone directly to James Rowland's house, as Jonet had assumed he would. Instead, he had walked a long distance up High Holborn, then gone into the Church of Saint Andrew, of all things, where he had remained for the better part of an hour.

Cox was hardly a swift thinker, but he had had the presence of mind to peek into the church to see if perhaps Amherst had gone there to meet someone. But Amherst had been alone, engrossed in his meditation. Afterward, he had strolled down to The Mitre, a public house near Bloomsbury which was always filled with an odd assortment of actors and poets, and by a great many impoverished law students from the nearby Inns of the Court.

There he had ordered a light dinner, washed it down with two pints of cider, and politely refused both a game of cards and a willing prostitute. Amherst spent the remainder of the evening chatting, then went quietly home to a respectable set of lodgings in Red Lion Street. Strange behavior indeed for a nefarious spy. Suddenly Jonet choked on a swell of doubt.

Could she be wrong about Amherst? Or more to the point, could she be wrong about James Rowland? Was the man nothing more than the pompous prig she had always believed him? Such a possibility was unthinkable. The danger was too great to have been underestimated; too vile to attribute to the wrong party. If Jonet admitted that she might be wrong about James, she would have to acknowledge that she did not know who or where her enemies were. And were they even *her* enemies? Perhaps she had panicked unnecessarily.

During the initial hours after Henry's death, the nervous magistrate, Mr. Lyons, had intently questioned Hannah, the chambermaid, who was but one of many women who had warmed her husband's bed. It had been difficult indeed for Hannah to explain how she had been the one to discover the master lying dead in his bedchamber at three in the morning. Hannah had left the room a quaking bundle of nerves, but Jonet had no reason to believe the maid would have actually killed anyone, vain and silly though she was. Surely the girl could not have formed a real *tendre* for Henry? Nonetheless, Jonet had dismissed her, as she had all the servants, giving them two months' pay and a letter of reference.

Could Henry have died by his mistress's hand? Glorianna Lanier was a thin, energetic, rather volatile widow of questionable conduct. Not the sort Henry usually chose, for she was still accepted in society—but only just. Yet, surely Henry had been worth more alive than dead, as far as Mrs. Lanier was concerned? But there again—his own lofty opinion notwithstanding—Henry was hardly the most skilled or patient of lovers. Had his mistress killed him, it would likely have been out of sexual frustration, not torrid passion.

David had suggested that perhaps it was a political enemy, for he had been on the wrong side of several heated debates last year. Yet Henry's attendance in Parliament had been sporadic; he went only when his vote might benefit him. Indeed, though few would have admitted it, many had disliked him, for he had been both arrogant and self-indulgent. But one could trip over another just like him in almost any London drawing room, so common were men of Henry's ilk.

So why kill him? Only James, or someone within his family, had a true motive for that. Absently, Jonet slid her hands up and down her cold arms. Cole Amherst's departure seemed to have stripped the room of all its warmth and tranquility. Cutting off her foolish thoughts, Jonet rang the bell, deciding that a fire would be needed after all. As she waited, she took up her thin black shawl, wrapped it about her shoulders, and curled up in a chair by the hearth.

She was so bloody tired. So tired of being constantly vigilant. In Scotland, where she had gone to seek solace and safety, Jonet had begun to wonder if she would ever feel rested or warm or secure again. But now, she had the most fanciful notion that if Cole Amherst were near, she would feel immeasurably safer. Ha! Only yesterday she had imagined him to be her worst enemy. She still was not sure just who or what he was. Nor did she really like him, for she could sense his subtle air of moral superiority. And yet, his mere presence brought a sense of security into a room that not even David or Charlie could provide.

Agnes, her parlor maid, came in. Seeing Jonet shivering in the chair, she pursed her lips into a silent scold and began at once to build up a fire. Jonet managed a grateful smile. When she had been thrown into a panic in Scotland, Jonet had believed that if she surrounded herself with people she trusted—like Agnes and Charlie—they would provide her with a sense of security, but it had helped little. Dear heaven, how she hated that. The awful *uncertainty*. Jonet had never before been an indecisive person. What little had been hers in life to control, she had controlled with a strong sense of purpose. It had earned her nothing but criticism, and a reputation for being too willful. James Rowland, she knew, had been foremost among her detractors.

Well, they could all go straight to the devil as far as Jonet was concerned. Her world had been set on its ear the day she had given birth to her first child, for it was only then that she had realized that she was wholly responsible for someone other than herself. Suddenly, she had known that she must take command of her life. She could no longer afford to be sad or meek or sniveling. To go rambling haplessly through life, as if she had surrendered both her spirit and her sense. It simply would not do. What sort of children could such a pathetically weak woman hope to raise?

After her wedding, Jonet had tried to make Henry love

her; indeed, she had *tried* to love him. Too late, she realized that she had been nothing more than a challenge to his manly pride, and when he finally lost all interest in his much-coveted wife, Jonet had not felt the loss too deeply. But now that Henry was dead, her life and most everything in it was at last hers to control, and yet she felt more lost and alone than ever. More useless, more ineffectual. She longed for someone whom she could rely upon.

Good heavens, what was wrong with her? *Someone to rely upon?* How naïve! She could rely upon no one but herself. She had learned that lesson long ago, and learned it the hard way. Still, in her mind's eye, all she could see was Cole Amherst, with his tawny hair and lean hips. That determined, long-legged gait, the way he had of fixing his brown-gold eyes upon a person, then piercing through to their soul.

Jonet had never met a man who exuded such quiet confidence, such forceful, focused intellect—or so much raw power held in check. Her strange attraction to Amherst disturbed her to the point that, at times, she wanted to be deliberately sharp with him. She wanted to challenge him, and yet Amherst rose to the bait only on his terms. Strangely enough, Jonet had discovered that she respected that. How different life might have been had she had a real marriage partner. Instinctively, she knew that it *would* have been different, though she had seen precious few good marriages in her day. Certainly her parents' marriage had been a poor example, for her father's notorious indiscretions had put even Henry to the blush.

At last, Agnes put the poker back into the rack with a clatter and left the room. The greedy flames licked up beyond the kindling to eat away the coals, reminding Jonet that her day, too, was swiftly disappearing. Other than a quiet two hours with the boys, followed by dinner with David and Ellen, she had nothing more to look forward to.

What she *had* looked forward to, strangely enough, was dinner with Cole Amherst, but he had vexed her by claiming a previous engagement. Jonet burned to know where he was going, and with whom he would dine. Did he have perhaps a mistress? A sweetheart? She felt a stinging sense of disappointment at that thought. He could well afford to keep a wife in good style; Jonet could discern that much with one sweeping glance. And even had he been born a poor man, which Jonet rather doubted, a man such as he never stayed so for long. Which only begged the question of why he had come to school her children.

Jonet shook her head against the smooth leather of the chair. The villain she sought *had* to be James, she reminded herself with a measure of regret. There was no other reason he would send such a man into her house.

Cole walked with the butler into the hall to await Jonet's carriage, which was to take him back to his rooms. The morning breeze had been fierce, and Cole gladly took his greatcoat from the butler's outstretched hand, studying the man's face again as he did so. Curiosity finally bested him. "Sir, you look somewhat familiar to me," Cole said. "Lord Robert tells me you were in the Peninsula. I wonder—had we the pleasure of meeting? I was with the First Royal Dragoons."

Donaldson looked at him a little warily. "I'm no certain, sir. 'Tis possible, I'm sure."

"What regiment were you with?" Cole persisted.

"Royal Scots, sir."

"Ah!" said Cole appreciatively. "Quite gallant soldiers.

Such bravery at Salamanca. You seem to have made quite an impression on Lady Mercer's sons."

At last, the butler smiled. "Aye, they're good lads, sir. But young ones see only the heroic, never the brutality—which is as it should be," he added.

"Very true," agreed Cole, pleased that the butler's reticence seemed to be weakening. "Tell me—were you at Vittoria? I understood Robert to say you were wounded. Is that when you returned to England?"

"Aye, but tae Scotland, sir," the tall man corrected, looking rather chagrined. "I got the business end of a bayonet at Vittoria, I did. I was invalided oot and missed the rest o' the war."

"I see," said Cole solemnly. "What did you do thereafter?"

Donaldson blinked at that. "Why, I went back home, sir. To Kildermore."

"Kildermore?" Cole was a little surprised. "Do you mean Kildermore Castle? Lady Mercer's childhood home?"

"Oh, aye. Lady Jonet—that is t'say, Lady Mercer—took me back into service at once."

Cole considered that for a moment. "Well, Donaldson, you were a fortunate man. Not many soldiers came home to find gainful employment awaiting them."

The butler inclined his head slightly. "Most fortunate. But Lady Jonet made it plain that there would always be a place for me. She said I was t'go straight there, soon as I was discharged." The butler drew himself up another notch. "There've been Donaldsons at Kildermore for three hundred years. I was born there, and God willing, I'll die there, too."

Cole was amazed. "You have known her ladyship for quite a long time?"

"Why, all my life, sir. There's naught but six months between us, me being the elder." Suddenly, Donaldson clapped his mouth shut, as if he feared he had said too much.

Cole considered asking further questions, then thought the better of it. There was no need to press his luck with this man. But perhaps he had already learned something very important. He was not perfectly sure. Just then, the clopping and creaking of a team and carriage slowed to a halt outside.

"Well, Donaldson," Cole said briskly, "I shall return with my things shortly, but I must regrettably go out again for the evening. However, some night in the near future, perhaps you will give me a game of cards? Or permit me to stand you a pint? Then we old soldiers can exchange war stories, eh?"

For a brief moment, Donaldson looked taken aback. Suddenly, his amiable face split into a wide grin. "Aye, Captain. Suppose there'd be little enough harm in that."

In the late hours of the afternoon, Cole found himself completely unpacked and all his possessions neatly arranged by Jonet's efficient staff. Moreover, he was already dressed and ready for dinner in Albemarle Street, where he was to join his friend and fellow officer, Terrence Madlow. Absently, Cole tugged out his watch to see that he was, as usual, too early.

Lest heated thoughts of Lady Mercer again return to bedevil him, as they had done with a rather disturbing frequency these last few days, Cole looked about for something to occupy his mind. Suddenly, he remembered that he was in need of a good Latin dictionary for the schoolroom and that he had neglected to put it on the list he had given Lady Mercer. Undoubtedly, her vast library would contain such a thing.

A few moments later, Cole entered the book-room, which at first he took to be empty. Suddenly, a soft curse sounded from a poorly lit corner. Cole looked down the length of the room to see a tall, russet-haired woman of an uncertain age reaching up most awkwardly for a book perched upon a high shelf. Caught in mid-stretch, she looked at Cole, blushing effusively. "Oh!" she said softly, and drew back her hand.

"I beg your pardon, ma'am. I thought the room unoccupied." Cole turned to go.

"Oh, no! I wish you would not hasten away," the woman said. She came swiftly across the room, her head cocked inquisitively to one side, her hand outstretched in greeting. Her eyes were so pretty, her gestures so very like Jonet's, Cole realized at once that she must be a relation.

"I believe you must be Captain Amherst?" she said pleasantly. "Have I guessed aright?"

"Indeed. But I fear you have the advantage of me, Miss—?"

"Cameron. Miss Ellen Cameron, Lady Mercer's cousin," she explained, giving Cole a smile which softened her rather plain face. She leaned forward to rest her hands atop a high-backed settee. "Upon my word, I shall scold Jonet soundly. How very like her to forget to tell you that I am here. It is a pleasure to meet you, Captain."

"A great pleasure, Miss Cameron," he said, studying her across the furniture. "Indeed, I see there is much resemblance between you and her ladyship." In fact, there was a great deal of resemblance in the bones of the face, but Ellen Cameron was a larger, less dainty woman. She also looked serious and capable, and in that regard, very unlike her delicate flower of a cousin.

Under his gaze, the lady seemed to blush a little. "Oh, I rather fear that Jonet is the beauty in our family, sir. She has blue eyes, and her mother's thick, black hair. But I have the traditional Cameron coloring, with this mop of red, and eyes more green than blue. Jonet and I grew up together at Kildermore Castle." She looked at him carefully. "Do you know it?"

Cole shook his head. "No, I have not the pleasure."

Miss Cameron's eyes softened almost passionately. "How unfortunate for you! It is the most beautiful place on earth. So romantic! All craggy cliffs and stone turrets—with the ocean dramatically crashing down below." She laughed lightly, and Cole began to wonder if the lady was flirting just a bit. He looked at her again and quickly discarded the notion. She was a little silly, but unless he had badly misjudged, that was all.

Cole smiled back. "Well, castles and such aside, beauty is generally a fleeting thing, is it not, Miss Cameron?" he said, and without waiting for her answer, barged ahead. "Now, tell me, ma'am, may I help you fetch that book? I fancy I may more easily reach it."

She nodded, and Cole walked along the wall until she pointed it out to him. He slipped it from its place and passed it down to her. She lowered her lashes demurely, then promptly laid it aside. "You are most kind, Captain Amherst. You have come to teach the boys, have you not?"

"Yes," he answered. "And what of you? Are you visiting or do you reside here?"

"Oh, some of both, I suppose," she replied, absently skimming her finger across a shelf of books, as if she might choose yet another. "Generally speaking, I live in Cavendish

Square with my elderly aunt, but she often goes to Kent to see her son and grandchildren in the country."

Cole heard what was left unsaid. Ellen Cameron was an impoverished relative, a companion who was shifted here and there, yet she did not seem unhappy. Nor did she look like the type of woman who would yearn for a husband, though why he sensed that, Cole could not say. "You do not care for the country?" he lightly responded. "I confess, I prefer it."

"I like it well enough, but I prefer Scotland—the sea and cliffs! And the moors, too." She smiled briskly. "But I cannot go there at present, and just now, I think it best I stay with Jonet. Though I daresay I do plague her a little with what she calls my spinsterish ways."

"Not a bit of it, I am sure, ma'am. You are very good to think of your cousin. No doubt your aunt misses you."

Miss Cameron lifted her chin to stare up at him. "You are all kindness, sir. But my aunt understands, just as I do, that Jonet is not . . . not precisely *well*. She has suffered greatly from the loss of her husband, you see." She turned from the row of books she had been studying, the heat of her words intensifying. "People really do not understand, Captain Amherst, just how profoundly it has affected her."

"Perhaps you are right." Cole struggled to keep any hint of sarcasm from his tone. "Lady Mercer loved her husband deeply, I am sure."

Jonet's cousin circled around a brocade settee to stand nearer. "Oh, I am persuaded," she said ardently, "that in her own way, Jonet was quite devoted to Henry."

Cole smiled weakly, not wanting to disabuse Jonet's obviously starry-eyed cousin. Despite her age, which must have been near thirty, Miss Cameron still maintained the cheerful innocence of a woman who had never been married, and who had no idea that happily-ever-afters were rare indeed. Because Lord and Lady Mercer had wed, and had children, and lived more or less under the same roof, Miss Cameron probably assumed that the marriage had been blissful. Cole knew better. And he had learnt it the hard way.

But Miss Cameron sensed his skepticism. "I see you do not understand, sir. People persist in believing that Jonet and Henry hated one another. Oh, perhaps she was a little silly at first, wishing to marry for love and all that, but he was no worse than most men when all was said and done."

"Indeed?" Cole calmly replied. "I'm glad to hear it."

"Well, then!" said Miss Cameron brightly as she tugged a small book of verse from the shelf. "Shall I see you at dinner?"

Her question pulled Cole back into the present. "Why, no, Miss Cameron. Not tonight. I fear I have a previous engagement, but Lady Mercer has kindly said that I must dine with the family on most evenings."

Miss Cameron blinked. "Well, of course!" she responded. "Are you not a cousin, too? Jonet is very generous, and particularly so with her family." She smiled a little tightly. "That is one of the advantages to being securely on the shelf, Captain Amherst. I have the freedom to come and go as I please, and Jonet includes me in everything."

"Everything?" Cole was a little taken aback. "Were you here, then, Miss Cameron, on the night Lord Mercer died?" He blurted the question out quite coarsely, yet Jonet's cousin seemed to take no offence.

"No, but I was invited," she insisted. "As I said, Jonet invites me to *everything*. But I had been here for all of Christmas, and I really wanted to go home. To my aunt's, I mean. And so I said—well, really, I fibbed a little—and said that I had a headache in the afternoon."

"How shocking," Cole teased. "You must be very wicked indeed."

She made a sour, childish face. "Well, I will confess that I did not like many of the people who were coming to dine. But now, I feel inordinately guilty for having left poor Jonet here alone after what happened . . ." Lamely, her words trailed away.

"Yes, I think I see," said Cole gently. "But you must not feel guilty, Miss Cameron. I am sure you did all that you could. It was time for God to call Lord Mercer home."

"Was it?" she asked a little sharply. "There are some who might disagree, I daresay." Abruptly, Miss Cameron stacked up the two books she had chosen. "Well, delighted to have made your acquaintance. Shall I see you at dinner tomorrow?"

"Yes, perhaps." Cole paused to make her a little bow, then held the door as Ellen Cameron passed through it. He stood there for a long moment watching her skirts go swishing around the corner, until suddenly he found himself swept back into the book-room on a tide of boys and dogs, which had come rolling down the back stairs.

"Scoundrel! Rogue!" shouted Stuart ineffectually as the dogs circled around them, tails wagging violently. "Sit! Stay!"

"Captain Amherst! Captain Amherst!" chimed Robert boldly. "Did you really move your things in? Are you really going to stay here? Have you really come to teach us? Stuart said you'd not come back, but I said—"

"Did *not*!" interjected Stuart loudly, affectionately roughing the coat of the old collie as he passed by. "What I said was, he won't come back if he's got any sense."

Automatically, Cole lifted a leg just as Rogue came shooting between his knees. "Er—well, that rather settles it, doesn't it? I have no sense. I always feared that might be the case."

"Oh, who cares?" asked Robert rhetorically as the dog whipped another quick circle around him. "Mama says you're to stay, and that we are to work with you on our Latin—and our *cricket*! And she says we're to call you Cousin Cole, but only if you agree. Do you? Do you agree? *Sit down, Rogue!* Anyway, don't you think we ought to call you that? Cause now we know you're not a spy or a suspicious character—and Mama says that since we are in mourning for Papa, we may have only family here—and Lord Delacourt, of course," he belatedly added.

Cole glanced over at Stuart, who merely rolled his eyes dramatically. "You must get used to it. Robin never stops talking, whether or not he has anything meaningful to say."

With an amused smile, Cole pulled out his watch and looked at it again. His meeting with Ellen Cameron had made him very nearly late, which was all but unheard of. "I am afraid, gentlemen, that this discussion must wait. I am tardy for a dinner appointment." He glanced back and forth between them, his face grave. "But I have selected your first extracurricular assignment. Search this library from top to bottom until you find a Latin dictionary, then bring it—along with yourselves—to the schoolroom tomorrow at nine o'clock sharp."

"What's extracur'icler?" Robert looked suspicious. "It sounds like *something extra*. More work, belike." The boy crossed his arms over his narrow chest.

"Well," said Cole slowly, wondering if he had been engaged to tutor the youthful equivalent of a Spitalfields horse trader. "It is something in addition to your regular assignments. So of course, there must be, ah—*extra credit.*"

"Oh—?" Robert squinted one eye. "Of what sort?"

"Well, the gentleman who finds it will . . ." Cole paused to think of a suitable reward. "Ah, yes! Will accompany me to the best match of the season at Lord's. Eton versus Harrow!"

"Yes!" said Robert, suddenly agreeable. He danced off to begin, Rogue at his heels.

Stuart, however, did not move. "Mama won't permit us to go to a cricket match, sir," he said very quietly. "We are still in mourning."

The child looked so bereft and so solemn that Cole could not help but lay a gentle hand on his shoulder. "Perhaps I may persuade her, Stuart," he said softly. "The match isn't until mid-June, and it will have been almost six months by then. If nothing else, we shall take a carriage, and you may watch them play from the window."

The boy's face brightened a little at that. "Yes, I suppose we could do. Even Uncle James could not object to that, could he?" His dark brows drew into a little knot. "He's forever sending Mama scolding letters, you know. Telling us how we must go on, how we must show respect, and all that rot."

"Yes," murmured Cole, his jaw tight. *All that rot indeed.* "I am sure you respected your father a great deal, Stuart."

Stuart lifted his steady gaze to Cole's and nodded. "Oh, we did, sir. We liked Papa well enough. I cannot think why Uncle James persists in annoying Mama. She becomes quite upset every time his letters arrive." The boy shrugged his narrow shoulders. "We really could do without that just now," he added, sounding far older than his nine years.

Cole bent down to look Stuart straight in the eye. "Never you mind Uncle James. He's my uncle too, as it happens. And I learned years ago just how to manage him. Leave him to me. Now, go help your brother look for the dictionary, and I shall take you both to the match, right?"

"Found it! Found it!" screeched Robert from the back of the library, just as Cole walked out the door and into the hall.

Stuart's footsteps pounded toward the back of the room. "Oh, you simpleton!" Cole heard him say in the distance. "That's the *Greek* one."

"Same blasted thing," wailed Robert insistently.

"Oh, good Lord! It is *not!*"

"Is *too!*"

"Is *not!*"

"Horse's arse!"

"Dog turd!"

By now, Cole's hand was on the front doorknob. After hesitating a moment, he decided that he was officially off duty, then yanked it open and headed down the steps.

Despite his dire prediction of tardiness, Cole arrived at his club a few moments before his friend, and to Cole's great surprise, Terry Madlow was soon followed into the dining room by his widowed father-in-law, Jack Lauderwood, a retired army officer. The old colonel moved with great care nowadays, for he was almost completely blind. His illness had begun insidiously during Cole's first months in the army, but by the time the First Royal Dragoons had been deployed to Portugal, Lauderwood had been unable to see well enough to command the field. His son-in-law, Captain Terrence Madlow, along with Cole and many others, had sailed without their mentor.

"Amherst!" Lauderwood's huge fist swept across the table to shake Cole's hand with bone-crushing enthusiasm.

"Colonel! What great good fortune. I had not heard of

your return from Lincolnshire. I trust you found your estate well run?"

"Well enough," agreed the old man, taking the chair his son-in-law gently pushed him toward. Together, the three of them enjoyed a simple meal and bottle of wine, passing the time between courses by talking of the war. Cole enjoyed the opportunity to relax in the company of men whom he liked and trusted. Until that moment, he had not fully appreciated how much the situation with Lady Mercer's children had weighed upon his mind.

"Now then, Terry!" boomed the old colonel, settling back in his seat as the last course was removed. "My shot-bag is plump, so have that waiter fetch me a bottle of his best port and three glasses. You two must take up a deck of cards and never mind me, for I shall go on perfectly well."

With a wink in Cole's direction, Madlow rose to do his father-in-law's bidding. Lauderwood leaned amiably across the narrow table, his clouded eyes skimming over the room. "Cole, my boy," he said, returning to their dinner conversation for a moment. "I see very little these days, but even I can see that what we have here is a room full of fine officers gone to waste. The army has lost its sense of purpose, I believe, and I fear it shall never be recovered." His voice was a little tired.

"Perhaps, sir. But thank God we are at last at peace."

Lauderwood laughed genially and reared back into his chair. "Trust you to point that out, my boy! I am fond of you, Cole. Exceedingly so. But upon my life, I shall never understand how you made such a good officer. You really are not the type, you know."

Cole smiled lightly. "That is true, I suppose."

Lauderwood pursed his lips for a moment. "Now, tell me," he said, leaning forward again eagerly. "What of this tomfoolery Terry is giving out about your moving to Mayfair? Quite shocking, that."

At that moment, Terrence Madlow leaned across the table to set down a bottle, as well as the three glasses that were caught neatly in the fingers of his right hand. "I told you, Jack," he answered with a wicked grin. "Cole's just helping out his cousin, Lady Mercer."

Cole rolled his eyes, then focused on his glass as Madlow filled it. "You may recall, Colonel, that the uncle who raised me was the younger brother of Lord Mercer? He has become greatly concerned about his nephews, Lord Mercer's two sons."

"Ugh," grunted Lauderwood. "Nasty business. They do say Mercer was poisoned. Not surprised to hear it."

"But is that really true?" Cole asked impulsively, well aware that Lauderwood knew everyone in town. "I mean, I did hear that rumor put about, but no one seems to have been apprehended. Perhaps it was his heart? Mercer was not a young man."

"I know for a fact that it was suspected there was something in the wine he drank," answered the colonel as he took his glass from his son-in-law. "An old doctor I know—Greaves by name—lives just over in Harley Street. He was brought to the scene by the magistrate."

Madlow interrupted. "Yes, Jack—but they were at a dinner party, were they not? And did not everyone drink the same wine?"

Solemnly, Lauderwood shook his head. "No, this was afterward, as I understand it. Greaves was hard pressed to make a diagnosis. The few symptoms indicated heart trouble, but there was a decanter of red wine and a set of goblets kept in the sitting room which connected his bedchamber to his wife's. The decanter and one goblet were found empty on his night table. The dregs in the decanter appeared suspicious, but nothing could be ascertained."

Cole exhaled sharply. "And so he went upstairs to bed, poured himself a glass of wine, and collapsed onto the floor?"

"More than one." Lauderwood scratched his head. "So Greaves says. Now, mind me, Cole, this is quite confidential—but Mercer had apparently developed some sort of bilious complaint the preceding week. Nothing serious, but his doctor had suggested a little red wine before retiring. He did not normally drink it."

"I wonder how many people were aware of his doctor's recommendation?" mused Cole. "Not many, I daresay."

"Oh, I know precisely," answered the colonel. "Greaves was there when Lyons, one of the parish magistrates, interviewed the servants. The only people who knew were his butler—who kept the tray replenished—his valet who'd seen 'im drinking it, and of course, his wife."

Cole swallowed hard. This was very grim news. Very grim indeed. "And where does the investigation stand now, Colonel? Have you any idea?"

Lauderwood shrugged. "Officially, it is at a stalemate," he answered. "Greaves says the butler and the valet had no motive. And in any event, they have since been dismissed by her ladyship. To be sure, no one in the Home Office is apt to support charging Lady Mercer with the crime."

"Why?" asked Terry Madlow innocently.

Lauderwood made an exasperated sound. "She is a peer, for pity's sake. It just isn't done. Not without absolute proof."

"But there was an inquest, was there not?" insisted Madlow.

The colonel snorted. "Yes, and a bloody quick one, too. Just the way Lord Delacourt wanted it, if the rumors of his influence can be believed."

"And so that is the end of it?" asked Cole archly. "The coroner's report no doubt mentioned something vague about death by causes unknown, leaving Lady Mercer to be tried, convicted—and metaphorically hanged—by public opinion? That hardly seems fair."

"Fair?" echoed Lauderwood. "Better to be hanged by public opinion than by the end of a rope, I daresay. And there are a great many who feel that is just what she deserves. I am sorry, Cole, if that offends you, but that is the truth. She's a pariah now. An outcast. Only Lord Delacourt has continued his friendship with her. And there are some who say that dalliance, too, is swiftly coming to an end."

"To an end?" asked Cole, his heart lurching foolishly. "I will admit, the man looks a little vain and egocentric, but do you think he would cast her off on such scant evidence?"

The colonel pulled a rueful face. "Well, Delacourt is a great favorite with the ladies. Rumor has it that he has set up a new lightskirt—an actress—in Long Acre. Quite the dasher she is, too, so I hear."

Cole was stunned into momentary silence, remembering the elegant young man he had met, and the look of sweet anticipation on Lady Mercer's face when she'd greeted him. "But . . . are you sure, Lauderwood? How do you know?"

The colonel looked a little affronted. "I'm half blind, Amherst, not half dead. I can still get . . . well . . . *out* on occasion."

With a soft chuckle, Terry Madlow interceded. "Papa-in-law also has a *dear friend* in the neighborhood near Drury Lane, Cole. That is what he is trying to say."

"Oh," answered Cole, feeling the heat rise to his face. He

certainly had not meant to impugn his old mentor's sexual prowess.

"Mercer was not much younger than you, was he, Jack?" asked Madlow, diplomatically changing the subject. "Louisa said you were acquainted."

"Indeed?" interjected Cole. Louisa was Madlow's wife, and a particular friend of Cole's, for she had followed the drum across Portugal with them. He returned his attention to Lauderwood. "Did you know Mercer well?"

Lauderwood grunted again and took a generous pull from his glass. "Knew 'im? I suppose that I did in my salad days—or as well as a younger son of a mere viscount might presume to know a fellow like Mercer. We ran in some of the same circles—the Fancy, you know. Always loved a good turn-up, Mercer did. And it was a far more bruising sport twenty-five years ago. Not like it is today. Bah! The Pugilistic Club and all that rot! When we were young, a good mill was an honest mill."

Madlow sat to one side, smiling as he lazily shuffled their cards but making no effort to deal. It was an opportunity Cole could not resist. He leaned intently forward in his chair. "And so you saw one another with some frequency, sir?"

The colonel pulled a thoughtful face. "I'd say so. Races, boxing, the occasional cockfight—always something for a gent to fritter away his money on. But Mercer was usually in company with Kildermore and Delacourt—all three very thick in those days, don't you know. The rest of us were just lowly hangers-on."

"Delacourt?" Cole could not suppress his shock. The man he had seen was quite young.

"Aye, but the old lord," Lauderwood explained. "Not that young fop of Lady Mercer's."

Cole found it interesting that both Jonet's father and her husband had been good friends with Delacourt's sire. He tucked that fact away for further consideration and returned to his questions about Jonet's husband. "And what manner of man was Lord Mercer, Colonel? I should very much like to know." He gave a wry grin. "You see, as the family foundling, I was permitted in his exalted company for weddings and funerals only."

Lauderwood puffed out his cheeks and held his breath for a long moment. "He was pretty much the same sort of fellow that he was when he died, I daresay. Haughty, selfish, and a womanizer, too. But the first Lady Mercer was a timid sort. Gave him no trouble a'tall. Nothing like that she-devil second wife the poor bugger got!" The colonel laughed richly, then, just as quickly, his face became serious again. "Now mind what I say, Cole! Jonet Rowland is the sort of woman a man crosses at his own peril!"

Cole sipped pensively at his port for a moment. "And what sort of woman is that, Colonel? I hardly know her. And yet, I can plainly see she and her husband were ill suited. How did that come about?"

"Oh, it came about in the same manner as do most of life's troubles. Mercer asked for it. He and the Earl of Kildermore were two of a kind. Scoundrels and philanderers of the first order. And Kildermore had a wife and daughter tucked up in the Highlands, a fact he ignored."

"Oh?"

"Indeed! But as soon as the chit was old enough, Kildermore brought her to London to marry her off. Scots, you know. Wanted to get his heir through her as quickly as possible."

Across the table, Madlow snapped the cards into a neat shuffle. "I remember her come-out," he said, his voice a little wistful. "I was three-and-twenty at the time, and eager for a wife myself. Lady Jonet was by far the prettiest girl in town that season, and the most agreeable, too. No pretense or conceit about her, so far as I ever saw."

Grinning, Cole gave his friend a little jab with his elbow. "Were you in love, Terry? I cannot imagine anyone save Louisa stealing your heart away."

Terry Madlow almost blushed. "I fancied her a little, as did we all," he said softly, swirling the dregs of port in his glass. "But nothing came of it. Kildermore made it plain that fellows like me weren't good enough. He wanted his family linked to a great English title."

Lauderwood drained his glass and propped back in his chair as if planning a comfortable coze. "Aye, and he found one rather too quickly. His good friend Mercer was just six months out of mourning and keen for a new bride." He turned to wink conspiratorially at Cole and continued. "Mercer was desperate for an heir, as it happens. Couldn't have all that wealth trickling down to that pompous uncle of yours, could he? Much less that worthless scapegrace Edmund Rowland, eh?"

Cole felt a prickle of unrest at Lauderwood's words. It was perfectly true. Until Jonet Cameron had come along, his uncle James and cousin Edmund had been next in line for the title. Madlow slapped the deck facedown onto the table and looked uneasily around the room. "Speaking of Edmund," he said very quietly, "rumor has it that he's fallen in with a gang of blacklegs from the West End, Cole. It is not a pretty tale, either. Roly-poly this time."

"How much?" asked Cole sharply, keeping his voice low.

"Nearly a thousand pounds. On top of all else."

Cole slid a hand over his jaw. "Bloody hell! James will surely kill him this time."

Madlow elevated a brow. "It may well be less painful than what those West End sharps will do."

"Bah!" growled Lauderwood. "Let the blacklegs do their worst. Lord James shan't do a damned thing, for he hasn't the backbone. When all is said and done, Mercer did us a favor by getting his heir on the Cameron girl." The colonel cocked his head. "Don't think she was any too pleased by it, though."

"No, I fancy not," agreed Cole dryly, far more interested in Lady Mercer than in worrying about his tiresome cousin. "Even now, she makes little secret of it. Did Mercer apply to her father, and that was that?"

Lauderwood chuckled. "Oh, no! Mercer offered for her within a fortnight of her come-out, but Lady Jonet wouldn't have 'im. Said he was too old, which he was. At first, Kildermore refused to push the girl, but the season wore on, and the chit refused one offer after another."

"And so Kildermore pressed her?"

Lauderwood gave a puzzled frown. "It did not appear so, but by all accounts, Mercer was mad for the girl, and one can see why. He offered again, with wildly generous marriage settlements, and still Kildermore deferred to Lady Jonet. At the end of the season, Lady Jonet went back to Scotland, and all of us lesser mortals thought that was the end of it."

"But obviously it wasn't," Madlow interjected. "Though I never knew what happened."

Lauderwood shook his grizzled head. "Mercer got Kildermore drunk is what happened. Challenged him to some very high stakes. Kildermore was in very deep, hardly enough to impoverish him, but enough to aggravate. He was anxious to reverse his losses, and Mercer agreed to one more game, provided the earl would stake his daughter's hand." The colonel laughed softly. "Kildermore lost, but he got his revenge when he sobered up."

"How so?" asked Cole.

Lauderwood laughed. "His solicitors drew up the most god-awful marriage settlements ever a man was saddled with. 'Twas the talk of London. And a large part of why Mercer could not control his wife. That, and Kildermore's guilty conscience. It ate at him a bit, I always thought. In his later years, they did say that the old Scot mellowed."

At that moment, the door burst inward to admit two more officers from their regiment. Quickly, Terry Madlow pulled up more chairs, Lauderwood sent for more port, and the subject of Lord and Lady Mercer was tactfully postponed.

Later that night, as soon as the door thumped shut behind Lord Delacourt, Jonet flew up the two flights of stairs that led to the boys' rooms. As was their custom after dinner, the boys were playing with their soldiers in the middle of Stuart's bedchamber. "Mama!" cried Robert, leaping up to hug her. "Look! Look! Tonight we're the First Royal Dragoons!"

Laughing, she released him, and he dragged her across the room to see the game the boys had laid out across the rug. Gingerly, she knelt beside Stuart and ruffled his hair. "Yes, it looks like quite a bloody battle here," she said appreciatively, her eyes surveying the clutter strewn across the floor. "And is that . . . *heavens*! Is that my blue shawl?" Intently, she studied the long swath of silk spread down the center of the rug.

"Aww, Mama!" said Robert dejectedly, "it's not a *shawl*! It's the River Dos Casas! And these are Massena's cavalry. And see here"—his face brightening again, he lifted up her small chip bonnet which was situated far downstream—"this is Fort Conception!"

Stuart cast his mother a worried glance, but Jonet forced a smile. "Yes! To the trained military eye, it is obvious!" she agreed. "And let me guess—in your version, the brave Dragoons will crush Massena single-handedly? Is that it?" Robert nodded, then yawned broadly.

Jonet stood up and studied them both carefully. "I think you boys like your new tutor a good deal. Am I right?" Both boys enthusiastically agreed.

"Then I am pleased," she said, after a long, quiet moment. But in truth, she wished she were as comfortable with Captain Amherst as her sons quite obviously were. "Now! Off to bed with the both of you, sirs! Come, Robin, and I will tuck you in first."

After a restless night spent rethinking his conversation with Lauderwood, Cole arose from his bed in a somewhat foul humor. Ellen Cameron's naïveté aside, it was becoming increasingly obvious that Jonet Rowland had had more than ample reason to wish her husband dead, and Cole found it inexplicably disheartening.

One question kept tormenting him. Trapped in a loveless marriage, could Jonet have learned that her beloved David had formed an attachment to someone else? Could that have been the impetus which had driven her to such a desperate act? To free herself for the man she loved? Was Delacourt that important to her? Cole could hardly bear to think of it. Despite his intense dislike of Jonet, he was loathe to believe her to be a murderess. Indeed, at times, he felt strongly—perhaps even foolishly—that she could never have done such a thing, despite the fact that she had had means, motive, and opportunity. But in the next breath, Cole had to admit that it was not Jonet's, but his own shortcomings which he was reluctant to examine.

How lowering it was to realize that he could feel such a vast and intense range of emotions for a woman whose moral character was questionable at best. And there was no denying the fact that one of the most intense emotions he felt was lust, pure and simple. The breathless rush of tenderness he had felt for her upon seeing her fight back tears was almost as alarming. Perhaps more so, now that he fully considered it.

But the facts were plain. Jonet had never loved her husband, and she loved Delacourt very deeply. Cole had seen it in her eyes that day in the corridor of Mercer House. There had been no mistaking that look of feminine anticipation. Yes, the facts were damning. Incriminating enough to ruin her, but not to convict her. Cole wondered which was worse.

Perhaps the pressure of it all explained why Jonet behaved so strangely, almost as if she feared that James might seek to avenge his brother's death. Perhaps that was the explanation behind her hulking footmen and the other watchful servants. Nonetheless, had she admitted her fear of James, Cole would have reassured Jonet that his uncle did not have the guts for such an act.

Did he? In truth, Cole had found his uncle's indifference about Lord Mercer's killer rather surprising. He had been stunned when James had admitted that he did not think it would be possible to convict anyone of the crime. Ostensibly, James's only reason for sending Cole into the Mercer household was to control the welfare of the children, not to search for a killer, nor even to incriminate Jonet. Did James perhaps know that his sister-in-law was innocent? Did he have some reason to hope that the real killer would not be uncovered?

No, just as Cole believed Jonet incapable of a ruthless murder, he believed it equally impossible of James. But there was always Edmund to be considered. Edmund was lazy and extravagant, and wed to a woman who was even more so. Together, the two of them had elevated vanity and dissipation to an art form. Moreover, according to Terrence Madlow, Edmund had again found himself in serious financial straits, which was no unusual occurrence.

Still, Cole could not imagine Edmund summoning up the energy to have anyone murdered. Most certainly he would not have sullied his own gloves with such an act. And one murder would hardly have solved Edmund's problem. Jonet's sons had placed him far down the line of succession. Tormented by such questions, Cole shaved and dressed in haste.

It was not yet seven o'clock, and the house was still quiet. Although he did not yet know the habits of the family, Cole was sure he would have ample time in which to fetch his horse from Jonet's mews, go for a ride, and return in time for breakfast. Quietly, he crept downstairs and walked through the back of the house, only to hear a great deal of squealing and laughing just inside the breakfast parlor.

The double doors of the parlor were flung wide to reveal a small but sunny room which was already laid for breakfast. For a long while, Cole stood unnoticed in the shadows of the corridor, reluctant to intrude upon such a scene of domestic harmony. Robin sat perched upon his mother's knee, a red smear of jam across one cheek, squirming madly as Jonet tried to clean his face. She certainly looked nothing like a cold-blooded murderer.

"Do hold still, Robin," she ordered, the words coming out on a giggle. "You are like a sack full of puppies!" With a quick, careless motion, Jonet dunked her napkin into her water glass, then proceeded to scrub with vigor as Stuart, grinning, looked on.

"Ow, ow!" squalled Robert. "You're rubbin' off my jaw bone, Mama!"

"Good," chortled Stuart. "That'll be one less place to smear your food."

Jonet's brows drew together in mild irritation, but her smile never faltered. "Ah! And who is the young man who dumped porridge in his lap last week, *hmm*, Stuart?" Stuart pulled a rueful face as Jonet scrubbed the last bit of jam from Robert's ear. With arms that were surprisingly strong, Jonet lifted Robert from her lap and set him on his feet. "And it was an accident, was it not?" Her voice took on a cheerfully cautioning tone. "And had it been otherwise, such as the time you and Robert decided to pelt one another with scrambled eggs—"

"I remember! I remember!" Robert interrupted loudly. "We got a proper trimming for *that*! Then we had to wash ourselves!"

Stuart hung his head. "Yes. And the table linens, the floor, and our shirts, too."

"Quite so," agreed Jonet brightly. "Because servants have enough to do without cleaning up after naughty children. Now, who is for a walk in the garden?"

Still standing at her elbow, Robert looked plaintively at his mother. "Not the garden again!" he whined. "Why can't we go to the park? Why can we not have a ride on our ponies?"

Impulsively, Jonet encircled him in her arm, drew him to her side, and placed a smacking kiss atop his head. "Just because, poppet. We must stay close to home for a while yet."

His mood obviously soured, Stuart scowled at his plate

and gave it a disdainful shove. "Captain Amherst has promised to take us to St. John's Wood to watch Eton play Harrow." His voice took on a strident edge. "I daresay *that* will be too far from home as well."

"Oh, Stuart!" said his mother softly, stretching a hand across the table as if inviting him to take it. "I know you must feel very cross. It is just for a little while longer. I promise."

Loudly, Cole cleared his throat and stepped into the room. "Good morning."

Jonet looked over her shoulder and dropped her arm, allowing Robert to dart away from her and toward Cole. "Cousin Cole!" said the boy brightly. "Did you come to have breakfast with us? You're very late. Do you like kidneys? 'Cause Stuart ate the last one. Anyhow, I hate 'em. We've been here for *hours*. Look, I've finished. I got jam on my face and hair, too."

"Yes, so I see," murmured Cole, peering down at the sticky spot in the hair above Robert's ear.

"Good morning, Cole," said Jonet a little tightly, motioning him toward a seat. "I trust you passed a comfortable night?"

One of the footmen appeared with coffee and a fresh plate, but Jonet's penetrating gaze never left Cole's face. Her dark beauty was vivid this morning, as if a little of the fatigue that had lingered in her eyes had lessened. But there was something else in her eyes now, and Cole intuitively sensed that it was anger.

"Yes, ma'am. I slept quite well," he lied.

Across the table, Stuart laid down his fork with a clatter. His mother turned to him and gave him a smile that was obviously forced. "Stuart, if you've finished, take Robin into the garden, if you please. Cole and I must discuss the morning's lesson." Her spine rigid, Jonet rose to follow the children to the double doors, then pulled them both shut with a sweeping gesture. Before she had the chance to turn on him, Cole had steeled himself for the inevitable scold.

Deeply annoyed, Jonet whirled about to face the man who sat so casually at her breakfast table. She hated the fact that he looked as if he belonged there. And that he seemed so congenial, so unerringly polite, and so . . . so damned *decent.* What was worse, Cole Amherst—devil take him—appeared even more striking today, backlit as he was by the morning sun. His tawny hair gleamed in a dozen different shades of warm gold, the perfect complement to his skin, which was still lightly bronzed by his years on the Peninsula.

He seemed far too large for her parlor table, and yet he sat there looking graceful and elegant despite riding clothes which had obviously seen much use. Strangely, he seemed to take up every inch of space within the narrow room, filling it with his presence in a way Jonet could not understand. She did not like it one bit.

The fact that her children were already charmed by the man served to further aggravate her, an admittedly irrational response. It was of the utmost importance that the boys admire their tutor, and yet Jonet feared anyone who might be able to exercise undue influence over her children. It was quite a quandary, and in part, it was the reason she had avoided engaging a new tutor for so long. Slowly, Jonet stalked toward him. "Let us understand one thing, sir," she began with a lethal softness. "Where my children are concerned, you are never to undertake any sort of travel without my consent. Do you comprehend me? They are not to step foot from this house unless I have been apprised of it—or there'll be the devil to pay!"

Cole inclined his head very slightly. "Certainly, ma'am," he coldly responded. "But to my knowledge, they have not yet done so. Your indignation seems precipitous."

Jonet paced across the length of the room, then whipped about again. "You, sir, are arrogant and out of line," she shouted, raising her hand to point her finger sharply at him, to remind him of his place.

Cole apparently mistook the gesture. Roughly, he reached out and snared her hand, dragging her close—so close that she could not possibly slap him with the force he now deserved. "Do not you *ever* raise your hand to strike me, madam." He gritted out the words, his voice resolute. "I have had just about enough of your bad temper and shrewish tongue. I have no notion what manner of man you are used to heaping your abuse upon, but I'll not put up with it."

Still struggling to pull away from him, Jonet looked up into eyes so blazing that they sent a shiver down her spine. The line of his lips was hard and ruthless, the set of his perfect jaw almost cruel. And yet, Jonet knew instinctively that he would not hurt her, that he had merely misinterpreted her gesture.

In fact, perhaps she had wanted him to do just that! How horrifying. Had she wanted to test him? To further torment him? No, it was almost as if she resented needing him. As if she felt compelled to punish Cole for having such quiet strength and utter serenity.

Yes, that was it, wasn't it? And it was both unconscionable and dangerous. By God, she would not have it. Not from him. Not from herself. With one final effort, she jerked away from him. "Do not bandy words with me, sir," she said, softening her tone. "I merely meant to point at you!"

"Did you?" Cole's voice was laced with scorn, but his face was suffused with color.

"Yes—and don't you dare to change the subject, sir. You meant to take my boys off to a cricket match at Lord's."

Cole seemed to relax incrementally. "With your permission, I should very much like to do so," he agreed, his golden gaze steadying, his square chin now lifted a little arrogantly. "But calm yourself, madam. It is just a match amongst schoolboys, and yet some weeks away. I daresay we have time to iron out all the annoying little details."

The condescension in his tone snapped Jonet's temper again. "My children are not to leave this house!" she demanded. Her voice rose sharply, yet she was powerless to control it. "I shan't have it, do you hear? And don't you assume such arrogance with me!"

Cole's mouth fell a little open, and he stared at her for a long moment. "Let me understand you, ma'am," he finally snapped. "I am to educate your children, and undertake to improve both their riding and their athletics, as well. And yet, they are *not to leave this house?* Have you any idea how bizarre that sounds?"

Jonet was still pacing the room, her stomach tightening into a knot. She really was losing her mind. "I do not care how it sounds, sir! We have a back garden! We have a mews! You must simply manage, that is all there is to it. I cannot have my children dragged from pillar to post by people I do not know! People whom I cannot trust!"

At once, Jonet felt the room grew hotter, more narrow. She could trust *no one.* The walls shifted inward, squeezing out the air. Jonet was scarcely aware that she had pressed her palms to her temples as she paced. *No one!* Her pulse pounded. Her heart was in her throat. For a moment, the sunlit room faded. In her mind, she could hear a pistol shot. The deafening crack still rang in her ears. She felt the hum of the lead ball, skimming over her scalp, snatching away her hat. She could almost feel the horse beneath her tense, then rear.

When she spun about the next time, the vision was gone and Cole stood at her elbow. His breakfast napkin still in hand, he had managed to seize her, and drew her to a halt. "Jonet?" he said softly. Cole lifted one hand and tenderly turned her face back into his.

Dimly, she felt the warmth of his breath on the dampness of her forehead. She struggled to regulate her breathing, forcing back the walls of the room, which threatened to crush her.

"Jonet?" he said again, his eyes searching her face. "My dear, what is it? Please do not distress yourself. Let us not argue. I shall take care of the boys. I promise."

"N-n-*no*," she managed to say, leaning back against the edge of the table.

"Jonet." Cole pulled her a little nearer, one big hand still cradling the side of her face. His touch was cool and soothing. "I have no wish to quarrel. I care deeply for the welfare of your children, too. But they are active boys, and we simply cannot smother them. Perhaps you have not yet gotten over your husband's death? Perhaps you have some irrational fear that—"

"*Irrational* fear?" Abruptly, she shoved away his hand and exploded. "How dare you, sir? You know nothing of such things. They are not your children! You cannot possibly understand the love which a parent feels for a child!"

Jonet stepped away from him, her eyes wide and angry. "Even before a child is born, you must devote yourself entirely to its welfare. There are sacrifices one must make to ensure its safety. You can know nothing of that sort of devotion, sir. *Nothing!*"

Suddenly she saw Cole's face go white with anger. The muscle in his jaw jerked hard, and he spun away from her, hurling his napkin onto the table in one smooth, disdainful motion. "How very right you are, madam," he bit out, his back to her.

He half turned again to stare at her over his shoulder, his eyes dulled by an emotion she did not recognize. "I do indeed know *nothing* of it. How very kind of you to remind me." And on that remark, he strode rapidly from the parlor.

In the distance, Jonet could hear his heavy riding boots thunder down the hall and out the back door. Weakly, she collapsed into her chair and let her head fall forward into her hands. What had she done? What had she said? And when would this nightmare end?

5

In which Captain Amherst prevails

Cole and the boys were finishing luncheon in the schoolroom when a light knock sounded at the door. One of Jonet's footmen had just begun to clear the table. He set down the tray and opened the door to reveal his mistress standing in the corridor.

Looking past the footman's shoulder, Cole came swiftly to his feet. Framed in the lintel, Jonet wore a hat set at a rakish angle, its veil turned back, emphasizing the soft, full style of her hair. Over her arm, she carried a black shawl, and at her feet, Rogue and Scoundrel pranced like impatient ponies. Obviously, Jonet was on her way out, and the collies sensed it.

"Good afternoon," she said, her voice unusually hesitant. "I thought perhaps we ought . . ." She faltered a bit, shifted her gaze from Robert to Cole, then drew a quick breath. "That is to say, it is such a lovely afternoon, is it not? I think we should go for a walk. In the park."

"Oh, capital, Mama!" shouted Robert, shoving back his chair and giving his mouth one last swipe on his shirtsleeve.

Jonet's hand came up to stay him. "*If* Captain Amherst—Cousin Cole—says we may. We cannot go if you are behind in your lessons."

His anger still on edge, Cole wanted to sarcastically reply that they had barely begun their lessons and could hardly be expected to have accomplished anything in three short hours. And yet, he recognized Jonet's backhanded apology for what it was and held his temper in check.

Stuart, who had been staring out the window, turned to face his mother. "What about our being in mourning, Mama? What will Uncle James say?"

Jonet smiled, but without light or happiness. It tugged at Cole's heart in a way that a frown or a pout could never have done. "I do not think the bounds of propriety will be breached by my taking a little exercise in the company of my children, Stuart," she answered softly. Jonet transferred her gaze to Cole. "Shall we go, Cole? What do you think?"

Hands clasped tightly behind his back, Cole inclined his head. "By all means," he answered with clipped civility. "I have lessons to prepare."

"Oh, no," she said, stepping tentatively from the threshold and into the room, as if reluctant to trespass on Cole's territory. "I meant for all of us to go. Ellen—Miss

Cameron—is fetching her cloak." She looked across the room, where the footman was quietly loading the luncheon tray. "And Stiles, you must come as well. To—to help with the dogs, of course."

"Oh, I say, that'll be jolly!" answered Robert. "I shall take my ball, Cousin Cole. That way, we may practice a bit. And my bat, too. Do you think I might make a good bowler? Will you teach me? Will you? I think I might be quite good."

Stuart came away from the window to stand at Cole's side. "Let's do go, sir," he said softly. "We haven't been out since we came home from Kildermore. Won't you come along?"

And so it was that Cole found himself trailing through Grosvenor Square and across Park Lane shortly after one o'clock. Miss Cameron walked at his side, chattering amiably. Ahead of them strolled Jonet, her veil down now. She was flanked by her children, whose hands she held, with the dogs trotting dutifully at her heels. Behind her walked Stiles, holding the leashes. They entered through the gate near Upper Brook Street to find the park almost empty.

Inside, the beds and borders were in full bloom, tulips and daffodils splashing great, glorious swaths of color across the spring grass. Cole looked ahead to see a lone phaeton come wheeling through the gate at Hyde Park Corner. At once, a small brown dog scampered toward them, yapping madly, sending Rogue and Scoundrel into a frenzy of canine indignation. After the dog had disappeared and the collies had calmed, Jonet turned and knelt down to unleash them, her black skirts pooling elegantly on the pathway. In a stern voice, she instructed them to behave, then set them loose to run across the grass.

"May I give you my arm, Miss Cameron?" asked Cole

politely, trying to tear his gaze away from Jonet as she rose to shake out her skirts. "I fear this path is not perfectly smooth."

He looked down to see Miss Cameron blinking uncertainly. Finally, she took his arm, and the group resumed their leisurely promenade. Cole had not realized that his mood was so clearly reflected in his face, but apparently it was. At his elbow, Miss Cameron delicately cleared her throat. "One might get the impression, Captain Amherst," she said very softly, "that you do not approve of my cousin."

Curious, Cole stared down at her. "It is hardly my place to approve or disapprove of Lady Mercer," he calmly responded. "And I cannot imagine my opinion is of consequence to anyone here."

"Oh, but it is." Ellen lowered her lashes. "That is to say, Captain, that I daresay I understand how you feel. After all, I'm little more than an impoverished relative myself."

Cole forbore from pointing out that he was hardly impoverished, nor was he really very much of a relative. It seemed too cruel. "Miss Cameron," he quietly responded, "I wish you would not demean yourself by—"

"No, no!" She cut him off with a smile. "You must pay me no heed! In truth, I receive an adequate allowance, and despite aunt's dreadful attempts to marry me off, I manage to live as I please. But I am a little older, and a little more serious than my cousin, so if you find Jonet a little . . . well, *frivolous*, I would simply ask that you remember her situation."

Cole lifted his brows and stared at her in some amazement. "*Frivolous*, Miss Cameron, is not a word I would ever apply to your cousin," he responded. For a long moment, neither spoke as they trailed steadily along the path behind the rest of the group. At one point, Cole watched Robert look up at his mother, obviously pleading for permission to romp with the dogs, but his mother shook her head, then reached out to touch the child lightly on the shoulder.

Again forcing his eyes away from Jonet, Cole studied the speeding collies as they made darting forays across the grass. The dogs had clearly suffered from being confined. Now freed, they sped around trees and bushes with blazing energy, tongues dangling and feet flying. Nonetheless, at a single word from Jonet, they would skid to a halt and whirl about, returning to her side with breathless eagerness.

Eventually, the dogs worked their way toward the water, and animal instinct took over as they proceeded to herd the scattered ducks into a cluster away from the pond's edge. Circling one arm about Stuart's narrow shoulders as they walked, Jonet lifted her hand to point, and together, they laughed gaily at the sight of the birds, now flapping and quacking their displeasure. A particularly fat drake fluffed himself to full impudence and dived for Scoundrel's feet, but the old dog calmly paid no heed, continuing in his instinctive efforts to guard his flock.

With measured reluctance, Cole returned his attention to Jonet's cousin. Paired off with her as he was, he had little choice but to converse, though he had no heart for it. "Tell me, Miss Cameron," he finally said, the words slipping out before he could curb them, "do you believe the rumors about Lord Mercer's death?"

On his arm, Miss Cameron's hand suddenly tightened. "Are you asking me, sir, if Jonet hated her husband enough to kill him? Oh, I know what the gossipmongers say, but no marriage is perfect. How can it be, when marriage benefits men, not women?" Her voice was cool, oddly detached.

"My cousin's pride was wounded, but people rarely kill out of pride."

"Pride? I am not sure I take your point, ma'am."

Ellen stared absently toward the Serpentine, which glistened in the distance. "Unfortunately, Jonet married so young, she did not understand that men"—she cut her eyes up at Cole, then blushed—"that men require diversions. Of course it made her angry."

"What exactly are you saying, Miss Cameron?"

Jonet's cousin clutched at him a little awkwardly and tilted her chin up as if to study the light clouds that were scuttling across a surprisingly blue sky. "You are the scholar, Captain Amherst. What was it Congreve said? 'Heaven has no rage like love to hatred turned'? Something like that?"

" 'Nor hell a Fury like a woman scorned,' " finished Cole softly. "But that logic would imply that Lady Mercer loved her husband when she married him, and by all accounts, she did not, did she?"

Miss Cameron smiled tightly. "No, but she tried to." Abruptly, she came to a halt on the pathway. "But what idle talk this is! I believe you have tempted me to speak too boldly, sir. Jonet would never harm anyone, no matter how enraged she became. It is simply not within her nature to act with such . . . cold calculation."

"Nor with such violence, I hope?"

Miss Cameron's eyes flew open wide. "Why, certainly! That, too. Her temper is very bad, to be sure, but being possessed of a bad temper is hardly a sin. Or if it is, then one must suppose hell to be very crowded indeed."

Suddenly, Cole realized that Jonet had stopped on the path and was staring over her shoulder at him, her look intense but inscrutable. Strangely frustrated by something he could not name, Cole deliberately held her gaze, but her eyes did not waver. Finally, Cole gave her a little nod of acknowledgement and resumed his pace. Miss Cameron was obliged to come along.

The Serpentine was very near now. They drew to a halt beside Jonet, who looked anxiously at her cousin. "Ellen, the boys would very much like to walk along the water. What do you think? I do not wish to let them, but I daresay I am being foolish."

Beside her, Robert gave a little whine. "It's just a *pond*, Mama! Look, there are some other boys! The ducks are loose now, and I see a swan. A black one!" He turned a plaintive gaze on Miss Cameron. "Cousin Ellen will come with us."

Jonet shot her son a chiding look, but Ellen chimed in. "Yes, of course I shall."

"Do you mind?" asked Jonet softly. She gave her cousin a veiled look. "It would be very good of you, Ellen, since I should like to speak privately with Captain Amherst for a moment. I shall send Stiles along with you, of course."

Stuart and Robert shouted their happy agreement and set off with Ellen Cameron and the footman. The collies jerked up their heads, then dashed forth to greet them. Jonet pointed toward a long, low bench under a small copse of trees. "Will you sit with me, Cole?"

He nodded, and Jonet strode toward the bench, her slender figure graceful, her narrow shoulders rigid. Cole followed her, watching the black silk of her skirt hem trail over the tender spring grass, and trying to suppress the sudden, incomprehensible surge of longing that swept over him.

Lust. Yes—that was exactly what he felt. And something more. *Frustration. Apprehension. And yes, a good deal of admiration.* Cole shook his head. The feelings which Jonet

Rowland inspired in him were exasperating. Inconceivable and irrational, too. Did she have this effect on everyone? No wonder she drove men mad.

Good God, he was angry with the woman, as he had been since the first moment he had entered her drawing room, days ago. And yet, she engendered in him every protective instinct and all the masculine emotions he possessed, with desire foremost among them. Burning with a sudden shame, Cole ducked beneath the low tree limbs, the leaves brushing coolly against the heat of his skin.

Jonet sat down, then reached gracefully up to fold back the veil of her hat. Cole took a seat at the far end of the bench, and as if she could read his thoughts, a flash of humor lit Jonet's face, then just as quickly disappeared. Slowly, she turned to look at him through eyes that were shrewd, but not cold. "I daresay that I owe you an apology, sir," she said, her voice low and husky. "My behavior this morning at breakfast was inexcusable."

"We both behaved rather badly, I fear," Cole calmly replied. Good God, he had called the woman a *shrew*! Yes, he had meant it, but now the insult seemed so much uglier. He was ashamed of his ungentlemanly behavior.

Jonet gave a sad little shake of her head. "It was my fault. I fear that I spoke very harshly—and a little irrationally—this morning at breakfast. I hope you will forgive me for . . . for losing my temper."

Cole fixed her with a knowing look. "It was rather more than your temper which you lost, ma'am," he said pointedly. "Indeed, one might be excused for thinking you were frightened."

Jonet gave him another of her humorless smiles. "I believe my husband was murdered, Cole," she said levelly, looking away to stare across the wide swath of green that separated them from the children. "Would that not be enough to set anyone's nerves on edge?"

"*On edge,* perhaps. But not over the edge," Cole responded. He stared at her unflinchingly, determined to understand her. He dropped his voice to a more intimate tone. "Have you any intention of telling me, Jonet, just what it is which has you so thoroughly terrified? It might be better if you trusted me just a little."

She gave her head a small, unsteady shake. "No. I mean . . . pray do not try to change the subject. I merely wish to apologize. I was rude, and I said something which obviously angered you. I do not perfectly understand, but I regret it nonetheless."

Cole refused to back down, more anxious than ever to learn what was in her mind, his earlier anger all but forgotten. "I think I have a right to know what it is you fear, Jonet," he coolly responded. "You are quite obviously worried about your children. Do you not think that I, of all people, ought to be taken into your confidence? Or do you still imagine I might carry tales to my uncle?" His voice ended on a bitter note.

Jonet's eyes flared with indignation. "I have no notion what you might do. I confess, you strike me as an honorable man, far more so than I ever expected. But I simply cannot afford to trust you when the only things which matter to me are at stake."

"I think you are afraid of Lord James Rowland." It was a statement, not a question.

She drew a deep, shuddering breath. "My husband is *dead,* sir," she repeated, her voice hollow and haunted. "And your beloved uncle would like nothing better than to see me hanged for it! Yes, I am afraid of James! Would not you be? Particularly if your children were all which stood between him and the title which he has no doubt coveted all his life?"

His lips tightly compressed, Cole shook his head. "James would not do such a thing—"

"Your opinion is blinded by affection, sir!" she cried. "Someone *has* done it, and there is no one who has more to gain."

Cole looked across the bench at her. Beneath the black silk of her dress, Lady Mercer's thin body shook like a reed in the wind. "Oh, Jonet," he said softly, sliding down the length of the bench to take her trembling hand in his. "That is why you are afraid to allow the children out, is it not? And why you have dogs and footmen and guards all about your house? But James would harm neither his brother nor his nephews. I am blinded by nothing. I see him for what he is—a pompous old fool—but in truth, I have seen him do nothing that would lead me to believe he covets the title." Cole gave her hand a little squeeze.

"Indeed?" asked Jonet sharply, but she did not draw back her hand. "Then what of Edmund? He is a nasty piece of work if ever I saw one—and his wife is little better. Do you defend them as well?"

"No," admitted Cole softly, his gaze fixed blindly on the water. To the left, an obviously courting couple strolled along the water, seemingly intent on no one but themselves. Absently, Cole found himself studying them. They were approaching the boys, but they seemed to pose no risk. "No," he said at last. "I cannot defend them. Edmund and his wife are all that you say."

Jonet stared at him, shock overcoming her fear. "I cannot believe you would admit that."

"I admit only that they are untrustworthy," he

amended. "Edmund has not the guts to commit violence. I am . . . I am *sure* of it."

Jonet elevated her chin stubbornly, and the breeze caught the fine mesh of her veil, lifting it gently away from her hat. The smell of honeysuckle tinged with Jonet's own rich scent drifted on the air, teasing at him. "Of course you would trust them," she whispered. "But I cannot."

Cole shrugged. "I am persuaded, Jonet, that you do not fully comprehend the nature of my relationship with James and Edmund. You say that I am blinded by affection, but you are very much mistaken. I daresay no one knows either of them better than I. Believe me when I say James would do nothing to harm his brother, and that Edmund is incompetent to do so."

Jonet shuddered again. "But James would dearly love to see me hang."

"That may be true," Cole whispered. He stared across the grass at Stuart, who was running down the length of the Serpentine with the collies on his heels. "But only if he thinks you guilty."

"But I am not!" she cried stridently, crushing one fist into her lap. "Oh, I have grown so weary of this! Why will no one admit that *I* had no reason to kill Henry! Indeed, he was hardly worth the effort. We went our own ways long ago, and I am no better off for his having died."

"But now you are free to remarry," said Cole a little desperately, not knowing where such words had come from. He stared down at the dainty hand he held too tightly in his own, and felt a moment of sick regret.

"Oh!" she cried, dispelling it. "As if I would be so foolish as to take another husband!"

Cole held her gaze intently. "You cannot fail to be aware,

Jonet, that there are many who expect you to wed Lord Delacourt as soon as your mourning has ended."

Almost hysterically, Jonet began to laugh. "Oh, do they indeed? Then we must hope no one holds their breath in anticipation, or there shall be yet another funeral instead of a wedding." She threw back her head and stared into the trees overhead. Cole could see her blinking rapidly.

"Jonet—"

"David and I shall never marry," she cut across him sharply. "The very thought is ridiculous. He is my dear . . . *friend*. And that is all we shall ever publicly be. *Friends*. Why can society not accept that of me, when every other woman of the *ton* has a vast collection of escorts and lovers trailing after them?"

"Perhaps," he said simply, "because you are more beautiful and more bold than any other woman of the *ton*. Perhaps you . . . intrigue them." At that remark, her chin dropped, and her head swiveled toward him. Jonet's eyes were wide, her face blank with confusion. Cole could feel the heat rise to his cheeks, and he knew that despite his tanned skin, his face was red. He steeled himself for a set-down.

But there was none forthcoming. "I thank you, sir," Jonet quietly replied. "But beauty can be a curse, too, and I can see plainly enough that mine is not what it once was. I am thin, too drawn, and I look like . . ." She sighed sharply. "Well, like a haggard old crow these days."

A haggard old crow? Cole was arrested for a moment. Was it remotely possible that Jonet Rowland did not know that she was more beautiful now than she had been at eighteen? Such naïveté was incomprehensible. No doubt she was merely toying with him. And yet when Cole looked at her, she appeared to be perfectly sincere. Almost grateful to him, in fact. What a perplexing woman she was. And how he both longed and feared to know her better. Yet there was no denying that she had made him almost violently angry this morning in the breakfast parlor. Now, however, Cole was forced to admit that his heated response to her words could not be fully blamed on Jonet. He had, perhaps, overreacted by seizing her hand. And Jonet's comments had been calculated to make a hard point, but not to open an old wound.

How could it have been otherwise? The woman hardly knew him. Most certainly, she did not know his failings. No one did. It should have galled him, perhaps, to see her struggling so valiantly to do with her life just what he had failed to do with his, but it did not. Oddly enough, Cole's admiration of the lady seemed to grow in spite of their many setbacks and misunderstandings. In spite of the fact that she might be a murderess. Grudgingly, he released her hand and sat a little bit away from her on the bench.

With a facile brilliance, Jonet turned to smile at him. "Let us talk of something else. Will you share with me your impressions of my sons? Are they terribly behind in their studies?" Her voice regained its resolve and composure. "They are quite bright, are they not?"

Readily, Cole agreed that they were. In fact, little had suffered from the four months without schooling—except, perhaps, their discipline. For a long while he and Jonet talked of the boys; of their likes and dislikes, and of their weaknesses and aptitudes. Unlike some parents Cole had seen, it was quite clear that Jonet held no delusions about her children. She weighed both their shortcomings and their talents with an equal hand, and in all things, Jonet Rowland gave every impression of being a sensible, loving mother, and nothing like the shallow, selfish woman James had led him to expect. Indeed, if one could but ignore Jonet's dark beauty and volatile temper, she seemed perfectly . . . normal. A witty, vibrant woman whom Cole might have wanted as a friend, had circumstances been different.

Shifting her weight, Jonet propped her elbow on the back of the bench and studied the man who was seated next to her. Overhead, the leaves tossed lightly in the breeze, dappling sunlight and shadow over the hard planes of his face. The day had grown warm, and as she listened to the calming rumble of Cole's voice recount Robert's morning antics in the schoolroom, much of her unease settled. Together, they found themselves chatting almost companionably for the next quarter hour, until a sudden, awkward hush fell over them, as it so often does when two people who have resolved to dislike one another unexpectedly find common ground.

Quickly, Jonet spoke to dispel the silence, but her words were clumsy. "You are a widower, Cole, are you not?" She dipped her head, feeling the heat rise to her face. "That is to say . . . well, I seem to recall that you married shortly after Henry and I. That is why I remember," she finished awkwardly.

She sensed at once she had touched a nerve. The muscles of his face drew taut, and his throat worked violently. "Yes," he said at last. "My wife died while I was in Portugal."

"I am very sorry," Jonet said softly. "How tactless I am. No doubt your marriage was quite different from mine, and you miss her a great deal."

His eyes searched her face, as if he struggled to understand Jonet's question. "Rachel was a good woman," he finally said. "It was a great honor to be her husband."

Jonet noticed he had said nothing about love or devotion, and she wondered if the omission was deliberate. Had Cole felt passion for his wife? If so, one could not discern it from his words, and yet, he looked like a deeply passionate man. "A pity you had no children," she said lightly. "You are quite good with them."

There was a long silence during which Jonet watched the knuckles of Cole's hand whiten where he gripped the edge of the bench. She began to feel increasingly awkward. Good heavens, when had she lost all semblance of tact? Indeed, she sometimes feared she was losing her mind. First her irrational reaction this morning, and now this! Clearly, she had touched on another delicate issue. After all, what did she know of this man? Perhaps he *did* have children. Perhaps he was somehow estranged from them. Really, it was none of her business! She had grown entirely too interested in Cole Amherst. She had foolishly allowed herself to bask in the fleeting illusion of friendship, and in the process, had let down her guard, and possibly insulted him.

Cole's face remained flat and emotionless. "No, I have no children," he finally answered.

Jonet did not know what further to say. At the end of the bench, Cole shifted, then turned, as if he could not make himself comfortable. Finally, he made a vague gesture toward the Serpentine. "Your cousin, Miss Cameron, seems quite pleasant," he said tightly.

They watched as Ellen threw a stick and Rogue scampered toward the water after it. "She is very dear to me," agreed Jonet, turning to look sharply at him. "And on that score, I daresay I owe you another apology. I had meant to introduce you at dinner last night, but when you dined out instead . . . well, I find that my mind has been much occupied of late."

Cole inclined his head in acknowledgement of her apology. "I met Miss Cameron yesterday afternoon. In the book-room. Tell me, has she always made her home with her aunt?"

"Oh, no! She grew up with me in Scotland." Jonet sighed wistfully. "Her father was my father's younger brother. We are both devoted to Kildermore."

Cole's brows pulled incrementally together. "She has never wished for a home of her own? She has never wished to marry?"

The question gave Jonet an uncomfortable pause. *Did Cole find Ellen charming?* Clearly, he disapproved of Jonet rather keenly, so perhaps Ellen was indeed more to his taste. She certainly had not failed to note how Cole had offered Ellen his arm and escorted her through the park, his golden head bent to her darker one as they conversed in muted tones. Immediately, she felt ashamed. In many ways, Ellen and Cole would be ideally matched. Jonet should be pleased.

"No." Jonet lifted her shoulders in an elegant shrug. "Kildermore is her home, just as I consider it mine. Her parents died when she was young, and Papa brought her to live with us. We even came out together." Jonet wrinkled her forehead in thought. "But Ellen never really . . . *took*."

"Perhaps it is your family's tendency to breed women who are over-bold," Cole replied, and Jonet's head jerked toward him. She was relieved to see a teasing light in his eyes.

"No doubt you are right," she agreed with mocking good grace. "I daresay an inheritance the size of mine is sufficient to offset any number of dreadful faults."

"I did not say that boldness was a fault, my lady. Indeed,

it can be quite an asset, but one which some men may find too challenging to take up."

"You are prodigious good with words, are you not?" Jonet smiled faintly. Apparently, the devil had taken hold of her tongue again. Cole's gold-brown eyes narrowed, and he opened his mouth, no doubt to utter a cutting retort, but no words came out. Instead, the warm spring air was rent by the terrifying scream of a child.

Cole had no memory of leaping from the bench and racing toward the Serpentine. Indeed, he had no memory of wading into the water, nor of dragging Robert and Scoundrel out of it. He knew only that by the time Jonet reached them, flying over the distance with her skirts brazenly hiked up, both he and the boy sat in the grass, Cole's boots and breeches ruined, and Robert drenched to the skin. Beside him, the dog began to shiver.

"What happened?" Jonet screamed, falling heedlessly to her knees in the grass. She reached out desperately with both hands, cupping her son's wet, ashen face. "*My God!* What happened here?" Water from Robert's hair soaked her gloves and ran unnoticed down her wrists.

Scoundrel dipped his head, snuffling nervously at Robert's coat. At once, Cole became aware of Stiles anxiously hovering, and Ellen drawing in a sharp, sobbing breath. In the background Stuart stood immobilized, the other dog by his side. Ellen stepped closer to Cole.

"Robin! Tell me! What happened?" Jonet repeated, her voice edged with hysteria.

Robert screwed up his face and began to wail. "Scoundrel p-pushed me in!" he cried. "W-w-we were just playing in the water with a stick, and h-h-he wanted to swim!" The last word broke into another wail as Stiles dropped to his haunches next to Jonet.

Stiles looked bloodless and shaken. "I turned me back but a moment, m'lady, I swear it! I went 'round the bushes ter look for the other lad, and I reckon . . . why, I reckon the poor boy stepped over the edge." The stout footman gestured toward a stand of tall shrubbery. "Mayhap the dog did get in the way like. But it were an accident, nothing more."

"Miss Cameron!" Cole bit out, pulling the wet coat away from Robert. "What did you see?"

Timidly, she came forward and knelt in the grass beside Jonet. "Oh!" she answered on a sob. "I was just over there." She pointed at a level patch of grass. "And I think—oh, I *think* I was admiring a cloud . . . and oh, dear! It was dreadfully foolish of me to let my mind wander!" Her voice caught painfully. "I looked away but a moment, Jonet, and the next thing I knew, they were both in the water. And then Stuart screamed."

"Stiles!" shouted Jonet grimly, tearing her gaze from Robert. "Search the shrubbery."

The footman looked at her in amazement. "But my lady! T'weren't no one there! Just the boy and the dog."

Held tightly in his mother's arms, Robert shuddered. "Search it!" she ordered. "All of it."

With a tug at his forelock, Stiles leapt up and began moving swiftly through the clumps of shrubbery that lined the water's edge. Cole watched the footman as he moved, realizing how easy it was to intermittently lose sight of someone walking along the shoreline. In truth, with a little luck, half a dozen men could have made their way around the shore unseen.

And there *had* been someone in the vicinity. He remembered it now. "There was a couple walking from that direction." Cole pointed to the right. "A few minutes ago. Did no one else see them?"

Tearfully, Ellen shook her head. "I saw no one." Filled with unease, Cole returned his attention to Jonet and Robert, whose sobs were beginning to quiet. Almost automatically, he reached out to her, placing the weight of his hand firmly on her shoulder.

Her face swiveled up, her eyes still wide with terror. "Jonet," he said softly. "Are you all right?" Mutely, she nodded, but the trembling of her full, expressive mouth betrayed her.

"Listen to me," he said intently. "Robin is safe. Take him home. And get him out of those wet clothes. He's to have a warm bath at once." Gently, he squeezed her shoulder. "Jonet, do you hear?"

He waited for Jonet to nod. "Yes," she whispered hoarsely.

Cole looked grimly at her. "I shall remain behind—with Stuart," he added firmly.

Panic darkened Jonet's gaze again. "I will not let him from my sight," stressed Cole gently. "I will not so much as let go of his hand, Jonet. We are going to have a walk around, and see what, if anything, he remembers. Now go. Get Robin home. And trust me."

For a long moment, she looked as though her face might crumple, but she was obviously made of sterner stuff than that. Cole could see the thoughts flash through her mind, and he knew that she was weighing him, carefully measuring everything she knew, and everything she suspected. Cole prayed that she would trust him.

And he prayed, too, that she would not blame him for the near tragedy. Had he been wrong to disapprove of her vigilance? Was Jonet's fear more rational than it had first appeared? But it was too late for recrimination. Cole shook his head. Surely it was just an accident, and it had occurred essentially as Robert said. Somehow, in his enthusiasm, the boy had merely stumbled over the dog. Cole looked at Jonet again pleadingly.

He did not know why he so desperately wanted this woman to have faith in him, but he did. It had been a long time since he had cared urgently about anything at all, save the safety of his soldiers in the field. But this—! Oh, this was a different level of desperation altogether.

He massaged her shoulder gently with his hand, feeling the tension deep in her muscles, and hardly caring who observed the intimacy of the gesture. "Jonet—?" he whispered.

Jonet leaned incrementally nearer, still visibly shaken. "Yes," she whispered in a voice so low and unsteady that he could barely hear it. "Yes, but if any harm comes to my child while he is in your care, understand this: I will cut out your heart with my own knife. I swear it before God." Abruptly, she swept Robert into her arms and came smoothly to her feet.

"Stiles!" Cole shouted over his shoulder, and the footman bounded toward him. "Take Lord Robert from Lady Mercer and carry him home, if you please. Miss Cameron will manage the dogs," he said, glancing in her direction. White-faced, Ellen nodded quickly, and took the leashes from the footman's outstretched hand.

"Lord Mercer will remain with me," Cole explained. "I wish to look around."

In a moment, the group was off, walking toward Park Lane at an anxious pace. Stuart remained beside Cole, watching them go. True to his word, Cole held the boy's hand. He turned and stared down at him. "Now, tell me, Stuart. Just what did you see? You need not fear upsetting your mother now."

Stuart looked up, his eyes narrowed against the sun. His face held Jonet's keen intelligence and intense eyes. "I saw very little, sir," he answered softly. "We were just throwing sticks. Mine went wide, and I followed Rogue after it." The boy pointed to the path that skirted the Serpentine to the west.

Cole followed the route with his eyes. It would be difficult indeed to see the water's edge from that portion of the lawn. The intermittent clumps of shrubbery prevented it. It also provided ample cover for someone who wished to circle the edge of the pond unseen. The ground there was damp, and footfalls would make no sound.

"And you saw no one?"

"No, sir. The shrubbery blocked my view. But I heard nothing, either," he added, anticipating Cole's next question. "Nothing but Robin splashing, that is. I ran back, and saw him struggling."

"And then what happened?"

Stuart's eyes skimmed the shoreline, but it was obvious he was looking inward, not outward. "I saw . . . I saw Scoundrel grab his coat collar. Yes! I remember now. He had it in his teeth, and when I screamed—why, I daresay I frightened him. He . . . he let go. And then you came, sir."

Cole dropped to his haunches to look Stuart in the eyes. "Think hard, Stuart. When you ran back, was Scoundrel in the water, or out of the water?"

Dully, the boy shook his head. "I cannot say for sure, sir. I—I rather think *in* but I'm just not sure. It all happened so fast, and I was scared."

Cole laid a steadying hand on his arm. "Yes, of course

you were. I was, too. But the water is not too deep just there, and I daresay Robin was never in very much danger."

Not unless he had struck his head on one of the protruding rocks, or been unable to gain his footing, or been alone . . .

The awful thoughts ran through Cole's head, but he did not lend voice to them. To do so would have frightened Stuart unnecessarily. He turned his attention back to Stuart, who was looking calmer now. "Tell me this, Stuart," he said. "And think carefully. Do you think Scoundrel could have bumped Robin and pushed him in accidentally?"

Again, Stuart shook his head. "Not—not really, sir," he whispered. "Rogue might have done such a silly thing. He's still a little clumsy sometimes. But Rogue was with me, sir. I am sure of that."

Silently, Cole nodded. "Come along. We'll search the greenery around the water for footprints."

Together, they set off to circle the pond hand-in-hand. And they found footprints. Hundreds, if not thousands, of them. The moist earth around the pond apparently held the shoe prints of half of London, and all of the dogs and waterfowl. Absently, Cole let his eyes wander over the far shoreline and beyond, to Hyde Park Corner, where all manner of horses and carriages were beginning to drift in, as the *beau monde* prepared to strut their finery up Rotten Row in the late afternoon promenade. He sighed with resignation. There was nothing more to be learned here. Gathering Stuart closer, Cole turned around and headed for home.

Following Robert's accident, an atmosphere of quiet restraint fell over Mercer House. Over the course of the next three weeks, Cole often noticed Jonet pacing the house with a restless energy. It appeared as though she ate and slept little. For his part, Cole's anger toward Jonet had burned to a simmer, but his lust continued unabated—and despite all hope, it was a lust which did not lessen with familiarity.

The morning had dawned with the humid warmth of a summer's day, a fact that bode ill for the evening. Already, Cole could feel the air growing heavy with a gathering storm. In anticipation of the heat, Nanna had wisely thrown open the schoolroom windows at first light, and now the thick breeze rolled in, lazily undulating beneath the under-drapes and carrying with it the morning rumble of carriages and the jingle of harnesses.

Shortly after nine, a coster's cart rattled up to the servants' entrance, and the cook came out into the stairwell to loudly quibble over the price of his parsnips. The boys snickered a bit as the costermonger took the razor's edge of Cook's thick brogue, but otherwise all was peaceful until half past ten, when the sound of a heavy carriage drawing up to the door could be heard. Someone hastily alit, and plied the knocker with an impassioned vigor.

The boys looked up from the table, curious. Cole was curious, too. He almost rose from his chair to peer down into the street, then quickly shut away the thought. It was not his place to wonder at who Jonet's callers were.

The ensuing argument quickly changed his mind. In a few short minutes, the dialogue grew from a loud rumble to a veritable shouting match. Soon Jonet's words were carrying distinctly up the stairwell, her husky voice rising to a wild rage. The lower tones that followed her were audibly arch and defensive, and could belong to only one man. *Lord James Rowland.*

At once, Stuart and Robert lifted their eyes from their work, their faces pale with concern. "It would seem that

Uncle James has called," said Cole dryly, shoving back his chair. The thump of a slamming door vibrated through the house. "Sir, are you going downstairs?" asked Stuart, his face strained. "I think perhaps you ought. Mama gets very upset when James comes."

Just then, the sound of shattering glass rang through the house. "*Uh-oh*," said Robert ominously. "Mama got hold of that vase on the hall table."

"Right, then," said Cole, coming swiftly to his feet. "I'd best go down. Stuart, you will continue conjugating your Latin. Robin, when I return, I want all of those arithmetic problems corrected. You can and shall get them right."

The boys mumbled their agreement, and by the time Cole made his way down the two flights of stairs, a housemaid was already sweeping up glass in the hall, and Donaldson had somehow maneuvered the fray down the corridor and into the drawing room. The double doors were flung open wide, and the butler stood stoically upon the threshold, one protective eye on Jonet.

His hat still clutched loosely in his hand, James stood by the window, a shaft of muted sunlight illuminating the fleshy pallor of his face. A sheen of sweat was visible on his brow as James's eyes flicked back and forth between Jonet and Donaldson as if measuring his opponents. Heedless of Cole's presence, James's implacable gaze settled on Jonet. "I tell you, madam, I have every right to see those boys!" he insisted, his empty hand fisting spasmodically. "You may not keep them from me! I shan't stand for it any longer, and you may mark my word!"

Jonet threw back her head, her face a blazing mask of anger, her eyes dark and glittering. Cole had never known that a woman could look so utterly vicious. "Mark *my* word, Lord James!" she bit out, her light brogue thickening. "My children are at their lessons and they'll not be disturbed." Jonet took another threatening step toward James. "You, sir, may wait upon my solicitor, and make your appointments through him."

"And you, madam, should be confined in Bedlam, if not someplace worse! Newgate springs most immediately to mind!" James made a jerking, dismissive gesture with his hand, and Jonet took another step nearer and drew back her arm.

Cole had not realized until that moment that she had managed to lay hands on a thin black riding crop. His own, by the look of it. Urgently, Donaldson turned toward Cole, with *For God's sake, do something!* plainly writ across his face.

Cole cleared his throat and stepped into the room. "Why, it is Uncle James!" he said evenly, crossing the room to take a strategic position near them. "To what do we owe this unanticipated pleasure?"

Cole watched as Jonet and James turned to stare at him, both faces darkening to a shade near blood red. Together, they erupted into an angry tirade. "He has come to harass me!" insisted Jonet. "Is that not obvious?"

"I have come to see my wards! My nephews!" demanded James. "Do you not see, Cole? Is it not just as I said? She is an unnatural mother!"

"Out! Get out! Get out of my house, sir!" screamed Jonet, drawing back her hand again.

"This is *not* your house, madam!" countered James, pulling back just far enough to avoid the crop. "*Your* house is a rock pile hanging off the side of some godforsaken Scottish cliff, and I wish you would take yourself off and stay there! Mercer House belongs to Stuart, and I am the trustee! Now, I will see him, if you please!"

"Or what?" snarled Jonet, her chin jutting out, her stance aggressive.

"Or I shall bring my solicitors!" fumed James. "And then you will bring those children down here or I shall know the reason why!"

"It strikes me that we have more than enough children down here already," said Cole, calmly stepping between them. James scowled at him, but Cole turned his back to face Jonet, thrusting out his left hand, palm expectantly up. "Lady Mercer," he said softly. "I see I carelessly left my crop in the back hall again. How thoughtful of you to retrieve it."

In response, Jonet nailed him with her black gaze, her dark, arching brows drawn fully together. Her lovely lips drew into a stubborn line, but after a long moment, a shadow of angry acquiescence passed over her eyes, and she laid the crop smartly across his hand with a *thwack*.

"Thank you, ma'am," Cole glibly responded, suppressing a wince. "You are too kind." Palm stinging, he turned to his uncle. "Now, James, if you would kindly excuse us, I should like to speak with Lady Mercer privately, and then perhaps we might all have a little coffee?"

"*Coffee—?*" Jonet's voice was shrill.

"By all means, talk, if you think you can reason with her," growled his uncle, cutting Jonet a nasty, nervous glance. The whites of his eyes were bold and a little tremulous, like those of an uneasy stallion.

"No!" she protested sharply, even as Cole slid one hand gently beneath her arm. "I shan't leave him alone in my house. I shan't do it!" She moved as if to drag away from him.

"Jonet, he is not alone," Cole gently reminded her. "Donaldson is with him." Then, a little roughly, Cole gripped her elbow and propelled her from the room. With his eyes, he commanded the butler to stay put.

Donaldson discreetly pushed the doors shut behind them as Cole drew Jonet across the hall into the empty breakfast parlor. Cole tossed the crop into a chair and turned to face her. Obviously seething, she rounded on him, her black hems swinging wildly, her color high. Jonet's hands fisted angrily at her sides, and she looked dangerously beautiful in her fury. "You must be mad, sir! Perhaps you are on his side!" Her voice dropped to a raspy whisper. "Perhaps I was foolish to hope otherwise."

"Jonet, for God's sake, listen to me!" he said, sliding both his hands up her arms to lightly grip her shoulders. "I am on no one's *side*. But James is correct." He gave her a gentle shake and held her eyes with the calmest gaze he could muster. "Regrettably, he has every right to see the boys. It is very imprudent of you to play these games with him."

Jonet spat out an unladylike oath. "Do you think I care one whit for what is *prudent*?"

Cole held her firmly, realizing how deeply she trembled. "Jonet," he gently explained, "you may share guardianship, but James is the undisputed trustee of the Mercer estate. He can make your life difficult. Moreover, with just the right amount of maneuvering, he can probably take those children from you."

Angrily, she tried to jerk from his grasp. "Oh—! And I daresay you would like nothing better!"

Roughly, he dragged her a little nearer. "No, Jonet! That is precisely what I do *not* want." Cole stared intently down at her, but Jonet refused to meet his gaze. He gave her another shake, more firmly this time. "Listen to me, for pity's sake! James raised *me*. It is not a fate I would lightly wish on anyone."

"I do not believe you," she insisted wildly.

"Then you wound me," Cole softly returned. "Most deeply."

Slowly, she looked up at him from beneath lids that were heavy. The skin under her eyes was dark from a lack of sleep, and her mouth quivered uncertainly. "Dear God, I am the worst sort of fool," she finally said, her voice almost inaudible. "I cannot think why I trust anyone, let alone you."

"Jonet, my dear, I think you must trust someone." Cole spoke quietly. "I do not mean to be cruel, but I do believe you are on the edge of a mental collapse—and not without reason," he swiftly added. "But one cannot escape the fact that you were brandishing a crop in James's face. It won't do, Jonet. It simply won't do. Indeed, it gives him ammunition against you."

With a weak, tremulous shrug, Jonet looked away again. "What would you have me do?" she finally whispered. "I seem not to know what ought to be done any more. Dear heaven, I am too tired to think." Abruptly, she pulled one arm from his grasp and rubbed a palm against her temple.

"Let me bring the boys down to take tea with James."

Jonet's hand dropped. Her face jerked back to his, eyes flaring with alarm.

Cole shook his head. "Jonet, I promise you that I will not leave them. James will simply goad you into a temper, but if I take them, he'll have no further argument. After all, he has sent me here, and you have accepted that, albeit a little reluctantly." Cole forced himself to smile at her. "And if he is allowed to visit them, to see how they go on, then he shall have nothing further to quarrel over."

Jonet inhaled on a deep, shuddering sigh, and Cole forced himself to resist the urge to pull her into his arms.

Dear heaven, she looked so small, so very frail. Beyond the bay window of the breakfast parlor, the wind was already beginning to whip at the young birch trees, unsettling the branches and flicking the leaves upside down to catch the sun. With a soft sigh, Cole slid his hands a little further around her shoulders and patted Jonet lightly on the back, resisting the urge to drag her against his chest and press his face into her soft mass of black hair.

He knew that it was beyond foolish to hold such a woman. She was like quicksilver—tremulously brilliant, dangerously beautiful. He shut away the thought of how ripe and warm her mouth might feel beneath his, and searched his mind for words of mere comfort. But he did not attempt to convince Jonet that her concerns were without foundation. Not after what had happened yesterday. Nonetheless, Jonet could not continue to deny James his rights. Cole knew all too well what the man was capable of.

"All right," she said quietly, and half turned in his arms to stare through the window with him. She did not look at him as she whispered. "I will do as you say. Pray God that I am not gravely mistaken, but I trust you—or perhaps I ought to say *I need to trust you.*" Her words ended on a little choking sound. "But I doubt that makes any sense."

Cole still stood with his hands resting lightly on her shoulders, feeling the tension and the uncertainty within her. And in that moment, he ceased to struggle against his better judgement. Suddenly, it seemed the most natural thing in the world to draw Jonet a little nearer and place a light, tender kiss upon her temple. Again, he refused to carefully consider what he was doing, and when his lips should have left her skin, they lingered a moment longer than was wise, lending the caress an intimacy that went beyond a simple gesture of comfort. Her breath escaped on a small, almost wistful sigh. Jonet's hair was warm and soft against his lips, and for a fleeting moment, he felt her quicken to his touch.

And then abruptly, she jerked away. "Thank you," she said, her voice husky, as if the words had been stirred from sleep. "You are very kind."

"Ah," said Cole, forcing a lightness into his tone as he stepped away from her. "I seem to recall your saying those very words the first time I kissed you. My lips always have just such a devastating effect on women."

Jonet seemed unaware of his weak attempt at humor. "So you do remember that day?" she asked in a faraway voice.

"Your wedding day," responded Cole softly, looking across the room and into the distance. "Oh, yes. I remember it well."

"I . . . I do not. Not the actual wedding, at any rate." Jonet's gaze flicked up at him again, and abruptly, she changed the subject. "I will go up to the schoolroom and fetch the boys," she said reluctantly. "Give me a moment to collect myself, then I shall bring them to you."

"Yes, of course," agreed Cole levelly. He ignored an irrational wave of despondency, and forced himself to turn away from her and stride across the breakfast parlor.

Jonet watched him go, her gaze caught by his hand as he laid it flat against the door to push through it and into the hall. His hands were broad palmed, yet elegant. Indeed, she had studied them often enough. The strong tendons and heavy veins lent them character, while his years in the army had left them tan and a little rough. And now she knew that they were gentle, warm, and infinitely comforting. Jonet simply hoped the comfort was something more than a carefully crafted delusion. But dear heaven, Cole was right about one thing. She had to trust somebody. Did she dare to trust him?

The answer was no. Yet matters simply could not go on as they were. Indeed, *she* could not go on as she was. She really was beginning to lose control. It grieved her to admit it. Today she had all but brandished a weapon in James's face. The near tragedy in Hyde Park had shaken her far more than any of the previous accidents had. And *accident* was really not the proper word, was it?

Jonet was increasingly convinced that nothing which had occurred, beginning with Henry's death, had been an accident. Wearily, she sat down at the breakfast table and gazed across its width and through the window. She still did not know if she could risk trusting Cole. Her children's welfare was at stake. And Cole was James's nephew. Yet her every instinct pulled her to him, and the restraint which was required to resist that temptation was just another drain on her nearly exhausted mind.

Why had he accepted this position in her home, if he did not intend to do James's bidding? What other reason could there be for such a man—a soldier—to take up such a post? It had taken several weeks to thoroughly investigate him, but she now knew it was not money which motivated him. And she did not for one minute believe he had done it out of the goodness of his heart. Life had taught her that people were almost never that unselfish.

Yet it troubled her to admit how reassuring his embrace felt. Jonet was a tall woman. Few men towered over her the way Cole Amherst did. His chest was broad and his arms were sure. Jonet had wanted nothing so much as to dive into them and remain, sheltered against the wall of his chest, until the trembling inside her ceased and the madness dissipated. It was a luxury she had never known. One that she could not now afford.

How odd, and yet how natural, his touch seemed. And he had kissed her—an almost brotherly gesture at first. But then, it had felt almost as if he had lingered, as if he had briefly considered skimming his lips down her brow to turn the kiss into something more erotic than comforting. And Jonet had wanted him to do just that. She should have jerked away, mindful of his place in her household. But in truth, she no longer knew what his place in her household was. Effortlessly, and without any degree of arrogance, Cole Amherst took command of people and situations as if it were his duty. And thus far, she had been almost relieved to let him do so.

No, Jonet had not jerked from Cole's embrace. Instead, she had ached to lean into it, weakly convincing herself that it was perfectly natural to take a moment's comfort from him, because Cole was *family*—an idea she had found laughable but a few days earlier. The Rowland family had never brought her anything but grief. And yet, for the briefest of moments, Jonet had allowed herself to forget that her children were in danger, and that her worst enemy lay in wait for them just inside her drawing room.

Foolishly, she had savored the heat of Cole Amherst's sinfully erotic mouth against her skin, desperately wishing that he would slide his lips over hers and take her with a savagery sufficient to blind out all else. He was more than capable. Raw power and repressed sensuality boiled just below his steadfast restraint. A man was not gifted with such wicked lips, were he incapable of using them to every advantage.

And the rest of him was equally promising. With a little cry of despair, Jonet pushed away the thought. How dangerous! Oh, she had toyed with the thought of seducing him, and would willingly have done so had she thought it would keep her children safe. But whatever Cole Amherst's ambition, Jonet had come to suspect it would not be thwarted by seduction. That sensuous mouth aside, Cole was too driven, too self-possessed, to yield to feminine manipulation, while fear and fatigue had stripped Jonet of her usual cold, unyielding strength, leaving her susceptible to all sorts of foolish emotion. She had become weak, though she took great pains to hide it. Yet her hard veneer was cracking, and Jonet felt it all too keenly.

Sighing into the emptiness of the room, Jonet was further shaken by the realization that for the first time in her life, she almost missed her husband. At times, she had hated Henry, it was true. But the last few years of her marriage had finally brought a sense of peace; a poignant acceptance of the fact that her life was all it would ever be. Her children had been her reason for living, while David had been her comfort. And Henry had been . . . what? At least he had ceased to be her enemy. It was true that the gossip about David had finally enraged him, but Henry would never have carried out his threats. Given time, she could have brought him around. But fate had cheated her of the chance.

Well! There was nothing to be gained by regretting the past. She would bring the boys down as Cole suggested. But she had no intention of leaving them alone. Rationally, she knew James could not snatch them from her very drawing room, but it was the irrational that so often drove Jonet nowadays. It would be easy enough to go around through the book-room and stand by the double doors that connected it to the drawing room. Perhaps she might even learn why Cole had come to Mercer House. And like so many other sins these days, eavesdropping was no longer beneath Jonet.

6

Lord Delacourt issues a Challenge

The coffee had barely cooled when it became painfully obvious to Cole that James's interest in Robert and Stuart was superficial at best. Throughout the visit, which lasted all of fifteen minutes, it became clear that James was more interested in needling Jonet than in caring for her children. Eventually, he drew out his watch and peered at it with barely suppressed impatience. "Well!" he said, coming forward in his chair to heartily slap his thighs. "You two seem to be flourishing under your cousin's tutelage. It was a wise decision on my part, I can see that."

"Yes, sir," answered Stuart flatly. Robert said nothing, but fidgeted in his chair.

James gave his broad, disingenuous smile. "Right then! Well, off with you now. I must speak privately with your cousin for a few moments." Sonorously, he cleared his throat. "It was very good to have seen you at last." A hint of sarcasm laced his tone, but if the boys noticed it, they gave no indication.

"Good day, sir," said Stuart, sliding to his feet. "It was good of you to come, I am sure."

"Yes, sir," agreed Robert dully, following his brother's actions. "Good day, sir."

Together, they all but flew across the room and escaped

into the corridor. As soon as the door thumped shut, James leaned forward. "Well, Cole?" he said abruptly. "What have you learned?"

With calculated deliberation, Cole elevated his brows and studied his uncle carefully. "I have learned, sir, that Robert has charm, but his arithmetic skills are very poor. And Stuart has quite a flair for languages, but he is too quiet. But both are bright, and potentially—"

"No, no, no!" James interrupted, shaking his beefy jowls. "About *her.* What about her? Has she done or said anything that would give me cause to take charge of the boys? What sort of mischief is she about? Good God, Cole! Have you uncovered nothing in the month since I sent you here?"

Cole willed himself to be calm, but inwardly, he was far angrier on Jonet's behalf than he should have been. His feelings for her were sharp, almost painful, and he did not understand them. With one hand, Cole pulled off his spectacles, pinching the bridge of his nose with the other. James always made his head ache. "Sir," he said bluntly, "I shan't act as your spy. I believe we have already discussed that."

James puffed out his cheeks impatiently and drew his breath to argue, but Cole cut firmly across him. "Indeed, Uncle, I have something of an argument with you. I discovered too late that you failed to fully explain my circumstances to Lady Mercer. I daresay I ought to have left as quickly as I came when I learned that you had failed to secure her agreement."

"Agreement!" spouted James indignantly. "*Agreement,* do you say? One cannot reason with a madwoman, Cole. A horsewhip! The woman threatened me with a bloody horsewhip, for pity's sake!"

Cole suppressed a hiss of impatience. "Good heavens,

James! That was no horsewhip. Just a riding crop. Mine, to be precise." Casually, he leaned forward to refill his coffee, steeling himself to tell a blatant lie. "No doubt Lady Mercer was merely tidying up. I am sure she meant you no harm."

"Balderdash, Cole, and you know it!" James looked truly angry now.

"Do I?" he asked coolly, lifting his cup and staring over the rim with a hint of a challenge.

But James was having none of it. "You bloody well do! She would have striped the hide from my face had you not dragged her away from me! And I daresay the Marchioness of Mercer has little need to go about 'tidying up' after her fine Scottish servants."

"Pray come to the point, Uncle," said Cole a little grimly. "As it happens, the boys are awaiting my return to the schoolroom, and it is plain to me that you have not come to see them."

James's face flooded with red. "By gad, you're an unnatural nephew, Cole. Just think how it would look if I waited upon you without first asking for the children!" he blustered. "Lady Mercer would think I have given up! That I do not mean to assert my rights!"

"Precisely my point, sir." Cole pushed away the coffee he had just poured. "Now what do you want?"

"Nothing," said James coldly, jerking his ponderous weight out of the chair. "Nothing which you will tell me, that is plain enough."

Smoothly, Cole rose to his feet. "The boys do go on perfectly well, sir. And Lady Mercer, despite her rash temper, seems a loving mother." Cole softened his tone a bit. "Should I see anything to the contrary, surely you must know that you can trust me not to remain silent?"

"I am not entirely certain, Cole," grumbled his uncle, a

little mollified as they made their way toward the door. "I bloody well hope you have not fallen under that woman's spell." Abruptly, James halted and eyed his nephew up and down suspiciously.

Cole felt his face go tight with the indignity of it. The truth hit a little close to home. "I should hope, sir, that you know me somewhat better than that," he retorted coldly.

"Oh, I suppose so," muttered James gruffly. "She is hardly the type of woman *you* would consort with, is she? You are far too morally discerning, I daresay, to fall in with the likes of her."

"Let us just say that the lady is not at all to my taste, sir," replied Cole as he laid his hand upon the door handle. "Nor can I imagine that I am hers."

Jonet did not hear his last eight words. She spun quickly away from the doors and strode across the room to stand before the fireplace, her head bowed, her chest choked with an emotion she did not understand. A crushing sense of despair hit her, and she sank into the broad armchair by the hearth. Down the hall, the drawing room door clicked smoothly open, and heavy footsteps sounded toward the front entry. In the corridor, James's pretentious voice echoed as he called for his coachman and footman to be sent up from the kitchens.

Thank God he was leaving.

Wearily, Jonet toed off her slippers, curled up in the chair, and let the waves of regret and relief roll over her. There was little doubt now about what James wanted Cole to do—but apparently, Cole was not amenable to his uncle's scheme. That was something, was it not?

And yet, her sense of disappointment deepened, far outweighing the relief. There were other feelings, too.

Deep, perplexing emotions which Jonet did not want to consider, much less feel. It was as though a dozen different currents tugged at her, any one of which could drag her beneath the churning surface. She was strong, yes. But good God, was she strong enough?

Well, she had to be, did she not? She had no choice, and never had. Life had taught Jonet that she was a survivor, that she was *hard*. But Cole Amherst was harder. She knew it instinctively. And deep inside, Jonet also knew that she should be grateful that it was not he whom she was pitted against. Oh, yes. Better an unseen enemy than an invincible one.

It was clear that Cole was as in command with his uncle as he was with everyone else. And now, had there been any doubt, Cole had made it equally clear that he held her in no great esteem. Indeed! The proud Captain Amherst was apparently "too discerning" in his tastes to "consort with the likes of her," or so James had said. What lowering words those were, no matter whose mouth they came from.

At times, Cole could be exceedingly kind, it was true. But his air of moral superiority was real. She had not simply imagined it. She would never be the sort of woman Cole Amherst would . . . would *befriend*. Even the obtuse James knew Cole better than to think otherwise. And Jonet, who had always been a clever, confident woman, knew it, too. Why, then, did Cole's words cut her so deeply?

He was nothing to her. Brutally, Jonet shoved herself upright in the chair and jerked her spine perfectly straight. Amherst's opinion mattered no more than anyone else's—which meant it mattered not one whit! Jonet was not blind. On those rare occasions when she ventured beyond her front door, Jonet could hardly misconstrue the whispers, the stares, and—other than David—the almost total lack of callers. She, who had long been the toast of London—a woman who had had her choice of escorts every day of the season, and who had been invited to bed by half the House of Lords—was now a pariah to the *ton*.

Strangely enough, the loss of society's esteem had not surprised her. What had surprised her had been how little she had cared. Cole meant no more to her than they did. Absently, Jonet pressed the heel of her hand against her brow and rubbed. *Another headache.* She was dimly aware of the clock striking the hour as someone pushed open the drawing room door. Startled, Jonet snapped her gaze upward.

Ellen came into the book-room, carrying a swath of black silk draped over her arm. She pursed her lips into a vexed smile. "Oh, there you are, Jonet! Will you please have a look at this gown?" Her cousin crossed the room, her arm outstretched. "I have stitched these jet beads across the bodice, just as you like it. Now, have I enough, do you think?" With a sigh, Ellen dropped the gown into Jonet's lap.

Jonet looked down at the dress, lightly fingering the fine fabric. The work was exquisite. "Oh, Ellen!" Admiration battled with exasperation. "You need not be forever doing things for me. I can very well stitch my own beading."

Ellen looked aggrieved. "Is the work not to your liking?"

"Oh, Ellen! Do sit down." Jonet motioned to a chair opposite. "You are like a sister to me. It troubles me to see you behave as if you are anything less."

It was an old argument, and one that Jonet and Ellen had had many times before. Since marrying Henry, Jonet had tried to continue treating her cousin as a member of the family. But Ellen had resisted. And despite Ellen's arguments, her remaining alone at Kildermore had been quite out of the question, given her age and unmarried status. There had been a time when she'd assumed Ellen would want a home of her own, and so Jonet had dragged Ellen to balls and routs, introducing her to suitable men. But her cousin would have none of it. Ellen's wishes remained a mystery to Jonet.

Jonet drew a deep breath. "You are angry with me again, are you not? I daresay I have done something to deserve it, Ellen, but I know not what."

"I am not angry, Jonet!" answered her cousin. "It is you, I believe, who is distressed. Has Captain Amherst done something to upset you?"

"No, nothing," lied Jonet softly.

"Now, now my dear!" Ellen's face tightened, but her tone softened. "Indeed, Jonet, I fancy that you are just a little too intrigued by him. You cannot lie to me, you know."

Jonet gave Ellen a dry smile. "No, I cannot, can I? But I do not think that—"

Her words were forestalled by Charles Donaldson's entrance. Across the room, his eyes caught and held Jonet's for a long moment as a look of understanding passed between them.

"A caller, my lady," he finally announced, flicking a look toward Ellen. "It is Pearson from Bow Street. He has brought his final report on Captain Amherst."

"Well!" announced Ellen a quarter hour later as Donaldson escorted the Bow Street runner from the bookroom. "I must say, Jonet, you never cease to surprise me."

"In what way, my dear?" Jonet turned her pensive stare from the cold hearth to study her cousin's face.

Ellen shot her a wry look. "Uncle always bragged that you were hard as flint. I might have known you would not be so foolish as to trust Captain Amherst altogether."

Jonet jerked from her chair and crossed to the window,

bracing her hands on either side of the embrasure. Blindly, she stared down into the side street as her groom brought Pearson's horse around. "I trust no one," she finally responded, her voice low.

Ellen seemed not to have heard her. "I wonder what Lord James will do next."

Turning her face from the window, Jonet stared over her shoulder. "What do you mean?"

Ellen let her eyes drift over Jonet. "Oh, James is up to something, and no mistake."

Jonet snorted in a most unladylike fashion and pushed herself away from the window. "James has been 'up to something' from the moment I wed Henry, Ellen. To what specific iniquity do you refer?"

Ellen lifted her shoulders and looked up, her eyes wide. "I daresay he means to discredit your morals by setting up Captain Amherst as a credible witness. Perhaps he thinks to catch you out in some terrible indiscretion?"

"What are you saying, Ellen?"

"Why, my dear, I hardly think I know." Again, she shrugged equivocally. "Perhaps James is disturbed by your relationship with Lord Delacourt. Indeed, he may have chosen to believe—unfairly, of course—what is said of you two."

Carefully, Ellen folded her hands into her lap, hesitated but a moment, then spoke again, more gently. "In truth, my dear, mightn't it be best not to see Delacourt for a time? Just a few months," she swiftly added. "Your mourning will be over, and then you may—"

"And then I may do *what?*" interjected Jonet peevishly. "Marry David? *Et tu Brute?* Do you think I poisoned my husband as well?"

"That is not what I was suggesting, Jonet!" insisted Ellen

hotly, springing up from her chair. "I neither know nor care what you plan to do with Delacourt! I am merely suggesting you keep your distance from him—and from Captain Amherst, for that matter!"

"Oh, Ellen!" said Jonet softly, opening her arms and drawing Ellen into a light embrace. "I must mind my sharp tongue." Gently, she patted her cousin on the back. "Come, now! You can trust me to curb my Cameron wickedness in front of Captain Amherst!"

"I suppose so," came Ellen's worried response.

Jonet pushed Ellen back a little and smiled at her. "Do you think me so incorrigible, then? I can behave if I must. And I do not think Captain Amherst will pay overmuch attention to me. In fact, I have reason to believe he thinks me far beneath his notice."

Ellen sniffed with disdain. "Oh, that sort of man would, wouldn't he?"

A little hurt by Ellen's agreement, Jonet let her hands drop. "Perhaps you are more to his liking."

"How silly," insisted Ellen, snatching Jonet's black silk dress as they strolled toward the door.

Jonet held open the door as her cousin passed through. "Perhaps," she softly responded. "But neither of us can ignore him, particularly when he's to make a rare appearance at dinner tonight."

Cole dressed for dinner with a little more than his usual care. In light of his new duties, he had at last felt compelled to temporarily put away his regimentals and dust off his civilian wardrobe, which was plain to the point of severity. There had been no place for peacocks in the hallowed halls of Cambridge, and in truth, despite his financial situation, Cole had always dressed essentially as his father before him had done. Which was to say, rather like a vicar. And so he carefully attired himself in a plain gray waistcoat and matching breeches, then topped it off with his best black frock coat.

Well, that was that, he thought, turning to study himself in the mirror. A true country parson in the making. Ruefully, he poked through the heavy walnut wardrobe into which Jonet's servants had carefully placed his things. It was of no use. All of his coats were just as black and just as severe. Fleetingly, he thought of Delacourt's dapper wardrobe, and wished on his next breath that he looked half as slender and elegant. Then, angry with himself, he slammed shut the wardrobe door, very nearly catching the loose ends of his cravat in it. That simply would not do. He did not have—and did not want—the services of some puffed-up valet to press and re-press his linen merely because he had not the patience or the intelligence to care for it properly.

Ruthlessly, Cole lashed his cravat into its usual severe style, but a little tighter and a little higher than usual—not out of any point of vanity, but mostly to punish himself for being so witless and facile as to worry about how he looked in comparison to another man. His orderly Moseby had often remarked that Cole's attire wanted only a hair shirt to make it fully effective punishment. It was true that Cole liked to be turned out with military precision, but he had always seen it as his duty to look the part of a dedicated officer. Particularly at a formal occasion such as dinner.

Dinner. Good God, how he dreaded it. Lord Delacourt would be there, of course. He was more often than not in attendance. Since coming to Mercer House, Cole had seized every opportunity to dine out. But tonight, he had exhausted his excuses. Tonight, there would be no avoiding Jonet's haunting beauty and her vain young lover. And there would be no avoiding the spectacle Delacourt would undoubtedly make by fawning over her.

Abruptly, Cole jerked to a halt at the top of the steps, swearing violently under his breath. *Good God, what was wrong with him?* What the devil did he care whom Jonet Rowland dined with? Or bedded? It was her home. And clearly, she intended to do pretty much as she pleased in it, too. Cole had come to Mercer House for the sole purpose of educating her children. It was time he stopped acting like a jealous young swain where Jonet was concerned. The woman might be a tad unpredictable, but she was more than capable of defending herself. Indeed, at times she could be quite vicious—perhaps more vicious than Cole wished to acknowledge.

On impulse, he spun about and headed for the schoolroom, deciding that he had no need to join the household in taking wine in the drawing room before dinner. Better that he should spend that hour with the boys, and then go down just a few minutes before the meal was served.

Cole found Stuart and Robin on the verge of enjoying their own dinner, which was always served by a footman under the auspices of the stern but capable Nanna. As the boys greeted him warmly, the dogs leapt up from their positions beneath the table to eagerly wag their tails. Cole responded by drawing up one of the larger chairs to the table just as Cox set down steaming plates of kidney pie and an assortment of stewed vegetables.

Immediately, Robert pulled a face. "Oh, yuck! I *hate* kidney pie," he groused.

"Och! Hate it do ye?" asked Nanna archly as she set down two brimming mugs of milk. "Well, that's all there's tae be, and eat every bite ye surely will, or go tae bed w'naught else. And that means no pudding, mind!"

Robert scowled, but after a long hesitation, he began to pick at his vegetables. Cole turned his attention to Stuart. For a few moments, Cole engaged the young marquis in casual conversation, watching to be sure that he ate, and that he seemed settled enough for sleep. Last night, Stuart had been terribly restless. Cole knew it, because he too had lain awake. Three or four times, he had found himself crawling from the warmth of his bed to prowl up and down the lamp-lit corridors of Mercer House. And for no good reason that he could determine. Indeed, there was nothing that he could identify or explain in even the vaguest of words. It was just that feeling, that ominous sensation of a malevolent presence, which was all too familiar to a battle-scarred soldier.

Once last night, Cole had met Cox coming up the back staircase. The man had nodded silently, then gone on about his business. And in the wee hours of the morning, he had seen Charles Donaldson lightly dozing in a ladder-back chair in the rear hallway. The big Scotsman had bolted instantly awake at the sound of Cole's bare foot on the top step, and his chair, which had been tipped back against the wall on its rear legs, had flown forward with a clatter. Through the balustrade their eyes had met, and in the dim lamplight, a knowing glance had passed between them. Slowly, Cole had gone back up the stairs, knowing that all of them watched for the same thing.

Nothing. *Everything.*

It was then, at the top of the stairs, that Cole had seen the shaft of weak light shining beneath young Lord Mercer's door. Cracking the door ever so slightly, Cole had peeked in, just to be sure that the boy was all right. The hinges had been perfectly silent. Stuart, his back to the door, his open book turned toward the lamplight, had not known that he was being watched. This morning, Cole had asked Donaldson to have every door hinge in the house tightened down until it squalled, and if that did not work, the hinges were to be replaced with new. Again, the knowing look had passed.

Tonight, however, Stuart looked marginally less worried, but like his brother, he ate little. Nudging his pie to one side, the boy picked at his vegetables and nibbled at a thick slab of bread, then pushed the plate disdainfully away. It had become painfully apparent that his young lordship shared some of his mother's fears. Cole was very much afraid that a little vigilance was necessary. He wished only that he knew why. For a long moment, Cole merely studied Stuart's face, but gradually, he became uncomfortably aware of Robert, no matter how hard he tried to ignore the boy.

And try he did, for the truth was, Robert was busy shoveling his dinner beneath the table, and allowing Rogue to lick the spoon. Inwardly, Cole could not help but chuckle at Robert's antics, not to mention his composure. Oh, the lad might look like the very image of Delacourt, but Cole was very much afraid that Robert had inherited his mother's shrewd ways.

Nanna, however, was not so admiring. It did not take long before the keen old Scotswoman caught young Robert in the act. She launched into a swift reprisal, which included dire threats of near starvation and no sweets for weeks to come. Bravely, Robert owned up to his crime. "But I'm not eating any more of that kidney pie," he warned with a shrug, "if I've already lost my pudding."

Undaunted, Nanna surveyed their plates. "Aye, weel suit yourself, my fine laddies," she announced grimly. "I daresay you'll be earning the privilege to turn up yer nose at perfectly gude food when yer stomach grinds all night." Plaintively, both Stuart and Robert looked up at Cole.

He immediately jerked out of his chair. It would soon be time for dinner downstairs, and Cole knew better than to interfere with Nanna and her methods. Cole had recently learned that Nanna had nursed both Jonet and Ellen, and had half-raised Charles Donaldson, as well as most of the other servants. She was a battleaxe in wool worsted, but Nanna loved the boys. And so Cole patted the boy firmly on the back. "Sorry, Robin! You must take your punishment like a man."

Dinner was indeed a miserable affair. Ellen Cameron babbled on aimlessly, but Jonet was surprisingly quiet, almost sullen. To his utter consternation, Cole could not keep his eyes from her face, despite his constant efforts to do so. Delacourt, too, seemed absorbed by their hostess.

As if he sensed her mood, the young man kept touching her gently on the arm, leaning solicitously toward her, and inquiring as to the taste of her food. As if it were his own home, Delacourt ordered the footmen to fetch first one thing, then another—more sauce for the fish, more pepper for the beef, a dozen little things—in an attempt to encourage Jonet to eat. And yet, she did not.

Twice, Delacourt caught Cole's gaze as Cole tried to drag his eyes away from Jonet. Boldly, Delacourt stared across the table, a look of dark challenge etched upon his handsome visage. And then, just as quickly, he dropped his chin and turned away, arrogantly snapping his fingers for the footman to refresh Jonet's empty glass. Wine was the one thing she seemed to be consuming at a prodigious rate.

Cole soon became grateful for Miss Cameron's incessant chatter. Under normal circumstances, he would have found her lighthearted inanity grating, but tonight, with tension thrumming through the room, her banter maintained at least the semblance of civility. At some point, the subject turned from the depressed economy to the London stage, a subject Cole had little interest in. Delacourt remarked upon the current schedule, and dimly, Cole half listened as Miss Cameron mentioned some particular play which was set to open at the Theatre Royal toward the season's end.

"What do you think, Captain Amherst?" Miss Cameron inquired, leaning eagerly forward. "Does that not sound delightful? Have you ever seen him perform? I vow, he is my favorite actor."

"Oh . . . delightful indeed," murmured Cole, rousing himself to attention. With no notion of whose talent was in question, he tried to look inquiringly at her. "But I am afraid I have not had that pleasure, Miss Cameron. No doubt he is most excellent."

Her gaze dreamy, Ellen Cameron paused with her empty fork held aloft and rolled her eyes heavenward. "Oh, yes!" she exclaimed, her voice rich with awe. "I saw him last year in *Titus Andronicus*—I do so love a good tragedy, don't you know—and he was inspiring."

Delacourt pulled a sour face. "Ugh! What a violent piece, Miss Cameron. I cannot think how it lasted the fortnight it did before closing."

Miss Cameron's dreamy expression vanished abruptly. "Yes, it is rather appalling, is it not? I daresay *Measure for Measure* will be even better." She turned her eyes upon Cole. "What do you think, Captain Amherst? Would you care to go when it opens?"

"Ellen!" interjected Jonet harshly, her wineglass again empty. "Might I remind you that we are a house in mourning? Upon my word, I cannot think what has come over you."

Ellen put down her fork with a clatter. "*I* am not in mourning!" she hotly insisted. "No one expects me to put on my black for a year!"

"But good heavens, Ellen!" insisted Jonet, her voice strident, her face flaming. "You are an unmarried woman! It is entirely inappropriate for you to suggest—"

Ellen coolly cut across her. "I merely meant that perhaps Captain Amherst would give his escort to Aunt and me when she returns from Kent." She lifted her chin a little stubbornly. "I daresay that there is nothing so terribly wrong about that."

Cole tried to intercede. "I should be most pleased to accompany you and your aunt, Miss Cameron." In truth, he had no desire to escort Jonet's cousin any further than the front door, but at that moment, he'd have gladly agreed to drive her to hell and back, merely to put an end to the conversation.

Though addressing Ellen, Jonet turned her gaze on Cole, carelessly setting down her wineglass and striking the rim of her dinner plate. "I am sure Captain Amherst is merely being polite, Ellen," she remarked, her eyes narrow and cold. "Indeed, he is a man of very *discerning* taste and high principles. I daresay he considers the frivolity of the theater beneath him—perhaps even morally corrupting."

Delacourt promptly choked on a mouthful of food.

Cole jerked himself upright in his chair. "How kind you are, my lady, to think so well of me," he replied, allowing a hint of sarcasm to lace his words. "Be assured I am hardly worthy of such praise."

"Praise?" echoed Jonet stridently. She drew another

deep breath, but Delacourt interrupted, speaking directly to Cole for the first time since the meal had commenced.

"Do tell us, Amherst," the viscount quickly interjected. "How does a scholar come to leave his vocation and go into the army? I must say, I have often wondered at that."

"There was a war, my lord," Cole coolly answered. "I believed it my duty."

Duty be damned thought Jonet irritably as Cole and David continued to discuss the army and the postwar economy. Oh, yes! Cole Amherst was very assiduous in *doing his duty.* Though the plight of unemployed soldiers was a subject which normally stirred deep concern in Jonet's breast, tonight she really did not give a fig about them. But then, she had consumed more wine than was prudent. Well! She didn't give a fig about that either. Lightly, she tapped the rim of her wineglass, and Cox quickly filled it. David paused in mid-sentence to shoot her a disapproving look. Jonet ignored him and let her mind return to her discussion with Pearson.

As with the conversation she'd overheard between Cole and James, the results had been either disappointing or reassuring, depending upon the light in which one viewed them. Had Pearson's last report uncovered something, Jonet would finally have felt justified in throwing Cole out of her house, and thereby out of her life. But the truth was, she was coming to depend upon him. To *want* him.

How dangerous! Slowly, she lifted her eyes from the glass and let them drift over his golden hair, his high, striking brow, and his full, sensual mouth. How truly brilliant the man was in choosing his wardrobe. The starkly elegant clothing and high, simple cravat would have set him apart from the crowd had the room been filled by London's handsomest bucks and beaus. A less refined gentleman might have overdressed, but Cole knew how to set off his golden good looks with flawless elegance.

So tempting. So tormenting. And so *morally discerning,* as James had said. In her confusion and anger, Jonet wanted to strike out at him for it. Instead, she emptied half her wineglass. It seemed the surest way to dull the pain of knowing how different they were. It was, perhaps, a pity Pearson had uncovered nothing. It seemed Cole Amherst was a man of mystery—or at least a man of discretion. But as she had suspected, he suffered no financial difficulties. In fact, it appeared he had extensive landholdings which were unencumbered and unentailed—and in which he seemed inexplicably disinterested. Following his marriage, Cole had left his university post with high recommendations and would now be welcomed back in a trice.

Within the ranks of the army, he was considered a valiant officer and strategist, whose easy manner made him a favorite with the enlisted men. Pearson confirmed that Cole was childless, a widower, and that his late wife's reputation was also above reproach. He kept no mistress, and courted no one. There was nothing that might leave him open to bribery or blackmail, nothing that would even require him to earn his keep. In short, Cole was considered a brilliant if somewhat reticent gentleman who was disposed to intellectual pursuits and athletics such as riding and cricket. Just as he had said.

Oh, yes. *A paragon of manly virtue.* Damn him straight to hell. She forced her gaze from him and stared blindly down the table, across the wealth of silver, crystal, and porcelain, all of which meant nothing to her. Cole was everything she had once admired and wanted in a man. He was perfect for her—or would have been ten years ago. Before she had changed so inexorably. Before her father's scheming had thrust her into a world she had been ill prepared to deal with.

Yes, she had fulfilled her Cameron legacy, inasmuch as any woman could. She had grown callous, sophisticated, and wary, until at times it seemed she was little better than her father had been. She felt a sudden urge to escape the room. Her life. Everything.

The footman was in the process of serving the cheese when Jonet rose abruptly from the table, shoving back her chair a little roughly. "Gentlemen," she announced, steadying herself as the floor dipped a little precariously. "I believe we shall leave you to your port."

Delacourt and Cole jerked out of their chairs as soon as she rose. The viscount caught her eye with a sharp, sidelong glance. "But my dear Jonet," he said with a light laugh, "they've just brought in the last course. Surely you would wish to join us in—"

Jonet cut him off with a wobble of her hand. "No." Then, forcing a solicitousness she did not feel—indeed, what she felt was mild nausea—Jonet remembered to look inquiringly at Ellen.

Ellen also stood. "Quite so," she swiftly agreed, stretching out her hand to her cousin, her face a mask of sympathy. "I couldn't eat another bite. Come, Jonet, let us go into the drawing room."

Cole had no inkling of what had prompted Jonet to leave the table so abruptly. All he knew was that he was now left to stare across the snowy linen at Delacourt, profound dislike seething through his blood. As the two footmen cleared the uneaten course they had just laid, Cole carefully examined his feelings. He could find no rational explanation for such heated enmity. What he should have felt was guilt. Though the viscount's conduct toward Jonet had been annoyingly attentive, Delacourt had behaved with all propriety. Why, then, did the young nobleman's demeanor so aggravate him?

Because Delacourt was a duplicitous, false-hearted bastard, that was why.

Cole suddenly realized that Delacourt, too, was eyeing him suspiciously. Normally, the viscount asked Jonet to remain when port was served, but this time they were alone. Cox filled the last of the two heavy goblets with the dark red wine, settled the bottle on a small salver at the viscount's elbow, then drew shut the double doors. Smoothly, Delacourt lifted his glass in a toast. "To our lovely hostess," he said softly, staring across the rim at Cole.

"Indeed, to our hostess," agreed Cole brusquely. He sipped from the glass, then put it down again.

"The vintage does not suit?" asked the viscount lightly. "Or is there something else, Amherst, which is not to your taste?"

"I have no notion what you may mean, Delacourt," answered Cole evenly. "The port is fine. I thought the meal quite excellent."

"Yes, Jonet's cook is splendid, if perhaps a little conventional," agreed Delacourt. "Nothing, of course, that can compare with Jacques, the chef who was recently let go."

"Was he indeed?" asked Cole, already weary of the viscount's superior air.

"Indeed," echoed Delacourt. "But as it happens, that is not the issue to which I was referring."

Cole felt his impatience rise. "Delacourt, I fear the army has worn away whatever polish my social skills may have had," he said caustically. "In truth, I have no taste for witty after-dinner repartee. I wish you would simply say what you mean."

Lord Delacourt smiled wickedly, his teeth wide and glittering in the candlelight. "Excellent! Then let me be perfectly blunt—indeed, almost ungentlemanly. I wish to say simply this: I have my eye on you." He dropped his voice to a lethal softness. "Just as surely as you watch her, I watch you."

"I do not know what you mean, Delacourt," Cole answered, his voice low and serious. "And what business is it of yours whose eyes are where, come to that?"

Delacourt seemed completely unruffled. "I am speaking of Lady Mercer, of course. I have taken it upon myself to . . ." The viscount cast his gaze aloft as if searching for just the right phrase. "To look after her interests, shall we say?" he finally finished.

Cole fought a scalding burst of anger. "It is my opinion, Delacourt, that your despicable behavior has precluded your rights in that regard," he retorted, his teeth nearly clenched shut.

The arrogant viscount threw back his head and laughed richly. "Why, now I must confess my own confusion, Amherst. I have not a clue as to what you are trying to imply."

Cole felt a wave of bone-deep mortification. Dear Lord, he was on the edge of saying something that was entirely out of line. Worse, he very much feared he might be wearing his heart on his sleeve, and Cole had no intention of giving the haughty Lord Delacourt something else to peer at through his quizzing glass. Slowly, he drew a deep, steadying breath, and spoke as calmly as he could. "Just this, Delacourt. Lady Mercer has already suffered greatly. To now be heartlessly betrayed by someone for whom she cares deeply would be a cruelty beyond bearing."

The color seemed to drain from the viscount's face.

"Pray continue, Amherst," he said coldly. "I confess, you have my full attention now."

Cole held his gaze without wavering. "If you care for Lady Mercer as deeply as you would have others believe, then I beg you to be a little more solicitous of her welfare."

"You'd best explain yourself, sir," retorted the viscount, his voice blatantly hostile now. "Those words sound perilously like an accusation."

"Make of them what you will," growled Cole.

Delacourt leaned halfway across the table, an ugly snarl marring his handsome face. "See here, Amherst—you can go to the devil if you mean to imply that I would do anything which is not in Jonet's best interest—"

Cole cut rudely across him. "I speak not of her interests, Delacourt, but of yours, which I am given to understand have recently been fixed elsewhere."

After a long, expectant pause, the viscount settled marginally back into his chair and took up his glass again. "You know nothing of my interests, Amherst, and nothing at all about where they are *fixed*."

"Very little," agreed Cole grimly. "But I daresay it would deeply wound Lady Mercer to learn of your little love nest near Drury Lane."

Delacourt looked up from his port, his eyes wide and mocking. "Why, that sounds like another threat, Amherst. I was given to understand you were the quiet, studious type. Do you now fancy yourself Jonet's protector?"

"I fancy only that you are a self-serving young coxcomb who spares no thought for the welfare of others."

The viscount gave another bitter laugh, then took a healthy pull from his glass. "By God, I should call you out for that, Amherst." But oddly, his temper seemed to have cooled.

Delacourt's sudden equanimity served to further inflame Cole. "By all means. But you would be a fool, sir. For you will lose."

"I daresay I might," agreed Delacourt with a casual half-shrug. "I have heard that you have a steady hand. Are you an exceedingly good shot?"

"Quite."

A smile seemed to play at one corner of the viscount's mouth. "Well, then! I should dislike above all things to ruin a good coat in a duel which I am destined to lose. Perhaps we ought to reconcile our differences, lest our wardrobes suffer to no good purpose." The viscount took up his glass once more, his anger quite obviously spent.

Cole was incensed. "By God, sir, I believe that Lady Mercer's honor is a very good purpose," he said stiffly. He was beginning to wish Delacourt would call him out, despite the fact that in his saner moments, he harbored dark and serious doubts about Jonet's honor.

"Oh, come now, Amherst! Lady Mercer and I are just old friends." Delacourt gave his light, elegant laugh. "You are simply jealous. Confess it."

"I am her children's tutor, Delacourt."

"True," agreed Delacourt flippantly. "But if you want Jonet, I say *carpe diem,* old boy. One never knows—perhaps she fancies you. One can never be sure."

"Good God, you really are a fool, Delacourt." Blood lust thrummed through his veins, and Cole, who had never fought a duel in his life, was suddenly more than willing.

"Ah, perhaps!" He smiled wolfishly again. "But I am not a coward, which I daresay you are, Amherst. Drawing a sword takes but a moment's bravado, you see. Opening one's heart to pain, to rejection—or even to passion—requires a far more sustained courage."

"What the devil are you talking about, Delacourt?" Cole fumed. "I swear, you speak in circles."

One of Delacourt's dark brows arched high. "Oh, I think perhaps you want Jonet," said the viscount softly. "But you are afraid to pursue her. Admit it."

Cole shoved back his chair with every intention of hauling Delacourt out of his, but he was forestalled. The double doors burst open simultaneously and a panic-stricken Robert bolted into the room. Stuart was at his heels, his face bloodless.

Robert hurled himself at Cole, seemingly oblivious of Lord Delacourt. "Come quick, sir!" the boy cried. "Come upstairs at once! It is Rogue. He's—" Suddenly, grief overcame the child, and he began to heave with sobs.

Holding Robert tightly in his arm, Cole snapped his head about to look at Stuart. "What is it?" he demanded. "Tell me what has happened!"

"Rogue. He's sick, sir," Stuart answered, his mouth tremulous. "He staggered around a bit, then crawled beneath the sofa. He—oh, he looks very ill, sir. He won't come out at all."

"Oh, he's going to die," wailed Robert, pulling one hand from Cole's neck just long enough to wipe his nose. "I just know it!"

The haughty Lord Delacourt completely forgotten, Cole rose from his chair, put Robert down, then strode from the room with the boys at his heels. "Stuart," he ordered, "find Nanna. Tell her to bring her basket of herbals—and any other medications she might have."

Ten minutes later, the kitchen beneath Mercer House was deadly quiet, the clanging of pots and pans now stilled, the scullery maids long since sent away. Only Cook remained, while Cole and Nanna stooped low over the dog, who now lay limply across a rug near the hearth.

"Aye, it's a poison o'some sort," whispered Nanna under her breath. Cole shuddered at the words he had dreaded to hear. He had arrived in the schoolroom to find Rogue under the schoolroom sofa, his breathing shallow. Cole had carried the dog belowstairs, saying he needed constant supervision.

But the truth was, he wanted neither Jonet nor the children present if matters took a turn for the worse, as he very much feared they would. On his knees beside the dog, Cole ran a soothing hand down Rogue's spine, looking up at Nanna as he did so. "What do you think happened?" he asked softly as the collie shuddered beneath his hand. "Could this be the same thing which killed Mercer?"

"Aye, p'rhaps, but this time we're like tae lose something a wee bit more valuable," hissed Nanna as she clawed through her basket. "Sheepdogs earn their keep, and niver do ill toward the innocent."

Cole let that remark pass without response. The old woman was clearly too distressed to guard her tongue. "Did the dogs go outside this afternoon?"

Nanna stopped rummaging through the huge willow basket she had carried into the kitchen and looked pensively down at him. "Aye, Stiles took 'em down tae run in Green Park—just as usual." Suddenly, relief passed over the old woman's face. "Aye, mayhap that's it. Like as not the dog took it intae his head to eat something he oughtn't."

"Perhaps." Cole studied the dog. "I suppose what we need is a purgative?"

Nanna shook her head. "Nay, I think no' a purgative . . .

t'will just force the poison intae the bowels. If it isna already there. T'would surely help to know what the poor wee thing ate."

"What then?" asked Cole anxiously. "What would you do if one of the boys had eaten something which you suspected was poisonous? Give milk? Induce vomiting?"

"Aye, an emetic," she answered swiftly, still poking through her basket. "T'will force up whatever may be left in the belly and keep it from the bowels." Suddenly the old woman produced a stout brown jar with a cork. "Ipecacuanha root," she announced in a satisfied voice.

"Will that make him vomit?" Cole asked anxiously.

"Oh, aye. It will do." Nanna nodded solemnly. "Mayhap t'is too late, though." She looked down at Cole, her broad, wrinkled face anxious. She pulled two more vials from her basket, then looked down at Cole. "Are you to help me, then? T'will no be a pleasant job, I'm telling you straight out."

Cole slicked his hand down Rogue's coat again. "Yes, I am going to help." Nanna stared down at him for another long moment, looking as if she might say something further. Then abruptly, she called Cook to the hearth, and in calm, precise tones, she began to explain just what things would be needed.

7

In which the Captain suffers a Sleepless Night

It was almost midnight when Cole trod wearily up the three flights of stairs from the kitchen to the schoolroom. Above stairs, all was quiet, with no light visible beneath the children's doors. Jonet, it would seem, had finally managed to ease their worry, at least enough to permit them to sleep a bit. Cole very much feared that he would not be so fortunate. The entire evening had been a nightmare. The ordeal he and Nanna had suffered through had temporarily obliterated the embarrassment of his argument with Lord Delacourt. Now, with poor Rogue asleep downstairs, the horror of it came back in full force.

What had he been thinking? And what the devil had Delacourt meant by his veiled insinuations? Cole did not know. He knew only that he had humiliated himself in his ineffectual, and probably unnecessary, attempt to defend Jonet. And Delacourt, damn and blast him, had seen through it. Yes, Jonet's scornful young lover had somehow glimpsed what Cole wanted no one—not even himself—to see. That he was already half in love with Jonet Rowland.

There. It was out at last. How mortifying it was to feel such a potent mixture of strong, almost unmanageable emotions for another person. A person one hardly knew, and dared not trust. Tonight, he had been angry with Jonet for drinking too much, aggravated by her capacity to drive him mad with sudden lust, frustrated with her inability to see what a vain popinjay Delacourt was—and yet, he had felt compelled to protect her. And in so doing, Cole had all but accused the viscount of infidelity.

But Delacourt had not bothered to deny it. Cole snorted in disgust. Yes, it would be very convenient for the viscount if Jonet were to turn her attentions elsewhere. Then he could snuggle into his new love nest without that most tormenting of emotions—guilt. Cole realized that he was standing at the schoolroom, one hand clasped over his face as if to shut out the truth. Slowly, he noticed that someone was tugging at his shirtsleeve, his waistcoat and frock coat having been left somewhere in the kitchen. Cole looked down to see Stuart at his elbow. The boy was barefoot, attired only in his nightshirt.

"Sir," he whispered plaintively. "Is Rogue going to be all right? Mama said we must remember him in our prayers, then go to bed. She said that you'd take good care of him. But I just cannot sleep."

Gently, Cole encircled the boy's shoulders with his arm and drew Stuart into the schoolroom. Through the deep windows that fronted the house, Cole could see that the rain had finally begun in earnest. In the distance, lightning flickered, too far away for the rumble of thunder to be heard. Along the walkway below the windows, the watch was calling midnight, his lantern swinging eerie shadows up the walls of the house across the street. Nanna, bless her, had left a lamp burning low on the table.

Cole propped one hip on the corner of the table and stretched out his hand to tip up the boy's chin. "Listen, Stuart—Rogue is still quite ill. But I do believe he will be all right in a day or two."

"Can I see him, sir?"

Gently, Cole shook his head. "You need your sleep, as does Rogue. And the dog must rest. He is very weak, because we gave him something which helped him to vomit whatever it was he had eaten."

Stuart jerked his eyes away and stared across the table. He looked small and very frightened. "What he ate was Robin's kidney pie," said the boy softly.

A long, dreadful silence hung in the air. Finally, Cole sighed. "Yes, I know that," he answered gently. "But no doubt he gobbled down something in the park today."

Stuart cast up a doubtful glance. "Collies are pretty smart dogs, sir," he answered.

Cole considered it for a moment. It was a very good point, and it nagged at him. "Well, it is very hard to say what it was," he answered calmly. "Do you think you can sleep now?"

In the pale light, Stuart nodded solemnly, his young face still rather drawn. Affectionately, Cole patted his narrow shoulder. "Then take yourself off to bed, Stuart," he said softly. "I plan to work a bit, but you have only to call out if you need me. Do you understand?"

Solemnly, the boy nodded, and rose from his chair. Then, like a stealthy ghost in his flowing white nightshirt, the boy drifted out. As the door clicked shut, Cole stared down at his pile of paperwork and immediately gave up. Frustrated by things he did not want to consider, he tore off his spectacles and tossed them on top of the heap. He was weary, but not sleepy, and he could not bear the thought of an empty bed, so Cole simply flung himself across the long, leather couch and dragged an arm across his eyes. Unfortunately, it shut out nothing but the light and did little to calm his tumultuous thoughts.

Ruthlessly, Cole kicked off his shoes and stretched out his legs. Stuart's remarks had raised a chilling issue. There was no escaping the fact that his altercation with Delacourt ought to be the lesser of his concerns this night. Cole's pride would not kill him. But something had very nearly killed Rogue.

Neither Nanna nor Cole had spoken the words aloud, but it had been plain that they'd both realized, just as Stuart had, that the dog had eaten food intended for Robert. Stuart had thrown his away, and the scraps from dinner were long since gone. Another quick conversation with Cook had indicated that the meat had been bought fresh at the usual butcher's the previous afternoon, and had been served in one form or another at all three meals. Had there been complaints? *Why indeed not!* Was there anyone ill among the staff? *Heavens no!* And it had required all of Cole's charm and a touch of Nanna's authority to smooth Cook's feathers following that little exchange.

Cole forced himself to recall that not six months ago, someone in this house had likely been poisoned, and if so, the murderer was still at large. It was of some comfort that these dreadful happenings exonerated Jonet, at least in Cole's mind. Jonet's face when she spoke of her sons was lit by a maternal light so bright that there could be no mistaking the depth of her devotion. With the lamp still low, Cole lay on the sofa, listening as the wind whipped the rain back against the glass in spattering sheets. Summer rainstorms always left him melancholy and restless, even under the best of circumstances.

Another discomfiting memory stirred in the recesses of his mind. Yes, it had been just such a night—a rainy summer's evening—when he had gone to his late wife's house to ask for her hand in marriage. How far away it all seemed now. And yet, not far enough. God, no. Never far enough.

Cole had known Rachel only as the daughter of his mentor, a man whom Cole had both admired and emulated. Her father, Thomas, had taken Cole under his wing during his early years at Cambridge. Cole, ever hungry for a father figure, had been glad when their friendship had deepened into something more when he joined the faculty. He and Thomas had shared much, and when his old friend had lain dying, Cole had been stricken by a grief more profound than anything he had felt since the death of his own parents almost twenty years before. Of course he had asked what he might do to alleviate Thomas's suffering. Strangely, it had come as no great surprise when his friend had asked him to look after Rachel and—if he could find it in his heart to do so—to take her as his wife.

It had seemed like a small thing to do for a man who had given so much. As trustee of Thomas's perfectly adequate estate, Cole had made it plain to Rachel that he would always be there for her; that she need not wed him in order to be assured of his care and friendship. And so five days later, when she'd said yes, Cole had sincerely believed that Rachel harbored some secret affection for him. He had been pleased. He had been genuinely fond of her, although he had not known her well. Rachel had seemed perfect; serene, lovely, and gently feminine. When her mourning had ended, they were quietly wed.

Cole had begun the marriage with hope in his heart, but too late, he'd realized that Rachel had married because she viewed it as God's intended role for women. What he had taken for serenity went well past that, and into an emotion so restrained he could ill define it. Rachel had had no interest in cultivating any sort of mutual passion. It was, he soon learned, an emotion that made her acutely uncomfortable. In Rachel's view of marriage, gentle subservience was a wife's duty, and she had summarily placed housekeeping and lovemaking into that same category, with considerably more enthusiasm attached to the former than to the latter. Yes, Cole's bed had been almost as warm as his hearth, but neither had felt especially welcoming.

Rachel had loved him with half a heart, seeking only a contented existence. Inexperienced in the ways of love, Cole had come to believe that the fault was his; that he was incapable of stirring true passion in a woman. Now, despite a good deal more experience, he secretly feared it still might be true.

But good God, how Rachel haunted him. Even in the dimly lit schoolroom, he could almost see her, the crisp white nightrail tied at the throat, the long plait of cool blonde hair that fell across one shoulder. He could see her face, too. Full and pretty, with wide-set blue eyes filled with a childlike innocence. But Rachel had been four-and-twenty, hardly a child. Cole swallowed hard and looked into the lamplight, willing away the vision. Many men would have been happy with a quiet, undemanding wife. He, however, had not been. After three years of such a placid existence, Cole had realized that he still did not know his own wife, and the knowledge had left him sick with disappointment. Again, that had been his failing. But why now, of all times, should Rachel torment him?

Or better put, why was he deliberately torturing himself? Initially, he had not loved her, it was true. But he had wanted to. Many good marriages began with less. Cole had always believed that love was like a delicate flower that required cultivation and warmth. Had he been so wrong to think that his love for Rachel would grow? This wild, hot thing that bloomed in his heart for Jonet Rowland was no tender, delicate rose. That emotion had sprung quickly to full flower, its blood red petals unfurling as if impelled by a tropical heat beneath a searing sun. More passion than reverence, more lust than admiration, it was a desperate emotion, one that was beyond Cole's realm of understanding.

Restlessly, he shifted his weight on the sofa and watched another bolt of lightning split the sky. A shaft of fire. Yes, that was precisely what he felt in his gut—and in his loins—when he touched Jonet. Such a thing could not be love. A man could not love with such mad desperation a woman he did not fully understand. A woman who, at times, made him wild with anger and reckless with lust. Perhaps Rachel had been right all along. Surely this sense of having one's heart torn out of one's chest was worse than a safe and tepid affection. He could not be at peace in the same room with Jonet, and yet, when she passed from his sight, it was as if a part of him had been torn away.

Last night, Cole had slept poorly. In his imagination, he had been driven to a heated madness by sultry dreams of Jonet, when he should have been worried about the children. That was his job. And yet, twice he had awakened bolt upright in bed, wondering where their *mother* was. Then he would find himself obsessively wondering if Delacourt had somehow managed to creep into her bed. Damn it, he wanted to *know.* And as he had begun to drift back to sleep, Cole had unwittingly begun to fantasize about the wicked things he would do to Jonet Rowland if he were to share her bed.

In the whole of his life, Cole had never been in love with anyone, not even the woman he had married. And now he was beginning to fear that he had allowed himself to do what everyone—Lauderwood, Madlow, and yes, even his insensible Uncle James—had warned against. Suddenly, the rain increased its tempo, rattling wildly through the downspouts. In the western sky, lightning flashed again, and this time, the low rumble of thunder could dimly be heard. On the table, Nanna's lamp sputtered and went out, submerging the room in darkness. Cole dragged his arm over his eyes once more, and his awareness of the storm melted away.

"Psst—!"

The soft, insistent sound roused Lord Robert Rowland from a near dead slumber. One fist screwed into his eye, the boy sat up in bed and peered into the darkness. "Iszat you, Stuart?" he managed to mumble. Robert listened as his elder brother's footsteps trailed lightly across the carpet to the edge of his bed then paused.

"Psst—!" came the sound again. "Robin, did you hear a noise?" Stuart's whisper fell somewhat short of brave. Robert felt his brother's weight settle onto one corner of the mattress as he continued explaining. "Because I thought I heard voices. And then a *thump*! It might have come from the attic. Didn't you hear it?"

"All I heard," grumbled Robert sleepily, "was you jabbering to Cousin Cole." Robert collapsed back into a heap of feather pillows with a breathy *whoosh!* "Now, for pity's sake, Stuart! Go to sleep! You've been hearing things in the night since Papa died."

Stuart crept a little further up the mattress. "No, honest, Robert! I heard more noises after I left the schoolroom. I think someone is hiding in our attic. Probably in that closet near the maids' rooms."

"Oh, *go back to bed, Stuart!*" groaned his brother, dragging the covers over his head. "It's just a thunderstorm."

"I swear there was a noise, Robin!" insisted Stuart. "Anyway, you sleep like the dead. A herd of vicious elephants could come in here and eat you alive—"

"Awww—elephants don't—"

"And you would never hear it!" insisted Stuart, ignoring his younger brother's interjection. "I daresay I ought to sleep in here with you. It would be safer, don't you think?"

"Noo—!" wailed his brother. "I don't *think*. You kick, and you steal the sheets. Now go back to your own bed. We're safe. Cousin Cole is just down the corridor. Depend upon it, Stuart! He will catch anyone who comes skulking down the hall."

The squall of newly tightened door hinges slowly stirred Cole to a hazy wakefulness. He had no notion what was wrong, just the vague sensation that something was not . . . *right*. How long had he slept? And where the devil was he? Silently, he listened, trying to bring his senses to full alert.

Ah, yes. The schoolroom. Hinges shrieked again. Cole's body jerked taut. Was it Stuart? Or had an intruder slipped past Donaldson? Outside, the rain beat down relentlessly, suppressing all sound, swathing his senses in cotton. But someone *was* in the room.

His thoughts still disjointed, Cole spun to a seated position and stood. In the windows behind the sofa, lightning flared. Too late, Cole realized he had been silhouetted against the glass. Thunder rolled ominously. Cole darted toward the door. A sharp, powerful shoulder caught him low in the spine, sending him facedown into the floor with a breathless grunt.

Coming fully awake, Cole moved to throw off his attacker, but the sharp prick of a blade beneath his chin forestalled all resistance. He froze. Something was very wrong. Suddenly, it occurred to him—just as a bead of warm blood rolled down his throat. The attacker splayed half across his back felt taut and powerful—but absurdly light. *Far too small to be either Donaldson or one of the footmen.*

"Aye, don't even twitch, you bastard," rasped a cold, feminine voice against his ear, "or I swear, I'll slit your throat from ear to elbow." As if to reinforce the threat, she shoved his face hard against the floor.

"Oh my God," whispered Cole, his cheek pressed to the cold planks, his words unsteady. He could feel the point of the blade quiver against his skin. "Have you utterly lost your wits?"

The shapely feminine form atop him stiffened for a long moment, and then collapsed, her mouth slack and panting against his ear. "Oh . . . *shite,*" came her tremulous whisper.

The blade fell to the floor.

Smoothly, Cole twisted about until he could pitch his attacker to one side. He did not need light to know that it was Jonet he held in his arms. He could smell the deep, sweet scent of her, feel her breasts and belly pressed to his. Judiciously, he reached for the knife, tossing it from her reach.

"Jonet?" he said softly, squeezing shut his eyes despite the dark.

Against his chest, he felt her begin to tremble like a green soldier who has just survived his first brush with death. *"W-w-what?"* she finally answered.

"Jonet, where did you learn that disgustingly vulgar word?"

Her breath came out on a wispy little sigh. "F-f-from Charlie Donaldson, I think."

"I see," he said with utter calm. "I wish you would not use it again. I find it offensive."

"Just let me go, Cole," she whispered, but she made no move to roll away from him.

Vaguely, Cole wondered if he would ever be able to do what she asked. He knew he had no business touching her. She felt too good, smelled too enticing. But blast it, the woman had jumped him in the dark, and he damned well ought to teach her a lesson. Just then, another bolt of lightning split the night, lighting up the schoolroom. *Good Lord—Jonet was wearing nothing but a plain cotton nightshift!*

"Oh, Cole—!" As if the sight of his face had somehow unleashed her tension, Jonet collapsed in his embrace. Her trembling intensified to a bone-deep shudder. "I—I hurt you . . . I'm sorry."

Cole made no move to let her go, telling himself that it would be wrong to do so when she was so obviously distraught. "Jonet," he said, folding her tightly to his chest and speaking softly into her hair. "What do you mean by behaving so rashly? For God's sake, you're shaking all over."

She said nothing, and after a long moment, Cole looked down. In the gloom, he could not see her face. But he could sense that her breathing was still shallow, and he could hear the little hitch of fear in it. "A noise," she said, her voice muffled by his shirtfront. "I was checking on the boys, and then . . . I *thought* I heard a noise in the schoolroom. Did you? Did you hear anything at all?"

"No." Uneasily, Cole tried to shift his weight incrementally away from her. Relief was obviously flooding through Jonet, but he was far from relieved. Feeling rather like the word he had just ordered her *not* to say, Cole tightened his embrace, feeling his arousal leap to full flame. Good Lord, what a prince he was. Jonet had been scared witless, and now his cock felt like an axe handle shoved up against the softness of her thigh. Cole prayed to heaven she would not notice, but he couldn't make himself move away.

"It's just a storm, Jonet," he said softly against her hair. She smelled surprisingly innocent; warm and inviting, like apple blossoms and spring grass under a cloudless sky. Like a woman a man could lie down and sleep with. But not him, of course. Cole lifted his head away. "Jonet, the weather worsened rather quickly. Perhaps a rumble of thunder awakened you?"

"I . . . yes, perhaps," she said uncertainly. Slowly, her characteristic composure returned, and she pushed him away a little. Cole levered himself up onto one elbow, trying to bestir some shame. A gentleman would have been on his feet by now, helping her up from the floor, and warning her not to be so heedless. But Cole was doing neither, and Jonet did not seem to expect it. "Jonet," he finally whispered, "perhaps we oughtn't be . . . on the floor like this?" Lightning flashed again, more muted this time, and he glimpsed her face. Her eyes were wide and luminescent now, the lines of her mouth soft and suddenly inviting.

"Perhaps not," she replied. Long black hair cascaded over Jonet's shoulder, heavier and more wavy than Cole had expected. He began to be painfully aware of just where all their body parts were pressed together. Absolute lust—hotter and more intense than anything he had ever known—surged through him, pulling him toward her.

Nearly sightless in the gloom, Jonet looked up at the man whose body half covered her own. Even in the dark, he was huge and overpowering. The relief she had felt upon realizing it was Cole she had tackled had been quickly—too quickly—replaced by the sensations of deep, shuddering need. Though lust was an emotion she had had little experience with, Jonet knew it for what it was. She knew, too, that she should be ashamed of what she was thinking. *Of what she wanted.*

A bitter smile curved her lips. Perhaps she was not, strictly speaking, the type of woman Cole Amherst would ordinarily *consort with,* but it was rather obvious that his lofty morals had failed to inform his nether regions. Pressed against her thigh, Cole's rod was as hard as his heart. And at the moment, Jonet wanted them both. With a calculated deliberation, she reached up and drew Cole's lips to hers.

It was as if someone had sent a blazing oil lamp crashing to the floor. Heat and flame rolled over them with a fierce intensity, burning up every shred of resistance, every scrap of dislike, and every grain of suspicion. On a slow moan, Cole dragged his mouth over hers, then surged inside. Hotly, harshly, he plunged into her, again and again, giving her no chance to respond or refuse. Fleetingly, Jonet wondered just what she had unleashed, and then carelessly pitched herself headlong into the fire.

Her mouth open hungrily against his, Jonet listened in feminine satisfaction as a second groan—deeper, far more urgent—rumbled through Cole's chest. She felt his erection grow even harder against her leg. She felt the stubble of his beard rake across her face. Willfully, she skimmed both her hands along his sides, feeling the ripple of big ribs and taut muscle. And then, she felt his hands come up to roughly shove her shoulders hard against the floor.

In one smooth motion, Cole rolled her fully onto her back and dragged himself over her with powerful arms, rucking up the hem of her nightdress with his knee. Jonet felt a second moment of alarm, and then inexplicably relaxed again when she remembered that it was Cole whose hardness was now pressed between her thighs. She let her fingers come up to slide through his hair, but Cole mistook the motion. He captured her hand in his own, and dragging it up over her head, held it knuckles-down against the wood for a long moment, still kissing her.

Cole. *Oh, yes!* Jonet let herself move suggestively against him. She wanted and wanted. Oh God, how she wanted him. She yearned to forget her troubles in the shelter of Cole Amherst's arms. It was weak and wrong—even sinful—to want *anything* in such a desperate way. Tomorrow she would no doubt feel humiliated. Tonight, she simply did not care. In that instant, Jonet would have given up everything she possessed just to have this man slide deep inside her. The need was fierce, frightening, and wholly unlike anything she had ever known. Her mouth still under assault, Jonet tilted up her hips and pressed herself eagerly against his shaft.

Arms braced wide above her shoulders, Cole jerked his mouth from hers just as light flickered through the room again. "*Jonet*—" he whispered, his voice thick with desire. "*This is wrong.*" His wild, golden mane fell forward, and Cole froze, his eyes glassy, his face stark with unleashed need.

With her silence, she dared him to deny the depth of the emotion which both of them felt. He could not. On another feral groan, Cole's head dropped forward to take her breast in his mouth. He drew it between his teeth, into the warmth of his mouth, sucking hard through the sheer fabric of her gown. Desperately, Jonet deftly slid her hand down his ribs, feeling his flesh quiver at her touch, until she reached the bearer of his trousers.

Slowly, she let her fingers skim beneath it, then worked her way down and down, until Cole sucked in his breath and she captured the sweet weight of his rod in her hand. Greedily, she wrapped her fingers around it and felt it twitch powerfully against her palm. Cole jerked his mouth from hers, his breathing raw and rasping in the darkness.

"*Ahh . . . yes.*" Jonet breathed out the words against the damp skin of his throat, reveling in the heat and the weight of him. "Take me, Cole. I'm so tired of being alone. Just take me to your bed. Give me this. *Please . . .*"

Cole had her off the floor and in his arms before she could draw her next breath. Wedging his bare foot into the door, Cole kicked it halfway open and strode through the darkness toward his bedchamber.

Cole kept waiting for Jonet to protest, to claim that he had misunderstood her words. He kept waiting for sanity to flood back, all the while forcing it away. With one shoulder, he shoved open his door, then carried Jonet through his small sitting room, into the bedroom, and deposited her unceremoniously into the middle of his half-tester bed. Hastily, Cole began clawing at his cravat, whipping the linen from around his neck. He knew—oh, by God, *he knew*—that come tomorrow he'd regret this.

But nothing would now stop him from spreading the Marchioness of Mercer across his bed, stripping her naked, and plunging himself into her up to the hilt. That he would undoubtedly be plunging into something far worse seemed suddenly a worthwhile risk. Indeed, he could no longer recollect precisely why he had been trying to resist her attractions. Ripping his shirttail free, Cole dragged his shirt over his head and pitched it to the floor.

On his nightstand, the housemaid had left a lamp burning brightly, and the light should have brought back some semblance of reality, but it did not. By God, he'd had just about all the temptation he was able to tolerate. The woman had teased and tormented him from the moment he'd first laid eyes on her. And if she wanted it, he decided as he tore off his stockings, then he was determined to oblige.

Suddenly, Jonet came up onto her knees on the edge of his bed, swallowed hard, then pulled her nightrail over her head. The fabric slithered elegantly up her long, pale body, and when it came off, her black hair settled around her shoulders like a cloud, and her eyes held Cole's with a startling intensity. Just like that, the woman of his dreams was naked in his bed.

In that timeless moment, it seemed to Cole that she was the most perfect of God's creations, breathtaking in her beauty. For a split second, lust gave way to an almost holy sense of awe, and then came roaring back. Jonet's breasts were high, pale—and despite her too thin frame—surprisingly full. Her rosy nipples were puckered into hard buds of desire, and as he watched, her head tipped back, her mouth parted, and her hands came up to caress them invitingly.

Still watching Jonet stroke herself, Cole's hands went to the fall of his trousers. His fingers, suddenly big and awkward, struggled through the buttons, and then, in a spurt of pure frustration, nearly ripped loose the tapes that fastened his drawers. *Good God, he was going to explode.* He simply could not keep watching her touch her breasts that way. Foreplay became a foreign concept. Cole had to be inside her. The sound of rending fabric tore through the air. Still on her knees, Jonet shifted toward him.

"Please," she said softly, lifting her wide, seemingly innocent gaze to him. "Let me." With hands that shook only a little, she deftly freed the knotted ties, allowing the linen to drape loosely about his hips. Skimming her hands around the curve of his hipbones, Jonet made a little hum of pleasure deep in her throat and slid her palms down to cup his buttocks. With another gentle tug, she drew him right to the edge of the bed. Cole balanced his fingertips on her bare shoulders, feeling the silk of her hair drag across his knuckles as Jonet bent low and turned her head, nuzzling her cheek, and then her open mouth, against the shivering flesh of his belly. The gesture was sweetly tender—and wildly erotic.

One more nudge, and Cole's drawers and trousers slid onto the floor, his manhood springing free of the tangle. Jonet lifted her head and took the weight of his rod into her hand, sliding her fingers down his length. For a moment, he was almost certain she meant to pleasure him with her mouth. *Surely not!* And though Cole had little experience with that kind of pleasure, he knew that it was not what he wanted. Not tonight. With a growl of impatience, Cole bent his knee to the bed, pushed her over, and followed her onto the mattress.

"Do you want me?" she asked breathlessly.

"Since the moment I first laid eyes on you," he rasped, his desperate confession almost inaudible against the tender flesh of her neck.

Jonet felt Cole's weight bear her down into the softness of his bed. The coverlet had been turned back by an efficient housemaid, and the starched white sheets were cool against her skin. As if it were an afterthought, Cole lifted himself to kneel over her, one big hand holding the impressive weight of his cock, the other skimming up her inner thigh. Seductively, he slid his long, capable fingers into the slick folds of flesh between her legs to test her readiness.

She was. Need like nothing she had ever known knifed through her. "*Ah, ah . . . a-a-ah,*" she breathed, arching off the bed, one hand knotting into the bedcovers. Mouth open,

Jonet turned her head into the down of the pillow, wanting to drown in the dusky, masculine scent that lingered on Cole's bed linens. She yearned to feel his skin against hers, hungered to taste the heat of his passion, needed to draw in his scent and become, if only briefly, a part of Cole.

In the flickering lamplight, Jonet looked up at him. His knees braced on either side of her thighs, Cole towered over her, his long, elegant fingers still caressing himself, still caressing her. She drew in her breath and let her eyes drink him in, stunned to realize a man could look so . . . dangerously, deliciously masculine. His eyes were black and glittering, his hard jaw heavily shadowed with an unexpectedly dark beard. Sweet heaven, but he was a big man. *Everywhere.* The lamp cast a golden glow over the taut skin of his chest and arms, which were perfectly sculpted and lightly corded. A fine trail of hair led from his breastbone and down his lean belly, growing thick and dark at the base of his manhood.

As she watched, Cole drew his hand down the length of his shaft once more, and, no longer able to resist, Jonet made a choking, desperate noise in the back of her throat and reached out for him. Everything happened quickly then. A little roughly, Cole shoved her knees apart. Eagerly, she let her hands skim down the small of his back and over his taut hips, feeling the muscles tense as she urged him hard against her. And then he was on her, probing, hot and urgent, at her entrance. Only the sheer size of him cut through the haze of sensuality, and fleetingly, Jonet considered asking him to go slowly.

A desperate knock upon Cole's door made that unnecessary.

Atop her, Cole's entire body drew taut. His head jerked up, like a wild cat sniffing the air for danger. "*What—?*" he rasped heatedly.

A long moment of silence held sway. "It's j-j-just me, sir." Stuart's voice was small and terrified. "I th-think there is something under my bed."

And then his body jerked away from hers. Sick, Jonet felt the mattress dip and creak as Cole rolled to one side. Worse, she felt the revulsion and shame that flooded through him, washing away all desire for her. She felt shame, too, but she shut it away, for at that moment, her every instinct drew her to Stuart. *What had she been about to do?* Her children were alone and frightened, and she lay naked in their tutor's bed like a common slut. It was unconscionable. Biting her lip, she turned her face into the pillow again, dragging up the hem of the sheet to cover her shame.

"*Go—!*" she whispered urgently, giving a little shove against the small of his back.

Without looking at Jonet again, Cole sat up at the edge of the bed. He exhaled once, sharply, then dropped his head into his palms, his broad back and shoulders limned in the lamplight. "It is all right, Stuart," he said, his words unerringly gentle. "You're safe. Sit down at my desk. I'll . . . be right out."

Jonet watched as Cole stood, hitched his trousers up over his narrow hips, and dragged on his shirt, roughly shoving his arms through the sleeves. His flaming desire had burned down to a smoldering anger, which seethed through the room like a palpable, living thing. But was it directed at her? At himself? Jonet could not be sure, and at that moment, she did not care.

She cared only that Stuart was frightened. She had heard the terror in his voice. Even now, it took every drop of willpower she possessed not to go to him. But she couldn't very well let Stuart see her crawling from her would-be lover's bed, could she? Again, she had failed her child.

Cole buttoned the close of his trousers and turned to whisper over his shoulder without really looking at her. "Jonet," he coldly mouthed the words. "Go back downstairs to your bedchamber."

Levering herself anxiously onto one elbow, Jonet looked at him. "No," she whispered, shoving a heavy length of hair back over her shoulder. "I must be sure he is safe. That there is nothing . . ."

Through clenched teeth, Cole looked at her, his face hard in the lamplight. "There *is* nothing. Just a stormy night. If I discover otherwise, I will knock on your bedchamber door and tell you so." Then, with an icy calm, Cole picked up his lamp and went out the door.

Jonet listened intently as, in the sitting room beyond, Stuart began to explain. "It is probably just my imagination, sir," he said, sounding marginally less frightened now. "But you did say, sir, that I ought to wake you. And really, I thought it better for you to have a look than to wake Mama or Nanna. Was that . . . was that all right?" He sounded sheepish.

"Perfectly all right, Stuart," came Cole's soft response. The rest of his soothing words were lost to her as they left Cole's suite and went out into the hall.

His feet bare, the throat of his shirt open, Cole walked slowly along the corridor, the lamp held aloft in his left hand, his right laying lightly upon the young marquis's back. Rhythmically, he patted Stuart as they walked. Inwardly, however, he cursed himself for a fool. An irresponsible, libidinous fool. Dear heavens, what if Stuart had not paused to knock? What if, terrified by something real or imagined, he had simply burst into Cole's bedchamber, only to see his lecherous oaf of a tutor pounding himself inside his mother? Oh, what a comforting sight that would have been!

Cole wanted to reach around and kick his own arse. Stuart was nine years old, and boys of that age were not altogether naïve. He would have had some idea of what was going on. Most certainly, he would have known that it was *wrong*. The vision made Cole's gut clench with shame. What had he been thinking? Good God, what had Jonet been thinking, come to that? The woman was going to bring him nothing but trouble, and he had known it since the start. They were neither of them any better than rutting animals, clawing, licking, and panting all over one another. Now, his cock limp with humiliation and his chest tight with fear, Cole realized that he had made a terrible misjudgement.

Was it possible that what he had taken for Jonet's terror in the schoolroom had been nothing more than her own lust? Perhaps she really was just that shameless. Cole hardly knew enough about women to be sure. Perhaps she had merely wished to spite Delacourt. Or perhaps her willingness was motivated by nothing more than pure physical desire for him.

Oh, of course! he thought sarcastically. There was the answer! He was irresistible. And perhaps he should have felt flattered by it all, but he bloody well did not. What he felt was *used*.

Jonet waited but a moment before crawling out of Cole's bed, yanking on her nightrail, then wrapping a blanket lightly about her shoulders to follow them. Stuart's door stood half closed, probably Cole's way of encouraging her to make a discreet disappearance down the stairs. But Jonet had no intention of leaving her son when he was so obviously frightened.

After dinner tonight she had sent David straight home so that she might curl up with the boys on the sofa in her sitting room. There they had remained, Jonet trying to comfort them, until Cole had come up to say that Rogue was indeed on the mend. Yet Jonet now chided herself for not realizing that there would be aftereffects of such a crisis, particularly with Stuart, who was both sensitive enough and old enough to take seriously things that often escaped Robert.

Jonet was comfortable with her femininity—too comfortable, in fact, to continue to reproach herself for desiring a man like Cole Amherst. But she deserved a scathing scold for failing to anticipate her children's needs. It was yet another sign of just how precariously taut her thread of logic had been pulled. Was it wrong to want him as desperately as she did? Certainly it was wrong to be anything less than circumspect about it. Making love to a man on the floor of her children's schoolroom was not discreet. Undressing him without locking the bedroom door was so witless as to defy justification.

But that recrimination also fled as she turned the corner into Stuart's room to see Cole on his hands and knees, his narrow hips in the air, his head thrust beneath the bed. The boy lay facedown atop the mattress, peering rather anxiously over the edge. Cole's lamp sat on the floor beside him, and in the yellow glow that shone up into his face, Stuart looked pale and drawn.

The sight broke Jonet's heart. Rashly, she rushed toward him. "Oh, Stuart!" she whispered urgently. At once, Cole jerked at her voice, and the heavy crack of bone against wood sounded beneath the bed.

"*Damn it!*" came Cole's swift response. He emerged from beneath the mattress, assiduously rubbing the back of his head and glaring at Jonet, who now sat on the bed, Stuart caught in her embrace.

Cole was obviously annoyed that she had disobeyed him, but he was wise enough to direct his words to Stuart. "There is nothing under there, Stuart," he explained calmly. "I believe you may safely go back to sleep. Indeed, I suggest that that is what we *all* should do." He turned to look pointedly at Jonet. "And the sooner the better."

Despite the fact that Cole's shirt billowed loose at the throat, exposing a rather enticing expanse of chest and muscle, Jonet ignored him. Instead, she turned her attention to Stuart, pressing her lips fervently to his head. "I thought I heard a disturbance—and of course, I came up to investigate," she murmured.

Stuart lifted his head from his mother's chest to stare at Cole. "See?" His eyes widened again. "Mama heard something, too."

Cole merely darkened his glare and began to shove in his shirttail with sharp, violent motions. "I think what your mother meant, Stuart, is that she heard us rummaging around. Is that not right, ma'am?"

"Yes! Yes, of course. That is what I heard." Nervously, she licked her lips. "And so I became worried that perhaps you were ill or frightened. Was that not very silly of me?"

Stuart nodded, hugging his mother tightly. "I was a *little* frightened," he confessed in a small, whispery voice, "but I did not want to upset you any more, Mama. Cousin Cole has poked his lamp under my bed, and there is nothing there. Perhaps I just had a bad dream, and thought it up?" He stared up at his mother for confirmation.

Gently, Jonet eased him back into bed and pulled the

covers tightly up around his chin. "No doubt that is just what happened, Stuart. In fact, I believe I had a foolish dream myself tonight." Lightly, she kissed his pale forehead. "Now sleep tight, my darling. You did the proper thing by going to Cole."

Together, they left the room, and Jonet pulled the door shut as she came away. A long, awkward moment passed, and then almost roughly, Cole seized Jonet's hand and dragged her toward the schoolroom. "No," she whispered as they reached the door. "Not here, for pity's sake! Let us go back into your rooms where we may be private."

Cole held the lamp high, his face a mask of stone. "You mistake my intentions, madam," he said coolly. "The schoolroom will suffice." So saying, he dragged her inside, set down the lamp, and shoved shut the door.

Roughly, she jerked away from him. "Perhaps you mistake mine, sir," she retorted.

Ignoring Jonet's words, Cole turned on her abruptly, his expression impassive. "I find that I owe you a most abject apology, ma'am," he said, inclining his head very formally. "I fear that I forgot myself. Inexcusably. I beg you will forgive me. That is all I have to say."

Caught in a tangle of emotions, Jonet stepped a little too close to him. "Well, that is a very pretty speech indeed," she said bitterly. "You *forgot yourself*. You wish to *apologize*. You are ever the gentleman, are you not?"

"I would that that were true, but I continue to prove otherwise." Cole put his hands on her shoulders and thrust her a little bit away from him. "I am sorry, Jonet," he said softly, his eyes squeezing tightly shut.

Jonet's mouth came open, then closed again. "You are . . . *sorry?*" she finally echoed, then took a step back from him. "Yes, I think I see. I am to be . . . dismissed, is it?

Just another befuddled child who cannot discern reality from a dream?" Her voice caught on the last word.

Cole turned his back and strode across the floor, leaning down to snag something in his hand. He returned to the table and slapped down her knife alongside the lamp. "Go back to bed, Jonet. And take that if you feel you must." He paused, and swallowed very hard. "But for God's sake, use it only for defense. Do not ever attack a man again, do you hear me?"

Cole looked up to see that Jonet's head now hung low, as if she did not hear him. Good God, how dare the woman sulk when he was trying to do the right thing. And trying to keep her safe! Her insolence galled him, and he was in no mood for it. A little roughly, he took her by the shoulders again and gave her a little shake. "Jonet, for heaven's sake, listen to me!" he whispered. "You have a house full of men who are perfectly capable of coming to your aid. Just shout! *Scream!* But do not ever be so foolish as to attack a man in the dark again."

To his acute dismay, Cole found his temper rising with his own words. He really did not want to admit the truth of how desperately he had wanted her just a few short minutes earlier. Nor did he wish to acknowledge how greatly he feared for Jonet's safety—not even to himself. But now the words were out, impelled by fear. And panic was beginning to gnaw at him again. Dear God, she could have been killed! It had been an exceedingly reckless thing to do.

But Jonet was glaring at him as if he'd said he ate puppies for breakfast. "Oh, for pity's sake!" he hissed. "Don't look at me like that! You're safe in your own home! Really, Jonet, I sometimes think you are just a bit too melodramatic."

Cole never saw the blow coming. Jonet's hand cracked

across his jaw and snapped his head halfway around. Eyes watering, face stinging, he stared at her, open-mouthed. Jonet's face was tight with emotion, her bottom lip trembled, and her eyes welled with tears. "You arrogant, self-righteous swine!" Her voice was a rasping whisper. "How dare you tell me what I can or cannot do inside my own home to protect my own children? You know nothing!" Her voice took on a hysterical edge. "Do you hear me? *Not one bloody thing!*"

She came at him again, smacking and clawing like a wildcat. Not knowing what else to do, Cole threw his arms around her waist, pressing her arms to her sides. Kicking and flailing, Jonet hissed like a cornered animal, then sunk her teeth into his shoulder. Out of desperation, he yanked her off her feet, resolutely carried her to the sofa, and collapsed. Jonet landed awkwardly, half across his lap. For a moment, she continued to flail ineffectually, and then suddenly, she fell against him like a dead weight.

After a long, silent moment, a deep, wrenching sound tore through her chest. Sweet heaven, she was crying. Jonet Rowland lay across his lap, her face pressed to his chest, sobbing as if her world had just ended. *And just what was he supposed to do about it?* Gentlemanly instinct surged forth, but could not find a foothold. Lightly, he patted her on the back. "Shush, shush," he whispered. "It will be all right, Jonet. It will be fine."

Cole cast his eyes heavenward, but divine guidance was not forthcoming. He saw only the high, shadowed ceiling of the schoolroom hanging over his head. Good Lord, what a horrible night! First dinner, Delacourt, and then the dog. Now, he had a case of sexual frustration he would likely never see the end of. The only thing hotter was the throbbing lump on the back of his head, which burned like the devil's doorstep. And in between, he'd been stabbed—well, *severely poked*—in the throat with one of those nasty little Scottish knives. It only wanted this—a weeping female!

Cole patted her on the back some more and jiggled her up and down a bit. Was that what one did? He could not remember ever having seen a woman cry so unabashedly. Cole's mother had been effervescently cheerful. His Aunt Rowland had been too proud to cry openly. And as for his wife . . . well, Rachel had simply not possessed passion sufficient to fuel such an emotional outpouring.

Clearly, Jonet suffered from no such limitation. Indeed, he was beginning to wonder if the woman possessed any restraint at all. In his arms, she sagged pitifully. Deep, tremulous sobs tore through her. Pressed against his inner arm, her too-thin ribs shuddered and heaved. But oh, God! How sweet she felt. Weakly, Cole realized that he was still in serious trouble. Even more so, perhaps, than he had been when Jonet had lain naked in his bed.

His traitorous shaft began to stir at the memory. Just then, as if matters could get any worse, the schoolroom door cracked open. Charles Donaldson stood framed in the darkness. Given the commotion, and Cole's run of luck, he realized he should have expected it. In the light of the low-burning lamp, the butler looked embarrassed and confused, the huge Adam's apple in his throat working furiously.

Abjectly, Cole stared back with what he knew was a bewildered expression. He realized how unseemly he must appear in the butler's eyes, but Cole did not know what else to do. Should he put Jonet down? Give her to Donaldson? No . . . somehow that did not seem at all proper.

But Donaldson made the decision for him. Apparently, overwrought females did not fall within the scope of his duties, either. Returning Cole's perplexed expression, the Scotsman gave a little shrug and quickly shut the door. His meaning had been plain. *Better you than me.*

Jonet still sobbed, but a little gentler now. Quietly, and despite his better judgement, Cole shushed her with breathless little noises, his lips pressed close to her temple. It seemed the only decent thing—*oh hell, be honest!*—it was what he *wanted* to do.

"Now, now," he soothed. "What is this all about, Jonet? I think you had best stop crying and tell me." He smoothed one hand down her back.

"N-n-noo," she whimpered, her grip on his shirtfront tightening. "Just le-le-leave me alone."

Cole had no notion of what he ought to do next. Plainly, she was not rational. And despite some of his uglier accusations, Jonet did not strike him as an irrational woman. Arrogant, infuriating, volatile, and lusty—yes. But she was irrational only when she was distraught. And she was distraught only when her children were in danger. Cole exhaled on a sigh. Perhaps there was some seed of logic here after all. "Jonet, darling," he coaxed, barely hearing the endearment he used. "What is it? Is it Stuart? Robert? Is it the dog? *What?*"

"Y-y-es," she breathed into his chest. Cole could feel the warmth of her tears through his shirt.

Deliberately, Cole bounced her a little as one might a distressed child. "Now, now, Jonet," he crooned. "Poor old Rogue is fine. The boys are asleep. It was just an accident. The dog simply ate something he shouldn't have."

"Oh, yes," she answered bitterly, lifting her face from his chest. "*Something* he shouldn't have. *Something* that was intended for Robert. *That* is what he ate."

Her explanation chilled Cole to the bone. He did not like having his worst imaginings cast into stone cold words for yet a second time this awful night. "I think you ought to tell me what you imagine has happened, Jonet." Cole paused. "In truth, I begin to think there's a great deal you ought to tell me."

Slowly, Jonet slithered off his lap and sat a little bit away from him on the sofa. In her lap, she clasped her hands tightly. Snuffling like an abandoned orphan, she looked nothing at all like the arrogant noblewoman who had greeted him with such open disdain just a few weeks earlier. Jonet's hair was a mess, and the blanket she had purloined from his bed was now slipping off one shoulder, taking her still unfastened nightrail along with it.

To preserve his own sanity, Cole reached out and pulled up the thin fabric, carefully tucking the blanket about her. Jonet remained silent, her hiccuping sobs fading away. "Jonet . . . ?" Cole encouraged.

Eyes fixed on his knees, she exhaled sharply, then dashed away a tear with the back of her hand. "It is obvious, is it not? Someone put something in Robert's food."

Cole knew better than to insist that she was wrong. Thus far, firm, stoic denial had gotten him nowhere. And in truth, had not that very thought crossed his mind? "I considered that possibility, Jonet," he confessed. "In fact, I asked a great many questions of the kitchen staff."

Her head jerked up at that. "Did you?" Jonet seemed almost relieved. She had the look of a woman who had been carrying a heavy burden alone for far too long.

Cole was blindsided by a wave of shame. He should never have belittled her reactions. Jonet's fears were quite real, and not without foundation. "Yes, I did ask, Jonet. But there was nothing . . ." He let his words trail away, then picked them up again, his tone more plaintive. "Jonet, the dog ate only a few bites of his pie. Cook bought the meat and prepared it herself. And no one was in—" Cole blanched, realizing the lie before he spoke it.

"What . . . ?"

"I was going to say that no one unknown to us had access to—"

"*James,*" hissed Jonet. "His servants—where did they wait this afternoon?"

"In the kitchens," he reluctantly admitted. "But my darling, I daresay Cook would have noticed if two strange men had gone poking through her pantry."

Cole winced at his own words. *So he was back to "my darling" again*. Strange how those endearments kept popping out of his mouth. It had to stop. He simply ought not think of Jonet Rowland, the Marchioness of Mercer, as his *darling* or his *love* or even his *dear*—because she was not and never would be any of those things. Not really. Not to someone like him. But Jonet was softly speaking, and Cole dragged himself away from the bleakness of his future and back into the danger of the present.

". . . and these things just seem to keep happening," Jonet was quietly explaining. "I really begin to fear that I will go mad if one more so-called accident occurs. And that will do my boys no good at all. None whatsoever."

Cole turned to face her on the narrow sofa and took her hands into his. "Jonet, perhaps I have no right to ask, given what just . . . what we almost . . ." Words failed him, and he exhaled sharply and began again. "What I mean to say is that I think that you must trust me enough to tell me everything."

"Everything?" she echoed. Jonet looked tired and confused.

Cole nodded. "Yes. Begin with your husband—with Henry's—death. I am sorry to ask you to do this, but I think you must tell someone."

Wearily, she shrugged. "To what end? I have been over the last six months a thousand times, and the conclusion seems obvious."

"And that is?"

Jonet's face remained expressionless. "Why, that I poisoned my husband."

Cole simply stared at her. "Even you suspect it," she said softly. "I know that you do. But I *did not* do it."

Cole felt relief surge forth. He wanted so desperately to believe her. And yet, for a moment, she had frightened him very badly. And deliberately, too, he thought. "Just tell me exactly what happened the night your husband died," he ordered flatly.

Eyes bleak, she nodded. "What harm can it do?" she asked rhetorically. And then, in a voice that was surprisingly calm and neutral, Jonet began to speak.

8

Lady Mercer's dark and dangerous Tale

Jonet's story was simple enough. The New Year's Eve dinner was a tradition at Mercer House. Despite the fact that much of society removed to the country for the winter, a table of a dozen or so close friends and family members could always be counted upon each year. This year the evening had been relatively informal, and the meal unremarkable. No one had been taken ill, although most had imbibed heartily of both food and drink. Afterward, a few guests had withdrawn to a card table at the far end of the drawing room, while the more energetic had danced until the early hours of the morning.

"And who was in attendance?" asked Cole. "Can you recall?"

"Oh, I shall never forget," Jonet answered hollowly. "But why am I telling you all of this?" Her distant gaze drifted across the room, refusing to hold his. "Why do you care? I do not understand you, Cole."

It was on the tip of his tongue to tell her that he understood himself no better than she did. "Just tell me, Jonet," he answered instead, his voice too rough.

Succinctly, she nodded. "Yes, all right. There was Lord James, of course. And Edmund and Anne Rowland. William and Lady Constance Carlough. And David—"

"You mean Lord Delacourt?" asked Cole sharply.

"Yes, of course," answered Jonet, as if there was nothing unusual about a lady of the *ton* inviting her lover into her husband's home.

And indeed, there was not. Cole found such understandings distasteful, but they were hardly unusual. Moreover, his opinion was of little consequence. "Yes, go on."

Jonet snared her lip as if struggling to remember. "There was Lord Waldborogh, and his widowed sister, Lady Diana Trimble, whom I believe Henry ogled for the better part of the evening. Oh! And Lord and Lady Pace."

"Pace?" Cole frowned. "I thought he and Mercer were on opposite ends of most debates."

Jonet smiled weakly. "Henry was always on the end which best suited his purposes. I believe that of late, Lord Pace had persuaded him to his side on a number of issues, but nothing of any consequence." Cole filed that fact away for later consideration. Jonet's tone was still emotionless, as if she had considered these very same details a hundred times. Perhaps she had.

"And who else, Jonet?" he gently prodded.

"Sir Ronald Holt, Henry's gaming companion, and his wife." She drew a deep, shuddering breath. "And of course, there was Mrs. Lanier." Her voice dropped a note. "I dare-say you know who she is?" Jonet's tone made it plain that she did.

Cole paused for several seconds, then discreetly cleared his throat. "I understand," he answered carefully, "that she and your late husband were . . . close."

"As often as possible." Jonet gave a harsh laugh. "But Glorianna seemed harmless enough."

Cole caught the strain in her voice. " 'Seemed'? Have you now reason to believe otherwise?"

Jonet shrugged, sending the blanket slithering back down her shoulder. Inwardly, Cole sighed, but he dared not touch her again. "Oh, Ellen wants to believe Glorianna killed Henry—but I cannot agree. He was too valuable alive."

With the back of her hand, Jonet swept away her hair, which kept tumbling seductively over her shoulder. Cole's stomach did a flip-flop, but he stayed the course. "Jonet, there was talk about an argument that night. It was said that you and Henry quarreled."

She paused for a long moment. "We quarreled often. But not that night."

Cole sensed that she was being deliberately vague. "Jonet—there *was* a quarrel."

Jonet pursed her lips stubbornly, then, finally, she looked up at him with surrender in her eyes. "Toward the end of the evening," she said bleakly, "Henry and David had an argument in the book-room."

Cole looked pointedly at her. "Precisely what happened, Jonet?"

Jonet looked reluctant. "I overheard the beginning of

their quarrel from the corridor. And so I went in, and told them that their voices could almost certainly be heard through doors which connect it to the drawing room. Those doors close quite loosely, you know and—" For no discernable reason, Jonet's explanation jerked to a halt, and she colored furiously.

"No, I did not," said Cole dryly.

"Well, they do," she answered, then lifted her chin and continued. "And so I pointed that fact out to them, and they finished their discussion in more hushed, if not more civil, tones."

Cole studied her for a long moment. "Did they quarrel over you, Jonet?"

Jonet chewed at her lip for a moment. "You must understand—it was not that Henry cared about my relationship with David, it was simply that that gossip had gotten out of hand."

"Did they quarrel over you, Jonet?" Cole repeated, his voice more demanding.

In her lap, Jonet's hand fluttered uncertainly. "Yes," she said at last. "If you must know, Henry insisted that David and I stop seeing one another. He had already tried that with me, and I told him to go to hell. And so he threatened David instead."

Cole felt suddenly ill. "With what did he threaten Delacourt?"

Jonet avoided his eyes. "He made several wild suggestions," she said vaguely. "Initially, he said he would seek a divorce. He said that all of society believed us to be lovers, and that he could no longer tolerate the humiliation. He said"—her voice choked for a moment—"he said that, if necessary, witnesses could be paid to give the evidence needed to charge adultery."

Cole realized at once she was not being entirely honest, but the horror of what she had said stunned him. "My god, Jonet! You would have been *ruined*."

"Oh?" She looked at him disdainfully. "And what am I now, Cole? Something less than a picture of moral rectitude, would you not say?"

Cole had no answer for that, but some very unpleasant thoughts were beginning to take shape in his mind. "And what was Delacourt's response to Mercer's demand?"

"Nothing," she said hesitantly. "I stopped them, saying that if they must quarrel, to be discreet. I was shaken, but I suggested that we all go into the drawing room, and behave as if nothing untoward had occurred."

Cole sensed that Jonet was holding something back. "Did anyone notice that you had all come in together?" he probed.

"I daresay they did. And that horrid man—that Mr. Lyons, the magistrate—he thought that it was I who had started the quarrel. He implied as much by the look on his face."

"Did you tell him that it was Lord Delacourt and not yourself?"

Jonet drew herself up to her full height, and suddenly, despite her pink nose and disheveled nightclothes, she looked every inch the haughty noblewoman. "I did not. He did not ask. He merely hinted at what he believed—and it will be a cold day in hell before I stoop to defend myself from idle gossip."

"But Jonet," Cole persisted. "Did you not clarify this during the inquest?"

"Oh!" Jonet pulled a stubborn face. "And just what was I to say? Would you have me discuss my private life in public? Besides, at the time, I was just so *sure* Henry had died of natural causes, and the inquest happened so quickly . . ."

Cole sighed and ran a hand down his face. He was afraid he was beginning to see what part Jonet's pride might have played in this whole debacle. "Yes, very well," he muttered. "Let us return to the dinner party. Were there any other guests present? What happened next?"

"No others," said Jonet. "Lord Pace was the last to leave, at about two. I remained behind with the staff. Henry disappeared, as he often did. I supposed he had arranged to meet Mrs. Lanier." A shadow of pain flickered in her eyes. "But I was wrong. It seems he went straight to his room after all."

"And did you see him again? Did you go to his room for any reason?"

Jonet shook her head, and refused to look up from the fists she held clenched in her lap. "We had not that . . . that sort of relationship."

"I did not mean to suggest—" Cole felt heat suffuse his face. He was glad Jonet was not looking at him. "What I meant was, perhaps you went in to say goodnight? Or to try and reason with him?"

Beneath the lawn of her nightrail, Jonet's slender body jerked convulsively. "No," she answered, her voice a choked whisper. "We didn't even have *that* sort of a relationship."

"Yes, I see . . ." In the dim lamplight, Cole watched her quietly for a long moment, and slowly, Jonet recovered herself. His heart ached for this woman—the one who gave every impression of having been deeply affected by her husband's death. She seemed so far removed from the cold, insolent marchioness whom he had met upon his arrival at Mercer House that Cole could scarcely reconcile the two. And what of the woman whom he had almost bedded tonight? Ah! She, too, was different—but in yet another way.

In the back of his mind, of course, he could hear his Uncle James warning him, cautioning him to be wary of Lady Mercer's sharply honed feminine wiles—laughing at him, even, for taking her so recklessly to his bed. Cole struggled to shut away the noise. Almost making love to Jonet had been a dreadful misjudgment, yes, but surely Jonet's grief was real?

But upon careful consideration, Cole realized that it was not so much *grief* that seemed to torment Jonet as it was a deep and abiding sadness. A kind of distant regret, a wistful longing that her marriage could have been different. Admittedly, she had not loved Lord Mercer. It was almost as if she needed to mourn for her husband—and came away as saddened by the fact that she could not, as she was by his very death. How well Cole knew that sort of anguish.

But perhaps he was merely painting her with the pigments of his own torment. How foolish that was. Jonet had little reason to mourn a man whom she had been forced to marry; a man who had never harbored any intention of honoring his wedding vows. Indeed, some would suggest she had had cause to hate her husband. James would insist that hate him she surely did.

But neither hate, nor guilt—nor even lust—had anything to do with Cole's purpose in talking so openly with Jonet now. Slowly, it had dawned on him that he must get to the bottom of Lord Mercer's death, and not just for his own peace of mind. Something evil was afoot. And he had known it, and tried to ignore it, from the very first. Mercer's death was at the center of a much larger mystery. And Jonet *was* hiding something, though Cole was less and less convinced that it had anything to do with her husband's death. But it might very well have something to do with Lord Delacourt. What might she do to protect him?

"Jonet, why are you so sure Lord James is behind what happened with the dog tonight?"

Jonet's head jerked up, her eyes again blazing. "Why are you so sure he is not?"

Cole refused to be baited into another of Jonet's arguments. "I am far from *sure* of anything. I just think it unlikely. Tell me, on the night of the dinner party, did you see James—or even Edmund—do anything suspicious? Did they perhaps go upstairs? I mean . . . forgive me for repeating gossip, but I had heard that there may have been poison in Lord Mercer's wine."

"Yes, I daresay it is possible." Her delicate brows furrowed. "The decanter had been nearly one-quarter full earlier, but when the magistrate came, he noticed it was empty." Jonet shook her head. "As I said, at first, I was certain Henry had died of natural causes."

"And now you are not?" Cole asked with uncharacteristic sharpness.

As if she were now lost in thought, Jonet seemed not to notice his tone. "My father died in a similar fashion. They said it was his heart. And Henry's death seemed so very much the same. Never did I dream that someone would . . . *Oh, God!* It's too horrid to speak of." Jonet began to shiver lightly.

"Was the wine yours, Jonet?" Cole asked softly.

She looked up at him, and in her eyes he saw the same sort of pleading he had earlier seen in Rogue's—a sad, almost guileless hope that she would not be further hurt. "Yes," she admitted quietly. "It was. I often took a glass just before bed. I had done so for years, but Henry rarely drank wine of any sort, unless with a meal. And then he preferred white."

"But he had recently begun to drink it, had he not?"

Jonet's expression chilled. "You are amazingly well informed. But yes, his doctor had recommended he do so. And since I always kept a decanter in our sitting room, it became his habit to drink from it. I . . . I really never thought anything of it."

Cole considered her answer. "When had you last poured from it?"

"Why, the night before, I suppose." Jonet paused as if to further consider his question. "I really cannot remember."

Against his better judgement, Cole reached out and tucked an errant bit of hair behind Jonet's ear. She looked up at him with some surprise, and Cole felt his face flush. "And what happened after you spoke with the servants that night?" he quickly asked.

Jonet seemed to wither. "About an hour after Lord Pace left, I went upstairs and rang for my dresser. Only moments later, I heard a loud cry, and Hannah—one of the upstairs maids—came running through our sitting room, then burst into my bedchamber." Jonet dropped her head into her hands and stared at the rug for a long moment. "Hannah was sobbing and gasping for breath," she finally continued. "I could make no sense of her. At first, I thought that she and Henry . . ." Without looking at Cole, Jonet let the words trail away, then exhaled on a sharp sigh. "Henry was not always gentle with—with the servant girls who . . . well, you know."

Cole froze. No, he had not known. Or rather, he had never considered it. Nor had he really stopped to think about the effects of a husband's infidelity on his wife. "I am sorry," he said gravely. "I ought not to have begun this discussion."

"I am fine," she insisted, despite evidence to the contrary. Her hands fisted in his blanket, which she still wore. "I want to tell you. I want to have done with it." Jonet drew another deep breath and began to gently rock herself back and forth on the sofa. "I went into Henry's bedchamber with Hannah. He lay upon the floor in his evening clothes. I knelt down beside him. He was warm, but there was no pulse. I knew at once that he was dead. I think . . . why, I think I screamed then."

Cole tried to swallow the lump in his throat. "Jonet, you do not need to continue."

Jonet balled up a handful of his blanket in her fist and wrenched hard on it. But her voice was amazingly steady. "I . . . really recall very little after that," she continued. "Someone—it may have been the butler—summoned the watch. It never occurred to me to wonder if someone had *killed* him. I could not get beyond the fact that he was gone! I could not begin to think what I would tell the children!" Nervously, her gaze shifted from one darkened corner of the room to another.

"Jonet, stop—!" Cole softly pleaded.

It was as if she could no longer hear him. As if her mind had turned inward again, to that place of dark despair. Cole had seen that look before, even on the most hardened of soldiers.

"I could not bear it," she finally said, her voice hollow. "The awful thought kept running through my head—that morning would come—and I would have to tell my boys that their father was *dead!* I sent the bootboy to fetch David. I did not know to whom else I might turn. Shortly thereafter, the magistrate came. And then the doctor. I did not know then that a horrible nightmare had just begun."

Cole leaned into her and gently pulled the blanket

snugly about her narrow shoulders, shoulders which now looked frail and overburdened. "Jonet," he said softly, "you did not answer my initial question. Why do you now think your husband was murdered?"

Jonet's head came up, and she looked at him through eyes that were suddenly dark and narrow. "Because someone is determined to kill my children," she retorted, her voice flat and cold. "Someone wants them dead, and only one man has a reason to wish both my husband and my sons out of the way."

Cole felt his heartbeat slow, then almost stop. "James."

"Yes."

Cole took her hand in his and lightly rubbed it. "Jonet, I know the accident at the Serpentine frightened you, and that you are worried about the dog, but I hardly think such simple incidents mean that someone is trying to harm your children, my dear." But the reassurance rang hollow, even to his own ears.

Then, in a voice that shook only slightly, Jonet spoke the words which Cole had long feared to hear. "There have been a half dozen such happenings, Cole, and they cannot all be 'accidents,' as much as I would like to think otherwise. Did you think that this—this horror was something new to me? I have been living in a nightmare for months!"

"What sort of happenings?" Cole tightened his grip on her. "Why did you not tell me?"

"Why am I telling you now?" Through long, damp lashes, she looked up at him, her eyes dark and still a little mistrusting. "Perhaps that is the better question."

"Because," he said quietly, "no matter what else you may think of me, you know in your heart that I could never hurt your children. That I would never side with James against you. *Tell me,* Jonet, that you *believe* me."

"I . . . yes, I do," she said quietly, then drew a long, deep breath. "And yes, if you wish it, I shall tell you everything, Cole. I will tell you just what my children's lives have been like since their father died. But you will think me quite mad. The very worst was when someone tried to shoot Stuart."

"Someone shot at Stuart?" Ice-cold fear shafted into Cole's heart.

"Oh, yes!" Jonet whispered. "And it was my fault! I thought, you see, that I had taken them to a sanctuary. To Kildermore, my home! Strange things kept happening in London, and I thought we would be safe in Scotland. Now, I realize they were in danger even before we reached the castle walls."

Cole felt his blood drain away. "I think you had best explain yourself, Jonet. Are you saying someone shot at Stuart along the way?"

"I—*no.*" Jonet shook her head as if to clear her mind. "I am not making sense, am I? The shooting came two weeks after our arrival. We were riding, the boys and I. We went inland, toward the forest, and when we reached it, Stuart asked to borrow my horse."

"Your horse?" Cole forced a smile. "Fancies himself on the cusp of manhood, does he?"

Jonet looked up at him and smiled weakly. "Poor Stuart has grown a little weary of being forever relegated to a pony, and Heather—my old mare at home—is docile, so I agreed to switch. Within a quarter mile, the shot was fired. It came so close, it took my hat off. I was thrown at once. Thank God I had not far to fall. Only my ankle was injured."

"Jonet," Cole said softly, "perhaps it was a poacher. An accident. There are many relatively innocent reasons such a thing could happen."

"No," she said firmly. "Someone shot directly at Stuart's bay pony—and it was only then that I remembered the damaged carriage wheel. We'd lost one not ten miles outside the village. David saw it from horseback, and said we were very lucky that the resulting accident was not worse."

"Was the damage deliberate, then?" Cole asked, trying to ignore her use of David's name.

Jonet lifted her shoulders in an elegant gesture of surrender. "I now think so. The smithy said it looked as though the bolt had been weakened by something other than normal wear, but at the time, I was so eager to see Kildermore, I did not properly question him."

"Did you report it?"

"No!" she said stridently, falling wearily back against the sofa. "No, I didn't. I hardly know whom to trust! I can scarce bear to let my children from my sight. I tell no one anything which I do not have to tell them. My husband's family wishes me hanged for murder! And now, I'm talking to you! I really am quite mad!"

It was plain to Cole that she was fatigued to the point of near collapse. "Jonet," he said softly, rising to his feet, "it is late. We cannot solve this dreadful problem tonight. You need your rest. Tomorrow you must ask Donaldson to find some extra men. Unemployed soldiers are begging for work, and he will know best who to hire."

Cole could see the toll his probing had taken, in the tightness of her lovely mouth, the drawn skin of her face. "Very well," she whispered. "I will tell him." Hysteria again edged her voice, and he felt a wave of heated shame for having questioned her at all.

In silent invitation, he extended his hands toward her, and she took them without argument. Gently, he helped her to her feet as the blanket slithered onto the sofa. When he might safely have done so, he did not release her hands as he ought to have done. Instead he allowed himself the small pleasure of touching her for one last moment. "I am sorry for what happened between us earlier," he finally said.

"I—I don't know if I am sorry," she admitted, her words but a whisper.

Cole pretended not to have heard her. "My behavior was inexcusable," he said simply, "but I thank you for explaining to me why you have been so deeply troubled. I need to know these things, Jonet, and as long as I am here, you must always tell me."

"Do you believe me, then?" Her voice was strained yet hopeful.

Cole drew in his breath. Briefly, he considered trying to assuage her fears once more—to convince her that she had misinterpreted what she had seen—but Jonet was not a fool. "I wish that I could say I do not believe you," he answered. "Let us leave it at that for now. Just trust me when I say that I will do everything in my power to keep your children safe."

"Yes." She nodded once. "All right. And Cole—?"

"Yes?"

"I'm sorry that I . . . that I stabbed you."

Cole forced a bland smile. "Oh, I've had worse from a badly stropped razor, Jonet."

Mutely, she nodded, then turned her back to go.

"Jonet—?" His voice brought her spinning back around.

"Yes?"

"Did you ever love your husband?" It was not a question he had meant to ask. It burst from him, like a sharp breath after a blow to the stomach, though impelled not by force but by a deep, twisting emotion which was part grief and part foolish, frivolous hope.

In the lamplight, she shook her head once. "No."

"I am sorry."

"So am I."

And then, Cole led her gently from the room, and watched as the pale fabric of Jonet's nightrail floated through the gloom and down the darkened stairway. In the lower hall, he could hear the clock strike three, the melancholy sounds echoing off the walls and up the stairwell. Long after she had disappeared from his sight, Cole still stood. Watching. And knowing that after the strange night he had just spent with Jonet Rowland, his life would never be the same.

Dawn came all too quickly for Jonet. By seven, she found herself rushing about the kitchen, pouring tea and toasting bread. Between pulling out the thick crockery plates and scrounging about for the butter, she paused to dust off her hands and scowl darkly across the kitchen table. "That will be quite enough, Robert!" she cautioned. "Nanna says you must give Rogue just a little food every hour."

From his position, bent solicitously over the dog, Robert looked up at her. "But Mama, he's so hungry. Look! Look at his sad eyes! I think he's starving to death." Rogue responded with two weak wags of his tail.

Hands on her hips, Jonet sighed. Stuart dutifully leaned down to take up the bowl of gruel, placing it on a high shelf beside the mantel. "Mama is right, Robin," Stuart warned. "Just remember how sick he was last night. His belly is still queasy."

"That's right. Now come and have your breakfast," Jonet said, turning to place a rack of toast in the center of the well-scrubbed worktable. She looked up just as Cole came through the door, attired in his riding clothes.

Jonet drew in her breath. He stood frozen in the doorway, one broad hand set at his hip, the other holding his black leather riding crop. Memories—both erotic and embarrassing—of the preceding night flooded back. Four hours ago, she had been wrapped in his blanket, pouring out her heart to him. And just before that . . . oh, God. *How humiliating.*

For a long moment, Cole did not move. Instead, he merely watched, his gaze shifting from the boys to Jonet, obviously taking in the fact that she stood in the kitchen with an apron on. If he found it odd to discover the better part of the noble House of Mercer dining belowstairs, he gave no indication. He smiled lightly, but it was an expression more formal than she would have liked. "Good morning, ma'am," he said in a voice so low that the boys seemed not to have heard him. "You are up very early."

Jonet realized at once that she must look a fright. Nervously, she put up a hand to check her hair, finding the same untidy knot she had fastened so haphazardly early this morning. But the emotion she saw in Cole's face did not appear to be disapproval at all. The unguarded look in his eyes was one of confusion, perhaps even an element of appreciation.

Or perhaps she was merely being hen-witted. "I fear that I've always been an early riser." She forced a bright smile. "Have you come to join us for breakfast?"

"Cousin Cole! Cousin Cole!" Robert leapt up from his seat on the floor and rushed to his side, Stuart on his heels. "Look at Rogue! He is almost well again."

His face shining with a rare happiness, Stuart chimed in. "Yes, he really is much better, sir. Look! Nanna made him some special food. We are to feed him a little bit every hour."

"Ah, I am inordinately relieved," he returned. Then, with another glance at Jonet, as if to reassure himself of his welcome, Cole stepped fully into the room.

She heightened her smile another notch, and smoothly, Cole draped a companionable arm around each boy's shoulder, and together they strolled across the room and knelt by the hearth, scratching and petting and murmuring over the dog. How handsome—and how very grave—he looked this morning. Clearly, he was still angry with himself, and perhaps with her as well, about what had almost happened between them last night. She had not thought to come face to face with him so early on a Sunday morning, for it had seemed his habit to attend early services. Perhaps they were both afraid that a cloud of hypocrisy might follow them through the church door. Now, Jonet found that she could not bear to think about all the intimacies that had passed between them.

Good Lord, she had stripped herself naked before him, literally and figuratively. And he had wanted her, too. Rather desperately. And yet, something more than simple guilt had held him back from her. She feared it always would. Jonet watched, her mouth dry, as Cole stroked one of his long, perfect hands down Rogue's spine. In response, the dog's tail thumped with renewed vigor. Clearly, Cole's touch was comforting. Inwardly, she sighed. She would never know *how* comforting—not even for the one fleeting moment she had hoped.

And Cole would not likely give her another opportunity. Driven by desire, he had succumbed to his baser instincts last night, but he was a strong man. Such a man did not often surrender to his own needs when his mind and his heart said otherwise.

His opinion of her had changed little, she feared, and she was a fool to hope that he could come to feel any strong affection for her. But could she, perhaps, salvage some element of friendship from the whole ugly mess? Certainly, there had been something deep and meaningful between them late last night, even after the passion and anger had burned to ashes all about them.

Yes, Cole *had* stayed with her, and under circumstances that would have led many a man to make an expedient escape. She had not behaved well, and she knew it. And yet Cole had seemed to understand. She looked at them again, the three heads bent so intently over Rogue's makeshift bed by the fire. Cole and her sons looked casual and content, as if they belonged together, despite the distinct differences in their coloring and appearance.

Jonet did not wish to consider the picture of domestic bliss that thought conjured up. It wounded her in a way which she feared would hurt too much, were it to be examined too closely. And most assuredly, it was the sort of wound that a simple friendship would never assuage. But he did care deeply about her children. She was sure of it now, though she would have been hard pressed to explain why.

Through some strange twist of fate, it seemed that God had sent a decent, honest man into her life, and at a time when she had least expected to see one, too. Jonet was not sure she deserved even the friendship of such a man, but she was not a fool. She had made compromises all her life, and would gladly make another to have his friendship. Abruptly, she cleared her throat. "Boys, will you come to the table, please? And Cole, you will join us?"

Cole looked up at her, his expression inscrutable. "I did not mean to intrude, ma'am. As it happens, I merely came down after my ride to look in on the dog." He paused to look about the room. "Where is everyone? Cook, I mean—and the staff?"

Jonet gave him a crooked smile. "I fear you are looking at her—er, them."

"Mama gives the staff Sunday mornings off so that everyone can go to early services," added Stuart helpfully.

Cole snapped to soldierly attention, his eyes suddenly narrow. "Not everyone, I hope?"

"No," admitted Jonet softly. "Donaldson and Stiles are still upstairs."

"And we're to have porridge and toast and bacon and boiled eggs," added Robert, oblivious to Cole's sudden disquiet. "And milk and tea, too. There's plenty of food. Mama likes to cook. Sit down." The boy resolutely dragged out an oak chair that was as heavy as he was, leaving Cole no way to graciously refuse. With obvious dismay, he stared down at his riding clothes.

Jonet gave him her warmest smile and set down a pitcher of milk in the center of the table. "You need not change, sir, to dine with us in the kitchen," she said lightly. "And I fear you shall have little choice. You must risk my cooking, or wait until Cook returns from kirk." She took her chair and motioned that they should do likewise.

"Then I shall gladly join you," he agreed, and settled in next to Robert. Suddenly, Cole looked up at her, a ghost of concern passing over his expression. "You have not forgotten, ma'am, that you are to speak with Donaldson about hiring extra footmen?"

Jonet felt a sudden warmth course through her, but it was not a sensual feeling at all. "I have already done so," she answered. "Cox has been dispatched to recruit some more of their fellow soldiers." For the next several minutes, Jonet busied herself by pouring milk for the boys. Just as Stuart sent the toast around, Ellen darted in, almost skidding to a halt on the threshold.

"Good morning, everyone!" she said, looking at Cole with some surprise. "And how nice of you to join us, Captain Amherst."

"Ellen!" said Jonet, leaping up to fetch another mug, "I had no idea you were up."

"Yes, I am." Suddenly, Ellen's gaze shot from the table to the hearth, then she flew across the floor to kneel by the dog. "Oh, poor puppy! He's looking much better today." She turned to smile over her shoulder. "I believe Captain Amherst and Nanna worked something of a miracle last night."

"Quite so," agreed Jonet. "Now come sit down, Ellen, and see if this bacon is fit to eat. I believe I have it just the way you like it this time."

Dutifully, Ellen took her seat. Jonet watched in silence as the others ate and chattered gaily. How different the children seemed this morning, now that all danger to their dog was past. Last night, they had nearly broken her heart with their weeping. Jonet had not known what to do. It seemed her poor boys were beset by misfortune on all sides. First their father's death, then the series of so-called accidents, and all of it compounded by a mother who—she had to admit it—was no longer entirely balanced. On top of everything else, it seemed patently unfair that their beloved pet should be taken ill. But there was no question that the dog was rapidly improving, and no question that she had Cole to thank for it. Clearly, he had astonished Nanna with his efforts. Jonet had been subjected to a long recital this morning as her old nurse had sung Cole's praises. Though she was far too stubborn to admit it, Nanna had been completely won over by his willingness to roll up his cuffs and help.

Jonet stared down the table, studying the perfect angle of his jaw as Cole turned to laugh at some jest that Robert had made. How kind he was to the boys. Inwardly, she sighed. How wonderful it would be to spend every morning like this. Then she sharply chastised herself for returning to the forbidden topic. But the sad truth was that Jonet had never wished for a title or any part of the lifestyle which went with it. All she could ever remember wanting was this; her family surrounding her, especially her children and the man she . . . she . . . what?

Loved?

But good Lord . . . *did she?*

The realization stole upon her quietly, and wrapped itself around her heart, just as she watched Cole reach across to help Robert butter his toast. As usual, the boy had made a mess of it, and Cole was calmly wiping butter from both table and child, his golden hair falling forward to catch the morning light. Jonet froze, a mug of tea halfway to her mouth. She had never known a more desirable man, but the coursing river of emotion which she felt for him ran far deeper than simple lust. Yes, that was undoubtedly love.

And she had walked into it blindly.

In a very short time, Cole Amherst had somehow—certainly not deliberately—managed to melt her stone cold heart to a puddle, wreaking havoc with all her well-laid plans. The fact that he certainly had not set out to do so hardly mitigated the damage. Her resolve, her mistrust, her carefully calculated aloofness—all of it lay in ruins within days of meeting him. And her pride had followed last night.

Ellen brought her back to reality. "Well," her cousin said briskly, "what does everyone have planned for the day?"

Tearing her sidelong gaze from Cole's elegant jaw, Jonet

looked at her cousin, trying not to stutter. "Plans? Why, I daresay that the boys and I will go to church later, then pass a quiet afternoon at home. I hope you will join us." She returned her gaze to Cole. "And you too, Cole, of course."

For a moment, he looked taken aback. "I—no, I thank you, ma'am," he responded. "I attend a church near High Holborn, and I—"

"Well, that seems too far away!" interjected Ellen. "You must go to St. George's with us."

Jonet noticed that Cole looked distinctly uncomfortable, and she came to his rescue. "Ellen, I daresay Cole has a personal preference with regard to his church. We should accept that."

Ellen dabbed at her mouth with her napkin, then shrugged amiably. "To each his own. For my part, I plan to spend the afternoon working in Aunt's gardens." Her brows drew together in concern. "Do you know, Jonet, since old Manning died, her gardens have really deteriorated."

"Have they indeed?" Jonet returned.

"Oh, it is quite sad!" confirmed Ellen, cheerfully stabbing into her bacon. "I often remarked to Aunt that she really should dismiss that obnoxious young gardener whom Lady Pace recommended. The man does not know a weed from a root! What was she thinking? That is what I should like to know!"

Jonet, who knew nothing of gardening, murmured some polite response.

"Do I take it, Miss Cameron," interposed Cole, "that you are fond of gardening?"

Ellen, who was always reticent about her skills, looked suddenly shy. "Why, I quite like it well enough I suppose. There are so few hobbies available to us ladies." She smiled brightly. "And how shall you spend your afternoon, Captain Amherst? Have you plans of your own?"

Jonet watched as Cole's eyes hooded over. "Very pleasant, indeed," he said quietly. "I plan to pay a call upon a very dear friend."

In the early afternoon, Cole set aside his pen, put away his books, and rose reluctantly from his desk. For some months since the war's end, he had been engaged in an examination of Descartes's study of nature, and while he disagreed with a few of the man's theories, the work gave his mind some respite from his constant thoughts of Jonet. Cole stared down at the tidy desk and sighed.

He knew perfectly well what he was doing. It was not the first time that he had used his work as a means of escaping a personal relationship which seemed beyond his understanding. Descartes's philosophies were deep, yes. But not nearly as deep as his confusion over Jonet. Nonetheless, the afternoon was upon him, and Cole was in dire need of both fresh air and good advice. And so he carefully put on his red and gold regimentals, dusted off his hat, and went downstairs.

For a long moment, Cole paused upon the top step. For once, the London air was almost as fresh as it would have been at home in Cambridgeshire. Relieved to have escaped the confines of the house, Cole drew in a deep, satisfying breath, then very nearly choked on it. Bowling around the corner was a very familiar looking carriage. It bore the Rowland crest, but this carriage did not belong to Jonet. Which could only mean one thing.

Damn. Not again.

"Whoa up!" cried the coachman, tipping his hat to Cole as they drew alongside the stairs. At once, the footman leapt down to open the door and put out the steps. But to Cole's increasing irritation, it was not Lord James Rowland who stepped out after all. It was worse.

"Cousin!" cried Edmund, his arms open wide in an expansive gesture. "What great good fortune to find the prodigal returning to his very doorstep! It will save me the dread inconvenience of battling my way past Jonet's gargoyles!"

"I fear you very much mistake me, Edmund," returned Cole, stepping deliberately down onto the footpath and slapping his hat onto his head. "I was just on my way out."

Edmund's long face seemed to fall in disappointment, but even he could not dissemble the mocking glint in his eyes. "Oh, come now, Cole! Surely you can spare a moment for your brother? After all, I am nearly that, am I not?"

Cole was not fooled by his cousin's humble demeanor. Edmund had always hated him, and despite Cole's efforts to the contrary, he found he liked his cousin even less than his uncle.

But in all fairness to Edmund, his cousin's hatred was not, strictly speaking, irrational. While it was true that there had never been any love lost between Cole and James, in those early years, they had needed each other. Or perhaps *used* each other was a more accurate way of expressing the bond they had once felt. Orphaned at age eleven, and without the skill to make his way in the world, Cole had wanted his uncle's love and approval very desperately.

For his part, James had made good use of his wife's young nephew, for he made a practical tool with which to occasionally flog his adored but otherwise indolent son, Edmund. And for a time, Cole had deferentially borne the brunt of his cousin's consequent jealousy.

For a time. But it was long past. "What do you want, Edmund?" he asked quietly.

"What do I want?" Edmund's brows flew elegantly up. "Why, I want to *not* be seen gossiping in the street by half the residents of Mayfair, for one thing. Might we go in?"

Still, Cole hesitated. Jonet would not want any of her Rowland in-laws in her house. But Edmund was correct. Already, passers-by were looking at them curiously. "Yes, of course," Cole finally responded. "However, I can spare but a moment."

They went down the hall to the drawing room, and Cole motioned his cousin to a seat. "May I offer you a glass of something, Edmund?"

Edmund settled back, smoothing his hands along the arms of his chair in a gesture that made Cole's skin crawl. "Ever the gentleman, aren't you, old boy?" he answered mordantly. "Here you are, wishing me to the devil, but striving to maintain that gentlemanly façade. By God, I credit you. Small wonder you were always Father's favorite."

Cole stood rigidly, hands clasped behind his back. "What do you want, Edmund?"

His cousin's mocking eyes flashed again. "Why, perhaps I merely want to inquire as to how dear Cousin Jonet goes on. After all, you were sent here by Father to . . . to do precisely *what,* Cole?" The dark brows went higher still, and his voice took on an unmistakable edge. "I mean, correct me if I'm wrong, but are you not here to help ensure that the poor widow gets just what she deserves? And yet, weeks have passed without so much as a word from you. Such inattention to duty becomes you very ill."

"I am here to educate the children," answered Cole, taking one step toward Edmund. "And what Lady Mercer deserves is to be left in peace to grieve for the loss of her husband."

"Indeed? And what of those children, Cole?" asked his cousin sharply. "What do they deserve, do you imagine? To have Lord Delacourt as a stepfather? Does it not occur to you how much better off they would be under the supervision of Father and me?"

"No child deserves to be torn from a loving mother, Edmund."

"Ha!" he barked. "A *loving* mother? A woman whom all of society knows to be a cold-blooded—"

"You will hold your tongue, Edmund!" interjected Cole harshly, his hand coming up to stay him. "You insult Lady Mercer at your peril. She is an innocent woman, and I'll not stand idly by whilst you imply otherwise."

"Innocent?" Edmund laughed, but it was a strange, almost desperate sound. "You forget, dear cousin, that I was here on the night of Mercer's death."

"No, Edmund," replied Cole calmly. "That is one fact which most assuredly had not escaped me."

"I find I cannot like your tone, Cousin." Edmund's chin went up a notch. "I never left this room, save to go in to dinner. Try to find a witness who will say otherwise, if you will."

"That sounds rather like a challenge, Edmund."

A lazy smile curved his cousin's mouth. "Oh, if it is a challenge you are interested in, my friend, then it is a pity you did not overhear Delacourt's quarrel with Mercer that night. Several of the dinner guests did. Not that it was any secret what Mercer meant to do. It is a nasty business, divorce."

Cole's voice was icy calm. "Another word from you, Edmund, and we shall be meeting at dawn on Hampstead

Heath. And I know you dislike above all things to bestir yourself before noon."

The desperation in Edmund's eyes could no longer be hidden. Abruptly, he jerked from his chair. "I do not fear you, Cole," he hissed, but his face belied his words. "I simply want what is best for the family."

"Do you?" said Cole quietly. "Then it would appear that you and I possess vastly different views of what is best for this family. I am afraid I must ask you to leave."

Cole did not trust himself to see his cousin out. The temptation to shove him down the steps might be more than his Christian fortitude could bear. And so he rang for Stiles to escort Edmund to the door, desperately hoping that Jonet would not get wind of their cousin's visit.

He watched his cousin go, an aching bitterness in his heart. Edmund must be very desperate indeed to call upon him at Mercer House with such bold questions. What did he hope to gain? Did he imagine that if young Lord Mercer and his fortune were entirely at James's disposal, that James would be more inclined to settle his gaming debts? Or had he something more sinister in mind? Cole was not certain, but he knew one thing. He was more than a match for Edmund.

When his temper had cooled to a manageable level, Cole took up his hat and started toward the front door again, whereupon he very nearly tripped over Ellen Cameron, who was dressed to go out, a small wicker basket swinging neatly from her elbow.

"Good afternoon, Miss Cameron." Cole pulled open the door to allow Ellen and her basket to pass through. "Are you on your way up to Cavendish Square?"

Ellen smiled brightly up at him. "Indeed. Are you off to call upon your friend?"

"I am." Noting that no carriage awaited in the street, he touched her lightly on the arm. "Do you go alone, Miss Cameron? May I give you my escort?"

Ellen stepped lightly down onto the cobbled footpath that lined the street, the hems of her green muslin walking dress swishing neatly over the steps. "I thank you, Captain Amherst, but it is a short walk up to Aunt's house. I daresay it is out of your way."

Cole fell quickly into step beside her, suddenly anxious to discover what light Ellen might shed on Lord Mercer's death. "Then let me see you across Oxford Street, at the very least," he insisted, relieving her of her basket. "Even on a Sunday, it can be quite busy."

"If you wish," Ellen answered blandly. They reached the corner, and Cole gave her his elbow. The intersection was empty, save for a coach that turned up David Street and continued into the heart of Mayfair, its black leather harnesses jingling brightly beneath the warm summer sun.

As the clatter receded, Cole looked down at the woman on his arm. "Miss Cameron, you seem rather subdued today."

Wearily, she sighed. "I am a little worried about what happened to Rogue."

Cole wanted to question her further, but he was unsure of just how much Jonet shared with her cousin—or with anyone, come to that. "Do you think it was someone intent on deliberate malice, Miss Cameron?" he finally ventured.

For once, Ellen did not have a ready answer. One hand came up to push the hair back from her face in an awkward, uncertain gesture. "Well, it is not my place to say, but ever since his lordship died, awful things certainly . . . seem to happen."

It was on the tip of his tongue to ask her if she thought

Lord Delacourt capable of murder, but he dared not. They walked a few paces further. "Tell me, Miss Cameron," he said in a musing tone, "do you think one of the servants might have poisoned him? Lord Mercer, I mean?"

Ellen's hand tightened upon his arm. "Initially, I would not have dreamt of such a thing," she finally responded.

"And now?" he encouraged.

"I cannot think *why* they would do," Ellen reluctantly responded. "Of course, there was Hannah, the chambermaid. I often thought her rather too saucy with Lord Mercer. But that means little."

"Did you share your concerns with Lady Mercer?" Cole probed.

Ellen hesitated, very nearly halting on the footpath. "Sir, it was hardly my place to interfere in Jonet's . . . understandings with her husband."

Ellen had opened the door for yet another question, and a rather dangerous one at that. Cole wondered if he dared to pose it. In the distance, he could see New Bond Street, filled with the clamor of afternoon traffic. He took a deep breath. "Lady Mercer tells me that you also suspected a—a friend of Mercer's. A Mrs. Lanier?"

"I was not aware, sir, that my cousin confided in you to such a great extent."

"I believe her ladyship is worried on behalf of her children, Miss Cameron," he said smoothly. "They are entrusted to my care, and so I begged her to make me aware of the situation in every detail."

Slowly, Ellen nodded. "Well, I suppose that is only prudent. And yes, I did say that perhaps Glorianna had poisoned Mercer, but I daresay that was wishful thinking on my part."

"Wishful thinking?" A hackney coach passed a little too

near the footpath, and Cole urged Ellen a little closer to the wall. She looked up at him in some surprise, but whether from the question, or from the fact that he had pressed her a little nearer to him, Cole could not say.

"Oh!" she said sharply, coming away from the wall. "I do not wish her ill, if that's what you mean! It's just that I do not know Glorianna Lanier very well. And I suppose one hates to think of those whom one *does* know well as being—well—*murderers.*"

"I take your point," responded Cole dryly. Soon they turned left onto New Bond, and Ellen made a few banal comments on the heat and the rain, but she still sounded sad. At last they reached Oxford Street, and Cole led her carefully through the scattering of Sunday traffic to the corner of Vere. He had pressed her as far as he dared. "If you are sure, Miss Cameron, that I cannot see you further, I will bid you a good afternoon."

"Yes, thank you for your company. Shall I see you at dinner?"

"I am not certain," Cole answered carefully. He looked at her again, at the pale, tight skin of her face. "Miss Cameron? Are you truly all right?"

"Oh, well enough, I suppose." She made a pathetic, dismissive gesture. "But I grow increasingly concerned for Jonet and the boys. And for myself. I really do wish we might go away. To Kildermore. I cannot help but feel we would be so much . . . *safer.*" Her voice was wistful.

Cole tried to look sympathetic. "Safer? Indeed! I do not comprehend, Miss Cameron."

"Jonet needs to escape London. And I need to escape my aunt, who is increasingly determined to see me wed. Just yesterday she wrote, saying she'd found a widowed solicitor who was perfect for me, never mind his forty-five years and six children." Ellen tried to laugh and failed.

"And you have told your aunt your opinion in this matter?"

Ellen looked up, her eyes empty. "Sir, I am an unmarried woman. We do not have *opinions.*"

Lightly, Cole patted Ellen on the arm. "No one can force you to wed, Miss Cameron."

"Of course not," she said with an accepting shrug. "And you are very kind. Now, I mustn't detain you when your friend awaits." And on those parting comments, Ellen Cameron turned away.

Cole retraced his steps back along the empty footpath and down to the main thoroughfare, musing upon his conversation with Ellen. What was it about her that left him feeling puzzled? One certainly could not describe her as flirtatious, which was always a relief around unmarried women of a certain age. Cole had learned early on to avoid that sort. They toyed with a man in a way that Cole did not understand. But that was not Ellen Cameron's problem. The fact was, she reminded him of someone . . .

Suddenly, it came to him. *Rachel!* Oh, she and Ellen looked nothing alike, it was true. Ellen, with her dark hair and eyes, was striking, but far from beautiful, while Rachel had been a pale flower, a traditional English beauty. And yet, they both had that same facile pleasantness that many men found charming. Today was the first day Ellen had ever spoken of her own wishes, but only briefly.

It was the way of many women, he had come to believe. A price exacted by a society that was ruled by—and based almost solely upon the needs of—men. As a theologian, it had troubled him deeply. And he had deliberately taken great pains to give Rachel alternatives. At times, it had seemed as if he had spent every moment of his marriage working to find a way through the shell that shrouded her individuality; to discover her hopes, her dreams, her needs.

Perhaps he should have spent more time preparing himself to step into his father's shoes, to assume the vicariate of St. Ann's, as had been his lifelong goal. Certainly, Cole had had the bishop's blessing. It had been but a matter of time.

And yet, all of his emotional energy had been focused on his marriage, a marriage that to all outward appearances seemed happy enough but beneath the surface felt cold and barren. How could he have safeguarded the souls of his parishioners when his own knew no peace? His heart had cried out for something untamed, something more compelling. Not *excitement,* precisely—but something which would stimulate his mind and open his heart to life and passion.

In his own quiet way, Cole had always needed to *feel* strongly, no matter what circumstance life brought his way. And since life had brought him Rachel, he had simply altered his circumstance. After convincing himself that he was answering the call of patriotic duty, or attending to the will of God, or some such balderdash, Cole had circumvented his failure to instill in his marriage the passion he had yearned for by making his own challenge. He had gone off to war.

But it had surely not been God's will that his child would die as a result?

He could not get past that question. He never would.

He had left his wife, and inadvertently, his unborn child. Cast them to the winds of providence, while he was out gallivanting about on the Continent. He could have served, perhaps, as a chaplain, but that thought had never occured to him. He'd wanted a war to fight in, not to pray over. Too late, Cole had realized that the impetus behind his glorious military career had had nothing to do with God, and everything to do with his own shortcomings. That lesson had been taught to him by means of a letter from his parish priest, a letter which had arrived months after his wife and child were dead and buried. And their loss had been Cole's fault, as surely as if he had done the deed himself.

Perhaps it was what he deserved, but it was most assuredly not what they had deserved. Despite all the years—and all his prayers and tears—there had been no babe to bless his union with Rachel. What a stunning blow it had been to learn that she had been with child at the time of his leaving. He rather doubted that she had known it. But now, years later, he still wondered, tormented by the uncertainty of it. Surely she would have told him, had she known?

Surely his own wife would not have denied him the honor and the right to care for her and his unborn child at a time when he would have been most needed? But in truth, he simply did not know. Rachel had accepted his decision to enter the army with the same quiet acquiescence that she had brought to every aspect of their life. She had offered no strong objection, she had shed no tears.

But his wife and his child were gone, and a hundred ugly questions had been left to haunt him. Had she felt alone or frightened? Had she eaten properly? Had she rested as she should have? Had the midwives, the surgeons—even the priest—been fetched at the appropriate times? And good God, had she suffered? Had the child suffered?

But the sad truth was, Cole did not know the answers to

these questions. Nor had he asked. Since coming home to England, Cole had been unable to dredge up the courage required to go home—to Elmwood—and find out. He, who had fought so bravely for King and Country, could not now bear to return to the home he loved, for if he had stayed at home in the first place, keeping fast and faithfully to his marriage vows, none of it would have happened.

9

Colonel Lauderwood issues an Order to retreat

After leaving Ellen Cameron near Oxford Street, Cole turned east and set off for Montague Place, to an address not far from his old lodgings in Red Lion Street. He paused to shake off the memories that troubled him. Trying to take account of his surroundings, he was rather surprised to realize he had made his way to Bedford Square. Cole quickly crossed it, and finding a familiar doorway just a little further beyond, he thumped twice on the ornate brass knocker. He very much hoped that Jack Lauderwood was still in town, for he could think of no one else he would be comfortable discussing his present situation with.

Well, perhaps not all of it—but heaven knew he needed to speak with someone rational. Of course, he had thought at first to go to the Madlows', but Louisa's father was by far the better choice. Not only was the colonel a man of discretion, but for all his hearty bluster, he was also surprisingly well informed. Moreover, he was not apt to pry quite as deeply into Cole's business as Terry and Louisa would undoubtedly have done.

Cole was greeted at the door by Lauderwood's manservant, and shown immediately into a cheery, sun-washed parlor, where it was evident that the colonel had just awakened from an afternoon snooze. Lauderwood hefted himself into a seated position on a worn leather sofa, which was surrounded by rather wrinkled copies of the *Morning Chronicle* and the *Times*. Obviously, someone had been reading to the colonel earlier in the day.

Lauderwood ran one hand down his face, then gave himself a good shake, like a grizzled mastiff trying to stir from a nap. Then, realizing that Cole had already entered the room, he sprang to his feet. "Come in, come in, my boy!" he said effusively, motioning Cole toward the seat nearest his. "To what do I owe this pleasure, eh?"

"Must I have a reason for calling on my commanding officer, sir?" Cole smiled broadly, and took the proffered chair.

"No! No!" boomed the colonel cheerfully. "No reason a'tall! Been awhile, though, since I commanded much of anything. But if you have no purpose in coming, you won't object to reading to me for a spell, will you?" The colonel paused to poke a finger at the heap of newspapers, a mischievous grin spreading across his face.

"Nothing could give me more pleasure, sir," Cole returned, taking up the newspapers.

"Right, then," said Lauderwood briskly, leaning back and making himself comfortable. "Just finish reading the obituaries, eh? Need to know if I'm to bury friends or enemies this week. Louisa ran out on me. Wanted luncheon with her husband, and won't be back until it's time for my tea."

"Umm." Cole's answering smile was laced with doubt, and the old man let the pout slip from his face. Louisa was the most devoted of daughters, and they both knew it.

"Just the *Times*, mind," Lauderwood added, still waving his finger as Cole settled his spectacles onto his nose. "And then we will get down to what you have really come for, eh?"

Cole passed the next quarter hour finishing off what the allegedly indolent Louisa had left undone. When all of the paper had been finished, Cole folded it neatly and returned it to the table, at which point the colonel reared back in satisfaction and stared at him. "Fine and good," he said. "Now—! It is your turn, Amherst. I know perfectly well you have come here for information!"

"Frankly, sir, I wanted to revisit that conversation we had last week about Lord Mercer's death." Cole leaned a little forward in his chair. "Such things would normally be none of my concern, but the children . . . well, it is a most awkward situation."

"Yes, yes. I comprehend!" said the colonel, sliding a little deeper into his seat and crossing his hands over his ample girth. "Go on, Cole. You'd not ask such things without good cause."

Cole thought of how Jonet had looked in the kitchen this morning, and in his bed last night, and was no longer sure his questions were quite so honorable. But he was tormented by doubt. Just what was the truth about Jonet, her life, and her husband? Although it was a moot point, for he could never permit it to be put to the test, Cole yearned to know if he could trust her in any measure at all where his heart was concerned. "There is something, sir, which troubles me, and I can make no sense of it, particularly in light of our talk last week. You see, I have heard that Lady Mercer . . . well, never mind what I have heard. What I want to ask about is Lord Delacourt. Have you met him?"

Lauderwood nodded. "Yes, I have had that . . . *pleasure* if one may call it so."

Cole's eyes narrowed. "Then you may understand when I say that there is something about the man which I cannot trust. He is entirely too smooth, indeed, almost treacherously so, and I find myself wondering—" Cole paused, then tossed discretion to the wind. "Wondering if he had anything to do with Mercer's death."

"Other than comforting the grieving widow and hastening the inquest, do you mean?"

Cole smiled grimly. "Yes, other than that."

For a long moment, Lauderwood said nothing. Finally, he spread his hands open, palms up. "*Cui bono,* Cole," he answered. "That is what you must ask if you seek to find Mercer's killer. And I do not see how it can be Delacourt."

"Yes, *who benefits,* indeed," said Cole in a musing tone, unwilling to violate Jonet's trust and tell Lauderwood of Mercer's quarrel with Delacourt. Still, something did not fit. "And so you are suggesting it must be James or Lady Mercer who killed Henry?"

"I think one must consider every possibility," replied the colonel evasively.

Cole found himself wanting to argue on Jonet's behalf. And yet, to do so would mean breaching her confidence with regard to her fear for her children. But he was not yet done with Delacourt. "Does Lady Mercer's close . . . *relationship* with Delacourt have anything to do with the fact that both her father and her husband were friendly with the previous Lord Delacourt?"

Lauderwood screwed up his wrinkled face a moment. "Oh, no, I fancy not! That friendship fell out when she was but a babe. As I recollect, Kildermore and old Delacourt quarreled rather nastily during a house party at Delacourt's.

Anyone who was anyone—which is to say, the most well-bred of London's worst scoundrels—always gathered at his Derbyshire estate for the hunting season. Delacourt was a widower then, and his ne'er-do-well friends came and went at their leisure."

Cole mused over that. "And over what did they quarrel, sir? Have you any idea?"

Lauderwood grunted, and rubbed the stubble of his beard with one hand. "No one seemed certain. 'Twas said one of Kildermore's hounds turned on one of Delacourt's while they were in the field. Not at all the thing, you know! Others said 'twas a bad turn of the dice. Eventually, there was a duel. Mercer stood as second for Kildermore, and after that, Delacourt cut 'em both off. Removed to Derbyshire for good, and never spoke another word to them."

"How odd!" Cole stared at the old man for a long moment. "Given all that, I marvel at Mercer's tolerance of his wife's friendship with young Lord Delacourt."

Lauderwood lifted his bear-like shoulders in an amiable shrug. "Oh, I rather doubt Mercer cared whom she saw, so long as she didn't cuckold him publicly. The devil was infamous for flaunting his mistresses all over town. Lady Mercer went her own way after she gave him his heir. Delacourt is but one of the many peacocks who have flocked after her."

"Indeed," said Cole dryly. "I understand Lady Mercer has had several admirers."

"Many women of the *ton* have admirers, Cole," replied the colonel sagaciously. "Collect 'em like bric-a-brac, some do. Damned hard to know if any of it is serious. Lady Mercer is but one example."

Cole struggled to keep his tone casual. "It is said that she has had many lovers, too," he pressed, feeling a little sick with dread.

"Certainly she has had many *offers*," chuckled Lauderwood. "And little enough reason to turn many of them down, I daresay. But since young Delacourt came to town some years ago, she has thrown nothing but crusts to the others."

Cole could not suppress a scowl. "I cannot think what she sees in that pompous fop."

Lauderwood eyed him narrowly. "I rather fancy his being young, rich, handsome, and influential cannot hurt. The old man left him a vast fortune."

Cole fiddled nervously with his cuff, finally arranging it to his satisfaction. "And other than Delacourt, whom has Lady Mercer—er, favored, do you know?" he finally managed to ask.

Lauderwood shrugged noncommittally. "Oh, there have been a scad of 'em, though as I said, none as constant in their attentions as Delacourt."

"I think it a poor measure of constancy when one keeps a lightskirt set up," Cole bitterly retorted. "Does he still do so, do you know?"

Lauderwood merely stared at him for a long moment. Cole felt a piercing shaft of anger when he realized how greatly the colonel's answer mattered to him. *Why?* He did not know. He knew only that he was torn in the most visceral of ways, half hoping that Delacourt would be decent, and honor whatever commitment he had given Jonet, and half hoping that he would forsake her altogether, leaving the way clear for . . . *for what?*

Good God, what madness! Yes, he was a man—and like most of them, his flesh was weak. Since his wife's death, there was no denying that he had taken women to his bed from time to time. He was not proud of it, but his need was often raw and undeniable—and now, infinitely more tormenting for his having lived under the same roof as Jonet Rowland.

Now that sanity had returned, Cole knew he would never presume—or lower himself—to take a lover. It would be wrong for a dozen different reasons, not the least of which was morality. Better to look about him for a wife—one from his own social class—if he could not manage his needs. But the thought of another such marriage—and the horrid ring of the words *duty* and *convenience*—made Cole ill.

The colonel cleared his throat, eyeing Cole suspiciously. "So far as I know, Delacourt is still seen regularly in the environs of Drury Lane." Cole felt an irrational wave of relief. Abruptly, Lauderwood motioned toward a table between the windows. "Now be a good chap, Amherst, and pour us a drink. Gossip parches me."

Grateful for the delay, Cole agreed. He found a decanter of madeira, poured out two healthy measures, then returned to his chair. "Ah," said Lauderwood appreciatively. He downed a third of the glass, then, despite his clouded eyes, leveled a steady gaze in Cole's direction. "Now, in all seriousness, Cole," he said coolly, "I hope you are not fool enough to fall victim to the lady's charms? I daresay James initially sent you there to snoop about a bit, eh? Just do it, and get out, man."

"He suggested something of that sort," Cole reluctantly agreed.

Lauderwood nodded thoughtfully. "Yes, he thinks Lady Mercer rid herself of her husband in order to wed Delacourt. And he means to find out how, does he not?"

"Well, actually, no," Cole admitted. "Much to my own

surprise, James seems to hold out no hope of bringing his brother's killer to justice. It seems his pride is wounded, and he is more intent on controlling the children. Indeed, he wishes to take them under his wing and raise them as he sees fit. But Lady Mercer will have none of it. She hates and distrusts him."

"Perhaps James does not wish to think too much about his brother's murder," mused Lauderwood. "Mayhap he fears the suspicion might fall too near home."

"I've considered it," admitted Cole.

The colonel drained his glass and pushed it toward Cole. "Well, never stand too close to a cockfight, Cole. 'Tis family business—and not *your* side of the family, no matter how much James whines." His eyes narrowed. "And another word of warning—watch your step! Any man with a set of ballocks between his legs is going to be smitten by Jonet Rowland if he isn't damned careful."

Cole tried to shrug indifferently, and at once, the colonel jerked forward in his seat, the buttons of his ivory waistcoat straining. "Understand me, Cole," he said urgently. "I neither know nor care what the lady is guilty of. If she'd bludgeoned Mercer with a coal shovel, I wouldn't give a damn. Never liked him. He was indiscreet. Can't forgive a man that, myself." The old man sniffed disdainfully. "But the fact remains that Lady Mercer is a *femme fatale* of the first water. I have no wish to see you hurt while trying to protect her. She is more than capable of taking care of herself."

Cole felt a flash of anger. Why must everyone assume that because a woman was strong, she needed no one? What if Jonet was *not* capable of taking care of herself this time? Perhaps this time, something more than a few loyal servants and a faithless lover would be required. The circumstances into which Jonet had been thrust were treacherous enough to try the most hardened of soldiers. Indeed, he was beginning to think that neither Lauderwood nor society knew the woman who stood so proud and so alone behind what he was beginning to believe was nothing more than a beautiful, brittle façade.

They had not seen her clasp her children to her bosom, fighting for them as the most ruthless tigress might guard her cubs. They had not seen her in her apron, with her hair askew, looking as untidy—and yet as serene—as the most cheerful of scullery maids. And they certainly had not seen her pulling off her nightrail, her cloud of dark hair settling all about her shoulders, her breasts heavy, her nipples taut with . . .

"Cole—? Are you listening to me, boy?"

A little brusquely, Cole dragged off his glasses and tossed them onto the pile of newspapers. "Sir, I really do not think we need to discuss—"

"Now, mind me, Cole!" interjected Lauderwood, his face full of reproach. "Forget James's dirty work. What you want is a wife. Give up the army—it's gone to hell anyway—and go back home to Elmwood. Speak to the bishop. Tell him that you are ready to do what you have spent a lifetime preparing for, Cole. Get that black-haired siren out of your blood before she dashes your heart on the rocks."

Cole gripped the arms of his chair, thrust himself out of it, and strode to the window. He could feel the heat of irrational anger and suppressed lust coursing through him again. With one hand set at his hip, the other dragging his hair back from his brow, he stared blindly through the glass and into the modest garden beyond. "Jack," he finally said, speaking over his shoulder, "you need not worry that I will involve myself in an illicit affair. Certainly not with a woman above my station. And most assuredly not with one who already bestows her favors on another. I should hope you know me better than that."

Lauderwood said nothing. Cole turned away from the window to face the sofa. His strident words seemed to hang suspended in the parlor for a moment, floating unanswered, along with the dust motes, in a low shaft of sunlight until Cole began to wonder just who he was trying to convince.

"Oh yes, Cole, I know you." Lauderwood's gentle tone broke the silence. "And I know that underneath all that military brass and moral resolve, you have a heart too soft for your own good."

"Please, sir, I beg you! Flatter me no further!" Cole tried to smile, failing miserably. "Now, if you will excuse me, I'd best take myself off. I am wanted elsewhere."

"Ah, yes! That's it. Pry out all my information, and refuse my good advice." Lauderwood grumbled a bit beneath his breath, then looked up at Cole, his thick white brows drawn together. "Well! Am I to see you at dinner soon?"

Bending low, Cole took Lauderwood by his gnarled hand and clasped it hard between his own, his irritation all but forgotten. "It would be my great pleasure, sir. Shall we say one day next week?" The old man nodded, and Cole headed for the door. Suddenly, another question occurred to him, and he turned about abruptly. "One more thing, sir. What news, if any, of my Cousin Edmund's predicament?"

Lauderwood chuckled. "Bad, and getting worse, as I understand it. Shall I make inquiries?"

Cole shook his head. "No, but Edmund surprised me with a visit this afternoon. And I must tell you, Jack, he did not look well. Moreover, I cannot think why he called upon me. We barely speak."

The old man smiled grimly. "Oh, the worthless bastard wanted something, Cole. Depend upon it. Perhaps to borrow money? Or perhaps he is merely a vulture, preening over his uncle's carcass, and hoping that eventually there will be something for him to pick from the bones."

Cole returned to Jonet's house, carefully considering all that he had learned from Jack Lauderwood. Despite the colonel's probing suggestions, Cole had found it a relief to talk to him. But Lauderwood's rather poor opinion of Jonet reminded Cole of one very important thing. He could not leave the situation with Charles Donaldson unresolved. Indeed, as a gentleman, he should have sought a private moment with the butler first thing this morning. Last night, the butler had seen him in what had looked like a very compromising position with his mistress. Indeed, she was Cole's mistress, too, and he ought to take pains to recall it. He was by no means her social equal, as his afternoon with Lauderwood had so painfully reminded him.

Nonetheless, Cole would take every possible step to safeguard her reputation. The fact that Jonet's reputation was not particularly pristine was hardly an issue. Cole would not have it worsened by his own conduct. Moreover, he had a deep-seated curiosity about the former soldier who now served Jonet so steadfastly. Cole entered the long formal dining room just as Donaldson pushed through the swinging door from the china closet to set down a pair of exquisite Georgian candlesticks. The butler placed them carefully atop a mahogany sideboard, then stepped back as if to admire his handiwork.

"Afternoon, Donaldson." Cole leaned one shoulder casually against the doorframe.

The butler spun quickly about. "And a gude afternoon tae you, Captain," he said solemnly, his dark brows going up in mild surprise.

"A little spit and polish, I see."

"Aye, sir. We've set the lasses tae work on the silver. A loovely pair, is it not?"

"Indeed," Cole agreed absently, stirring himself from the door. "Listen, Donaldson—you'll recall that I promised you a pint awhile back. Come with me down to the Drum and Feather and let me square it. What do you say?"

"Now?" Donaldson looked concerned. "Thank you, sir, but I oughtn't—"

Cole cut off his objections. "The house is full of former soldiers," he gently reminded him. "I daresay it will be all right for us to step out if we don't go far, and I rather need to have a word with you in private."

Donaldson bowed his head. "Aye, then. I'll be but a moment to fetch my hat, sir, and tae have a word wi' the lads."

It was almost dinnertime when Ellen returned from Cavendish Square. Jonet was in the hall, carefully rearranging an assortment of lilies in the vase she had chosen to replace the one she'd hurled at James's head. She was taken a little aback when her cousin came swishing blithely through the front door, a strange young lady at her elbow. The visitor was tall and willowy, with a riot of red-gold hair that was cut and curled in a most becoming arrangement.

Cox reached out to take Ellen's hat as Ellen, oblivious to Jonet's presence, continued amiably chattering to her guest. "Yes, it is a lovely day indeed," Ellen said, surrendering her burdens to Cox. "Now if you will be so good, miss, as to let me rid myself of this basket. There! Now, it is a pleasure to meet you I am sure! You must be a very dear friend of Captain Amherst's, to have gone so far out of your way. But—oh, look! Here is my cousin, Lady Mercer!"

Ellen turned toward Jonet, leaving the young lady, who looked exceedingly bewildered, simply standing in the middle of the hall. "Jonet!" Ellen began brightly. "This young lady and her father, Colonel Lauderwood, are friends of Captain Amherst's. I've just this moment discovered Louisa here, standing on your front step with her hand on the knocker." Ellen opened her glove. "Look! Is she not kind? Louisa has come all this way to return Captain Amherst's spectacles. He spent this afternoon reading to her father."

Jonet paced down the hall toward them, feeling a little weak-kneed without really understanding why. "Why—how exceedingly kind, to be sure," she managed to say.

"Your ladyship." The young lady curtsied awkwardly, looking even further confused. "The spectacles were of no consequence, I do assure you. As I said, it was on my way." She turned as if to go.

"Will you not await Colonel Amherst's return?" asked Jonet politely, ignoring a vicious prick of jealousy. It seemed the mystery of Cole's afternoon visit had just been solved. A *dear friend,* indeed! The lady really was quite appealing, with a vivid, yet innocent, sort of beauty. "I think we may expect him back shortly. No doubt he would wish to thank you personally."

"No, I thank you, my lady," replied the visitor, lowering her lashes respectfully. "Just give him the spectacles, if you please, and thank him for his kindness to Papa. Now if you will excuse me, I believe another spate of rain is imminent. A pleasure, I am sure, Miss Cameron."

And with that, she was gone. "Well," said Jonet, forcing a bright smile. She was not about to discuss her crushing sense of despair with Ellen. "How did you find your aunt's gardens? Were they as dreadful as you feared?"

"Oh, worse!" declared Ellen at once. "And I am parched from the heat, too! May we go into the parlor and have a cup of tea?"

By six o'clock, the low drone of conversation inside the Drum and Feather had swelled to a roar, interspersed with harsh, sporadic laughter and the occasional *whoosh* of a deck being vigorously shuffled and dealt onto the worn oak tables. The afternoon heat had given way to another drenching, and through the open windows, the rattle of passing traffic could be heard swishing through the puddles. Beyond, in Carnaby Market, a few pedestrians were beginning to stir, laughing and moving from one public house to the next.

Cole turned his gaze from the window and leaned back against a wooden settle, trying to focus on the tall, rangy fellow who sat across from him. Eyes lowered, Donaldson was methodically sucking the foam off the top of his tankard, giving every impression of savoring each drop. Cole had savored a few himself—perhaps a few more than he ought, but the Scot was matching him two to one. Cole began to wonder where the man was putting it. Once, from the corner of his eye, he thought he saw Donaldson tip his mug toward the open window. No. Surely not?

Like most soldiers, Donaldson had turned out to be an amiable drinking companion. He and Jonet's butler had spent the better part of the last hour reminiscing about their army days. Thus far, they had carefully avoided any discussion of the happenings inside Mercer House. Now, in the midst of a desultory game of cards, Cole carefully laid down a trump and drew yet another trick across the scarred wood of the table.

"My game, Mr. Donaldson," he said, trying not to slur his words. He was a little discomfited by the amount of effort the task required.

The Scotsman fanned his remaining cards faceup across the table with a grunt of displeasure. "By God, Cap'n, you've the devil's own luck, that ye 'ave," he replied, his brogue thickening.

Cole tried without much success to lift his eyebrows elegantly. "Since the winner pays the shot, Donaldson, I cannot think you've suffered overmuch," he said dryly. "In fact, why do I begin to suspect you might be giving away the game?"

"Aye, Cap'n!" Donaldson smacked the table with the flat of his hand, grinning broadly. It looked perilously close to a drunken leer. "Niver trust a Scotsman w'yer purse! But I'll say one thing—not much gets by you, Amherst, I do'na think."

"Nor by you, I daresay," returned Cole. For a long moment, he stared across the table at his companion, then he drew a deep breath. "For example, Donaldson . . . about that *situation* you observed in the schoolroom last night. I would not wish to besmirch Lady Mercer's reputation in any way, and so I felt I ought—"

"I know when tae keep my clap shut, sir!" interjected the butler a little querulously. Donaldson shoved away his empty tankard with a disdainful gesture, looking more like an inebriated infantryman than a stately Mayfair butler.

"I am sure, Donaldson, that you do," Cole responded gently. "But I felt that perhaps I owed you an explanation. And the fact is, Lady Mercer was very distressed, and I was simply trying to comfort her." Cole exhaled sharply through his nose. "But I daresay it might have looked like something altogether different."

Donaldson looked concerned. "Poor wee thing! Had anither of her spells, did she?"

Something in the butler's protective tone set Cole's hackles up. "*Spells?*" he archly responded. "The poor wee thing tried to *stab* me."

Donaldson winced knowingly. "Och! 'Ad 'er blade, did she?"

Cole drew himself up a little straighter on the settle. "You were aware she roamed about in the dark of night with a knife clenched in her teeth?" he asked incredulously.

"Oh, aye," confessed the butler, his eyes wide and bleary, his head hanging low. "Gave it to her myself, I did—but I did'na know she'd took tae carryin' it between her teeth."

"She wasn't, Donaldson," Cole said dryly. "I was trying to make a joke."

"Oh? Gude, then." Donaldson wobbled a little on the settle and opened his hands in an expansive gesture. "And ye must pay no mind to her ladyship's fits, Cap'n. Known her all my life, I have. She's a hellcat, tae be sure—but she wouldna harm a livin' creature. Not without provocation."

Cole wanted to argue that snoozing on the schoolroom sofa could hardly be considered provocation, but he wisely held his tongue. Most of that night's troubles he had brought upon himself, and there was a great deal more he would like to ask Donaldson, who was now well plied with alcohol. Cole picked up both tankards and carried them to the tapster for refilling. He returned just as Donaldson, beating a rapid tattoo on the tabletop with his index fingers, burst into a rousing Scottish folk song.

Cole set down the heavy pewter with a thud, bringing

the song to an abrupt halt. Oblivious to the laughter which rippled through the taproom, the butler peered at the tankard for a long moment, as if struggling to recollect from whence it had come. "Haven't been out in a while, eh, Donaldson?" Cole asked lightly.

Donaldson pulled a gloomy expression. "Verra li'tle, sir." Then he roused again, his head hanging low and loose. "But I do na' mind, really! Lady Jonet needs me—or she wouldna ha' brought me down here to this stinkin' shite hole of a city."

"So I may take it that you do not care for town?" asked Cole, flashing him a wry grin.

"Noo!" The butler's black brows snapped together. "Nor she nither, come to that."

Cole was mildly surprised. "Does she not? I rather thought she preferred it."

Donaldson tried to shake his head, but he was now slumped back into the corner of the settle. "No, I do na' think so." He looked perplexed for a moment. "Left to her own ways, she'd close up the London house, take doon the knocker, and hie back tae Kildermore."

Cole was surprised to hear it. "You grew up there, did you not, Donaldson?" He felt the heat flush up his face, but he was in too deep to back out now. "I mean, Nanna said so, and I must confess, I have often wondered what Lady Mercer was like before—before . . ."

"Aye, say na' more." Donaldson waved a limp hand. "I know what you're saying, and aye, she's changed a vast deal. 'Twas her father's doing, too. That, and her marriage tae auld Mercer."

"Changed? Changed in what way?" Cole needed to know the truth about this woman whom he was very much afraid he had come to love against his will.

The butler shrugged equivocally, his glassy eyes focusing somewhere in the depths of the darkened room. "There's a hardness aboot her that wasna there before," Donaldson mused. "A darkness, a wariness which troobles me, and yet I canna blame her. No, I canna blame her a'tall." His gaze snapped to meet Cole's, his eyes looking suddenly sober. "That is all I can tell you," he said quietly.

Cole let a moment pass. "But Donaldson, has she always been . . . well, so overly *emotional?*"

"Wha' would you be meaning, sir, emotional?" asked the butler in all innocence.

"Well—prone to stabbing innocent people, for one thing," returned Cole. "*No, no—!* Ignore that! I realize she was overset last night. But has she always been so . . . so intense?"

"Oh, aye! Ye mean the fits and the spells." Donaldson shook his head. "No, no' a'tall. 'Tis true that as a girl she was a wee bit unruly," he admitted. "But no lass e'r had a better heart. And her feelings run deep, that they do. Once, you could see 'em plain on her face, too, but that was before . . ."

Cole looked at him expectantly, hoping that he would go on without being prodded. He felt shameless enough for discussing Jonet as it was. The butler took the bait. "But that's how we grew up, sir," he added, peering intently across the table as if he were explaining something of great importance. "Running wild along the seashore and o'er the moors—all of us—Miss Ellen, sometimes, too. Lady Jonet could'na know what sort of future she was tae have. We were too young to understand titles and duties and expectations."

Cole sighed inwardly, feeling just a little of the shock Jonet must have felt when her life in Scotland had jerked to a halt, flinging her into the arms of a man whom she had not wished to wed, and apparently, into a lifestyle she had wanted even less. But Donaldson was still staring into his tankard and mumbling about the past.

"And if you want to know about her temper," the butler was saying, "it is true that Lady Jonet has always been her own person—a passionate and stubborn lass, too. But on edge like this? No. 'Tis something altogether recent. But it's hell she's been through, no mistake. T'would unhinge anyone."

"Yes, I daresay it might," Cole admitted. For a time, he sat quietly, simply staring into the darkness of the public house. A nagging sense of urgency dogged him. Urgency not just in the sense that they needed to return to Mercer House, but also in that now familiar sense that something was terribly wrong, and that he had very little time left in which to rectify it.

"Tell me," Cole said suddenly, "what was the late Lord Kildermore like? Did you know him?"

It was as if a dark cloud passed over the butler's eyes. Donaldson put down his tankard and pensively ran his finger around the rim. "Aye. Knew him well enough."

Cole leaned urgently across the table. "Then tell me, what manner of man was he? I must confess, I have heard little which is flattering. Perhaps you have a more balanced view?"

"Ah, I doot it," he said bitterly. "He was a laird who kept servants in their places, and tae his way of thinkin', that meant tending his cattle, scrubbin' his castle, or warming his bed. Reckon someone forgot tae tell him that the right of first bedding went out with the Jacobites."

Cole gave a grunt of disgust. "Not a very pleasant sort, it sounds." Suddenly, he was struck by an appalling thought

"Donaldson, you're not—I mean—he's not your . . ." The ugly question was almost past his lips before he could stop himself.

The butler's fine black brows went up at that, and suddenly, he looked startlingly sober. "D'ye mean was he my father, aye?" he said grudgingly. "Weel—go on! You're not the first tae ask. And the truth is, I do na' know. Kildermore was na' in the habit of claiming his bastards. My mother was a chambermaid, but she died giving birth—"

"I am sorry," interjected Cole, aghast. "It's none of my concern. I merely wish to ascertain Kildermore's nature. I suppose I hoped to find some decency in the man, but it seems there was little."

"Decency?" Donaldson shook his head, then, almost as a begrudging afterthought, he lifted one shoulder. "In his own way, he seemed fond enough of Lady Jonet. Doted on her a bit when he was home, which wasna often, mind. And when Miss Ellen's parents died, he took her in straightaway." The butler's eyes narrowed a bit. "But for the most part, he was thought tae have no conscience a'tall. Yet when his health began to fail, I think the guilt caught up w'him."

"The guilt?" Cole lifted his gaze to meet Donaldson's.

"Aye, for having married off his daughter to Lord Mercer. No one knew better what sort of man the marquis was than did Kildermore." Donaldson gave a bitter grin. "Birds of a feather, they were."

Reluctantly, Cole drew the watch from his waistcoat and stared at it. It would soon be time for dinner. "Look, Donaldson," he said abruptly, "it grows late. I daresay we'd best return. Might we continue this discussion later tonight?"

The street was almost empty when they stepped out of the Drum and Feather. Cole paused for a moment on the footpath to look down the lane into Carnaby Market. In the fading light, the cobblestones glistened with rain, as the last of the day's heat rose up from the street, bringing with it the odor of damp horse manure and old soot. Grateful to have at least escaped the smoke and noise of the public house, he walked quietly beside Donaldson as they set off toward Mayfair.

Donaldson's stride was long and straight, and Cole wondered yet again if the man was as drunk as he wanted Cole to believe. He had carefully led Cole to reveal more than he had meant to say. Admittedly, Cole's relationship to James gave Jonet's staff cause to be suspicious. But if it had been the butler's way of measuring Cole's character, Cole was certain he had passed.

10

Lady Mercer seizes Command

Late that evening, Jonet sat alone in the book-room, staring through the thick glass as rain descended over Mayfair yet again. The normally comforting smells of beeswax, old books, and well-burnished leather went all but unnoticed. Tonight, there was no fire, and none should have been necessary. She should not have been cold. But she was. The insidious damp felt pervasive, as if it had crept into her soul. With quick, jerking motions, Jonet dragged her damask shawl tighter, then drifted toward the window.

Behind, in a distant corner, a mahogany longcase clock dolefully tocked off the minutes, each slower than the one before. As the clock struck half past the hour, a watchman appeared in the street below, his call lost in the clatter of a passing carriage and four. In the aftermath, an oppressive silence fell over the house like a heavy blanket. Jonet dropped her forehead to the cool glass. *Oh, God!*

She was lonely. The knowledge fisted hard in her stomach like a driving blow.

"*But why now?*" she whispered into the heavy darkness. Why now—after all the years of being alone and empty—why had it begun to torment her almost past bearing? Tonight was a dark sheet of emptiness, like the rain which slicked the cobbles and ran down the windowpanes, sliding silently into another empty tomorrow. There was no one—nothing save her own black thoughts—left to bear her company tonight. Now the emptiness, like the fear that so often haunted her, was a tangible thing.

Jonet had sent David away immediately after dinner, and the children had been long since tucked into their beds. She wanted *Cole*. She had *willed* him to come to her. But he had not. He was avoiding her. And now she was left to acknowledge the almost girlish naïvetée that had brought her to this empty room alone. She had hoped to meet him here.

Jonet had often seen Cole linger in the book-room at odd hours of the day, his head bent to some thick, musty tome, his long, elegant fingers splayed carelessly at his temple, and his gold wire spectacles slipping, unnoticed, down his nose. She could almost see his quick hand sliding the quill across the page, then darting toward the inkhorn and back again. As with all his motions, his reading and writing were possessed of a smooth, economic grace which never seemed hurried; merely certain and solid. And so, after dinner she had made her not-so-subtle excuses to David and she had come here to wait, hoping against hope that

Cole might seek her out—or at least stumble upon her unawares. She would take what she could get, it seemed.

All through dinner she had watched him, yet he had guardedly avoided her eyes. No doubt there was something in his gold-brown gaze he did not wish her to see. With every unspoken word, every subtle gesture, it had felt as if Cole was emotionally distancing himself from her tonight. And as she had stared at him across a chasm of white linen and glittering crystal, Jonet had been left to wonder if it had anything to do with the woman who had called for him earlier this afternoon.

That classic face and shock of red-gold hair were indelibly imprinted on her mind. The lady's air of youthful innocence had utterly disarmed Jonet. Indeed, in her confusion, she hardly remembered Ellen explaining who the woman was. Exactly what had Ellen said? And what had she called her? *Louisa . . . Lauderwood.* Yes, that was it. And undoubtedly, Cole had found it no great sacrifice to spend the afternoon reading to her and her father. She had seemed just the sort of woman who would appeal to him—in something more than just the baser physical sense.

Jealousy, an emotion Jonet had virtually no experience with, had begun to claw at her gut as soon as the woman had swept past Ellen and out the door to her waiting carriage. Jonet had wanted to confide in her elder cousin, to cry on her shoulder as she used to do as a girl, but she had been too ashamed to let even Ellen see her humiliation. And in that moment, she had found herself blindly and bitterly *hating* the lovely Miss Lauderwood.

For pity's sake, when had she become so acrimonious? With such a childish attitude, it was no wonder she had found tonight's dinner interminable. Not even Ellen's cheerfully sustained efforts at conversation could have concealed the fact that Cole and David had been looking daggers at one another again. Jonet had no idea what they could possibly find to quarrel over. David was a little arrogant, yes, but it was a part of his attraction. And as for Cole, his normally steady disposition seemed a degree less so today. No doubt she had driven him to exasperation with her behavior last night. Perhaps he had even been repulsed by her.

No! Damn it, that was *not* it. Heat suffused Jonet's face and throat, and spread lower still. She knew that Cole had found her more than attractive. The evidence—the heat of his stare, the desperation in his touch, and yes, the urgent quickening of his body—had been all too apparent. And if he had desired her once, albeit briefly, could he not be made to do so again?

At breakfast this morning, she had been convinced that he would never be so persuaded, and she had been willing to accept that, and settle for something less. Now, all Jonet's noble thoughts of compromise—of grasping Cole's tentative gestures toward friendship instead of tempting him to something more passionate—had all but vanished in the aftermath of Miss Lauderwood's visit. Dear heaven! She could not bear the thought of another woman having him.

Jonet lifted her head from the glass. It had been so long since she had thought about anything other than her children's welfare that she found it hard to believe lust could have seized her with such a stranglehold. But it had, and most inopportunely, too, for she'd wanted Cole Amherst the first day she'd seen him. Raw, unslaked desire had knifed through her shield of fear and rage, and nothing had been the same since. Perhaps she ought to seduce the man and get him out of her system? Could it be just that simple? Could she do it? And more importantly, would *he*?

Was it not said that men found her a sorceress? Jonet had never understood it, but enough of them had thrown themselves at her feet to make her realize that she must possess some superficial quality that engendered the inane devotion of men. Indeed, there had been a time not so long ago when it had been wildly fashionable to court her. With a persistence that bordered on the farcical, the bucks and beaus of town had desperately vied for nothing more than a waltz, or the opportunity to see her safely home. Wagers had been lost, swords unsheathed, and ill words spoken amongst men who had accounted themselves friends mere moments earlier. And all the while, Jonet had looked on, confused.

Young, inexperienced, and bored to distraction, she had not done enough to sharply discourage them. Her actions, she now knew, had been born of some foolish hope that her husband would regret his shabby treatment of her; that through the eyes of her many suitors, he would come to see her as someone worthy—and not just of his bed, but of his devotion. Jonet laughed aloud at her own naïveté.

Cole wasn't fool enough to imagine her a sorceress. And there was no manipulating him, for from the very first, Cole had proven impervious to her greatest weapons. Her initial line of defense—to outsmart him—was hopeless, since the man had a brilliant mind. Flirtation was of no use; his disdain could chill blood. And her attempts at condescension left her feeling shallow and unworthy, as if he had won every encounter by virtue of rising above her mean behavior.

Indeed, it often seemed Cole had a way of picking out her every human shortcoming and gently holding it up for her inspection. One could never persuade such a man to do anything that was against his nature. Nonetheless, he was a *man*—every golden, rock-hard inch of him. Which only begged the question again. *Could she seduce him?* There was only one way to find out.

With one boot propped high on the brass fender, Cole stretched out in his chair and listened to the rain with the satisfaction of an old soldier who is snug and dry, and knows too well the value of being so. Across the narrow surface that served Charles Donaldson as both table and desk, Cole and the butler eyed one another smugly as the second wave of rain began to spill from the downspouts and gush past the foundations of Mercer House.

Belowstairs, the damp could not reach them, for the butler's abode was strategically placed on a wall which abutted the huge kitchen hearth. Tonight, Cole found it an exceedingly comfortable haven. After suffering through another miserable dinner with Jonet, Ellen, and Delacourt, Cole had accepted with alacrity Donaldson's invitation to resume their discussion over a "wee dram of whisky." The wee dram had quickly become the better part of a bottle, and Donaldson's hospitality showed no sign of abating.

"Will ye have anither, Cap'n?" asked Donaldson, his voice cutting through the haze of Cole's thoughts. The butler tipped the bottle unsteadily forward. Smoothly, Cole shoved his glass in place just in the nick of time, then raised it high as Donaldson topped his own.

"And to whom shall we drink this time, sir?" Cole asked, cheerfully striking the rim of Donaldson's glass with his.

"Ah—! I have it!" proclaimed Donaldson. "To the River Zadorra! May it e'er run red with Frenchie blood!"

* * *

By midnight, Jonet still had seen nothing of Cole. No light burned beneath his bedchamber door, the schoolroom lay dark and empty, and both boys were still sound asleep in their beds. As so often was the case, Jonet had found herself roaming the empty corridors of Mercer House like a restless spirit. It was the sound of loud, argumentative voices that caught her attention belowstairs. Carefully, Jonet made to her way through the darkened kitchen. The sound, she quickly realized, was coming from Charlie's sitting room. Just as she made her way past the hearth, her fears were subdued by a burst of loud laughter.

"No, no! I must beg to differ, Donaldson!" she heard Cole loudly assert. "I claim that honor on behalf of the cavalry! Had they not smashed the French rear guard, the battle might have dragged on interminably."

Relief coursed through Jonet. *War stories.* They were not arguing at all, and it was no longer a secret just where Cole had hidden himself for the evening.

"Aye, weel," she heard Donaldson growl, "the last thing I remember was taking a Frenchie bayonette in the arse, so I canna argue w'what I didna see, but it was the infantry that carried the day, and no mistake, Cap'n! I wish I hadna missed the sight of those Frogs bolting for Pamplona, tha' I do!"

Swiftly, before her courage could fail, Jonet knocked loudly on the door of the butler's pantry. Immediately, a hush fell over the room, much as it did when one caught Stuart and Robert making mischief in the attic. "Come!" Donaldson finally barked.

Jonet pushed open the door to a sight that, had she not been weak with dread, would surely have left her whooping with laughter. Donaldson sat tipped back against the wall in a high-backed chair, his stocking feet propped upon his desk, and his black coat tossed into a nearby heap. Across the narrow room, Cole Amherst sprawled in a worn armchair by the hearth, one boot propped on the fender, his cravat gone, and his hand clutching a fistful of Scotland's best.

"Your ladyship!" answered Donaldson as both men snapped to their feet. The butler's chair fell to the flagstone floor with an awful clatter.

Cole politely inclined his head as the butler scrambled to right his furniture. "Lady Mercer," he said coolly, "I believe you have caught us unawares. Do excuse us." His unruffled tone was belied by the color flushing up his face.

Staring at the open throat of Cole' shirt, Jonet's courage very nearly faltered. "I—no, not at all," she managed to stutter. "Do sit down. I merely wished—that is to say—I wondered, Captain Amherst, if I might have a word with you in my sitting room? At your convenience."

Cole looked at her in some surprise. "My lady, it is past midnight. The children—?"

"Are perfectly well," she interjected. "But if the hour is too late, we may speak another time."

His expression guarded, Cole set down his glass. "I am at your service, of course, ma'am," he said cautiously. "If you will but give me a moment to restore my cravat to some semblance of order, I will wait upon you shortly."

The *haute monde*, who had once watched in mute amazement as the most dashing men amongst them paid court to the Marchioness of Mercer, would scarce have recognized her tonight. The woman who now paced anxiously across the floor of her sitting room bore little resemblance to the *femme fatale* who had so proudly sauntered her way through the salons and ballrooms of London.

As she paced, she clutched her hands before her in a nearly white-knuckled grip, for it seemed to Jonet that hours had passed, and still Cole had not arrived. Perhaps he had already sensed the torment which had sent her searching for him. Perhaps he knew what she wanted. He seemed just that sort of man, capable of seeing past her defenses and into her heart with an ease which left her reeling. But in truth, it would have taken little to see through the façade she had thrown up. Jonet knew that for a woman who was considered the epitome of boldness, she had faltered badly in making her request to Cole.

Suddenly, he appeared in her open doorway, his height and broad shoulders nearly filling it. Despite his size, he still looked graceful, his hips almost lethally lean, as he halted just across her threshold. He did not, however, look altogether pleased to be summoned to her private quarters, and Jonet wondered if his earlier civility had been displayed as much for Charlie's benefit as for her own.

Now, he leaned one shoulder negligently against the lintel and regarded her in a moody silence. His warmth of this morning seemed to be burning down into something else altogether. His indolent grace was a dangerous sign. Of course, she knew that he had been drinking off and on all evening. Not heavily, but consistently. And although the sharp, military precision of his movements had softened, his steely gaze had not. Jonet stood rapt before the cold hearth. "Will you come in?" she asked quietly.

Cole came away from the door then, and pushed it shut behind him. "What is it, Jonet?" His deep voice was soft, suspicious, and mesmerizing.

Jonet deliberately widened her eyes and forced her voice to steady. "I simply wished to reassure myself that all is well between us," she said, motioning him toward the sitting area near the fireplace.

His eyes hooded over. "I don't think I perfectly understand—"

"Tonight at dinner," she interjected sharply, settling herself into one of the wing chairs which flanked the hearth. "You seemed rather distant. I wanted to be certain that what happened between us last night has not created a rift." Jonet said the words coolly, willing the emotion from her face.

Cole stepped a little closer, finally taking the chair opposite her. He seemed distant, yet all too near. "Then you may set your mind at ease, Jonet. Last night was a dreadful lapse in judgement, and I hope that I am man enough to accept my part in it. You need have no concerns on that score."

"Need I not?" she asked, rather too sharply.

Cole shifted his weight in the chair as if to rise. "No, and if I have laid those concerns to rest," he said quietly, "I should bid you good night, Jonet. I daresay you need your sleep."

But Jonet did not dismiss him, knowing full well that he was too much the gentleman to simply walk out. Instead, she rose from her chair and crossed the room to a small desk, leaving Cole with no polite alternative but to stand at the edge of his seat.

Absently, she picked up a small porcelain figurine and began to toy with it. "You had a caller today," she said lightly, spinning around to face him. "I believe her name was Louisa? She returned your spectacles."

"Did she?" Cole looked vaguely surprised. "I own, I had not missed them."

"I believe you will find them on your desk in your sitting room," Jonet said quietly. "I must say, your Louisa is quite dashing. Is she a very dear friend?"

"Quite." Cole narrowed his eyes and gave her a dark, warning look.

Jonet tore her gaze from him and turned back to her desk, putting down the porcelain with an awkward clatter. "And would it be terribly presumptuous of me to ask if you have—ah, if you have formed an attachment of some sort?"

Cole hesitated, until at last she was compelled to turn about and look at him. He smiled lightly, but it was forced and humorless. "Jonet, you may be assured that had I any such *tendre* for Louisa, I would hardly hasten to confess it. Her husband is too sure a shot."

"Her—her *husband?*"

Suddenly, Cole paced toward the desk. "Come now, Jonet," he said softly, a skeptical look spreading across his face. "What is this interrogation all about? You cannot possibly have any interest in the wives of my fellow officers. I think you'd best come to the point." His words were unerringly polite, but there was no mistaking the challenge they held.

It seemed Cole meant to force her hand. His pride, perhaps, would not allow him to go so easily down her path. She should have sensed it the moment he entered the room. Perhaps he found her discomfort amusing. No doubt many women propositioned him in just such a fashion. He was a handsome, wealthy widower surrounded by an aura of intelligence and intrigue.

But those were not the reasons she wanted him. Hers were reasons she did not wish to examine too closely. Instead, Jonet sank into her desk chair and looked up into his piercing, golden stare, willing her gaze to hold steady. "Is it not obvious?" she asked pointedly. "I want an *affaire d'amour,* Cole. I want to finish what we started last night."

Abruptly, the room was plunged into silence. For a seemingly endless moment, Cole simply stared down at her, his eyes hard, his face set in implacable lines.

He was going to refuse her! Pride almost got the better of Jonet, as it so often did. By heaven, she had never begged for a man's affection in her life—not her father's, not David's, and certainly not her husband's. She surely would not begin doing so now. "I am asking," she said steadily, "if you will be my lover."

Briefly, she saw a heated anger flare in his eyes. Cole leaned down into her face, bracing his powerful arms wide on the chair, to stare at her. She could smell Charlie's best whisky on his breath as his heavy gold hair cascaded forward to shadow his face; a face so close she could see the light sheen of sweat across his upper lip. "Why, you make very bold indeed, madam," Cole whispered into the dim light. "Could you perhaps be more explicit? Is this to be a trial? Are we to discover whether or not I am man enough to replace Delacourt?"

"Do not be ridiculous," she hissed. "I have told you that David and I are friends."

His nostrils flared, and he looked suddenly dangerous. As if he might strike her. Or kiss her. Or damn her into the fires of hell.

But he did none of those things. Instead, he jerked himself erect again and spun away from her, all of the rage leaving on a sudden exhalation of breath. Slowly, he walked across the room, his heavy boots thudding hypnotically across the heavy carpet, one hand going to his forehead, the other positioned lightly atop his hip, in a now familiar gesture of frustration.

Jonet rose from her chair. "You want me, Cole," she said in a gently preemptive tone. "Do not try to deny it. I have asked you to be my lover. I have been given to understand that most men would find such an invitation tempting."

"Tempting?" he echoed bitterly, refusing to turn and face her. "Ah, yes, Jonet! You are all that—and so much more."

Boldly, Jonet crossed her arms over her chest and leaned back to stare at him, stubbornly setting one hip against the corner of the desk, and allowing the black fabric of her dress to cling somewhat revealingly. She had humiliated herself by asking, and she was bloody well going to have an answer from him. Tension lay thick across the room, but despite it, her breasts felt full, her nipples already taut with desire. He was teasing her, tormenting her, and making her want him all the more.

As if answering her challenge, Cole turned and stepped incrementally closer. Even in the lamplight she could see the hardness of his jaw and the beard that now shadowed it. But even his . . . his *anger,* or whatever his tightly tethered emotion was, did not dissuade her. The deep dimple in the center of his chin was more prominent tonight, and Jonet could scarcely restrain herself from rushing forward to touch it. Heaven knew she'd fantasized about it often enough.

Indeed, there really was no point in playing games. The piercing look in Cole's eyes said that he saw through her. He always had. Cautiously, she drew a deep breath and came away from the desk, jumping into she knew not what. Swiftly, she crossed the room and laid her hands flat against the wall of his chest. As she had suspected, the man did not flinch. Instead, he stood stoically, allowing her hands to roam over him, allowing her to feel the warm wool of his coat, the very beat of his heart, beneath her fingertips. Emboldened, she slid her hands beneath his lapels, running one of them around to caress the back of his neck, while with the other she lightly brushed her thumb across his silk waistcoat and over his taut nipple.

Cole did step back then, yet she followed him, slowly rising up to lightly brush her lips to his. He drew in his breath sharply and jerked his mouth away. "God in heaven, Jonet—just *don't*—" he rasped.

"Don't what?" she whispered huskily, sliding her hand into the thickness of his hair. "Don't touch you? I've told you what I want."

"Don't encourage me—this—*us!*" Almost imperceptibly, he backed against the wall. "Don't let us make the same mistake twice."

Shamelessly, Jonet followed him. "How can it be a mistake?" she whispered thickly. "I cannot help what I feel. I need you, and I cannot think that you are indifferent to me."

"Perhaps you want me," he roughly answered, bringing his hands up to caress her shoulders, then gently pushing her away. "But you don't need me. They are very different things."

His eyes were blazing with an emotion Jonet did not entirely recognize. She resisted his unspoken warning to step back. "I don't think you understand what I am asking," she urgently responded. "I do need you. And I want you in my life."

"Jonet, you want me in your *bed*," he responded harshly. "I cannot be a part of your *life*. Not in any way which matters. It simply is not possible."

The words hurt, but Jonet urged her body closer, sliding one hip against the joining of his long, muscular thighs. *Ah—!* Those sinfully lush lips lied. He did want her. He was hard and ready. She lifted her eyes to meet Cole's, opening them widely, guilelessly.

"I am a man, Jonet," he responded to her unasked question. "Don't read too much into it."

In response, Jonet teased at his nipple with her fingertips, feeling his manhood pulse against her hip. "You lust after me," she challenged again, elevating her chin a notch.

"Good God," he rasped, tearing his gaze from hers. "Is there no end to your arrogance?" But Jonet could feel his grip on her shoulders slowly tightening, she could sense his pelvis pulling into hers, and the faint stirring of motion in his hips. His face lingered near hers, his lips hungrily parted. Oh, he burned to have her. But apparently, he meant to torment her to within an inch of insanity first.

"Would you have me beg you, Cole?" She asked the question lightly, still urging herself against him like a Limehouse whore. "Are you, perhaps, attempting to humble me?"

At that, Cole eased himself incrementally away from her hip. "I daresay a little humility—not to mention restraint—would be in order here, yes," he snapped.

His remark angered her, taunted her. "Ah—!" she returned. "And are you man enough to humble me, Cole?" Wickedness, impelled by lust, drove her to skim one hand down between them. Without hesitation, she slid her fingers around his swollen shaft, caressing the hot length of him through the fine fabric of his breeches.

Cole let his head fall back, his breath coming out sharply. "Oh, mercy, Jonet!" he moaned. She could feel him shaking, she could hear the surrender in his voice as he urged himself harder against her hand. "Leave me in peace! You don't want this. Not the way I am tonight. Not *ever.*"

"I do want you," she insisted, easing her hand down the promising length of him. "Now. *Please, Cole—!* I am tired of wanting, wanting, and never having. Of being so achingly alone. So empty."

"For pity's sake, Jonet! There are risks. Risks which could involve someone far more innocent than you or I. I think you know what I mean."

"I won't become with child," she said softly. "Not—not right now." One hand still entwined behind his neck, Jonet lifted her other to the close of his breeches. Amazingly, her fingers shook not one whit, slipping the buttons loose with a rapid ease. She could feel him beneath the crumpled layers of fabric; hot, desperate, pulsing with life. Jonet could not ever remember wanting anything with such a visceral desperation. "*Please,*" she whispered urgently.

As her hand slid beneath the linen of his drawers to take the velvet weight of him in her hand, Cole drew in his breath on a hiss. In response, Jonet slowly eased her fingers up and down his length, feeling the blood pulse beneath the velvet surface of his skin. Deep, shuddering need passed through him, and as it faded, Cole gave her a rough shake.

"So you want that, Jonet?" he growled. "I am to simply pleasure you? To set aside my principles so that your noble ladyship can have her way with the *hired help?*" He shook her again. "Because, by God, if that's what you want, then you'd better make damned sure it's worth my while."

Jonet lifted her gaze from his erection and stared at him unblinkingly. "Oh, I didn't hire you, Cole," she softly corrected. "But I *will* make it worth your while."

With a slow deliberation, she slid one hand down his impressive length again, feeling him vibrate with suppressed lust. Atop her shoulder, his hand trembled, his fingers digging into her flesh. *Ah, sweet, sweet heaven!* How she wanted to lie beneath him, to feel him come deep inside her. "Are you still reluctant, Cole?" she softly teased, tightening her grip at the base of his manhood. "Can I perhaps persuade you with—"

In a flash of movement, his fingers came up to drag her other hand from his neck, jerking it to his crotch to join the hand that still cradled him. In a cruel parody, he pressed both her palms against himself, and eased them up and down. "Persuade me with what, Jonet? With that sinfully wicked mouth of yours?" Cole all but sneered at her. "Oh, yes, your ladyship—! Why don't you get on your knees and show me just how far you're willing to go to get your way with me?" The one hand still balanced on her shoulder began to urge her down into the floor.

It was as if his anger were suddenly contagious. Rage spiked through her, hot and quick. "You impudent dog!" she hissed, jerking away and bringing one hand up to strike him.

Cole was lethally quick, snaring her hand in mid-flight like a starved falcon. For a moment, he held it high, a slow, bitter smile curving one side of his mouth and deepening the hard lines of his face. Then roughly, he yanked her full against him. Dragging her hand to his mouth, he turned her inner wrist to his lips, his tongue flicking out to caress the tender flesh of her pulse point.

Jonet moaned, a deep, primitive sound, and Cole's eyes dropped nearly shut, his sinfully long, dark lashes feathering across his tanned skin as he drew her closer still, his tongue slicking a trail of heat down her inner arm. Jonet was suddenly lost; plunged in a sensation so carnal that nothing else existed but Cole's tongue sliding down her flesh.

That they were both still dressed and standing in her sitting room made no difference at all. A shaft of pure lust spiked through her, tugging at her breasts, her belly, and her womanhood in a quick, urgent motion. And then, his mouth opened, drawing in the tender skin of her inner arm, and she feared her knees might buckle. He suckled her there for a moment, his long, strong fingers encircling her wrist, his eyes holding hers with a frightening intensity.

The utter arrogance of his gesture escaped her, and when his mouth left her arm, she craved its return. He held her there for a long moment, her breasts now pressed high against him, and Jonet was taken aback to realize that she now stood—quite voluntarily—on her tiptoes and that her other hand was still urgently caressing him.

She still wanted him. Oh, yes. And with a second blaze of intuition, Jonet realized that Cole's reaction to her need had little to do with sex or morality. This was not *right* or *wrong.* He was fighting some inner demon she knew nothing about, and inside, he trembled with it. Jonet's hands slid away, and he let them go.

Before her, his face began to blur in the lamplight, and she found herself fighting against the hot press of tears. What *was* she willing to do to have him? If she did not know, how could he? Perhaps she should humble herself just a little. Slowly, gently, she slid her hands beneath his shirt and skimmed her palms lightly down his belly, feeling it ripple and quicken with sensual awareness.

She was, as he said, too arrogant. But he was not the man who had made her so. And yet, so often these last few days, he had paid the price for it. Cole was simply the man she desired above all else, and perhaps he deserved to know it. When she took him in her hands this time, he sucked in his breath on a gasp. When she shifted her weight to go down onto her knees and take him in her mouth, he exhaled sharply.

Jonet sensed the change in him but a split second before it occurred. She had not a moment in which to respond. With a feral, anguished cry, Cole shoved her away and turned, drawing back his fist and slamming it into the wall behind him. Plaster cracked as her balance faltered, and Jonet barely saved herself from tumbling to the floor.

Cole seemed wholly unaware of her. For a long moment, he simply stood there, saying nothing. Slowly, Jonet drew near, pressing herself against his back and wrapping her arms about his waist. Cole did not move as she settled her cheek against the back of his coat. She had come here, she had convinced herself, to seduce him. But he was now the seducer, drawing her closer, enticing her further, with his pain and pride and need. "I'm sorry," she whispered.

Still, he remained motionless. She could sense that there was a deep, hungry darkness in him, which all of his golden beauty and masculine strength could not cloak. The bitterness which was welling up inside him was all too recognizable to Jonet. And there was loneliness, too. It clawed at one's gut like a living thing. *Ah, yes.* She knew all too well what that felt like. Suddenly, Cole turned in her arms to face her, his face bleak. He jerked his head stiffly to the right, his blond hair tumbling down across one eye. "Is that the door to your bedchamber?" he rasped.

Mutely, she nodded, and he slipped his hand into hers, dragging her away from the wall in one smooth motion.

Pulling Jonet by the hand, Cole pushed through the heavy oak door that separated her bedchamber from the sitting room, finding himself in the midst of a large but sparsely furnished room. The decor was surprisingly masculine, the heavy furniture simple in style. A huge, mahogany bed with plain hangings of ivory brocade dominated the room.

For one sickening moment, Cole feared he had dragged her into her late husband's bedroom by mistake. But there could be no mistaking Jonet's scent in the air. Impatiently, he pulled Jonet to the edge of the bed and sat down, dragging her awkwardly across his lap.

Slowly, he reached up and slid his fingers deep into the mass of her hair to turn her face into his. Briefly, he studied Jonet, her dark eyes soft and alluring now, all of the rage burnt out of them. It was over, he realized, as he lowered his mouth to capture hers. He felt Jonet tremble with need. Yes, he was going to make love to her; to take what could never be truly his, and thereby ruin his life in the process. A man could not lie with a woman like Jonet just once and ever be whole again. She would take away a part of him.

But Cole's efforts at resistance had never stood a chance, and perhaps he had not wanted them to. She—fate—or perhaps the devil himself—had won. And now, he wanted Jonet so badly he would have fallen to his knees and begged should she have suddenly changed her mind.

Ah—but she wouldn't. Jonet was too bold to play games. And so he took what he had been offered. Hungrily, deeply, he kissed her, driving her head backward, one arm lashed tight about her waist. He held nothing in check. What was the point? He could no longer do the right thing, and so he simply did as he pleased. He kissed her and kissed her, thrusting his tongue deep into her mouth, almost into her throat, and still she did not hesitate.

As Jonet returned his kisses, matching his heat stroke for stroke, Cole let his other hand drift up to caress the nape of her neck, and then slide lower, to slowly unbutton the back of her dress. She whimpered and pressed herself against him, making Cole keenly aware of what he had vaguely suspected earlier. The black-eyed witch wore not a stitch beneath her black silk dress. No stays bound her ribs; not so much as a chemise covered her breasts.

She had set out to seduce him good and proper, had she not? Cole pushed her slightly away and stared down. A mere two inches from the curve of her neckline, Jonet's nipples were clearly visible, hard beneath her widow's weeds. Desperately, Cole continued to struggle with her fastenings, and when he finally lost his patience somewhere near button number six, he simply jerked the fabric down to expose the full, white mounds to his greedy lips.

A little roughly, he drew her right nipple into his mouth and closed his teeth around it. For a long moment he suckled, tormenting her with the tip of his tongue, then biting down until Jonet gasped. Then, reconsidering his haste, he eased her off his lap. "You have nothing on beneath that dress, have you?" he suggested, his tone rich with accusation.

Jonet stepped back a pace, pulling up her sagging bodice in an awkward gesture of embarrassment. "M-my maid undressed me after dinner and went to bed," she answered uncertainly. "I did not wish to disturb her."

"Just take it off." He rasped out the command.

Obediently, Jonet tugged the dress down. One button popped off and flew into the darkness, but one more was all that the job required. Jonet's hips were so slender, the dress slid to the floor in a heap, and what was left of Cole's pride soon followed. Lamps burned low on either side of the bed, bathing her naked body in the soft light, and the sight left him completely undone once more.

Jonet stepped out of the dress and lifted her gaze to Cole's. It appeared that her momentary uncertainty was gone. Now, she seemed entirely comfortable with her nakedness. Perhaps she had undressed just this way on countless occasions for countless men. Cole told himself he didn't care. Jonet stood before him proudly, the light of a challenge returning to her eyes, and then smoothly, she lifted her arms high and began to pull the pins from her hair.

The motion served to lift her heavy breasts even higher. Cole's mouth went dry as he watched the weight of them bounce and shift as Jonet drew out one pin after another, dropping them carelessly onto the thick Turkish carpet beneath her feet. And suddenly, that hair—that mass of glorious, bewitchingly black hair—was cascading down her shoulders in shimmering waves of curls that covered her breasts and brushed her hips. Cole could remember how that hair smelled, how it felt brushing low against his belly. A groan slipped from his lips, and fleetingly, Cole feared he might come just looking at her. After an unsteady moment, however, he managed to dredge up a small measure of self-control, and jerked to his feet.

Quickly, he went to her, urgently loosening his cravat with both hands. His skin felt feverish, desperate to rub against Jonet's, and when her hands came up to help pull away his neckcloth, the temperature leapt up yet another notch. In a matter of seconds, Cole's coat and waistcoat were strewn across the floor, his shirt quickly following. The close of his breeches still hung open, and it was a simple task to shuck the rest of his clothes and boots.

And then he stood before her, completely naked. It had been a long time since Cole had been so with a woman, and never with a gently bred lady. Rachel had preferred he come to her in a nightshirt, and of course, he had obliged. And yet, he had craved the touch of skin against skin, the scent of feminine arousal, and the faint heat that rose from the human body during the act of lovemaking. But Cole was not a vain man. Under any other set of circumstances, he would doubtless have paused to worry about what Jonet thought of him, but he was well beyond caring now. Instead, he took her in his arms and dragged her high against him, completely off her feet, until her feminine mound was pressed hard and hot against his throbbing cock.

He urged it against her. "Is this what you need, Jonet?" he asked softly, one hand around her waist, the other cradling the swell of her buttocks. "Do you want this inside you? Do you want it now?"

Jonet's head tipped back and her eyes closed, her inky black lashes fanning low across her cheeks. "*Yes,*" she moaned, bracing her hands wide on his shoulders and arching into him. "*Now!*"

With a little grunt, Cole braced himself, then hefted her up and let his straining cock slide into the sweet valley between her legs. Already she was wet and slick with need. Carefully easing apart her hips, he slid her down, gritted his teeth, and impaled her ever so gently.

Cole felt her hands spasm atop his shoulders, and then Jonet's nails sunk into his flesh. "*Ah, ah . . . oh, Cole, please! . . .*" she moaned, and Cole braced his legs and shoved himself in another half inch. It was all he could do not to drive himself deep on one last stroke, but her position was precarious. And for the world, he would not hurt her.

And then, over Jonet's shoulder, his eye caught on the huge mahogany bed—its ivory hangings neatly pulled back, the clean, fresh sheets long since turned down—and then he looked at what he was doing to Jonet. Suddenly, it seemed somehow . . . *wrong.* Even a little crude. A man might, in an occasional moment of blind desperation, take a whore that way, particularly in some limiting circumstance. He'd done it himself once, after the horror of a particularly brutal battle, when he'd been half drunk and too dazed to be properly ashamed. But despite Charlie Donaldson's very fine whisky, Cole was not precisely drunk—or if he had been, the look on Jonet's face when he'd entered her sitting room had sobered him up. He had known at once what she wanted. And now that he had agreed to give it to her, he ought at least to do the job properly. Jonet did not deserve to be taken standing up, like a common whore, simply because he was angry with himself for being vulnerable.

Cole was only dimly aware that he had ceased to move.

"Cole—?" Jonet's question came out on an urgent, breathless whimper. Quickly, he kissed her and lifted her off. Jonet's protest began before her feet touched the ground, her hands still clutching his shoulders stubbornly. "No, *Cole—*" she pled desperately, her voice thick with need. She gave him a hard shake. "Damn it, you *cannot* do this to me! Not *now*. Not after I begged—"

"Shush, Jonet," he whispered gently, holding her gaze as he encircled her waist and lifted her heavy hair over her shoulder. More gently this time, Cole pulled her tight against him and pressed his damp erection against the softness of her belly. Opening his mouth against her throat, Cole allowed himself the luxury of drinking in the warm smell of her skin.

In his arms, she still quivered with feminine anticipation, her hands coming up to spear eagerly through the thickness of his hair. *"Please, Cole!"* she begged. "Just don't stop."

Cole slid his lips around the curve of her jaw and up to find the dampness of her temple. "I won't," he said softly. "I just want to take you to bed, darling. Let me love you properly. Not like this."

Finally, Jonet pulled away to look up at him, her tongue slicking a layer of moisture across her full bottom lip, and his breath caught hard in his throat. Between them, his erection bucked hard against her belly. Sweet heaven, the woman was going to drive him insane.

"Then come with me," she said, and pulled him toward her bed.

Jonet was perched on the edge of desperation. She rolled to one side of the bed and dragged Cole's big body with her. He reached for her then and pulled her close, placing one warm, heavy hand over her breast in a sweetly possessive gesture. "Oh!" she said softly, mouthing the word as her greedy fingers sought him again. Cole's erection was thick and smooth, and as she stroked him up and down, a pearl of moisture appeared at the tip. She watched it, mesmerized, as a fog of sensuality clouded her brain.

Suddenly, Cole was halfway on top of her, tearing her hand from his shaft and bracing on one elbow to stare down at her. Eyes open wide, he kissed her again, lingering more tenderly this time. Then, very deliberately, he took her hand and pulled it to the moist curls between her legs. Guiding her fingertips into her secret place, he languidly began to rub them back and forth, guiding her with his hand until she began to arouse herself.

Then his hand left hers, and Cole sat back on his haunches and watched. Expectantly, she looked up at him. "Oh, *Jesus*, Jonet," he said hoarsely. "Just don't stop. Please."

Emboldened by his urgency, she did as he asked, becoming quickly lost in the sensation of self-arousal, and helpless to do anything save gasp for breath. Cole watched her every motion, his eyes wide in the lamplight, the muscles of his sinewy throat working up and down as his breathing became rapid and shallow. Quickly, Jonet's own dew slicked her fingers, and then her palm, until she was arching off the bed and crying out for him.

Mercifully, Cole straddled her then, his thighs bulging, his gaze hot and focused. Shoving her thighs wider apart, he looked deep into her eyes and grasped himself with one hand. Jonet twisted restlessly atop the covers. Her skin was on fire. Was he *never* going to give her what she needed? "For God's sake, Cole—!" she finally managed to gasp. *"Just do it!"*

Cole spread the palm of his hand flat against her mound, and with his long, elegant fingers, spread her wide to take him. With his other hand, he guided himself to her opening, and thrust partway in. A moment later, the mindless fog cleared sharply. *Merciful heaven, but he was a big man!* Jonet sucked in her breath on a gasp, but it was far too late. Cole braced himself high, then rocked back his hips and drove deep. One stroke. All the way.

Jonet did scream then, a little cry of pain and pleasure, but Cole seemed not to hear. His arms drew taut, their muscles bulging as his spine arched. He threw back his head to reveal the grim set of his jaw and eyes that were squeezed shut. Cole shuddered once, drew in a deep breath through nostrils flared wide, and then stroked her deep again. And again. It had been a long time, but the perfect strokes and knifing pleasure quickly overcame any discomfort. Instinct grabbed hold of Jonet, and her hips tilted up to take Cole deeper still. He settled into her, his rhythm strong and deep and infinitely comforting.

For a time, nothing broke the stillness of the room save

for Cole's harsh, rhythmic exhalations and the gentle creaking of the bed. Across the strong bones of his brow, a damp sheen appeared, and Jonet hungrily inhaled the scent of his soap and his sweat. Urgently, Jonet lifted one leg to wrap it high around his waist, moving with him as he drove into her. It wasn't enough. She craved more, needed to curl around him, crawl inside him. Like a cat, she twisted and snaked until her belly brushed his and her fingers clutched his buttocks, the nails digging into his flesh. And still, Cole pounded himself into her in that perfect, timeless cadence, his expression tight with control, his hair framing his face in a shimmering curtain of gold. At last, Jonet gave herself over to it, reveling in the long, heated strokes of his body inside hers, her breath coming out on a sigh.

"Ah, Jonet," Cole whispered, finally opening his eyes, his gaze piercingly clear. "I always feared that you were the stuff of which dreams are made."

He stroked her again, a little higher this time, and the fusion of motion and words unleashed something wild inside; something she thought had long since stilled. It was more than that glistening edge of pleasure that always tantalized; it was a deep and abiding joy, a singing of her soul. Jonet arched high against him again, and again. And then one last time, her spine drawn tight as she urged herself hard against the thickness of him. When she came, it was in an explosion of rapture and light. She clung to him for dear life as all about her the world splintered, leaving her only vaguely aware of Cole's incipient climax.

In that moment, nothing, but nothing else mattered to Jonet. All that had happened, all the pain and horror that had gone before, simply ceased to exist, and there was nothing but Cole Amherst, his head again thrown back, the corded tendons of his neck straining, and his hips working feverishly as he pulsed and drove and spilled himself into her womb. Cole stroked her deeply one last time, then fell forward, taking his weight onto his elbows and staring down into her face. And then, his eyes dropped shut and he kissed her lips, gently, almost reverently, his mouth soft and pliant, his lips half parted.

"Ah, Jonet," he whispered, his voice thick with awe. "I do love . . ." He stopped and swallowed hard. "I do love how you feel beneath me." Gently, he rolled away, taking her with him and burrowing deep into the covers. With one arm, he encircled her and drew her snugly against him. They lay there in silence, simply staring at one another through eyes that were slumberous and sated, until the beauty of his face simply became too much to bear, and Jonet was forced to shift her gaze away from him. She stared up into the bed hangings, seeing nothing.

Oh, what a fool she was! Jonet had irrationally hoped that if Cole bedded her once, her fascination with the man would cease. He'd still been hard and throbbing inside her when she had begun to realize what a mistake that had been. The thought that a man—particularly this man—could bring her such peace and joy seemed suddenly frightening. She had wanted him with something akin to madness, yes. But surely she could not *need* him that much?

Most certainly, Cole did not need her. Oh, she had given him great pleasure, Jonet was not naïve enough to think otherwise. But surely the intensity of what they had just shared was . . . almost *ordinary* to some people? People who felt a true passion for one another?

Jonet did not know. But she knew that this was her fault; she had pushed Cole into a situation he had honorably sought to avoid, and now she would be punished for her greed in the worst sort of way. By continuing to want what she could not have. Making love with him had assuaged nothing; it had merely taken the edge off her lust. And as she stared down at the hard wall of his chest, watching as his breathing deepened into the rhythm of sleep, Jonet realized that it would be a short-lived relief.

Throwing one arm across her eyes despairingly, she rolled a little away from him and onto her back, as if the distance might help. It was only then that she realized that Cole was not asleep. His hand snaked out to pull her back. "Please don't leave me," he murmured, his drowsy voice edged with desperation. Jonet wanted suddenly to cry.

Cole immediately sensed the sudden tension in Jonet's body; it was a blade of bittersweet pain slashing through his languorous warmth and masculine satisfaction. Perhaps his request had been too familiar, too demanding? Perhaps *he* was the one who was expected to leave? He had given her what she had begged for—and left her well pleasured in the bargain, he proudly acknowledged. But perhaps Jonet was now done with him. Slowly, he levered up onto one elbow to stare down into her face.

She did not look as if she was done. She looked . . . *lost.* Lightly, Cole smoothed one hand across the silken skin of her belly. Inside, she had been as tight as a virgin, and though she had carried two children, her figure showed no sign of it. His breath catching at the thought, Cole wondered what it would be like to feel his child stir inside her. He knew he should not think such things, but tonight he'd had a taste of her, and his emotions still ran too wild and feverish to control.

But Jonet was too thin, really, to bear a child. Just now, it would not be good for her. The stress of the last several months had taken a toll on her body as well as her mind. Yes, it would be far better to wait until Jonet was well, and then to hope for . . . *Merciful God—what was he thinking?*

It was as if she could read his thoughts. Languidly, she rolled her head to one side and stared at him through eyes that seemed deceptively heavy and sated. "What would you do, Cole, if I were to become with child?" she asked softly, her lush lips forming the words he could not bear to hear. "Would you, I wonder, do what you always do? Would you do the right thing?"

Still stroking her belly, Cole's hand froze. "Jonet, I thought you said—"

"I did. I won't." Her gaze left his as, lazily, she let her fingertips trail through the dusting of hair that ran from his chest to his belly, and then lower, until his traitorous manhood stirred to her touch. "But you are ever the gentleman, Cole," she continued. "Would you be a gentleman for me, Cole?"

Cole had the strangest impression that her languor was feigned; that somehow, Jonet cared more about his answer than she wished to admit. Nonetheless, it could not—*would not*—alter his response. He reached down to snare her hand in midstroke, drawing it to his mouth to lightly kiss her knuckles. He could not bear to look at her.

"Jonet," he said quietly. "I cannot believe we are having this discussion. You are speaking of marriage. I could not possibly marry you, and you would never be so foolish as to marry someone like me." Gently, he dropped her hand and slid his fingers into the dark mass of her hair, to push it away from her high, aristocratic forehead. He wanted to bend his head and slide his lips across the curve of her jaw, down her throat, and lower still. He wanted to make love to her again—but this time with his mouth and with his hands, openly giving her what little he did have to offer. In short, he wanted to do whatever it might take to somehow alleviate any pain that his plain words might have caused.

But Jonet did not appear to be in any pain. Her face was smooth and emotionless. Illogically, he felt a stab of disappointment. "Of course you are right," she said evenly. "But you are a delightful lover. Thank you for sharing a part of the evening with me." She turned her head on the pillow, her lips curving into one of her wicked, mischievous smiles. "And for giving in to a lady's whims with moderate grace. Can you find all your clothes, do you think?"

Her dismissal could not have been more gentle, nor more cutting. Was that what he had been? *A lady's whim?* Well? *Well—?* What the devil had he expected? Reluctantly, Cole pulled his fingers from the tangle of her hair, rolled to the edge of the bed, and began to dress in silence.

He kept waiting for her to reach out and touch him. He kept hoping that she would retract the words she had so coolly spoken, and plead with him to return to her bed and hold her in his arms until dawn. That, to Cole's way of thinking, had been an inherent part of their bargain, the most integral part of *making love.* Anything less was just *having sex,* and there was a big damned difference to him. But Jonet said nothing, and Cole was once again left feeling bitter and a little used.

Well. It seemed that they had simply had sex after all.

He could hardly complain. It wasn't as if Jonet had taken him by force. *Ha—!* He'd been hot, hard, and ready to shove up her skirts since the first day he'd met her. Indeed, he hadn't even liked her—and he'd *still* wanted her. But now, Cole had discovered that, most of the time, he liked her tremendously. That he loved her always. And that what he now wanted to do was to make love to her until the day they nailed his coffin shut.

But he had been a fool to come here. He had always known that it would be a mistake to touch her. Her reputation as a *femme fatale* was justly earned. And in his wild anger and uncontrollable passion, he had completely forgotten about Delacourt. He had lain with a woman who, by rights if not by God's ordination, belonged to another man. He had forgotten, too, about Stuart and Robert. Just as he had ignored his own family duty, he had ignored his duty to Jonet's children. The disappointment and despair began to twist in his stomach, sickening him.

If Jonet's sin was arrogance, his was surely selfishness. He had wanted her, and so he had simply taken her, sparing no thought for the consequences. That she had offered herself—indeed, pushed herself upon him—made not one whit of difference. And now, her question haunted him. What if she *did* become with child? It had been irresponsible of him to simply take her word that she would not. What would he do? Implicit in her question had been the suggestion that she would wish to wed him. But undoubtedly that remark had been casually made, born of that sweet, drowsy sense of intimacy that inevitably lingers in the aftermath of good sex.

Their marrying would, of course, have been out of the question, just as he had said.

No. His words had been a lie, had they not? If she conceived, Cole would force the issue to the depth and breadth of his ability. Given Jonet's wealth and titles, it could even prove difficult, depending upon her mood. But Cole would set aside both his pride and her happiness before he would bring another unprotected child into this world. Oh, yes. Marry him she surely would, even if he had to threaten her to get the job done. But no doubt she was right. Jonet was no green girl. Already she had demonstrated that she knew her own body unfailingly, as a virtuoso might know his violin. He must simply trust her word, and pray that . . . *pray that what?*

With a swift snap, Cole jerked his wrinkled cravat from the carpet, picked up his coat, and turned to face her. Yes, he loved her. Yes, he would ruin her life by marrying her, were there no other alternative left to them. Perhaps he ought simply to tell her and have done with it.

"Jonet, I—"

But Jonet was asleep, the perfect oval of her face smooth and tranquil in the lamplight, her mass of dark hair trailing over both her pillow and his. She lay halfway onto her side, one leg tucked high, the sheet rucked up beneath it, with the lamplight casting a sheen across the perfect turn of her breast and shoulder. Naked, beautiful, and unmistakably asleep.

And what had he been about to say anyway? Cole did not know. His lessons in gentlemanly deportment had taught him no words appropriate to this sort of situation. Slowly, he made his way around the bed, blowing out the lamps as he went. In the utter darkness, Cole gingerly made his way across the bedchamber to the door that opened onto the sitting room. Briefly, a shaft of light cut through the gloom and across Jonet's bed, and then the lock clicked quietly shut, plunging the room back into darkness. Jonet turned her face into her pillow and dragged it against her body, her fingers clawing into the softness as if she were drowning in it.

When the crying finally began, it was a letting go like nothing she had known before, as if the ice that had long shrouded her heart had finally melted and was coming up as tears. The air dragged from her lungs and pulled at her heart in great, heaving sobs.

Jonet cried until her pillow was wet, and then she cried until dry heaves racked her chest, forcing her to crawl from her bed in search of the chamber pot. She cried as she had not cried in all these many dark months and days, when her soul had been perched on the edge of despair. She cried because now she had gone over that black, black edge. And still, she could not stop.

11

In which Lord Delacourt is sadly Abused

The following day, a restrained and heavy silence descended upon Mercer House. Cole took great pains to avoid Jonet, and followed his usual custom of taking luncheon with the boys in the schoolroom. His afternoon, thank heaven, was to be free, since Nanna had arranged for the tailor to call upon Lord Mercer and his brother, in order that they might be fitted with half-mourning for the late summer months. It fell in perfectly with his plan to escape Mercer House and the painful memories of the preceding night, if only briefly.

Today there was to be an alumni match at Lord's. Nothing more than an informal game, but Cole was in the mood to work up a sweat doing something besides staring at Jonet. The rigorous exercise would suit him perfectly, and with any luck at all, the Eton alumni would pound the infidels to flinders, providing him with an outlet for at least a bit of his masculine angst. Cole dressed carefully for the match, then rummaged rather violently through his large trunk for his bat. Days ago, Jonet had made it plain that the boys would not be permitted to accompany him to any sporting events, and Cole no longer had the will to argue with her. In truth, today he needed to be alone. There was much he needed to consider.

And so he went swiftly downstairs, his bitter mood very little improved, only to find Jonet standing in the hallway, dressed in a green riding habit that was so dark it might have been black, and pulling on a pair of snug kidskin gloves. A gossamer black veil was rolled away from her face, which was pale and drawn, as if she had not slept at all. One of the dour Scottish grooms stood at her elbow, holding her whip.

She watched Cole descend, her eyebrows going up in mild surprise as her eyes settled on the bat he held loosely in his hand. "I see you've put on your whites, Captain Amherst. Do you mean to play today?" she asked politely, as if they were barely acquainted.

Cole came to an abrupt halt at the bottom of the steps. "Indeed, yes. With a few old schoolmates." He forced a polite smile. "And yourself, ma'am? It appears you mean to have a ride. You've chosen a splendid day."

"Yes," she said a little grimly. "I find I have a desperate need for exercise this afternoon. I simply cannot stay trapped inside these four walls any longer."

Cole gave her a civil nod and shifted his weight as if to go. "I comprehend your situation precisely, ma'am. I hope you enjoy your afternoon."

Damn it, thought Cole, the whole tone of the conversation was beginning to upset him. They spoke as if they were total strangers. Was this what his relationship with Jonet had come to? Had their deep intimacy merely served to drive them further apart? Would his one night of bliss in her arms now cut him off from the friendship he had begun to value so greatly? Certainly, it seemed so. And undoubtedly it was for the best. Her casual dismissal last night had wounded him too deeply.

Jonet gave the second glove a ruthless little tug and looked at him with a sharp, sidelong glance. "Do you go up to Saint John's Wood, then?" Suddenly, she stared directly at him, her eyes searching his face, and making his heart lurch forward in his chest. Something which looked like despair passed over her eyes. "I mean, if you do, I wonder . . . would it be terribly rude of me to accompany you? Merely to sit on the hillside and watch?"

Cole was taken aback. "Why, I cannot think that you would—" He cleared his throat and began again. "What I mean to say is that, of course, you would be most welcome."

Jonet's lush mouth curved into a ghost of a smile as she reached out to take her whip from her groom. "Rest assured, I have no wish to socialize. I will simply sit quietly while you play. I shan't be any inconvenience, nor cause any embarrassment."

"Do not be foolish," Cole answered, his voice roughening despite his best effort to steady it. "You could never be an inconvenience, nor any sort of embarrassment."

And so it was that Jonet found herself feeling just a little shameless while riding through Mayfair in the company of Captain Cole Amherst. Although a cricket match was quite different from a cotillion, she still had no business going out, particularly in the company of a man like Cole. But if anyone recognized her sleek black gelding, they gave no indication. One or two gentlemen of military bearing tipped a hat to them, but it was plain that it was Cole, and not her, whom they acknowledged.

Cole rode quietly beside her on the huge bay she'd watched him take out almost every morning since his arrival in Brook Street. No doubt he had been unaware of her observation, but Jonet had been unable to resist staring out her bedroom window, given its expansive view overlooking the mews. And in her rather discerning opinion, Cole sat a horse as well as any man of her acquaintance. It seemed that his long years in the cavalry had made him one with his mount, and Jonet found it an aesthetic joy to watch him ride with such grace and ease.

The distance through Mayfair and north to Lord's Cricket Ground was not long, and Cole at first seemed disinclined to conversation. Several yards behind, her groom followed. Cole had insisted upon it, explaining that heat and boredom might prove too much for her, and that he wished her to have a suitable escort with which to return. With airy good grace, she had agreed rather than argue, but Jonet had grown up in the saddle, and it took a good deal more than a little heat to put her under. And a woman would have to have ice water in her veins to become bored watching him. But let him think her delicate and feminine, if he would. Last night, his appreciation had been obvious.

As had his views of their future together. A little despairingly, she looked at him from the corner of her eye. Why in heaven's name had she asked to accompany him today? Did she mean to deliberately torture herself? But there was no ignoring the almost unbelievable passion that had exploded between them last night. She simply would not go on behaving as if nothing had happened.

"Cole—?" she asked, her voice low and controlled. "Do you not think we ought to talk about it?"

Cole looked at her with a startled expression, the reins

looped loosely through his long, elegant hands. "What is there to say, Jonet?" he asked gruffly.

Jonet would not be cowed. She had spent half the night sniveling pathetically, and she was done with it. "A great deal, I should think, given what we have shared," she retorted. Deliberately, she turned in her saddle and lifted her chin to stare at him. "I do not play simpering games, Cole. I think you know that. I have no hesitation in saying that you were—that you are . . . simply *magnificent.*"

"In bed?" Cole said archly. "Is that what you mean?"

Beneath her dark veil, Jonet felt the heat rush up her face, and she was inordinately glad he could not see how deeply the memory affected her. "Yes," she answered, her voice unnaturally throaty. "And as I said last night, I need you for . . . more than one night."

The grim angle of Cole's jaw went even more rigid. "You wish for a long-term *affaire?* Is that what you are saying?"

"Cole, I . . ." Beneath the veil, Jonet squeezed shut her eyes. He had already made it plain he wouldn't wed her, and she would sooner die than beg. "Yes," she said at last. "Yes, that is what I want."

"No." Cole said the word softly, the one syllable strong and certain.

"No—?" The pain in her voice must have been apparent.

Cole turned to look at her, the lines of his face softening ever so slightly. "No, Jonet. I am mindful of the compliment you pay me, but that is not the way I choose to live my life."

"I see," she said stiffly, her fingers tightening on her reins. In protest, the black snorted and skittered sideways, all too aware that his mistress knew better than to be so careless with his mouth.

Jonet easily reined him in, slackened her grip, then

shifted her gaze to Cole. "Then I must thank you for your . . . your *generosity* of last night. In many ways, the evening was the most pleasurable of my life. I hope to always have your friendship, if that's all you can offer."

Cole's eyes flared wide, as if from shock or pain. His hand lashed out in an instant, jerking her horse to a halt and drawing his close alongside. "*Always*," he said roughly, leaning halfway off his mount to look at her. On the cobblestones, their horses pranced uneasily, but Cole skillfully held them both, all the while keeping one eye on the groom to be sure he kept his distance. "Listen to me, Jonet! You will *always* have my undying devotion. If ever you have need of me, I will be there. In any way but that. Do you understand?"

Jonet was shocked at the vehemence in his tone. "Yes, I understand," she answered hollowly. "And I thank you. I will take what I can get, since I find my friends are few and far between of late."

"Then we are agreed," he answered, and urged the horses on down the street.

They rode along in silence until they had crossed over Oxford Street. But Jonet simply could not leave the awkward silence hanging between them. She began again in a more conversational tone. "Tell me, Cole—where do you go with your life after Mercer House?"

He paused, as if weighing his response. "I am not sure I perfectly understand your question."

"In the autumn, when you return to the army, do you go on to India? Or somewhere else?" With an upward brush of her arm, Jonet lifted her veil just enough to let him know that her smile was teasing. "I ask, you see, so that I may know where to send word if you are *needed*—as you said I might."

Cole nudged his horse around a parked dray, his leg

brushing against the pleats of her habit. "I am thinking of giving it up altogether," he said absently, as if the idea was just now taking shape in his mind. "I am a little tired, I think, of being away from England. And I begin to fear that I have wandered too far from my proper path in life, if that makes any sense."

Jonet regarded him in silence for a moment. "Indeed, I believe I understand all too well," she mused. "But tell me, where will you go to rejoin this path you seek? Not London?"

With a wry smile, Cole shook his head. "No," he agreed. "I suppose I must go home. To Cambridgeshire."

"*Ah*—to Elmwood Manor?" she asked lightly.

Cole looked at her in some surprise, then his eyes narrowed suspiciously.

"Yes," she admitted. "I took the liberty of making inquiries before permitting you inside my house. I needed to know your circumstances. Surely you can understand?"

After a long moment, Cole seemed to relax back into his saddle. "Yes, of course. And you are correct. I will go home to Elmwood."

Jonet tried to keep her voice light and conversational. "And what does your future hold for you there, Cole? What are your hopes and your dreams for this life you will lead at Elmwood? What is it that you feel passionate about?" She dropped her voice to a teasing tone. "I should very much like to know. After all, we are friends now. Can you not tell me?"

Again, Cole looked as if he had not fully considered it. "I daresay I shall resume some of my studies. I suppose I might even return to teaching." He paused for a long moment, his eyes suddenly unfocused and far away. "But I had thought one day to take up the vicariate of St. Ann's. I know that the bishop yet hopes that I will do so. St. Ann's was, as you may recall, my father's parish."

Jonet was astonished. "Yes, I did know it—but you . . . you have taken *orders?*"

"Yes, shortly before my marriage, but I fear I became rather unsure of my life's purpose." He smiled at her grimly. "Jonet, did you not understand? I tried to tell you when first we met."

Jonet shook her head as if trying to clear her vision. "I daresay you may have done . . . but I believe I did not fully grasp the—the reality of it all."

"Or perhaps you were too angry to listen," Cole mumbled under his breath. But Jonet barely noted the teasing sarcasm in his tone. Her mind raced. Cole had been intended for the church? She had never considered it, but it explained a great deal. And made a great deal more impossible.

Jonet Rowland aspiring to be a vicar's wife? That was truly laughable. She was considered the scourge of London. Cole certainly could not be saddled with a woman of her repute, particularly with the shadow of Henry's mysterious death hanging over her head. But she would have given up her status as the Marchioness of Mercer in a trice, she realized in some surprise, would Cole but ask it of her. Jonet had hardly wanted her own position, and she certainly hadn't wanted to wed Henry. But Cole's feelings for her were quite plain. Why was she dreaming? He desired her, perhaps he even liked her at times. But if he married again, and she was not at all sure he would, it would be to a woman like . . . like that *Louisa* person.

Jonet shut off that vein of thought at once, but yet another sprang immediately to mind. "Tell me about Elmwood Manor, Cole. Is it very lovely? Has it prospered?"

Carefully, Cole nudged his horse a little ahead of hers to make way between two parked gigs. When the street widened, enabling Jonet to pull alongside him, he still remained silent for a long moment. "I am told that Elmwood is very prosperous," he finally answered. "I have not been there since . . . in quite some years."

"Why?" she asked softly. "It is your boyhood home, is it not?"

Cole stared straight ahead and into the busy traffic ahead in Portland Place. "Old ghosts, Jonet," he said with a bitter laugh. "We all have them, I daresay."

"Ah!" she said knowingly. "At last, a subject on which I am an expert."

Cole turned to look at her quizzically for a moment, a bright shaft of afternoon sun catching the harsh planes of his face. "Yes," he said quietly. "I daresay you may be."

Jonet wanted to press him for details, so that she might better understand this man she had so disastrously fallen in love with. But it was clear that his pain was still raw. She did not have it in her to wound, merely to satisfy her own curiosity.

But to her surprise, Cole began to speak again. "I suppose that Rachel is the name of my ghost, Jonet," he explained in a low, unsteady voice. "She was my wife. We lived at Elmwood."

"I see," said Jonet calmly, but the pain in Cole's voice was like a knife in her heart. And yet, it was a knife she could not help but twist. She wanted to know about this paragon of virtue to whom she would never measure up. "Tell me, Cole, what was she like, your Rachel?"

"I really have no idea," he replied, his mystified words so quiet she could barely hear them.

"I beg your pardon?"

Roughly, Cole cleared his throat. "When she died, I knew her no better than I did on the day we were wed. Can you believe that?" he asked, his gold-brown eyes urgently searching her face, as if he hoped she might have the answer. "Can you believe, Jonet, that two people can share one life, one blood, and yet know nothing of one another? To . . . to come away with no understanding of that person's hopes and dreams and passions? Or worse—to begin to fear that they have none?"

Jonet was startled into silence. "No," she finally answered. "I cannot. It seems a foreign thing to me. I find that I cannot . . . *know* a person—or even care about them very much—until I understand which of life's many hungers drives them. Is it a thirst for knowledge? A passion for art or music? Do they crave wealth or power or sex?" She forced a self-deprecating laugh. "But as you know, I'm far too unrestrained. One can easily see through me. I daresay a wiser woman would strive to be enigmatic."

Cole shot her a look which might have been pain. For a long time, he simply stared at her, as if some sort of metaphysical truth had been revealed to him. "You are indeed," he finally responded, "like no woman I have ever known before."

Jonet did not know what to make of that remark, and had not the nerve to ask. For several moments, they rode abreast in silence, the streets of Marylebone quieter and less choked with carts and drays. The cricket field was not far beyond, and Jonet was beginning to wish desperately that she had not come on this journey with Cole, for a journey it had surely turned out to be. Regrettably, nothing she had heard so far made her love him or desire him any less.

"I want you to understand something, Jonet." Cole's

voice, tight and emotionless, came out of nowhere. He stared straight across his horse's head and down the narrow street, his hands tightly clutching the reins. "Rachel and I had a child together. He died. I could not take care of them because I was in Portugal." Cole said the words coldly, refusing to look at her. "And I will *never* bring another child into this world unless I am there to provide them with a safe and stable life."

Jonet bit her lip and shook her head. "But Cole, you cannot think that—"

Cole cut her off as if he had not heard. "You once told me that I did not know what it was like, Jonet, to sacrifice everything for a child. But you were wrong. I learned by not being there. And I can tell you most sincerely that failure is a far harder teacher than success."

"I am sorry," Jonet answered gently. Because she remembered what she had said to him that day in the breakfast parlor, and the memory made her feel like a heartless bitch. And because she knew nothing else to say to assuage his pain. Cole would not have thanked her for gratuitous platitudes, and Jonet had learned the hard way that people had a right to work through, and hopefully come to terms with, their own grief. And in their own way.

Over the field at St. John's Wood, the afternoon sun was settled high in the west. The forward fence of Lord's was coming into view. Their moment of intimacy was almost at an end, and Jonet was relieved. She wanted desperately to reach out to comfort Cole. But it simply would not do. And so instead, she lifted her hand to shield her eyes, watching as, on the corner beyond, a huge traveling coach drew up to disgorge a half dozen boys who looked to be a little older than Stuart. Giggling and jostling one another, the boys paused on the footpath to form a queue, and despite the emotion of the moment, Jonet found herself laughing. On the reverse of their coats, each wore a bright canvas letter pinned to the fabric. "H-A-R-R-O-W," she spelled aloud. "Please tell me, Cole, that is not your competition?"

Cole managed to flash her a weak grin. "No, we probably couldn't beat them. This is just an informal mix-up for alumni—a sort of last huzzah before rheumatism sets in."

But suddenly, his smile faded and his gaze focused straight ahead. In the shadow of the big coach, two gentlemen were rounding the corner and striding along the footpath toward them. The younger of the two was clearly dressed to play, while the elder walked with his hand laid lightly upon his companion's arm. Cole's smile shifted to a distinct scowl, but there was no avoiding them, and they clearly had no intention of allowing Cole to pass without a greeting.

"Ho! Amherst!" shouted the younger, a handsome man whom Jonet recognized at once. The sight made her regret the impulsiveness that had brought her here, but she could hardly turn her mount around now without looking excessively rude. She prepared herself to be snubbed.

Cole reined in by the footpath and touched his hat in turn. "Afternoon, Madlow. And Colonel, you are looking exceedingly well."

"Yes, yes," said the old man with an irritable toss of his hand. "As are you, one must suppose. Now introduce us, my boy, to this lovely young lady whom Terry tells me you have at your side." A smile played at his mouth, but his disapproving expression was painfully telling.

Mortified, Jonet wanted to sink through the street. Her presence must be an embarrassment to Cole. But if it was, Cole gave no indication of it. Carefully, he reined his horse closer to the footpath, and Jonet had no choice but to move up and draw back her veil. "Lady Mercer," he said calmly, "may I present Colonel Jack Lauderwood and his son-in-law, Captain Terrence Madlow? Gentlemen, my—er, cousin, Jonet, Lady Mercer."

Jonet leaned down and offered her hand, murmuring something suitably polite. But to Terry Madlow, she dredged up her courage and smiled. "*Captain* Madlow, is it now? What a great pleasure to see you again after all these years."

Jealousy bit like a horsefly at the back of Cole's neck as Terry Madlow's face split into an adolescent grin. "I should not have thought you would remember me, ma'am. I believe we have not met since your come-out. It has been too long."

Jonet's mouth curled into a wry smile. "Much too long, sir, and I daresay a little age has crept up on all of us. Indeed, my *cousin* here was just complaining to me of his rheumatism."

Insufferable minx! Cole could not bear the sweet look she was giving Madlow. How could she be so cool, so graceful in her manner, under such trying circumstances? And to Cole's undying frustration, it seemed his friends meant to keep them standing in the street all afternoon.

"Well, that is because Amherst is quite advanced in years, ma'am," Madlow countered, finally releasing her hand. "But you, *ah—!* May I say that maturity has merely lent a glorious patina to your beauty."

Jonet laughed charmingly. "You may certainly say it, sir, though I rather doubt we shall any of us believe it." Her eyes apparently took in his white attire. "Do you play today, Captain Madlow?"

Terry looked up at Cole and grinned. "Yes, for Harrow," he answered. "And I mean to hit a six on this big devil here—or die trying."

"How is Louisa?" interjected Cole stiffly. "I hope she is well?"

Terry's face went blank for a moment. "Yes! Yes! Very well, indeed. But like most women, she has no taste for cricket."

Throughout the exchange, Cole noticed that Colonel Lauderwood's eyes had never left him. Now, he gruffly interjected himself into the conversation. "Louisa brought your spectacles, did she not?"

"Yes," confirmed Cole, just as he noticed Jonet looking uncomfortably over her shoulder. In the street at either side of them, two brewer's drays were waiting to pass. "And now, gentlemen, we must walk on. It appears we are slowing the wheels of commerce. Madlow, I shall see you in the pitch shortly."

Cole exited the street and escorted Jonet away from the stands and around the bridle path that led to the far end of Lord's Cricket Ground. There, the crowd was sparse and the shade more plentiful. As a rule, Cole was inordinately fond of the game; prior to the war, he had played for Cambridgeshire, and following his return to London, he had quickly gained entree into the MCC along with many of his fellow officers. But today, the chastising look on Lauderwood's face had soured his mood. He was in no humor, particularly in the wake of last night's emotional encounter, to bear the brunt of the colonel's criticism. Cole tried to ignore his temper, and while Jonet's groom took the horses, he tossed out a blanket beneath a sheltering oak and settled Jonet onto it.

"You seemed to remember Terrence Madlow very well," remarked Cole noncommittally as he bent down to brush a little grass from the edge of the blanket.

Jonet looked up at him in some surprise. "Yes, quite. He

courted me most assiduously during the early weeks of my come-out, and for a time, I fancied myself rather madly in love with him."

"Did you indeed?" Despite his astonishment, Cole tried to maintain a conversational tone. "And what happened to disenchant you?"

Jonet looked suddenly far away. "My father quickly dispensed with any illusions I might have had about romantic love," she answered vaguely. "But I daresay I did not know then just how deep and complex that particular emotion could be."

After that, Jonet said little as Cole sat down upon one corner of the blanket to exchange his riding boots for shoes. No one paid them any heed, until a tall young man approached from the east end of the field, whistling a tune and swinging his bat as he went.

"*Oh, bugger me!*" hissed Cole under his breath when the man's face came into view.

Engaged in straightening the pleats of her habit, Jonet looked up from her position on the blanket. As the man drew up before them, Cole wondered if his day could get any worse.

"Why, what a vision of summer beauty!" remarked Delacourt, opening his arms in an expansive gesture, elegantly dangling his bat between two fingers of his right hand. "This blissful scene wants only a picnic basket and a book of sonnets."

"David!" exclaimed Jonet happily, bracing herself as if to leap to her feet. With a sharp jerk, Cole drew taut the lace of his shoe, very nearly ripping it apart.

Delacourt tossed his bat into the grass and bent down to brush the back of his hand across Jonet's cheek. Cole could have sworn the bastard was watching his reaction out of the corner of one eye. "You are looking splendid today, Jonnie," the viscount said a little wistfully. "Why do you not give me a scrap of that veil and let me be your champion?" Delacourt turned to look at Cole. "Amherst is a good chap. He shan't mind, shall you, old boy?"

"Do what you will, Delacourt," Cole sourly returned, "if you think it will help your game."

Delacourt tipped back his head and gave his elegant laugh. "Good God, Amherst! You grow more amusing with every passing day. One cannot but wonder what you will say next!"

"*David—!*" said Jonet in a warning tone.

Cole sprang to his feet and picked up his bat, giving his left instep a vicious whack. "Please tell me, Delacourt, that you do not play for Eton."

Delacourt grinned broadly. "Alas, no," he remarked. "I believe we find ourselves on opposing teams. Rivals, so to speak. What will that be like, do you think?"

When Cole made no reply other than to glare at him, the viscount turned his gaze to Jonet. "You know, my dear, that you are expected to dine at Delacourt House tonight? I trust you will not be late."

"Yes, of course I remember," she answered a little defensively, shifting uncomfortably on the blanket. "I very much look forward to it."

Cole turned his back on the pair. "If you mean to play, Delacourt," he said, swinging his bat over one shoulder, "you'd best get on with it. It's time to open the innings." And then, with unchristian bloodlust hot in his heart, Cole headed down the embankment toward the pitch.

Jonet knew little about cricket. In the social whirlwind which had constituted her life prior to Henry's death, she had rarely attended anything other than the most fashionable routs and balls. But cricket was becoming a popular fixture of the Season, and as she watched the gentlemen warm up, she began to see that the sport did indeed have some advantages.

Cole looked good on the field. Eagerly scooting forward to the edge of the blanket, Jonet watched the methodical movement of his arm as he pitched and caught the ball, and she remembered all too well the fine musculature and strong tendons that lay just beneath his clothing. In the afternoon light, with his dark blond mane catching every ray of the sun, he looked more glorious than any other player. He was taller, yes. But he was leaner and more agile, too, while his tanned skin made him look at home beneath the summer sun. When the teams went out to take the field, Cole took the position as the initial bowler, easily dismissing the first batsman, who just happened to be Terry Madlow. Captain Madlow merely grinned, wiped the sweat from his brow with the back of his cuff, and moved on.

Teams changed sides, with fieldsmen, batsmen, and bowlers alternating so frequently that Jonet quickly became confused. But as the afternoon progressed, Cole and another dark-haired man whom Jonet did not recognize rotated to bat, making several hits between them. Both batted with extraordinary skill, clearly frustrating the opposition and heightening the tension of the game. At some point, David had come into the field to take up one of the mid-positions, but Jonet paid him scant heed. She was far more interested in watching Cole's body move across the field.

Finally, the bowler pitched a good-length ball, and the striker hit it, but with measurably less skill. Both he and Cole began running; crossing and making good their ground with time to spare. Suddenly, Cole turned on his heel to return, his partner following suit, but even Jonet could see that this time it would be a tight race to the stumps.

In the foreground, she saw David's muscles bunch as he leapt up and out to catch the throw from the fieldsman. But Cole was still plowing ahead and straight for him. David made a lucky catch, snaring the ball in midair, but with a ruthless expression, Cole barred his teeth and pushed on, just as David's foot came down near his path. They came together and tumbled to the ground in an explosion of arms and legs, the wicket shattering, and bits of dust and grass settling over them like a snowstorm.

"Run out!" shouted a gloomy-faced gentleman behind the wicket, staring down into the fray with a disgusted expression. Dropping the ball, David stumbled to his feet, one sleeve pressed to his nose. There was no mistaking the bright red bloodstain which was rapidly flooding forth.

And there was no mistaking the fact that Cole had caught him across the face with a sharp—and almost certainly intentional—jab from his elbow.

By the time the arduous game ended, Jonet and her groom had apparently gone home. Cole was not disappointed. In truth, he had been dreading the ride home by her side. But his reluctance had little to do with her probing questions and insightful gaze, and everything to do with the fact that he was deeply ashamed of his behavior on the field.

He'd struck Lord Delacourt in a fit of masculine jealousy, and that's all there was to it. Two dozen people had doubtless seen him do it. What was worse, he had wholeheartedly wanted Delacourt to hit him back. The fact that they were in the middle of a gentleman's sporting event had escaped him completely. In his heedless rush toward the wicket, all he had seen was Delacourt—not Delacourt leaping up to catch the ball, but Delacout bending down to caress Jonet.

But that was no excuse. Cole had behaved abominably, and the eventual return of good breeding had required him to choke back his bile and apologize as soon as the inning was over. The fact that Delacourt had merely thrown back his head in laughter, proclaimed it an accident, and cheerfully pounded him on the back did nothing to alter the fact that what he had done had been coarse and ungentlemanly in the extreme.

His blood still boiling, Cole took his horse from a waiting groundsman, unstrapped his boots, and sat down beneath a copse of trees to remove his shoes. Halfway across the empty field, Delacourt was doing the same. Catching Cole's eye through the waning crowd, the viscount lifted his hand, grinned shamelessly, and gave Cole an almost affable wave. *Presumptuous bastard!* Did he take nothing seriously?

Suddenly, Delacourt looked uncharacteristically serious about something. His gaze still focused on Cole, but his eyes had narrowed to a glower that was pure evil. A chill ran up Cole's spine, and suddenly, he was struck with a faint misgiving about having made an enemy of a man who could focus his gaze with such pure spite. But what the devil had he done now?

At that very moment, however, someone standing near Cole's elbow cleared his throat delicately. Cole looked up from his boots just as his cousin Edmund's shadow fell across him.

Edmund grinned snidely. "Cousin!" he cheerfully proclaimed, fanning a handful of banknotes between his fingers. "It seems you have brought me good luck this afternoon."

"I certainly cannot see how," Cole remarked darkly as he clambered up from the ground, "since we had the living hell thrashed out of us."

Edmund showed his glittering white teeth. "Precisely my point, old boy! I had the foresight to bet on Harrow."

Ruthlessly, Cole shoved his shoes into his saddlebag. "*Christ!*" he muttered. "I cannot believe you would wager against your own school."

"*Tut, tut!*" cautioned Edmund. "We all saw you elbow poor Delacourt in the nose. Now you're blaspheming! Father will be crushed to hear that his golden boy has come down to tread upon this earth with us mere mortals."

"Oh, shut up, Edmund," retorted Cole. "Why do you not let it go! We're hardly schoolboys anymore. And I don't give a bloody damn what James thinks."

"Do you not?" Edmund folded the banknotes and restored them to his coat pocket. "Then it would appear that life with our fair cousin has brought about some sort of alteration in your personality, Cole. But then, Jonet does tend to do that to men."

Cole gathered his reins into one fist and threw himself easily into the saddle to stare boldly down at Edmund. "At least I am not floating down the River Tick," he retorted, "while being pursued by a gang of East End hoodlums. But let me assure you, Edmund, that if you utter one more word against Lady Mercer, you'll find your blacklegs a damned sight more compassionate than I shall be. For I shan't stop at maiming you. I'll put a bullet through you."

And with that parting shot, Cole reined his horse toward the gate. He watched a trembling, white-faced

Edmund hastily depart, leaving him to feel more like seven-year-old Robert with every passing moment. He had been reduced to hitting and cursing—not to mention committing fornication and threatening murder. Was there, he grimly wondered, a commandment he *hadn't* broken in the last two days? And he was still shaking with rage. Over Delacourt. Over Edmund. And yes, over Jonet. What the devil had that woman done to him?

Just then, *that woman* stepped from the shadows of the largest tree, her face a mask of anger mixed with satisfaction. "*Bastard!*" she hissed at Edmund as he hastened out the gate.

Swiftly, Cole dismounted and looked about. Jonet was alone. Indeed, the entire cricket ground was now empty. "Jonet, where the devil is your groom?" The words were sharper than he'd intended.

Turning to face him, Jonet regarded him with a sardonic smile. "Why, what an ill mood you are in!" she remarked, crossing her arms and relaxing against the tree trunk. "But I do thank you, Cole, for so boldly defending me against Edmund. As to my groom, he was bored. I sent him home."

Her nonchalance further galled him. Cole dropped his reins and paced toward her. "That was imprudent, Jonet."

Her eyes flashed, and her smile shifted to something far more knowing. "Why was it imprudent, Cole?" she softly challenged. "I am a twenty-eight-year-old widow with an already scandalous reputation. Can it simply be that you are jealous? Or afraid to be alone with me?"

He closed the distance between them. "Do not be ridiculous, Jonet," he hissed, fighting the urge to plunge his fingers into the softness of her hair and drag her mouth ruthlessly to his. Damn it, was he now to be further tortured? Delacourt had pushed him to the edge, and Edmund had very nearly shoved him over. Could she not see that it was dangerous to press him any further?

Apparently not. Jonet laughed, a gentle, incredibly feminine sound. "Oh, Cole! My dear, it is you who is ridiculous," she gently scolded. "And what was that bloody nose all about anyway? I vow, you and David behave as if you are little more than overgrown schoolboys."

Cole forced his hands into fists. "Thank you, madam, for reminding me of my humiliation."

Again, suppressed humor lit Jonet's eyes. "Really, Cole," she chided, "I should very much like to know what has come over you." Her hand came up to touch his shoulder, lightly brushing away a smear of dirt in a sweetly maternal gesture. The kindness of it merely served to heighten his fury.

Harshly, Cole caught her fingers in his own. "Damn it all, Jonet—why are you dining with him tonight?" he demanded, his voice a low growl. "Just tell me how you can lie with me one night, and go to him the next!"

"Just tell me why you care!" she boldly countered, lifting her chin and staring him square in the eyes. "I dare you, Cole, to be honest with us both. I do not play games."

Cole wanted to strangle her. By thunder, he really did. No doubt he'd intended to encircle her long, elegant neck with his fingers to make his point. But suddenly, he found himself kissing her instead. The beautiful oval of her face was captured between his filthy hands, and his rapacious mouth was driving her head hard against the tree. Rough and demanding, Cole's tongue invaded her, forcing its way past near-bruised lips, to drive deeply and repeatedly into the heat of her mouth. He bracketed her against the bark, trapping her and urging his body stubbornly against hers until he could feel her breasts and belly and warm, sweet thighs mold to his own. Cole neither knew nor cared if Jonet was responding, so savage was his need, so deep was his hurt.

But she *was* responding. Her mouth answered his hungrily. Her breathing rapidly ratcheted up to swift, desperate pants. Soft cries caught in the back of her throat as Cole plundered her mouth. And then, Jonet's eager fingers skimmed beneath his dusty coat to pull him closer still, and something inside Cole simply snapped. As roughly as he had begun, he stopped, jerking his trembling body from hers.

With a muttered oath, Cole lifted the back of his fist to his mouth and stepped away, dropping his gaze to the ground. Shame washed over him. "Fetch your horse, Jonet," he ordered quietly.

Jonet seemed to falter as she followed him away from the tree. "Fetch my horse?" she repeated, her voice soft and incredulous. "Perhaps I shall, after you've told me what that kiss was all about."

Slowly, Cole lifted his eyes to hers. "*That kiss*, damn it, was a lesson. I begin to tire of your willfulness, Jonet. Next time do as I say and just go home with your blasted groom."

"*Do as you say?*" she echoed. Her teasing tone was well and truly gone.

Cole ignored her indignation. "Just saddle up, Jonet. On no account would I make you late for your dinner engagement. Lord Delacourt's delicate soufflé might fall before you arrive."

Hands fisting angrily at her sides, Jonet glared at him. "Why you obstinate, overbearing ass! You are so witless as to defy all logic! Moreover, you know nothing about my dinner engagement!"

"Nor do I care."

"Well, you just asked—!"

"Another of my mistakes, your ladyship! I really wish to hear no more of it."

"Well, fine—!" The fists went to her hips.

Cole narrowed his eyes and lifted his hands heavenward. "Yes! Fine—! Now fetch your mount."

"I daresay that a gentleman would fetch it for me," Jonet insisted, tilting her head toward the horse, which was tethered but a few yards away. She steeled her gaze and pinned him with it.

"I believe, madam," he answered coldly, "that we have already established my many failings in that regard." But Cole relented, and after thrusting his reins into her hand, he stalked off toward her horse.

"Cole," Jonet said a moment later as he lifted her up into the saddle. "I'm sorry." She reached down to pat him lightly on the shoulder. "I really don't think you're an overbearing ass."

"But merely obstinate?" he growled, shoving her left boot in its stirrup and trying hard to maintain his stern expression. "And let us not forget *witless*."

Jonet's brows went up elegantly. "Well, my dear, if the shoe even occasionally fits—?"

Cole was afraid to say anything more. The ride home was long and silent.

Cole and Ellen Cameron dined alone that night. The meal was blessedly simple, and for once, Ellen had little to say. It seemed to Cole that she was distressed by something, but given the rate at which his social skills seemed to be deteriorating, it did not seem wise to broach the subject. Moreover, he had no wish to talk. He was too incensed by the fact that he'd very nearly ravished Jonet in broad daylight. And that Jonet had so boldly gone off to Delacourt's to dine alone with him. Both were scandalous, the former unforgivably so.

Over the meat course, Ellen finally began to talk desultorily about her day, and about the tailor's visit to Stuart and Robert. Then, just as the fruit was served, she shoved back her chair a little abruptly and set the back of her hand to her forehead. For the first time that evening, Cole looked—really looked—at her. All thought of his own tribulations fled at once.

Ellen's face was alarmingly pale, and a fine sheen of perspiration had broken out across her brow. "If you will excuse me, Captain Amherst," she said unsteadily, "I must beg to be excused. I find I do not feel entirely well."

At once, Cole leapt from his chair and snapped his fingers for the footman. Gravely concerned, he circled the table and touched Ellen lightly on the forehead. "She is burning up with fever, Cox," he said quietly. "Fetch Mr. Donaldson at once."

But matters quickly went from bad to worse. Donaldson could not help them. He had taken to his own bed not a quarter hour earlier. Cook, the scullery maid, and the bootboy had quickly followed suit. With Jonet away, in short order, the house was thrown into chaos, as Nanna, Cole, and the footmen rushed up and down the stairs toting water pitchers and chamber pots. Through all the illness, however, a burning fear began to nag at Cole.

In the midst of all the mayhem, Cole managed to pull Nanna to one side. The old woman looked shaken and tired. Cole was himself too terrified to feel anything but the panic that coursed through him. He had not seen cholera since the war, but he knew all too well the symptoms, and to his untrained eye, this looked dangerously like it.

"What is it?" he asked Nanna quietly as a pale housemaid carrying a stack of linen brushed quickly past. "Have you any idea?"

Breathing laboriously, the old woman shook her head and drew a handkerchief from her apron. "I canna say, sir," she answered, mopping her brow. "But whativer it is, 'tis verra quick."

Cole looked at her handkerchief with some alarm. "Good God, you are not—?"

Again, Nanna shook her head. "No, I'm weel enough, but we badly need a physician. I canna manage this."

Cole considered it for a moment. Ellen was beyond helping them, and no one else in the house had lived in Mayfair any longer than he had himself. He rather doubted that any of them knew the local physicians. But there was always Dr. Greaves, Lauderwood's friend. He lived less than half a mile away, and he had been to the house before. Quickly, before he could think the better of it, Cole stopped a passing footman and shouted out an urgent command to fetch Dr. Greaves, giving his address as just "Harley Street." As the frightened fellow darted off to do as he was bid, Cole returned his attention to Nanna.

He kept his voice to a whisper. "Can it be poison?"

Nanna's eyes welled with tears. "Och! What kind of animal could do sich a thing?" Clearly, she, like Cole himself had not wished to consider it. "Oh, I *hope* 'tis only a bloody flux, though God knows that would be bad enough!" The old woman twisted her handkerchief into a knot and looked at Cole a little desperately. "The boys—?"

Cole explained that he had somehow found the presence of mind to confine the boys to Stuart's room and set a footman to guard the door. But an hour later, as one footman fell ill to be replaced by yet another who did the very same, true panic begin to claw at Cole's gut.

Damn it! Where was Jonet when he needed her? The thought of her dining privately with Delacourt—if that was indeed all she had gone to do—had been painful enough. But now her entire household was falling ill, and Cole had no notion of what ought to be done. He had to know just what was happening.

Soon Agnes, the parlor maid, collapsed, and Cole carried her carefully up the back stairs to her room in the attic. It seemed but a matter of time before the boys, and perhaps even himself, became sick. With Donaldson and half the footmen abed, what then? Who would guard the house? Again, he stopped Nanna in the corridor.

"Nanna," he said urgently, " I want you to think over the last two days. Have any strangers been into the household? Has any food been served to part of us, but not the others?" The old woman merely blinked. "*Think,* Nanna!" he insisted. "I am trying to determine who among us may fall ill, and who may be expected to remain healthy. If we cannot determine this, I am very much afraid we need to get the children out of the house."

"Strangers?" Nanna licked her lips uncertainly, then nodded. "Aye, the chimney sweep was here not two days past. And Mrs. Trelawney, the cook across the street, called yesterday w'some clotted cream for Cook." The old woman paused. "That would be all, so far as I know."

Dr. Greaves was blessedly prompt in coming. After he had seen each patient in turn, he met Cole in the corridor. Together, they went into the drawing room, where Cole poured out two generous tots of brandy and motioned the physician toward a chair. With a weary glance, the old man set down his black leather bag, took the glass, and sank into the chair with a deep sigh. "You have a very sick household here, Captain Amherst," he said gloomily. "You must warn her ladyship that the next few days will be crucial indeed."

Cole slid forward in his chair, clasping the brandy snifter between his knees. He really did not like the question he was going to have to ask next. "Please, Doctor, I must know—is there any chance that this is poison?"

"Poison?" The doctor ran a gnarled hand down his face. "What a strange question. But I suppose, under the circumstances . . ." Greaves let his words trail away.

"*Well—?*" Cole grasped the arms of his chair tightly. "Are you saying that it could be?"

The doctor slowly shook his head. "Ordinarily, such a thing would never occur to me, Captain. And in truth, we may never know. But if I had to guess, given the symptoms, I would have to say we are looking at a simple case of dysentery."

"Dysentery?"

The doctor nodded gravely. "Yes, not that there is anything really *simple* about it, mind you. Nonetheless, if the victims are otherwise healthy, there is no reason they cannot survive it."

Still holding his glass, Cole leapt from his chair and began to pace the floor. He *had* to make sure the children were safe. He turned on his heel and stared pointedly at Greaves. "You must understand, Doctor, that young Lord Mercer and his brother are upstairs. There has already been, as you know all too well, one probable poisoning in this house. I must have your assurance that these children are safe."

Greaves shook his head sadly. "That, sir, I would be a

fool to promise. It could be any number of things; poison, spoilt food, or even some contagion. I do wish I could say otherwise, but I cannot."

Cole quickly drained the last of his brandy, then set down the glass with a clatter. "Then I pray you will excuse me, sir. I have things to which I must attend. Thank you for coming."

It took less than ten minutes for Cole and Nanna to dump out the contents of Cole's huge trunk, then shove it full of enough clothing for a long journey. By the time he had managed to drag it downstairs, Jonet's traveling coach was waiting in Brook Street. Then, at the last instant, Cole rushed back up the stairs, unlocked his top desk drawer, and withdrew the brace of pistols he kept secured there. But this was peacetime, not war. He felt inordinately foolish packing them. No doubt Jonet's coachman was in the habit of traveling armed, and there was probably a loaded pistol holstered inside the carriage. And yet, he could not help himself. He shoved them into his saddlebag, his every instinct screaming that this was war. But unlike the battles he had fought before, the enemy was unknown.

In the street below, the coachman was loading two portmanteaus, and together, he and Cole hefted up the trunk. Miraculously, the stable staff seemed to have escaped the illness. But Cole had taken no chances, and he had ordered everyone but the coachman to stay away. As the last leather strap was drawn taut, Nanna rushed the boys out of the house and into the waiting carriage. Quietly, Cole ordered the coachman to drive to Lord Delacourt's.

And they were off. The carriage rumbled slowly down Brook Street, gathering speed en route to Curzon Street, where Delacourt's town house was located. The utter humiliation of what he was about to do chilled Cole's blood. Perhaps he really was mad. Perhaps Delacourt would finally call him out for his audacity. But of course, Cole would have to sacrifice his honor and refuse him, because at present, he had far more important things to worry about than his pride. A small, sleepy voice interrupted his thoughts.

"Sir," Stuart began, his voice grave, "where are we going?"

Cole cleared his throat carefully. "Well, gentlemen, it is to be a surprise." *Yes, and a bloody big one,* he inwardly added. *Especially to me.*

"Oh, I just knew it!" interjected Robert, sitting straight up and clapping his hands with glee. "This is a surprise for my birthday, is it not? I knew—oh, I just *knew* that you and Mama would do something famous!"

"Your—your birthday?" Cole answered awkwardly.

In the dim light of the carriage interior, Cole could see Stuart cut a sidelong glance in his direction. "It's next week," he said quietly, in answer to Cole's unspoken question. As usual, the boy was too bright to be fooled, but his eyes were trusting.

Robert was still babbling. "Oh, yes! Next Thursday, I shall be eight years old!" he continued. "And I have been wishing and hoping and praying for a really wonderful surprise. And since I was so sick of being cooped up, I decided to pray for a trip to the country. That is what I should like above all else, to go to a place where we can ride and play. And that's where we're to go, is it not, Cousin Cole?"

"To—to the country?" echoed Cole.

Grinning, Robert gave a big nod. "Oh, yes. I know. I saw Nanna packing our clothes, just as she does when we're to go to Kildermore. Are we going all the way to Scotland again, sir? Or someplace else?"

Cole hesitated for a moment. "*Er*—someplace else," he answered vaguely.

It rather shocked Cole to realize that until now, he had no notion of where they would go. He had simply promised Nanna he would send word as soon as they were safely out of London. So desperate had he been to get the children out of the house that it had hardly seemed to matter where they went, as long as they went *away* from Mercer House.

Oh, he had thought vaguely of sending them down to Brighton, but there they would be too easily recognized, and Cole would not have been able to remain with them without further tarnishing Jonet's reputation. There was the Lake District, but that was far away. Nonetheless, there were hundreds of pretty little villages with adequate inns where tourists might spend a few weeks in relative obscurity. But suddenly, all of those ill-formed ideas went flying out the carriage window, and Cole knew where they would go. Where he *must* go—eventually. A place where there would be no prying eyes, nor any gossiping tongues.

They would go to Elmwood. Elmwood was little more than a day's journey by coach, and yet, it was far removed from London in a way which had little to do with time or distance. Certainly, there could be no safer place for a boy to romp and enjoy life. He, of all people, should know that. The first eleven years of his life had been spent there in utter boyhood bliss.

To be sure, he did not want to do it. He was not at all certain he was ready to return to the home he had once shared with Rachel, nor to face the memories they had left behind. And yet, what other alternative was left him? At least this way, he did not have to go alone.

Could he do it? *Yes.* But the decision left him feeling inordinately weary—and strangely, more achingly alone than he had felt in a very long time. Slowly, Cole let his head fall back against the velvet squabs and squeezed shut his eyes, feeling the rumble and sway of the well-sprung coach. Suddenly, they lurched hard to the left, and Cole knew without looking that they had made the sharp turn into Curzon Street. Dread lay in his gut like a cold, dead weight. The house was fast approaching. Dinner, even in the most fashionable of homes, would be long over. What would Jonet be doing now?

Cole shut his eyes tighter still, very much afraid he knew. And it hurt. Oh, God yes. It hurt. But he would disturb her—even from that, if he must. And he would shut away the envy and the anger and the pain if it killed him. But what right had *he* to feel angry? Some might call Jonet faithless. He, however, could not fairly do so, despite his ugly words of this afternoon. Jonet was rash, passionate, and deeply sensual—but she was not the wanton he had once believed. As to where she was tonight, Jonet had openly offered him the right to replace Delacourt in her bed, and he had refused her. That had been his choice. He could not now be angry with her for maintaining her relationship with Delacourt. Her lifestyle really was none of his concern.

Or was it? Perhaps her soul *was* his concern. He was ordained, was he not? He had made a commitment to God—albeit one which he had not always honored. In truth, he had strayed badly. He had proven himself unworthy. But no one, he reminded himself, was without sin. And the fact that he had not taken a parish did not obviate his duty to lead others, as best he could, down the path of righteousness.

Suddenly, Cole wanted to snort with disgust. The path of righteousness indeed! Yes, he had helped Jonet find heaven last night, but the only path they had taken had been the one from her sitting room to her bedchamber. He had stripped her naked, had enjoyed—*deeply enjoyed*—carnal knowledge of her body, and then had . . . why, yes—he had *refused* to make an honest woman of her! The fact that her question about marriage had almost certainly been rhetorical was hardly the point.

"Cousin Cole?" Robert's drowsy voice cut through the gloom.

Cole sat up and laid a hand lightly across the boy's knee. "Yes, Robert?"

"Do you think God always answers our prayers?" he mumbled.

"Our prayers?" echoed Cole uncertainly. His palms began to sweat.

"Like when I prayed to go to the country for my birthday," said Robert, his voice fretful from lack of sleep. "I mean—if there is something we need really, really badly, and we ask him for it, does he always give it to us?"

Weakly, Cole smiled at the innocent child. "Oh, yes," he replied softly. "He does indeed. Though not always in just the way we might expect."

And then, in the darkness of the carriage, Cole paused for just a moment to consider carefully what Robert had asked, and to ponder the accuracy of his own response. Perhaps there was some essential truth there; something that had almost escaped him. Something, even, that went far beyond the boy's simple question, or his own inadequate answer.

Suddenly, Stuart's soft voice interrupted his thoughts. "Where exactly in the country are we going, sir?" His tone dropped doubtfully. "And what will Mama say?" Just then, the coach began to slow.

"Why, I am taking you to my house, Stuart," Cole calmly

answered. "It is in Cambridgeshire. And I am going now to fetch your Mama. I am sure she will wish to go, too."

Cole was admitted to Delacourt's imposing town house by a tall, supercilious footman. If the servant was surprised to hear his master's knocker sounding so vigorously at such an hour, he gave no indication of it. Cole had not a second in which to take in his surroundings, for at that precise moment, the sound of rich, unmistakably feminine laughter drifted from what appeared to be a drawing room just beyond the entrance hall. And just as unmistakably, the laughter was Jonet's.

At least, Cole thought ruefully, he would be disturbing them from nothing more intimate than a glass of after-dinner brandy. Only now did he fully appreciate the fact that neither his temper nor his heart could have borne anything more. The realization made him want to shove a fist through the solid slab of oak which constituted Lord Delacourt's front entrance.

Ah, God! What he would have given to avoid coming here and humiliating himself in just such a way. He could already see the haughty, faintly humorous expression on Delacourt's face. But the children came first. Cole drew a deep breath.

"I apologize for the lateness of my call, but I fear I must disturb his lordship and his guest," Cole began, dropping his card onto the small tray the footman produced. "If you would be so kind as to give them this, I think that they will not object to seeing me."

The footman looked at him impassively. "I am very sorry, sir. Lord Delacourt is not at home."

More feminine laughter peeled out of the drawing room, but Cole barely noticed it as his emotions ratcheted up from simmer to boil. "What do you mean, not at home?" Cole demanded. "I know perfectly well that he is here, and that he is entertaining Lady Mercer."

The footman's mouth gaped open ever so slightly, and Cole realized that he should have expected to be refused admittance. But in that moment, the only thing that mattered was speaking with Jonet. Delacourt and his prevaricating servants could go to hell. Cole would not stand in the middle of the hall and plead. Not when time might be of the essence.

Impulsively, he pushed past the footman, who made no real effort to stop him, and strode down the hall toward the drawing room. The doors were already flung open to reveal a well-lit chamber, elegantly furnished in opulent shades of blue and gold. Just inside, two servants were engaged in laying out a coffee service. In his wrath, Cole did not notice that the room was just a little more crowded than he might have expected, and that the coffee service appeared rather generous for two people.

Instead, he stepped brazenly into the room. From across the wide swath of blue and ivory carpet, his eyes were drawn at once to Jonet, who sat in a delicately carved chair, her face alight with a charming, vaguely humorous expression.

"Excuse me, Lady Mercer," he began, his voice overbold, yet uncertain.

Just then, the servants stepped away from the table, and three sets of wide, feminine eyes swiveled toward him. But before Cole could assimilate the fact that Delacourt was nowhere to be seen, Jonet was out of her chair and anxiously crossing the room toward him.

"Cole?" she said apprehensively, her expression stark, her hands reaching out for his. "Cole, what is wrong—?" All of the color had drained from her face.

In the distance beyond her shoulder, Cole was vaguely

aware that an elderly, well-dressed woman was rising somewhat feebly to her feet. Beside her, a plain-looking lady of an uncertain age sprang from her chair to assist. Cole turned his full attention on Jonet as she slid her hands, small and cold, into his. "What is wrong?" she demanded unsteadily. "Tell me!"

"Calm yourself, Jonet," he said softly. "The children are well, but we must speak privately. In fact, circumstances require us to leave here at once. Can you make your excuses to—to these people, and go?"

Only now was it dawning on Cole that Delacourt was not there. Indeed, if one looked closely at the arrangement of chairs about the low table, and at the number of coffee cups laid out upon it, one was forced to conclude that he never had been. Suddenly, Cole realized that he knew nothing of the viscount's private life, and had no notion who these two anxious-looking ladies might be.

Jonet withdrew one hand from his and turned to face them. "Lady Delacourt, Miss Branthwaite," she said rapidly, "I believe you have not the pleasure of knowing my late husband's cousin, Captain Cole Amherst. Cole, this is Lady Delacourt, David's mother, and his elder sister, Miss Charlotte Branthwaite."

His face flushing with heat, Cole made his bow, but Jonet was still speaking. "And now, dear ladies, I must beg you to excuse me. I believe . . ." she returned her gaze to Cole, anxiously searching his face. "I believe that I am needed by my children?"

Cole urged Jonet from the room and down the hall, snaring her wrap from the footman as they passed. He knew that what they had just done had bordered on the edge of insult, but he found himself desperate to rejoin the boys. Mere seconds later, they found themselves standing alone on the front steps. Jonet's coachman leapt eagerly forward, but Cole threw up a staying hand and pulled Jonet a little nearer.

"Jonet, I must explain the situation to you quickly," he said softly, his eyes holding hers in the dim light. "I do not mean to press you, nor did I mean to be rude to your friends, but the boys are waiting in the coach."

Jonet's grip on his arm tightened spasmodically. "But you said they were well—"

"Yes, and I mean to keep them that way," he answered, placing his hands lightly upon her shoulders. "But I regret to tell you that almost everyone else in the house was taken ill tonight, unfortunately Mr. Donaldson and Miss Cameron among them."

Jonet drew in her breath sharply, but Cole continued speaking. "We know not why, nor who will be next. I sent for Dr. Greaves, but he cannot be certain of the cause of the illness, and out of an abundance of caution, Nanna has packed up the children and I have taken them away."

Jonet shook her head as if trying to clear her vision. "I do not understand. Where are you taking them?" Her voice was edged with rising fear.

Cole tightened his grip on her shoulders. "*Us*, Jonet," he said gently. "I am taking *us* to Cambridgeshire. To my estate. I think it is the safest place, but I have told no one as yet, not even Nanna. Please say that you will come with me."

Jonet's expression was tight. "You . . . you think it was poison, do you not?"

Cole shook his head. "No, in truth, both Nanna and Greaves think it's most likely dysentery. Someone—a friend of Cook's—brought clotted cream into the house yesterday. Do you remember eating any?"

Numbly, Jonet shook her head. "No, I . . . cannot think that I did."

"And what about the boys?" Cole urged.

"No." She shook her head more definitely this time. "No, the boys do not care for it."

Cole felt relief surge through him. Perhaps that's all it was, a mere accident. Nothing as black as he had imagined. Still, he could no longer afford to make such assumptions. "Then will you agree to this scheme, Jonet?" he asked, his voice soft, his mouth close to her ear. "Will you come with me to Elmwood? I swear, I will keep you safe. All of you."

Jonet lifted her gaze to his, and Cole could see a little glimmer of hope in her eyes. "Yes, but the boys . . . will they not be frightened?"

Cole shrugged. "Stuart we cannot hope to fool. But Robert thinks that it is a surprise trip for his birthday. I think that will make for as good an excuse as any. Once we are settled, and if none of us has fallen ill, then we can decide what ought next to be done. Or perhaps the doctor will be able to give us clearer guidance."

Mutely, Jonet nodded. Her only remaining questions were for the health of Ellen and her staff, and after reassuring her that they were as well and as comfortable as they could be, Cole bundled her into the carriage. She was immediately greeted by Robert, who hurled himself into her lap with exuberant thanks for his special birthday gift.

12

In which Mrs. Birtwhistle makes a Strategic error

After a late and restless night at a posting inn outside Loughton, they crossed over into Cambridgeshire in the early afternoon, and by teatime, Jonet heard Cole direct the coachman to skirt Cambridge to the east. Their route took them deep into the countryside, through a land so peaceful it made something hard and choking swell in Jonet's throat.

Cole now rode outside on the box, as he had done off and on since leaving London. Inside, however, the confines of the carriage were taking a toll on the boys. Initially, Jonet had anxiously watched them for any sign of illness, sending up a prayer of thanks when none was forthcoming. Quite the opposite, in fact, for they had quickly escalated from curious to rowdy, and were now fast approaching quarrelsome.

The day was hot and thick with the promise of more rain. Jonet's head pounded, and her stomach churned, and twice, as the boys' behavior worsened, she had threatened to cancel the trip, something that really was not an option. Cole would not have brought them here—and would not willingly have traveled in such proximity to her—had he not thought it absolutely necessary.

In truth, Cole had been assiduously avoiding her for the last several days, and almost everything that had occurred between them had been solely due to her maneuverings. She had first cajoled him into her bed, and then begged to accompany him to St. John's Wood, while he had done both without really wanting to.

But now, he was quite obviously taking pains to afford her no such opportunity. Last night at the inn, Cole had taken but one large room for both her and the boys, insisting upon one that was strategically placed at the end of a corridor. Throughout the night, he and the coachman had alternately stood watch outside the room's only door. Where, or even if, they had slept was a mystery to Jonet.

Moreover, she had not failed to notice that he had discreetly covered the crests of her carriage, and had registered them under an assumed name. What else, she wondered, had he done in his quiet, certain way? She had learned not to argue with him. Indeed, she had Cole's quick confidence to thank for this very journey, and although it was frustrating to be traveling just now, Jonet could not but think that what he had done had been for the best. And in truth, she was more eager to see his home than could possibly be wise.

At that very moment, Robert managed to poke Stuart in the ribs with the sharply whittled stick he'd coaxed off the potboy at the last posting inn. Stuart's ensuing scream and Jonet's snapping temper were enough to bring the carriage rocking to a halt. In a trice, Cole was down and jerking open the door.

"Out!" he bellowed, his brows a fretful knot. "Out, you rapscallions! That's quite enough. Up on the box and leave your mother in peace, or I swear, I'll have an inch of hide off the both of you."

Stuart pulled a face. "But sir, he start—"

"Did not!" interjected Robert swiftly.

"Did too!" insisted Stuart, elbowing his brother in the ribs.

Cole's jaw twitched. "I don't care!" he roared, one hand set stubbornly at his hip, the other stabbing violently skyward. "Up on the box! Account yourselves fortunate. At least you'll have something to look at."

The boys trundled out, tails tucked between their legs, though it was nothing but false piety and Jonet knew it. The opportunity to sit atop the box was a rare treat. As Cole settled into the opposite seat and dragged one hand wearily through his wind-tossed hair, Jonet could not suppress the smile that teased at her lips. "You played right into their hands, you know," she said calmly.

The coach lurched forward and the boys squealed with delight. A little defensively, Cole crossed his arms over his chest. "I daresay I did," he finally admitted, his voice softening. "But better that than to have them run you ragged."

Cole sounded so sweet, so truly concerned. Jonet did not know why it inspired her to such devilry and made her forget her pride. "You are very good, sir," she said calmly, her gloved hands folded demurely into her lap. "Not to mention practical and clever—and exceedingly attractive. Are you perfectly sure you'll not reconsider my offer of marriage?"

Cole looked both stunned and mystified, as if she'd clubbed him upside the head with his own cricket bat. "Oh, for pity's sake, Jonet!" he muttered, sinking a little lower in the seat and looking like a man beleaguered. "Not now—! Not on top of all else! I swear, I cannot think straight."

"Very well, *not now,*" she easily agreed. "I allow, it would be inconvenient. But if not now, when?"

Cole stared at her in stark amazement. "When *what?*" he asked, both his logic and his temper clearly frayed.

Jonet feigned total innocence. "*When* might you want to wed me?"

Every blasted minute of every blasted day, for as long as I live, thought Cole darkly. But what he said was, "Jonet, I do not recall your mentioning marriage except as a—a *necessary* measure. I understood you wanted an *affaire*—an offer which, though tempting, I cannot accept."

Suddenly, Jonet looked down and began to carefully rearrange the pleats of her skirts. "Then I am asking you now," she said quietly. "I have always wanted to marry you. There! I've thrown my heart beneath your bootheels! Use me and cast me aside if you will."

"Jonet, be serious," he whispered, letting his head fall back against the squabs. "You cannot possibly wish to wed me."

In obvious frustration, Jonet pummeled her fist into the velvet cushion. "Oh, for pity's sake, Cole!" she fumed, leaning impatiently toward him. "You are supposed to be possessed of a brilliant mind, but I begin to think you have no notion of what I want!"

Suddenly, the carriage lurched sharply, the left wheel striking a deep rut, sending Jonet bouncing off the edge of her seat. Instinctively, Cole reached out to steady her, dragging her slight frame up from the floor. For a long, timeless moment, their faces were almost touching, until slowly, Cole's eyes drifted down to the high swell of her breasts. "Well, I knew what you wanted two nights ago," he softly challenged, the words low and husky. "Did I not?"

"Oh, yes," Jonet admitted, lowering her lashes and turning her face into his. "You certainly did."

Her invitation could not have been more blatant, and as he watched her bottom lip quiver expectantly, Cole's carefully honed self-control blew off its hinges. His burning jealousy, his aching loneliness, and all of the seemingly endless days of despair and desire exploded, melted, then fused into something hot and irrepressible. Heedless of Jonet's attire, he dragged her up and into his lap, crushing her silk gown against him and sending her hat tumbling to the floor.

The kiss was open and carnal from the very first. Desire rose up from his belly unrestrained as her lips opened beneath his, eagerly inviting him to partake, urgently offering herself to him. Not that it would have mattered. The last several hours had driven Cole to near madness. He drove inside her mouth, yearning to take her, to possess her, to meld them together in a way which could never be torn asunder.

Sinuously, Cole wrapped himself around her, entwining their tongues, their arms, and seemingly, their very souls, until his every conscious awareness was of Jonet. He wanted her. God help him, but his blood rushed and his body throbbed with the wanting. And he was no longer sure he could say no to anything she might ask of him, no matter how wrong or imprudent it might be. And so, Cole let himself slide deeper inside, probing, exploring, and leaving Jonet whimpering with need. Through her thin black gloves, her hands were hot and demanding, flowing over him like molten heat, chasing shivers of desire as she touched him. Urgently, boldly, she kissed him back, her breath coming hard and fast.

Sweet heaven, but she was so easy to know. A man would never suffer the frustration of blindly wondering what she wanted. And as Jonet's hand slid up his inner thigh, he realized that what she wanted from him was all too plain. Unfortunately it was nothing he would—or even could—give her in the confines of a traveling coach. However, there was always tonight. *But tonight they would be at Elmwood.*

It was as if someone had dashed a bucket of damp sand over the smoldering embers of his passion. Damn! He was in a carriage. With Jonet and her children. In what was undoubtedly a very treacherous situation, on any number of fronts. And in a few short miles, they would arrive at Elmwood Manor, the one place he really did not wish to go.

Gently, Cole began to pull back, setting Jonet a little away from him. With one last tremulous kiss, her mouth reluctantly left his, her hand coming up to cradle his face so that he could not tear his gaze from hers. The ache he saw in her eyes said it all.

"Stop, Cole," she whispered. "Just stop trying to deny what is between us. What we have both known from the very first."

Cole had not the heart to jerk his face away, but as she had guessed, he could not bear to look at her. "And just what is that, Jonet?" he asked softly, closing his eyes and swallowing hard. "What is it that we both know?"

"That we need each other," she said, sliding reluctantly back into her seat. "That we were meant for one another. That we love one another."

Cole laughed, a hollow, bitter sound. "*Do* you love me, Jonet? Do you even know me? Have you any idea what a life with me would be like?"

Jonet's expression was suddenly sad. "And have you any idea what I want out of life?" she softly returned. "Perhaps that is the better question."

"I know what was meant to be," he said, staring into the depths of the carriage.

"Oh? And what will I do, Cole," she asked, her voice catching on his name, "when all this is over, and you are gone from my life? And please! Do not you dare give me that gratuitous tripe about 'being there' if I need you. I shan't listen any more, do you hear?"

Cole turned his face away to stare through the carriage window at the passing scenery. Every village, even the cow byres and cottages, looked familiar. This was his homecoming, and the green, open landscape should have felt welcoming. He should have felt comforted. But instead, Cole felt as bleak and as lonely as the day he had left it all behind and gone down to Whitehall to join the cavalry. "Perhaps you should marry Delacourt," he said quietly.

"Oh, my God!" Jonet's closed fist crushed into the fabric of her gown. "Is that what this is all about? Is it? I begin to think that the two of you will drive me mad."

Cole turned from the window to look at her impassively. "You seem fond of his mother and his sister," he answered quietly, as if that settled things.

"What—?" she rasped. "I seem *fond* of his family, ergo I should *marry* him? Cole, I play whist with them! I gossip with them! I wish for nothing more!"

"They are of your class, Jonet," Cole gently returned.

Oh, Lord. S*he was going to have to tell him.* Could she? Jonet could think of no other alternative. She had come to need him too desperately to go on without him. And yet, she had no real idea of when she had come to trust him. To love him. But slowly and inexorably, it had happened, and now, when they were apart, her consciousness was spiked with sudden, bittersweet thoughts of him.

If she closed her eyes, she saw him. Not just now, but every waking moment. And in most of her dreams, too. Cole, his spectacles sliding down his nose as he lost himself inside a book. Cole, bent solicitously over her boys, laughing at some inane jest. Cole, making love to her, his head thrown back in mindless passion. There was no escaping it. His strength, his decency, and his intelligence aside, the man was sheer beauty in motion as he walked, or rode, or played cricket with his unerring masculine grace. She could not possibly live her life haunted by memories the likes of those.

She looked at him again, his face bathed in the soft, afternoon sun, which shafted obliquely through the window. As they passed through the trees, the light shifted and changed, alternately shadowing then highlighting his strong, stark beauty. Never had she seen him look so bereft, so horribly alone. And yet, she resisted the impulse to reach out and touch him. It was not what Cole wanted.

And what of Cole? What about his needs and his wishes? Perhaps she was far too presumptuous in assuming that she knew what was best for him. God knew he was a strong and brave man who would fight valiantly for her. But perhaps not for himself, not against his own demons. Moreover, Jonet could not escape the belief that they were meant to be. In her arms, she had seen his almost unfailing reserve collapse. With her, he could be both firm and tender, in just the way she needed, but she had seen the wild abandon that took hold of him as he spilt himself inside her. And she had felt the peace that had flowed between them afterward.

He made her a better person, and returned to her some small part of the innocent girl she longed to be again. And she had dragged him from the shadows, to make him feel passion and anger and yes—*love* again. Oh, they were complete opposites in almost every way, but they made one another whole. Did he not feel that metaphysical symmetry—that bone-deep sense of emotional completion—as much as she did? Surely he must! Still, David stood between them. What would he say about all this? Jonet suspected he already knew where her heart was. And perhaps he was none too pleased. But David wanted her to be happy, did he not? And if that meant having Cole in her life, then David would simply have to accept her decision.

But would Cole? Certainly not without explanation. Nonetheless, many lives were at risk of ruin. And yet, after all that she and David had been through—the denial, the guilt, and ultimately, the deep and ceaseless devotion that no one else could ever understand—she knew that he wanted her to move forward with her life. To go beyond him, and find the man who was right for her.

And damn it all, she had. Oh, yes. And she would not let him go without a fight.

Cole sensed the turn to Elmwood long before Jonet's coachman slowed his team and drove them expertly between the tall brick gateposts. The gate itself was open, but the tiny gatehouse stood empty. Surely they were expected? He had sent a messenger ahead from the inn at Loughton. But as the carriage spun down the drive beneath the double row of old elms that sent the shadows sweeping over them, Cole's heart was filled with foreboding. The crunching gravel, the rhythmic sound of the horses' hooves, all served to heighten his anxiety. Good Lord, this had been a dreadful mistake. He ought not to have come here. He ought never to have come back again.

Abruptly, he reached forward and let down the glass, shifting his weight as if to look out through the window. Jonet's hand came out to gently stay him.

"She is not there, Cole," Jonet whispered gently. "There is nothing to see."

"I don't know what you mean," he answered, jerking back into his seat.

"Rachel," she said, her mouth forming the word almost silently. "Rachel is gone, Cole. I know how you feel, but that part of your life is over."

Cole opened his mouth to tell Jonet that it was hardly

her business, and that she knew nothing at all about what he felt. But in truth, she already knew a great deal more than he wanted her to. And perhaps it was very much her business. Was it? Was he about to make his life her concern? Was he about to foolishly lay open his heart and soul to this woman who seemed already to know him with the intimacy of an old lover?

He simply did not know. And at present, he was beyond thinking about it. The house was very near now. The carriage went rumbling over the bridge, and he could feel the coachman beginning to make the sweeping arc into the tight circular driveway. He could hear the happy cries of the boys as they sat perched upon the box. And then they rolled slowly to a stop.

Jonet's coachman leapt down to help the boys, and Mrs. Birtwhistle rapidly descended the front stairs to stand in the driveway, her spindly arms thrown open wide. Reluctantly, Cole pushed open the door and dropped down without the steps. Then, there was nothing for it but to catch his housekeeper in his arms and give her a little twirl. After all, she seemed to expect it. Certainly, she deserved it. She had known him and loved him since he was in leading strings, and for the last six years, he had more or less ignored her.

"Oh!" said Mrs. Birtwhistle breathlessly, when he'd set her down again. "Why, we'd begun to think, sir, that you might never come home again, and look how wrong we were! Oh! It will be just like old times!" The housekeeper let her eager, expansive gaze drift from the children to Jonet, who was being handed down by her coachman. She rushed forward a pace. "And please, ma'am, may I be the first to congratulate you?"

Jonet, whose rapt eyes had been drifting over the façade of

the house, immediately dropped her chin and smiled sweetly at the housekeeper. "Congratulate?" she said vaguely.

Too late, Cole realized he should have seen it coming. He should have leapt forward and clapped a silencing hand over Mrs. Birtwhistle's mouth. Instead, he froze as she blurted out the words, "Oh, congratulations indeed, ma'am! Why, we'd begun to fear that Mr. Amherst would never bring us a new mistress. And may I say we are all just beside ourselves with pleasure."

For a split second, Jonet's mouth hung gracelessly open. Then, as usual, her composure returned in full force. She gave a gracious laugh and leaned companionably forward, patting the old woman on the arm. "Oh, my dear Mrs. Birtwhistle!" she said lightly. "On that score, I must warn you that we are both one step ahead of Mr. Amherst."

"A step . . . ahead?" The old woman looked disconcerted.

"Indeed, ma'am, I am quite shocked at your acuity!" Jonet cut a teasing look in Cole's direction, then dropped her voice to an intimate whisper. "You see, I have indeed set my cap at him, but I have not yet convinced him."

"What sort of cap, Mama?" asked Robert vaguely, lifting his head from the fat, and rather obviously pregnant cat, which he and Stuart had been petting.

"Oh, my!" said the housekeeper, her attention snapping back to Cole. "But your message said—" A little desperately, she began to pat her apron pockets. "I had it right here, and I thought it said that . . . well, that there was a lady and her children to be made at home . . . and I daresay we mistook your meaning, and thought . . ."

Cole laid his hand lightly upon Mrs. Birtwhistle's arm. "Heaven only knows what my message may have said, ma'am," he said soothingly. "I wrote it in such haste, I wanted only to do you the courtesy of letting you know that our arrival was imminent. And I am sure that you have prepared as best you can on such short notice."

His remarks seemed to further distress poor Mrs. Birtwhistle. "Oh!" she remarked, one hand flying to her mouth in horror. "And I have made up the family rooms on the second floor."

"The second floor?" interjected Jonet brightly as her coachman began to toss down luggage. "I am sure that will do nicely. I always say that two is such a lucky number, do I not, my dear?" She slid her fingers possessively beneath Cole's elbow and shot him another spectacular smile.

The housekeeper looked as if she might say something more, but Cole simply nodded. "Mrs. Rowland is right, Mrs. Birtwhistle," he interjected, using the name they had agreed upon. "The second floor suite will suffice."

It was almost five by the time Cole finished reacquainting himself with his meager household staff, and nearer to six by the time he concluded his discussions with Moseby regarding the status of estate business. Overall, Moseby and his tenants had managed to patch things together during his absence, but after years of near neglect, many pressing issues demanded his personal attention. Time and again, he had cause to question the wisdom of his having stayed away so long.

Now, barns and granaries were urgently needed. Tenant houses required new roofs before another winter passed. The livestock required an infusion of new blood, and some serious decisions needed to be made regarding drainage and crops for the coming season. It seemed as if there was enough work to keep Cole at Elmwood for a full year without so much as an afternoon off. Here. Alone with his memories. It was a daunting prospect.

As the door to his father's old study swung shut behind Moseby, Cole crossed the room to a side table by the window and poured out a measure of brandy. His gaze drifted over the scene below—the perfectly trimmed grass, the graceful symmetry of the rose arbor, the cheerful white belvedere, all of it framed in a high hedge of boxwood—and he thought faintly of Rachel. How often had he watched her, just strolling through that garden in her quiet, solitary way?

He stood at the window for a long moment, simply swirling the amber liquid in his goblet and staring down into the shadows, both real and imagined. But that simply would not do. He tried to will away the vision. Through the open glass, he allowed himself to breathe deeply of the scents of warm boxwood, fresh grass, and newly tilled earth, discovering with some surprise that they were still quite comforting. Oh, yes. He had been away too long. He had left too many things ill tended, his own heart and soul amongst them, perhaps.

Suddenly, a shriek of feminine laughter tore through the silence, and Cole's eyes shifted to the little wooden belvedere that sat in a distant corner of the garden. Behind it, young Stuart appeared to be forcibly dragging his mother out of the shrubbery. "Found you, found you!" he chanted triumphantly. "Fair and square, Mama! Now you must seek while Robin and I hide!"

But Jonet was apparently unwilling to accept her fate with anything near ladylike grace. Still giggling, she resisted him mightily. A sprig of boxwood appeared to be protruding from her hair, which was rapidly tumbling down, and her skirts were a mess of dust and cobwebs. The hem of her black dress was caught on a dry twig, revealing a lovely ankle and a goodly portion of her well-turned calf.

Stuart jerked her free, then clapped his hands with delight, looking suddenly like the little boy he was supposed to be. Moving backward, he danced away from his mother. "Now, Mama, you must be sporting about it. Count, and go slowly now! You mayn't cheat."

Cole watched, entranced, as Jonet sweetly agreed, and then in a sudden flash of motion, darted across the open lawn after Stuart. She caught him easily, pulling him down into the warm, sweet grass and kissing him madly. Stuart shrieked and laughed, struggling to escape until his mother gave him one last kiss atop his head and then set him free.

"Aye, Stuart," Cole muttered under his breath as he tossed off a goodly portion of his brandy. "That's the way of her alright. Sweet one moment, willful the next. And before you know it, she's got you down and having her way with you."

But of course, Stuart could not hear him. He was off and running, his brother and their effervescent laughter trailing in his wake. Slowly, Jonet strolled up the steps into the belvedere, shut her eyes, and began to count in a loud, ominous voice. Tearing his gaze from the scene, Cole smiled, put down his drink, and went down the hall to begin to dress for dinner. It was only later—much, much later—that Cole truly understood that the sight of Jonet kissing her son in the lush summer grass had obliterated his irrational association between the memory of his late wife and the beauty of his garden.

Jonet could not stop looking at Elmwood. At its architectural core, the house was an elegant Elizabethan manor house, modernized with a brick façade and two graceful wings, the whole of it nestled like a rare jewel amongst ancient trees and simple gardens, then ringed with a moat, which had long since been permanently bridged.

Other than an hour spent romping in the gardens with the children, Jonet spent the whole of her first afternoon simply strolling through its elegantly landscaped perimeter, then drifting inside from one comfortable room to the next. The interior was rambling, and for the most part, cozy rather than ostentatious. The main hall boasted a sweep of darkly paneled walls and a fine Jacobean staircase. A dining room large enough to seat twenty, and a long, dark library completed the picture of country house elegance.

Cole had said that the house had once been the vicarage of St. Ann's, a fine old Norman church that sat at the southern edge of the village proper, hardly a stone's throw from Elmwood's rear lawns. If the cerebral tomes which filled the library, and the portraits of those long dead clerics which lined the upper hall were any indication, Elmwood had remained a vicarage, practically speaking, until very recently. Jonet was left to wonder what sort of tragedy could drive a man from a home he clearly loved, and a duty he was so obviously meant to take up.

In the drawing room, she began to understand. The portrait of Cole's late wife was set in a gilt frame, hanging high on the carved oak chimneypiece, the style of the clothing leaving little doubt as to the identity of the artist's subject. Rachel Amherst had been a traditional English beauty, with cool blonde hair and pale blue eyes. She had been painted in a high-backed Stuart chair, one hand resting limply along the arm, and the other lying across the Bible she held open in her lap. But it was the expression—or rather a lack of it—that brought Jonet to a halt in the center of the room.

She strolled closer, bracing her hands across the back of a settee that flanked the hearth, and leaned intently forward. The late Mrs. Amherst looked . . . *detached,* almost as if she were unaware of being painted. It was not a weakness of technique on the part of the artist. Nor was it a modesty of expression in the subject. But rather, a dull, almost placid look about the eyes. A sort of shuttered appearance which seemed to close in her own thoughts while shutting out the thoughts of those about her. Jonet's reaction was strangely visceral, as if icy fingers were touching the nape of her neck.

"Oh, she was a fair, pretty thing, was she not?" said a soft voice behind her.

Jonet screamed and whirled about.

"Oh!" chirped Mrs. Birtwhistle, setting down a huge vase of flowers and hastening toward the settee. "My dear Mrs. Rowland! I fear I rather crept up on you. Do forgive me."

Jonet looked down at the tiny woman and felt her face flush with embarrassment. "Oh, please!" she said, one hand still pressed to her heart. "I daresay I had no business snooping through the house like this, it's just that . . ."

Mrs. Birtwhistle nodded knowingly. "Aye, what with himself shut up in that study all the live long afternoon, like as not you're bored to death. But 'twill soon be time for dinner, ma'am, and if I know Mr. Amherst—and bless me, I do—he'll not be missing a meal."

The housekeeper flitted across the room to a wide mahogany sideboard. "Now, why do you not sit down right there, Mrs. Rowland, and let me pour something to settle your nerves."

In a moment, she returned with a measure of something that looked to be sherry, and Jonet sipped at it gratefully. Mrs. Birtwhistle, who was still looking at her expectantly, seemed disinclined to leave, and so Jonet seized the moment. "You have been here for some years, I take it?" Jonet asked pleasantly, letting her eyes drift toward the portrait. "I daresay you knew the late Mrs. Amherst well."

"Oh, yes," agreed the housekeeper. "She came here as a bride in '06, and stayed until she died, some four years later. Such a pity it was, too."

"She died in childbirth, did she not?" asked Jonet, deliberately keeping her tone level.

Mrs. Birtwhistle nodded sadly. "Indeed she did, poor woman. But I cannot say as how I was entirely surprised."

"Not surprised—?"

The elderly woman shrugged. "Well, it's not my place to say, ma'am, but she had that look about her, if you know what I mean. That wan sort of look—like a person who's not really a part of this earth, and just not terribly interested in it, either. Sort of like a—a fading away, before your very eyes."

"I think I have some idea of what you mean," said Jonet softly.

"Do you? It's fanciful talk, I daresay. But when the babe came, I was proven right—though I took no pleasure a'tall in it. Never had a chance, poor thing."

"Never had a chance? In what way?"

Mrs. Birtwhistle shook her head sadly. "Breech, it was. She labored for three days and simply had not the strength to deliver it. And by the time she did, well, 'twas simply too late."

"Oh, dear," answered Jonet hollowly. "How dreadful."

"Well, these things do happen, and 'twas no one's fault. Though that Mr. Moseby does say the master blamed himself when word came. But he oughtn't think such things, for he was a fine husband. Always bending over backward for her, and she seemed scarcely to notice. And she had the best of care for her confinement, and a fine doctor, too." Lightly, the housekeeper stroked the back of the settee, as if soothing a skittish colt. "But there now, Mrs. Rowland, let's not talk of that any more, shall we?" Her smile brightened. "Mr. Amherst has come home at last—and one oughtn't fret over the past."

Sleep did not come easily that night. Cole had not expected that it would, and so he had fortified himself with an extra pillow, a pair of lamps, and a well-thumbed copy of Milton's Latin elegies from his father's library. As he thumped his pillows into submission, Cole tried to take comfort in the fact that although his heart—perhaps even his sanity—might be at risk, at least the children were safe.

Everyone now slept in the family rooms on the second floor. Cole had deliberately given Stuart and Robert a large bedchamber to share, and placed Moseby on a cot in their dressing room. The man was a notoriously light sleeper, and his quick response had sent more than one careless French scout on to his great reward rather sooner than expected.

Yes, the children would be safe with Moseby. And as he had told Jonet over dinner, tomorrow he would send someone to speak discreetly with Donaldson to find out what, if anything, was known about the outbreak of illness at Mercer House. Then, as soon as it could be safely done, Ellen or Nanna—even Donaldson, if she wished it—could be brought to Elmwood, to stay as his guests until they had decided what next to do.

But he had made it plain that under no circumstance would he tolerate Lord Delacourt under his roof, nor would he even accept so much as her writing to inform him of their whereabouts. Jonet had jerked back, as if he had dealt her a physical blow. Nonetheless, after a short argument, she had reluctantly acquiesced. Cole only hoped that she would keep her word, because as soon as it could be safely arranged, it was Cole's intention to return to London alone. It was time, he had firmly decided, to have a long talk with Dr. Greaves and the magistrate about just who was behind the dreadful goings-on in Brook Street.

Through the dim light, Cole scowled at the door which led through his modest dressing room, linking his bedchamber to Jonet's. It was the devil's own temptation, that bloody connecting door. And there was yet another inexplicable thing—what the hell had he written to Mrs. Birtwhistle, anyway? She was old and a little flighty, but far from incompetent. Undoubtedly, he had written something that was as vague and misleading as the conflict which raged within his heart.

Slowly, as if he had willed it, his dressing room door creaked open, and Cole watched, transfixed, as Jonet appeared in a flowing wrapper, which caressed her body in all the right places. The soft fabric almost shimmered as she moved across the room, and Cole knew instinctively that she was naked beneath. In one hand, she cradled two glasses, and dangling from her fingertips, she carried a loosely corked bottle of wine. A wicked smile curved her lips.

"I pilfered your cellar," she blithely confessed, sauntering toward the edge of his bed.

Peering at her over his spectacles, Cole sighed, then closed his book and laid it to one side. "Why does that not surprise me, Jonet?"

With another faint smile, she leaned provocatively forward to put down her burdens on his night table, allowing her cloud of black hair to fall forward and her wrapper to slide open invitingly. "Really, Cole," she said throatily, as she pulled away the bedcovers and sat down to face him, "you did not honestly expect that I would be able to resist this, did you?"

"I do not suppose," he finally said, watching as she leaned gracefully forward and removed his spectacles, "that there is any point in telling you that you have no business whatsoever being alone with me in my bedchamber? Nor in warning you that we might be caught out?"

Jonet merely shook her head. "None whatsoever," she agreed. "If you're caught compromising my dubious virtue, you'll just have to wed me. But I daresay we both locked our doors, *did we not?*" She looked at him knowingly, one fine black brow quirking up.

"Yes," he confessed, his voice thick with sudden need. "Very . . . *tightly.*"

His heart in his throat, Cole watched Jonet's breasts shift and sway as she leaned over to fill the wineglasses. She made no secret of—nor any apologies for—what she wanted. And there was no doubt whatsoever that he wanted her. In fact, if he were completely honest, he would admit that his cock had been half hard since seeing her tumbling in the grass with Stuart this afternoon.

Inside, however, the memory of the last night he'd spent in Jonet's arms was as tender as a new wound. Oh, she had wanted him then, too. But he had very much feared that it was only that, and nothing more. And yet, today on the long carriage ride from Loughton, Jonet had very nearly laid open her heart to him. She loved him, she had said. She wanted to marry him—and in her usual obstinate way, Jonet had simply thrown her pride to the wind and asked.

Cole still did not see how it could possibly work, when he had nothing whatsoever to offer her. But abruptly, he found himself sitting fully up in bed and leaning forward to kiss her, threading his fingers lightly into the soft hair at her temples, cradling her face in his big, rough hands, and pushing his lips gently against hers.

"*Oh!*" she said breathlessly, as if the tenderness of his gesture shocked her. And then she kissed him back. Once, twice. And a third time, with her lips softly parted, her tongue lightly seeking. And then, with a shudder, she eased him gently back into the heap of pillows. "Let us be patient for once," she whispered hesitantly. "We have all night. I would have us learn about one another. May we do that, Cole?"

Ruthlessly, Cole stomped his fire down to a smolder and banked it. "As you wish," he agreed, lowering his lashes as he captured her hand and dragged her inner wrist to his mouth.

"*Cole—!*" His name came out on a sigh. "If you run that wicked tongue of yours down my arm again," she warned, "I shan't be accountable for the noise."

"Very well," he reluctantly agreed, restoring her hand to her lap. At once, she leaned forward and took up the wine glasses, now full, and passed one to him. Then, cradling the bowl of the glass in her palm, she tucked her knees under her wrapper and wriggled herself a little closer, until her hip was nestled companionably next to his thigh and they faced one another.

Cole held her eyes and raised his glass, lightly tapping the rim of hers. "To you, my dear. Now, what dread secret would you have me confess?"

Jonet looked suddenly mischievous again, her fingers snaking forward to toy with the throat of his nightshirt. "Well . . . first of all, I should very much like to know if you always wear clothes to bed?" She wrinkled her nose ever so slightly.

Cole felt a faint warmth flush across his face. "Not always, Jonet. But a nightshirt hardly constitutes *clothing*."

Deftly, Jonet slipped the single button loose and turned back the shirt facing to let her fingers play lightly down his chest. "That may be," she agreed, her voice soft and throaty. "But be aware, sir, that if I can persuade you to marry me, I intend to cut them all up into dust cloths."

Her hands felt like fire playing down his chest. "Jonet," he rasped, watching in fascination as her fingertips stroked lightly across his left nipple. "I really don't think we can have any meaningful conversation if you keep doing that."

Jonet's heated gaze came up to catch his. "Yes," she admitted, her lips parting softly. "You are perfectly right. Whatever was I thinking?" And then slowly, she returned the wineglasses to the table and began to unfasten her wrapper. Cole watched in wordless anticipation as she pulled open the silky fabric, letting it slither off her shoulders to pool around her hips, revealing her high, full breasts and her softly rounded belly.

Boldly, with her catlike grace, Jonet shifted her weight to climb over him, leaving her wrapper behind, tangled in his sheets as she straddled his knees. Then, she bent elegantly forward to slide her hands beneath the fabric of his nightshirt, pushing it to his waist, leaving his bare skin trembling with anticipation. Jonet's eyes never left his as her hands skimmed back down the jut of his heavy hipbones, then smoothed across the shivering plane of his stomach, and lower still, until she found what she wanted. "*Umm*," she said, the sound more of a moan than a spoken word.

"*Ah—!*" Cole sharply exhaled as Jonet took him, her strong, perfect fingers lacing tightly about the base of his rigid shaft, the other lightly cupping his testicles.

Cole had made love *to* a good many women, but in the whole of his thirty-four years, he could never recall having been made love to *by* a woman. However, despite the haze of sensual delirium which was rapidly possessing him, he realized that that was Jonet's precise intention. Cole had no more strength with which to resist her. And so he simply gave himself up to the inevitable, reveling in the long strokes of her firm, strong hands, and savoring the heat of her womanhood across his legs. But when her hair swept down over his belly, and he felt her breasts brush his thighs, the haze abruptly cleared, and his hands came up to stay her shoulders. "*No, Jonet—!*" he heard himself rasp. "Not like *that!*"

"Why?" Her voice was tender, the question soft. "Why may I not love you, Cole—in every way I feel drawn to?"

Why not, indeed? Because it was something only whores did? Because it was something he himself had rarely experienced? But Jonet's breathless plea made the first reason seem blatantly wrong. And the second was just a feeble excuse, tendered in the faint hope of holding back a part of himself from this woman who already threatened to possess him body and soul.

His hesitation was answer enough. Jonet's mouth was on him, drawing his shaft deep into her warmth as she caressed and stroked him up and down, slicking him with moisture, her tongue encircling and enticing him with ribbons of fire, her hand tight about his throbbing base. First enthralled, then wildly excited, Cole let his hands drift down to thread through her hair, resisting the impulse to both push her away, and to drag her nearer. She loved him greedily, wickedly, for long, timeless moments, until Cole hung suspended between exquisite pain and perfect pleasure. Until he was left straining upward with a desperate, visceral hunger, arching off the bed, and dragging her upward.

"Inside," he rasped harshly, his fingers digging into the flesh of her upper arm. Yet he was barely certain he had spoken the word aloud. Roughly—too roughly—he pulled at her shoulders, dragging her mouth from his pulsing cock. "I want inside you *now!*" he demanded, and this time Jonet's head jerked up, her eyes wide and limpid, her lush mouth wet and gasping. Obediently, she slid up his length, straddling his shaft.

"*Now, Jonet!*" he begged, his tone softer, his hands instinctively sliding around to lift and part her buttocks. Balanced delicately atop him, Jonet nodded mutely, then tipped back her head and impaled herself downward in one long, perfect stroke.

"Oh, God," Cole heard himself groan.

Jonet let out her breath in a whispery sigh, then lifted herself up and glided enticingly down again. Over and over she moved, until knowingly, his hands left the sweet weight of her hips and slid over her thighs. Settling one hand over the soft, damp curls of her mound, he let his fingers ease between her swollen folds, through the warm heat, and back again, to find what he knew would be her hard, eager nub. And it was. *Ah, yes!* It was.

He brushed it once, lightly, with the ball of his thumb, and Jonet began to pant wildly, her hair curling enticingly around rose-pink nipples that were hard and erect. She lifted herself high and slid down once more. After that, it was over very quickly. Jonet's thighs worked feverishly as she rode him, her tight feminine sheath pulsing up his length as she came, rendering him powerless, sucking the very life from him.

"*Oh . . . oh . . . oh . . . !*" she gasped. His hips came up, forcing her weight fully off the bed as Cole strained, mindlessly pouring into her. And then, he felt the sheets, cool against his back, and Jonet's weight falling forward to bear him deeper into the softness of the bed.

"Oh, my God," she whispered tremulously, her lips somewhere near his earlobe.

And then, the room was plunged into a deep, restful silence. Through the open window, a light breeze stirred across the bed, carrying with it the soothing sounds of a country night. After years of often sleeping out of doors, Cole could not bear being shut in. Now, it felt good to be away from London, in his own home, in his own bed, with the woman who was—or perhaps *could be*—his as well.

"Jonet?" Cole said softly, after they had drowsed for a bit. "Why did you come here? Was it for this? Or did you really wish to talk?"

"*Umm,*" answered Jonet sleepily, bracing her hands on his shoulders and pushing herself up to look at him. "All of those things, I daresay," she murmured absently, her eyes fixed upon his lips. Her mouth parted softly, and then she was kissing him again, pushing her lips against his and gently nibbling at one corner of his mouth.

"Have mercy, Jonet!" he muttered, urging her away. "I begin to fear you are insatiable."

"No," she said against his mouth, "you are irresistible." But finally, with obvious reluctance, she rolled off and stretched languidly out beside him. "Do you want the truth?" she asked quietly, after a long moment had passed.

Cole's experience at pillow talk was almost nonexistent, yet he knew instinctively that the answer was a resounding *no*. "Of course," he bravely lied.

To delay the inevitable, Jonet reached down to pull up the covers, then settled her head on his shoulder. Good heavens, but he smelled wonderful. Warm and faintly spicy, and underneath it all, the subtle tang of male sweat and sated desire. She drew in the scent of him, skimming one hand down his chest to rub little circles over his belly. "I like the way you smell," she murmured against his collarbone.

Swiftly, Cole's hand snared hers and dragged it back to his chest, pressing it over his heart and covering it with his own. "Don't change the subject, my dear," he warned. "You started this."

Jonet sighed and shifted a little away from him. "I just want to know about your life here at Elmwood. What were you like as a boy? What did you love? What did you dream?" she softly explained, staring up into the depths of the ceiling. "And I want to know if . . . if you slept here—in this bed—with Rachel, your wife. I want to know if you loved her. I want to know what she meant to you."

Cole dragged in his breath harshly. The tension rising inside him was almost tangible. "I never slept in this bed with Rachel," he said quietly, his gaze cutting toward the connecting door. "I always went to her room. May we let it go at that?"

"No," she whispered, but despair and doubt were swelling like a tide in Jonet's chest. She prayed she was not pushing this tenuous relationship too fast, and in the wrong direction.

Suddenly, Cole's arm snaked around her shoulder. His mouth came down against her brow, and she could feel his lips moving lightly against her skin as he spoke. "I never loved her, Jonet," he said softly. "Not in the way a husband ought. And what she meant to me was . . . hope. And a symbol of commitment to—to God, I suppose. I don't even know any more."

Jonet tucked her arm about his waist. "I think I understand," she said softly. "Will you—will you tell me about her? How you met her? What she was like?"

And so, for the next hour or better, Cole found himself doing precisely that. It was hard at first, and yet he found himself telling Jonet things he had never shared with another human being; truths and dreams and fears he had hardly understood himself. And somewhere in the process, he could never remember precisely when, the talk turned to his childhood, to the death of his parents, and to the cold, barren years spent under the auspices of Lord James Rowland. Strangely, peace began to flood his soul.

At some point, Jonet sat up in bed and refilled their wineglasses. By one o'clock in the morning, the bottle was as depleted as Cole's angst. By two, he had rolled Jonet onto her back and was thrusting deep inside her again; riding her hard and long, with no sense of her urgency or desperation, and no need to come again. Just slowly and quietly loving her, until she cried out softly, and rose up tight against him, tangling her fingers in his hair and curling her legs snugly above his hips.

Again, he slept. Deeply and dreamlessly this time, with no thought of the future and no fear of the past. There was only the present, and Jonet, her legs entwined with his, her arms tight about him. And then he was awake, but barely so, and Jonet was loving him, with her hands and her mouth, coaxing him to erection, teasing at his nipples with the hot, hard tip of her tongue.

Ah, how he needed her, this wild, reckless woman with her blue-black eyes and wicked hands. His desire had long ago turned to obsession, and had he been in his right mind, he would have known it and feared it. But tonight, he wanted only to make her his, and in a way no man ever had, or ever would again. Rachel—poor Rachel! She had never even tried to be woman enough for him. But Jonet—oh, she might send him to an early grave from sheer exhaustion.

Drowsily, he rolled over and dragged his weight on top of her, spreading her legs wide and pressing her down into the mattress. "What do you want, Jonet?" he asked hoarsely, his mouth open against the curve of her neck, his palms skimming up her arms, over her narrow shoulders, until he cradled her face between his hands. "Tell me."

Jonet sighed deeply, reveling in the weight of him, and in the feel of his hardness probing at her entrance. "Now?" she asked teasingly, one leg crooking high above his hips. "Or ten minutes from now? Or forever?"

Cole's head jerked up abruptly, his gaze clear and wide awake. "Forever," he said certainly.

13

The Widow Rowland gets what She deserves

By the light of the lamp, which had not yet burned itself out, Jonet stared into his eyes. The brilliant, golden gaze was back. The seriousness of it startled her, and she swallowed hard and jerked her eyes away. "I want . . . I want my children to be safe," she said, listening as her voice caught, and not fully understanding where the words had come from. "I want my children to be safe, and I want you to love me."

"I love you, Jonet," he said softly, letting his head fall forward until their foreheads touched. "You know that I do."

"Yes," she answered, certain that he spoke the truth.

"And your children are safe here with me," he softly vowed. "I swear it."

For a long moment, Jonet was silent. Slowly, she shifted from beneath him and crawled from the bed, then stared down to drink in the long, glorious length of him, stretched across the tumbled linen. Despite her sudden flash of fear and uncertainty, she knew that this night was not about her. It was about him. This man, who left her wild and breathless with the sheer beauty of his body, who made desire fist tight and hard in the pit of her belly. Cole was taut strength and hard bone, sinewed and muscled, and all of it protecting a heart that was honest and gentle and brave.

Slowly, she reached out her hand to him. "Come with me," she said softly. "Come to my bed, Cole, and love me again. Then fall asleep in my arms and stay with me there 'til morning."

His jaw hardened at an obstinate angle. It was abundantly clear he meant to refuse her. The memory of a cold wife—and perhaps an even colder bed—lay on the other side of that wall. But by heaven, Jonet meant to get rid of it. Slyly, she crooked one finger in invitation. "Come, sir," she teased. "Do you fear you're not man enough to please me again?"

Lightning quick, his hand lashed out, snaring her wrist and dragging her fingers to his mouth. Boldly holding her gaze, Cole drew her index finger between his lips and sucked deeply, suggestively, offering pleasure, promising ecstasy. Her womb tightened with a need that should not have been possible, and for a moment, Jonet was terribly tempted.

She could not get enough of touching him, or being touched by him, and when he jerked her closer to the edge of the bed, she came willingly, allowing his hand to slide down her belly and between her legs. Spearing his fingers through her damp nest of curls, Cole growled low in his throat and let his fingers probe, sending fire coursing through the pit of her stomach and up her spine, until her nipples drew taut and a deep, keening moan escaped her lips. Restlessly, she moved against his hand, instinctively shifting her hips back and forth as he deliberately tried to coax her back into his bed.

And then she remembered her purpose. Her hand came down to take his, gently easing his fingers from her wetness, and urging him out of the bed. Reluctantly, he stood, then dragged her into his embrace, letting the heat of his hands play over her flesh. "Mmm . . . *yes,*" he murmured, his fingers tracing over her breasts and hips, making her quiver. "That's it, my love. Come back. Come back to bed and let me pleasure you once more," he crooned, bending his head to her throat and sliding his tongue slowly upward.

"Oh, God, Cole," Jonet heard herself sigh as his fingers slid inside her again, his teeth nipping hard at the tender skin of her throat. Her knees went weak, and she shivered with need as he bit her again, more gently this time, sucking her flesh between his teeth and softly moaning.

Lord, but he was an obstinate man! Determinedly, she took a step backward, and he followed. He caught her and kissed her, then brushing his mouth over hers, he surged seductively inside on a long, endless stroke. "Don't you want it, sweet?" he murmured against her lips, lifting her high against his erection and urging himself against her. "Don't you want me to slide this deep inside you just one more time?"

"Yes—no—" she stuttered, feeling his shaft throb demandingly against her mound. "Yes, but in *my* bed, Cole.

Now—!" She jerked away, snatched up one lamp, and fled, leaving him standing in the middle of his bedchamber.

"My God, you're a willful woman," he growled, pursuing her across the floor, through the dressing closet, to stand in the center of her bedchamber, his hands set stubbornly atop his narrow hips. Jonet set down the lamp, flung herself diagonally across her bed, and looked at him through lowered lashes. Cole's face was a mask of lust and torment.

"Must you," he asked coldly, "always have your way?"

Jonet did not answer. Instead, she rolled onto her back and let her hand slide down her belly. Slowly, very deliberately, she parted her legs and began to caress herself, stroking one finger back and forth, then slicking it around and around. She watched as Cole's eyes glazed over with passion and his breathing became fast and shallow. Still, he stood obstinately in the middle of the room, his frustration warring with his lust. "*Mmmm . . .* you like to watch this, do you not, Cole?" she whispered thickly, letting her hips arch ever so slightly off the bed.

"What do you want of me, Jonet?" he rasped. "I've had about all I can take tonight."

Ignoring his question, Jonet continued to touch herself. "But I do not think, darling, that you would wish me to come like this? Not alone. Not here in this big, empty bed."

"No," he harshly retorted. "I would *not* wish it. Not tonight, at any rate."

With calculated deliberation, Jonet slicked her tongue over her bottom lip. "And what, sir, do you intend to do about it?" She twisted seductively atop the bed, one hand fisting in the sheet in mock ecstasy. "*Oh, oh, Cole—!*" she teased.

Cole looked at her darkly for a long moment. "Jonet, where are your stockings?"

Jonet stared at him blankly, her motions abruptly stilling. "My—my stockings?"

His expression forbidding, Cole took one step toward her. "Those damned stockings you wore today!" Cole looked about, his eyes catching on something near her dressing table. *"Aha—!"* he said, grabbing them up in one hand and stalking toward her.

Jonet's eyes narrowed. "Cole? . . . What are you doing?" she asked suspiciously.

Cole crawled on top of her with the full force of his weight. "Jonet," he said grimly, grabbing hold of one of her wrists and shoving it over her head, "I am about to tie you to this bedpost and give you the fucking you've been begging for since the first day I laid eyes on you."

Jonet tried to scramble backward, but there was no escaping Cole's weight. Or his determination. "And *not* some sweet, gentle pleasuring," he continued, looping the silk around her hand, "in which you tell me what to do, and I just blithely do it. But a good, hard one—and the way I want it, for a change."

To her undying shame, a little thrill chased up her spine and came out her mouth. *"Oh, Cole—!"* she said on a whisper.

" '*Oh Cole,*' my arse," he gritted, already lashing one of her wrists against the sturdy mahogany post. Ruthlessly, he grabbed the other hand and shoved it up over her head. "I have had quite enough of your willfulness, Jonet," he continued. "For all the weeks that I have known you, I have been civil, and I have been calm, and I have bitten my tongue and put up with your spells and rants and tantrums—when a lesser man might well have snapped."

"Oh, yes—!" she agreed breathlessly, craning her head

backward to watch his long, deft fingers lace the silken stocking about her wrist.

Cole seemed not to have heard her. "You have teased me and tormented me past bearing, Jonet! You have slapped me, stabbed me, and bitten me, and now, by thunder, your touching yourself like that is just too damned much for a good man to take. I know exactly what you need, and I'm bloody well going to tie you down and give it to you myself."

"Oh, *yes*, Cole!" she answered, quivering eagerly as he drew the back of her hand firmly against the coolness of the wood.

Cole laced one stocking through the other, then mercilessly yanked them taut, causing her breasts to arch high and her nipples to peak into hard, little buds. "*Umph,*" he grunted, tightening the last knot. "There, now! So if you mean to marry *me,* Jonet—"

"Why, I daresay I ought," she softly insisted. "I should be afraid to refuse."

"—then by heaven, you'll learn a little obedience," he finished, roughly shoving her legs apart.

"That seems only fair." Jonet tried to nod. "Else you might have to turn me over your knee and . . . oh, spank me—?"

"I just might." His head bowed, Cole stroked his hand up and down his erection, then probed rather forcefully at her hot, wet entrance. "So you'd best give me what I want, when I want it," he finished, shoving it in just an inch.

"Oh!" she said on a breathless jerk. "That seems very *firm* coming from a . . . a former choirboy."

"Curate," he corrected, roughly thrusting himself halfway inside.

"*Ahh*—," she moaned hotly, riding hard down onto his shaft. "*Yes-s-s!*"

Cole scowled darkly at her. "And when I say be still, Jonet, you'll do it, and no sass!" Abruptly, however, his mouth twitched, and Cole buried his head in the pillow above her shoulder. Too late. Jonet heard the little laugh that escaped. "At least—at least *once* in a while," he concluded, his words muffled.

"Yes, Captain Amherst, sir." She eased her pelvis up against his.

"Oh, bloody hell," he said on a choke of laughter. "Who am I kidding?" Atop her, Cole began to shake. Jonet kneed him gently in the thigh, until finally, he lifted his head and stared at her, his eyes watering with tears, his handsome mouth quirked tight with barely suppressed mirth.

"Well," she said, her eyes wide and serious. "Let this be a lesson to me! I'd best put my clothes away when I undress at night." Jonet smiled seductively and urged herself against him. "Now, my darling, are you going to give me the fucking I deserve? Or must I resort to something else?" Wickedly, she wiggled the fingers ensnared high above her head.

Cole's eyes narrowed darkly, his jaw went rigid, and he shoved himself fully inside with a grunt. "I'll take care of it," he hotly insisted, stroking fully out, and driving back in again.

And again, and again, until Jonet felt that sweet, fine edge of madness slide incrementally closer. She sighed and let instinct take over, but Cole pulled away, bending his head to capture her nipple between his lips. She arched off the bed as he drew her breast into the warmth of his mouth, sucking gently, then roughly, but always persistently.

When Jonet felt as if she could bear the pleasure no longer, she whimpered and tried to shift her hips higher, her hands and arms straining futilely against the silken stockings that held her fast beneath his thrusting hips and seeking mouth. Restlessly, she writhed beneath him, making soft, wild noises in the back of her throat until at last he released her nipple, only to turn his attentions to the other breast, giving it the same exquisite torment. Again, Cole withdrew from her, then drove deep inside, holding himself at a perfect angle. Mindlessly, she threw one leg around his waist, dragging her pelvis hard against his erection.

Cole lifted his head from her breast and laughed, a low, wicked growl from deep in the back of his throat. "Oh, no, my sweet," he whispered, his hand going around to force her leg back against the sheets. "This time, we do it my way." Again, he stroked his full, firm length into the wet petals of her feminine flesh, but this time, he held himself a little lower, deliberately cheating her of that perfect stroke of pleasure.

Her head thrashing back and forth on the pillow, Jonet began to plead. "Please! Oh, please, oh, *Cole!*" She panted hard, gasping for breath. "Harder. Higher. *Please!*"

In response, Cole slid his other hand between them to tenderly touch her, spreading her petals like a delicate blossom. Slowly, ever so lightly, he ran his finger over and around the sensitive nub of her womanhood until she started to scream. At once, his mouth came over hers, capturing the nascent sound and returning it with his tongue.

With his shaft still pulsing hungrily inside her, Cole made love to Jonet for long, sweet moments, alternately stroking her deep, then almost withdrawing, so that he might spread her wide with his fingers. Crooning to her with soft, tormenting words, he would slide his thumb over her quivering bud, holding her open and achingly empty, until she squirmed, then begged. "*Ah—ah—ah,*" she frantically panted. *"Ah—please, Cole!"* Fulfillment glittered and danced just beyond her reach.

With a lazy smile, Cole dipped his head to suck the tender flesh of her earlobe. "You want this?" he teased, withdrawing his hand and stroking her deep, touching the edge of her womb with the tip of his shaft.

"I . . . I . . . oh, I want," she gasped, "I want it hard. Please." Mindlessly, desperately, she struggled. But subtly, he shifted his weight and slid inside her, tantalizing, tormenting, and leaving her perched on the precarious edge of *petit mort.*

"Oh, no, my darling," Cole teased, almost fully withdrawing again. "I think you ought to have it slowly. Very, very slowly." Again, his strong hand spread her wide as he drove mercilessly inside.

Jonet stared up at the hard, handsome lines of his face. "Let go my hands, Cole," she began to plead, thrashing beneath his weight. "Untie . . . untie me and I will . . . I will . . ."

"Oh, yes, my sweet," crooned Cole thickly. "I know exactly what you will do with those wicked, wayward hands. But I would rather do it for you." Gently, he lifted himself and stroked her deeply and perfectly. The bright edge of pleasure slid nearer.

And again, he thrust. Harder and higher this time. Slowly, he rocked back, then into her again, bearing his weight forward onto powerful arms. His thick, blond hair fell forward in a shimmering, fluid curtain as he held himself over her, working her deeply, the taut muscles of his arms and chest bunching, his hot flesh slicking over her moist skin.

Mindlessly, Cole drove into her, until his arms began to tremble and his throat began to cord. "Come with me, Jonet," he begged, her pleasure intensifying. Cole's eyes tightly shut as he pounded against her. "Come with me, sweet. Now. Now. Yes! *Now—!*"

The explosion rocked the room. Jonet's awareness was swallowed up in a flash of light and ecstasy, until she could hardly separate her orgasm from his. She turned her head into the pillow and gave a soft cry as the hot rush of his seed filled her, and left her trembling.

She came back to earth to find Cole collapsed on top of her, air dragging in and out of his lungs, his heart pounding against her chest and in her ears.

It was a long, long time before Cole realized just what Jonet was up to. As their mornings at Elmwood turned into long, torrid nights, Cole knew only that his bleak past was rapidly becoming a distant memory. After celebrating Robert's birthday in good style, Cole and the boys tried to return their attentions to schoolwork, but it was a challenge, given that most of their books had been left behind in their rapid exodus from Brook Street.

While he patiently awaited the return of the messenger he'd discreetly sent to Charles Donaldson, Cole's afternoons were given over to estate matters, but his nights were reserved for Jonet. In her usual headstrong way, however, Jonet seemed disinclined to restrict her passion to the bedchamber. Over the next two days, there was hardly a room at Elmwood that Cole and Jonet didn't use to its full advantage. She begged him to ruck up her skirts one morning in the library. She drove him to madness with her mouth behind his father's desk on a rainy Friday afternoon. And one night after dinner, she dragged him to a chair in a dark corner of the dining room and sat—

Well, it should have been shameless, the things that they did—and perhaps it was. But never in his life had Cole been so grateful for a shortage of household staff. Alas, however, his luck was short-lived. When Mrs. Birtwhistle caught them mindlessly pawing one another in the still-room one morning, with Cole's shirt untucked and Jonet's hair tumbling down, he knew without a doubt that he was done for.

He was going to have to make an honest woman of the wayward Countess of Kildermore, or the Sorceress of Strathclyde, or whatever she was rightly titled. Mrs. Birtwhistle, who pulled shut the door with a huff and a glower, looked as if she might insist upon it. And somehow, marriage no longer seemed the rash, irresponsible thing Cole had once thought it. Moreover, Cole did not kid himself for one moment. Fornication was a sin. And he had been praying for strength since the first time he'd touched Jonet, knowing all too well that his flesh was weak where she was concerned.

The strength had come, albeit not in the form he had expected. Instead, he had found the strength to love and to trust and to feel hope for the future. He had grieved too long over Rachel. Yes, she had been a good woman. But she had never been a good wife, and perhaps she'd not been able. But Cole had done his best by her, and that was all a man could do. Now, it seemed that God had answered his prayers in an unexpected way. Jonet had shown him what a blessing love and passion could be. And it had made him feel whole. Healed.

Slowly, he had come to accept the fact that it was God's will—not to mention Jonet's—that they should be together. His only prayer now was that he would not get her with child before her mourning was ended. Society would find their match titillating enough without the added embarrassment of an early wedding. He could imagine the whispers at their first introduction as *Captain Cole Amherst and Jonet, Lady*

Kildermore. But that was not very fair, was it? Jonet didn't give a damn who he was or what he was called, and she never had. It had taken but a few short days alone with her to make Cole look past his stupidity and see what Jonet had tried to tell him; that all she wanted was love and a family.

In their whispered nights, they dreamed a hundred lovely dreams—wild imaginings that he had begun to allow himself to believe. After they were wed, they would spend summers in Scotland, going to London only when it was unavoidable, and spending the rest of their lives together here at Elmwood. The thought of it pleased Jonet, and it certainly pleased him. Moreover, Cole had made the decision to sell his commission. Someday, if he ever felt worthy, he might speak to the bishop about a return to the church. But for now, he had Elmwood and his marriage to Jonet to consider. Moreover, he had Stuart and Robert to think of, not to mention all the children he and Jonet dreamed of having. His life would be full. Their union would be blessed. He knew it with a certainty.

All the ecstasy and contentment aside, that afternoon Cole grimly decided that there was one last task he must take on. It had rained the better part of the day, and so he pulled on his shabbiest boots and went downstairs to find his old greatcoat, then set out across the rear gardens toward the squat, stone tower of St. Ann's and the churchyard that lay beyond. In his heart, he knew that he could not begin a new marriage until he had allowed his first to end.

Cole no longer questioned how or why he was aware of Jonet's presence when she was near; he simply accepted the fact that his intuition in that regard was unerring. On this particular occasion, Jonet was already in the gardens, apparently having braved the drizzle in order to take her afternoon stroll. She almost caught up with him halfway across the back lawn, and yet, she did not draw up along his side to walk with him up the narrow path. Instinctively, she seemed to hold back, and not even when he went up the three stone steps and pushed open the wrought-iron gate into the churchyard did she approach. Instead, she lingered in the shadows of the willow trees that fringed the low stone wall and waited for him there.

Jonet saw Cole the moment he left the house, and knew without a shadow of a doubt where he was going. And why. She told herself that it was time; that it was what she had wanted and encouraged. But the thought of Cole talking to—or even saying a prayer over—his dead wife made her heart hammer with jealousy. And yet, she was as ashamed of her own selfishness as she was proud of Cole's integrity. He was a far better man than she deserved, and she knew it well.

These sweet days spent as a family in the shelter of Elmwood had been the happiest of her life. Under the watchful eye of Cole's servants, her children had run wild and free for the first time in months. It gladdened her heart and made her all the more grateful for the strange twist of fate that had brought this man into her life at a time when all else had failed her.

The rain was over now. Only the occasional *plop! plop!* of water slithering off leaves and into the grass was left to remind her of the weather. Cambridgeshire was a lush, wet place, and Jonet did not mind at all. Indeed, she found it comforting to know that she might spend the rest of her life in this blissful haven. And so she spread open her cloak and sat down on a low stone bench nestled beneath the willow branches, and awaited Cole's return.

It was a long, agonizing interval until at last she heard the shrieking of the gate hinges and the sound of Cole's heavy boots coming down the steps and along the path. Jonet's head jerked up, and she went to him then, her hands outstretched. It was clear that he had been crying.

Heedless of prying eyes, Jonet pulled him to her breast, lightly circling one arm beneath his greatcoat, cherishing his warmth and his goodness. Cole bent his forehead to her shoulder, and they remained thus for a long moment. There seemed nothing to say, and nothing to ask. Plainly, Cole had made peace with his past. Gently, Jonet brushed the back of her hand across his cheek, and Cole turned his face into it, kissing her knuckles, then folding her fingers into his.

"The past is over and done," he said softly. "Let us look to the future, Jonet. It may be fraught with danger, but at least all of our old ghosts are being laid to rest."

Again, Jonet felt just a little bit ashamed. She let her arm fall from his waist and pulled him back toward the bench. "Come sit, my love," she said quietly. "I would speak with you privately, if I may?"

Cole looked at her in some surprise. Then, whipping off his greatcoat, he sat down beside Jonet and spread the coat over both their shoulders. He turned toward her, his eyes searching her face, even as his fingers came up to thread lightly through her hair. Suddenly, she wanted him to hold her, needed to feel his hardness pressed against her. Instinctively, he did so, kissing her gently, his long, dark lashes sweeping down across his cheeks. When he was done, long moments later, Cole slid his hands to her shoulders and set her a little away from him. "Now, my dear, if it is best said, then it is best said swiftly." Clearly, he sensed her hesitation.

Jonet looked down at her hands, now clasped tightly in her lap. "A man and a woman who are to be wed ought not keep secrets from one another," she quietly began.

Affectionately, Cole brushed his knuckles beneath her chin, urging her head up. "That is true," he gently replied, struggling to hold her gaze. "But be assured, Jonet, that there is nothing you might say which would alter my devotion to you. Have you some dreadful secret, my dear?"

Jonet looked at him plaintively. "Sometimes, Cole, there are secrets which are not fully ours to confess. Do you understand? I speak, as you may well guess, of my relationship with Lord Delacourt."

Cole's brows drew together. "Jonet! Really, my dear, must we talk of him? He is a part of that past which we intend to set aside. Is he not—?"

"Not . . . not exactly," she answered, softly mouthing the words. "Indeed, I would have you understand that as much as I love you, I cannot entirely set aside my friendship with him. I wanted to tell you now, and to ask your understanding."

She could see at once that Cole was deeply displeased. "Jonet, I see no redeeming characteristic whatsoever in that man," he answered grimly. "And although I love and trust you, I am not wholly without pride. Nor, I daresay, a measure of arrogance. I'll not be thought a cuckold even before I am wed."

Jonet tossed up her hands with a despairing little laugh. "Oh! Already you sound like my dead husband. But Henry deserved it. You, on the other hand, certainly do not."

"Good heavens, Jonet!" Cole sounded more worried than angry. "What has Henry to do with this? I wish you would speak plainly."

Beneath Cole's coat, Jonet shifted her weight on the bench until she faced him. Lightly, she laid her hands across the breadth of his chest. "You once said, Cole, that men like you did not marry women like me. But what would you say, I wonder, if I were a nobody? Or as near a nobody as a Scottish gentlewoman can get?"

Cole's hands came up to cover hers. "It would not matter to me, Jonet, if you were the scullery maid," he whispered, his eyes dark and serious. "I think you know that. In truth, I would almost be relieved, but such is not the way of life. We do not get to choose who we are, and oftentimes, not even what we will be."

Jonet smiled weakly, staring down at the cat, who had just darted from the shrubbery. "Oh, how well I know that!" she said, bending forward to trail her fingertips down the cat's fur. "I never wanted to be heir to Kildermore. I never even loved it the way Nanna or Ellen or even Charlie did! And most certainly, I had no wish to marry for position, nor to be fawned over by men who . . ." Her voice almost broke, but she caught it. "I just wanted a good husband, Cole. A man who would love me. I just wanted . . . a *normal* life."

Beneath his calm exterior, Cole was intently studying Jonet. She was deeply disturbed, more so than he had seen her in some days. His mind raced. Clearly, that bastard Delacourt was up to something. Had he somehow been in touch with Jonet? Probably. And what hold could he possibly have over her? Obviously, it was not a hold she greatly resented, and irrationally, that both angered and wounded him. He had thought a great deal about Delacourt since coming to Elmwood, and his suspicion had grown.

Over and over, his mind returned to Jonet's remarks about her husband's argument with Delacourt on the night of his death. Delacourt, who had pushed Lord Mercer's inquest to a hasty end. And Delacourt, who faithlessly kept a mistress behind Jonet's back. The man was nothing but trouble.

Cole forced his voice to be calm as he tipped up her chin again. "Jonet, my dear," he said firmly, "it is time you explained yourself. I must confess, you worry me with this strange talk. I begin to fear that Lord Delacourt is some sort of threat to you."

"Oh, no," she said stridently, shaking her head. "But our . . . *friendship* is quite complex." Jonet looked blindly down at Elmwood's expectant barn cat, who was now persistently twining herself around their ankles. "You see, David is—to my way of thinking, and perhaps even to his own—the rightful heir to Kildermore. Beyond that, I cannot say more."

Cole drew back an inch. "Jonet, I fear that makes no sense at all."

But Jonet continued on as if she could not hear him. "It is simply this, Cole. If life were fair, all that I possess—my estate and my titles and my wealth—all would be his. I would be plain Lady Jonet Cameron, a bad-tempered Scot of no particular merit. And if I wed you, society would account me quite fortunate to snare such a fine catch—just as I account myself now."

In astonishment, Cole stared at her. "But Jonet . . . surely you cannot mean . . . what you are really saying is—"

"I really do not think I can say anything more," she said softly. "You must trust me, Cole. And you must do so based on a half-truth. I am sorry for it."

Suddenly, a feeling of sick dread seized Cole. There were but few conclusions that could be drawn from Jonet's comments. None of them made sense. And none of them were pleasant. He grabbed her by the shoulders. "Darling," he said urgently, "listen to me! Did Henry know of this? Did he understand?"

Jonet laughed bitterly. "Oh, no one knew better! Indeed, I think he took a perverse sort of pleasure in it. Until the gossip became too much. And in the end, that is what so angered David. The threat that . . ." Shuddering, she let her words slip away.

"The threat that *what—?*" Cole rasped, his fingers digging into her flesh.

Jonet's voice dropped to a whisper. "Nothing," she said quietly. "Now, I have answered your questions as best I may. I can only hope that you will trust me, and let this be the end."

"Do not be ridiculous, Jonet." Cole jerked to his feet and paced away, leaving her on the bench, swaddled in the folds of his greatcoat. "You cannot begin such a tale as this and not expect to finish it! And if you cannot—or *will* not—then Delacourt most certainly shall."

Jonet leapt up, leaving the coat to slither unheeded to the ground. "What do you mean, Cole? Where are you going?" she demanded hotly, and Cole could sense that his briefly compliant fiancée was gone, and that her banked temper had burst into full flame.

He spun about to face her, his boot heel squeaking sharply in the wet grass. "I am going to London, madam," he said, biting out each syllable. "And when I get there, I am going straight to Curzon Street, where I mean to jerk Lord Delacourt up by the coat collar and shake a few answers out of him. I have meant to do so for quite some time, and now I see that I can delay no longer."

Jonet stalked after him, her fists balled tightly at her sides, the pregnant cat bounding awkwardly at her heels. "You have deliberately chosen to misunderstand me, Cole!" she shouted, her voice rising as they moved swiftly toward the house. "And I shan't have it, do you hear! That sanctimonious shroud of yours is worn perilous thin, sir! I see the truth—that you can be just as petty and obstinate and jealous as the rest of us!"

Stopping cold in the middle of the garden, Cole ran an unsteady hand down his face and stared at her. "I daresay I may be, Jonet. But I am not—and never have been—a fool."

By the time Cole was ready to set out for London, Jonet was in a true fit of temper. She had paced the floor of her bedchamber, alternately searching for something to hurl at his door, then consigning almost every man she'd ever known to the fires of perdition, her father, her husband, David—and sometimes even Cole—amongst them.

She and Cole were barely speaking. Following their heated discussion in the garden, he had stalked into the house and immediately begun shoving shirts and stockings into an old leather saddlebag. For a few moments, Jonet had tried to reason with him, dogging his footsteps from bureau to wardrobe and back, circling around the bed until she was breathless, and ripping out clothes as fast as he packed them.

As usual, it had all been for naught, since Cole was the most implacable, exasperating man she had ever known. And so she had resorted to threats. She was never going to touch him again. She wished his penis would wither and die. Most assuredly, she was never going to marry him. No, she *was* going to marry him. And then she would make his life a living hell.

The result had been predictably laughable. With his long, hard jaw set at its obstinate angle, Cole had merely stared at her as if she had taken leave of her senses. "Jonet," he'd finally said, as he'd fastened the buckle of his bag, "you are a sharp-tongued shrew. But you are my shrew, and I mean to keep you safe. Long may I live to regret it."

"Oh, God!" she had cried, clawing madly at her hair. "I *hate* it when you are reasonable."

"Which is all of the time," Cole had firmly responded.

And so she had ceased to argue. By heaven, let him go rail at David if he wished. Perhaps that was the best solution of all. Let those bold, brash men unbutton their breeches, whip out their cocks, and measure them against one another. Then, they could simply settle it—whatever *it* was—between themselves.

Oh, she loved David dearly, and yet she spared him precious little pity, either. He had brought much of Cole's antagonism upon himself, by means of his usual high-handed arrogance and deliberate provocation. And now that it had come to this, what would David tell him? One never knew what he might do. Perhaps he would tell Cole to go to the devil. Or perhaps he would merely laugh, and spill the whole ugly truth. Certainly, it was his to spill. As usual, she was little more than a hapless bystander in this farce which seemed to constitute her life.

Soon, Jonet found herself standing in the circular drive of Elmwood, her arms crossed resolutely over her chest, one toe tapping furiously in the gravel. Mr. Moseby had brought around a sleek, long-legged chestnut, which looked as if it might well eat up the ground from Cambridgeshire to London. With a little grunt of displeasure, Cole hefted over the saddlebag and deftly secured it. They were alone in the drive. He really was going to leave her. Suddenly, Jonet's resolve melted, and she started toward him. "Cole," she said softly, "if you must go, you will travel safely, will you not?"

Cole looped his reins loosely over the saddle and turned to face her, placing the palms of his hands lightly upon her shoulders. "Yes, I will travel safely," he promised. But his voice was weary, his face lined with fatigue, and Jonet was left to recall how willingly and unselfishly he had taken on the responsibility of her children's welfare. And how very much she needed him.

For a moment, she considered forswearing David altogether, if Cole would just stay with her and not go to London. Twice, Jonet opened her mouth to speak, and could not find the words. "Cole," she finally managed to say, "you must understand that David would never do anything to harm me or my children. He has no reason to do so."

"I suppose that I must pray that you are right," Cole grimly responded.

"Oh, Cole," she said despairingly, her hands going up to cup his face. "I know that David has been rash, perhaps outright rude to you. But he is young, and his burdens are many. If there is something which must be settled between you, then by all means, go. Just be mindful of the fact that you are both older and wiser, and so it is left to you to be reasonable. And above all, you must remember that David would never hurt me."

Cole looked at her sadly. "Perhaps that is so, Jonet," he softly admitted. "But what might he do to protect you? Or to protect his honor? Or the honor of someone else?"

Steadily, Jonet held his gaze. "Do you not think, Cole, that I have considered such a thing? Do you believe me such a blind fool as all that? But when all is said and done, David would never hurt my children. And that is why this whole thing makes no sense."

Cole opened his mouth to tell Jonet that at the least they did agree on one thing. It did indeed make no sense. But further debate was forestalled by the sound of a carriage rumbling across Elmwood's moat. He stepped from behind the chestnut to watch as the coachman drew around the circle and stopped. At once, the door flew open, and Nanna's round, wrinkled face popped out. Eagerly, Jonet hastened toward the carriage, both hands extended as if to help the old woman down.

It was only then that Cole realized the carriage was driven by Charlie Donaldson. Thank God. In short order, the steps were down, and Nanna and Ellen Cameron were standing in the driveway. The old nurse looked to be her usual acerbic self, but Donaldson looked measurably thinner and more pale, while Miss Cameron looked even worse. Clearly, the illness had taken a toll on them. As the ladies greeted one another, Donaldson secured the team, then motioned Cole to the far side of the carriage.

Discreetly, the butler returned to Cole the engraved breastplate of the First Royal Dragoons. "Verra quick of you, Capt'n, to send that along with your messenger," he whispered, cocking one dark brow. "And I came wi' all haste, but as you see, Miss Cameron is no' verra well."

Grimly, Cole looked at Ellen, then back to Donaldson. "No, she isn't, is she? Nor, by the look of it, had you any business driving them here. But tell me, what caused the illness? Does Dr. Greaves know?"

Donaldson looked chagrined. "Aye, sir, it must ha' been the cream," he confessed, lifting one shoulder apologetically. "There was a footman and tweeny laid low across the street."

"So . . . not poison after all?" Cole murmured. "Perhaps I overreacted."

Donaldson shook his head. "Ye canna be too careful, sir. You did what was best." His eyes drifted down Cole's riding gear, and over to the horse's saddlebag. "But where d'you go now, Capt'n?"

Cole's eyes had drifted toward Jonet. "To London," he said quickly, his attention snapping back to the butler. "And I don't mind saying I'm relieved to see you. But listen, Donaldson—you did not by chance tell Lord Delacourt of our whereabouts, did you?"

"Indeed not, sir!" He drew himself sharply erect. "I told no one, as you ordered. Why?"

"Because I mean to have a few answers from him," answered Cole grimly, watching as Nanna picked up the cat to stroke her sagging belly. "If he should come here, Donaldson, tell him that I have said he is not welcome. Under no circumstances should you let him in."

Jonet's butler shifted uneasily. "Have ye some cause to think ill of him, sir? I mean, I daresay her ladyship might take exception to his new mistress an' all—but I do na' think he means any harm."

Cole studied Donaldson appraisingly, realizing once again that not much got past old soldiers. He realized, too, that there was little he could say to Donaldson regarding his uncertainties about Delacourt. They were too nebulous, and potentially too damaging.

Moreover, he was beginning to understand that Jonet might well know, and probably did not care, about Delacourt's mistress. Perhaps he should have been relieved, but he was far from it. The tangle of truth and suspicion, heightened by Jonet's reticence, had conspired to give Cole a splitting headache, and that grave feeling of unease which had lessened since leaving London was back in full measure.

On top of that, he wanted to strangle Delacourt, but a long, tiresome journey lay between Cole and his quarry. In exasperation, he lashed his riding crop ruthlessly across the shank of his boot. Damn it, he could not hope to lay hands on Delacourt before midmorning at the earliest, and would probably have to roust the insolent bastard from his bed at such an early hour. For the nonce, he must console himself with the fact that Donaldson had arrived at Elmwood to help ensure the safety of Jonet and the boys in his absence.

14

In which Lady Delacourt tells All

Cole arrived in Curzon Street the following morning, still burning with a righteous indignation. But underneath his re, there was now a measure of fear, and it had grown ncrementally with each passing mile. Throughout the long ide from Cambridgeshire, he had thought of nothing but onet and their argument. And he prayed to God that he ad not dashed all hope for their future by his rash, and dmittedly obstinate, behavior. At every posting inn, he ad considered returning to her side.

And yet, he had not. Driven furiously toward London y a force he did not understand, he had pushed both himelf and his horse to the edge. He knew only that he needed o see Delacourt, and hear the truth from his lips. Only hen would he be able to fairly judge the viscount's intenons toward Jonet. Perhaps, as Jonet said, Delacourt meant er no harm. Cole could only hope that that was true. He ad no wish to see Jonet hurt by another man to whom she as so clearly devoted, no matter how much that devotion isturbed him.

But in truth, it now seemed as if no one had had a better notive than Lord Delacourt for wishing the Marquis of

Mercer dead. And that motive, Cole now understood, was something far darker than a desire to protect or befriend Jonet. Mercer's threat, if Cole had guessed correctly, would have cost the arrogant viscount his pride, and quite possibly, a great deal more.

In the back of Cole's mind, he kept reliving his conversations with Jack Lauderwood. It seemed as if it had been years, instead of mere days, since Lauderwood had recounted his story of Delacourt's father, and of his quarrel with Kildermore and Mercer. A duel amongst friends was an ugly business, and Cole was beginning to suspect it had had little to do with anything as mundane as ill-tempered hounds.

Cole was greeted at the door by the same haughty footman he'd met the previous week. Coolly, he stated his wish to see Delacourt, and deposited his card onto the salver. Without comment, he was shown into a small salon to wait. But when the footman returned, he escorted Cole not to one of the formal rooms in the house but to a small parlor in the rear. The footman threw open the door, and Cole stepped inside to see that it was not Lord Delacourt but his mother and his sister who awaited him.

Today, the old lady sat in a wheelchair alongside a bank of French windows. Through the glass beyond her stooped shoulders, Cole could see a small, carefully landscaped garden with a fountain. The pale, elegant décor made it obvious that this was Lady Delacourt's private morning room. No doubt the windows and the gardens were arranged just for her benefit. Her ladyship was very fragile, and given the withered look of her arms and legs, she appeared to have been so for quite some time.

As Cole suppressed his foreboding and made his bow, Lady Delacourt lifted a gold lorgnette and studied him in some detail. And then abruptly, she turned to the middle aged woman at her elbow. “Charlotte, my dear, leave us if you please.”

With a look of mild surprise, Miss Branthwaite rose, set aside her needlework, and quit the room, bidding Cole a very pleasant morning as she passed him to go out the door.

Lady Delacourt returned her assessing gaze to Cole. “I am told,” she said rather coolly, “that you have come to see my son. I should very much like to know why.”

Gripping his hands behind his back, Cole nodded respectfully, for her ladyship had a voice that unquestionably commanded it. “I regret, my lady, that my business with Lord Delacourt is of a personal nature. Might I wait and speak with him, if he is not presently at home?”

Her brows went up at that. “Indeed, you may.” Reaching o one side of her chair, Lady Delacourt took up a small, gold-knobbed walking stick and jabbed it toward a chair. “But in the interim, you will sit there, sir, if you please.”

The old-fashioned English schoolboy in Cole would not llow him to refuse. Obediently, he sat. She put down the ane and studied him. “Did Lady Mercer send you here?” he challenged.

“No, ma’am, she did not.”

Lady Delacourt nodded in satisfaction. “No, I did not hink that she would do so . . . but I daresay she has been he cause of your coming. Indirectly, of course.”

Cole sat very rigidly in his chair. “I can assure you, nadam, that Lady Mercer had nothing whatsoever to do vith it.”

“Indeed?” The old lady’s eyes narrowed. “I wonder, oung man, just what the two of you are up to. Jonet has een very different of late, and the affection with which she reeted you here last week seemed particularly telling. erhaps you would be so kind as to explain your intentions toward her? As you may know, she is very dear to me, and so I do not ask this question lightly."

Feeling more and more like an errant schoolboy, Cole clasped his hands in his lap. He hoped most sincerely that Lady Delacourt could not guess what he and Jonet had been 'up to,' but she possessed both the tone and perspicacity of a steely-eyed governess.

"My intentions toward Lady Mercer are honorable," he answered quietly. "Since you are her friend, I may tell you in confidence that I have asked her to be my wife, once her mourning has ended."

"Oh?" Lady Delacourt's pale brows went up. "And she has said—?"

Cole felt himself blush. "At first, I believe she was inclined to accept my suit. But now I am not entirely certain. We will, I daresay, work something out."

The old lady nodded, and rolled her chair a little to the left, in order to face him square on. "You have quarreled over David, have you not? I suppose animosity is to be expected between two such forceful young men under these circumstances. Jonet has told you, I take it, that David is her brother?"

It was just what Cole had expected to hear; confirmation of the appalling suspicion that had tormented him all the way to London. And yet, he was stunned. "No, ma'am. Not in those precise words. But I was left to draw my own conclusions, and that is why I wish to speak with your son."

Lady Delacourt shook her head sadly. "I daresay I can obviate the need for such a meeting, Captain Amherst. Do you truly mean to marry Jonet?"

"Most assuredly, ma'am, if she will have me."

For a moment, she nodded quietly to herself. "Well,

have always known it eventually would come to this, I suppose," Lady Delacourt finally said.

Cole looked at her in some confusion. "Come to what, ma'am?"

The old woman did not answer, choosing instead to change the subject. "I believe, Captain Amherst, that you have taken orders, have you not?" she said lightly. "Indeed, Jonet said so just last week. So I'll ask you to consider my words as a sort of confession. You will honor such a request, I daresay?"

Cole was growing increasingly uncomfortable. "Ma'am, I can assure you that you need tell me nothing at all. I have come to see Delacourt, and I fully intend to do so."

"Oh, and see him you surely shall," she said grimly. "No doubt my coxcomb of a son will insist upon it. But this story is mine, and so I shall tell it."

Cole did not know what to say. "If you insist," he answered softly. But it was clear that Lady Delacourt intended to have her say, and already, her gaze had turned inward.

"Many years ago, Captain Amherst," she quietly began, "I made my way in this cold world as a governess. My blood was a rather rural shade of pale blue—I daresay you know the color I mean—and I was accounted fortunate when I achieved every governess's fairy tale of marrying her employer. But in my case, my employer was the late Lord Delacourt, and he wed me out of guilt, not love."

"Guilt?" asked Cole softly. He really did not want to have this conversation.

The old woman's gaze was strong and certain, yet Cole could see her knuckles, white against the chair arm. "You see, I had been employed for some years as governess to his only child, dear Charlotte. We lived quietly at the family seat in Derbyshire, and his lordship often visited, bringing his friends for hunting parties. All went well until one autumn night when I made the dreadful misjudgement of going down to the kitchen for a mug of milk."

Cole was beginning to feel sick. "Milk, ma'am?" he echoed softly.

Lady Delacourt squeezed shut her eyes. "Why, yes. I do believe it was milk," she whispered weakly, but then, her voice took on a bitter strength that Cole had not expected from such a delicate woman. "In any event, I went down the servant's stairs—a regrettable choice, I confess—and whilst doing so, I was accosted and raped by a drunken houseguest. It was, as I am sure you have guessed, Jonet's father, Kildermore. Accompanied by his cohort Lord Mercer, who was kind enough to stand guard to"—the old woman paused to laugh bitterly—"why, to ensure my modesty, I do not doubt."

Cole could bear it no longer. He jerked from his chair and went to her, lightly placing his hand over hers, and Lady Delacourt's eyes flew open wide. "My lady, I beg you will not continue. This is most assuredly not what I came here for."

The old woman blinked once. "Oh, but I believe that it is, Captain Amherst."

Cole took her slender, wrinkled hand in his hand and knelt by the wheelchair. "Lady Delacourt, I would never wish you to distress yourself on my behalf."

"Yes," she said softly. "That has always been David's concern, and Jonet's, too. But I find that this story distresses you young people far more than it does me nowadays. My life has not been without joy, sir. And the late Lord Delacourt attempted to defend my honor as best he could given the circumstances. Moreover, when it became apparent that I was with child, he married me."

"That was—that was very honorable," Cole admitted, his throat constricting.

"Yes, and something few men of his rank would have done," she added, her voice soft and introspective. "And so, Captain Amherst, my son has inherited a fortune and title he now believes is not his by rights. And Jonet has one she feels is rightfully his. For as you may know, the Scottish earldom of Kildermore can convey to a female—but only if the titleholder leaves no male heirs. Legitimate ones, of course." She looked at him quizzically. "You did understand that, did you not?"

"Yes, I suppose that I did," he said weakly. Suddenly, the room seemed hot and far too small. There was something . . . something troubling him . . . *but what the devil was it?* Absently, he rubbed one palm against his temple, trying to answer Lady Delacourt's question. "In truth, ma'am, I am but a soldier and a scholar. I think very little about such things as rank and title. I recall, however, that at the time of her marriage there was talk of Lady Jonet's title being nearly the equal of Mercer's."

"And both of them grander than my son's viscountcy," she quietly returned. Suddenly, Lady Delacourt's other hand came up to cover Cole's. "But I do hope you understand, sir, that David displaced no one. My husband had no heir, for unlike Kildermore's, Delacourt's title could not convey through the female line. Had he died without a son, my stepdaughter Charlotte would have been left nearly destitute, whilst the title would simply have gone into abeyance."

"That seems . . . terribly unfair."

The old lady nodded. "It is. So my husband deprived no one of anything which was rightfully theirs, and provided for his daughter in the bargain. But confidentiality is essential, sir. Charlotte knows nothing of this. And regrettably, David's bitterness has caused him to make enemies, many of whom would be well pleased to see his name and title challenged. And yet, were it not for that devil Kildermore, my son would never have had to know the truth of his conception."

In amazement, Cole sat back down in his chair. "Do you mean to tell me, my lady, that the Earl of Kildermore *confessed* this dreadful sin?"

Lips pressed tight, the old woman nodded. "Quite shocking, is it not, Captain Amherst? But as a soldier, I do not doubt that you have seen what the fear of death can do to a guilt-ridden conscience. So it was not enough that Kildermore took my innocence. He had to take that of my son, and of his daughter as well—in some faint hope of assuaging his own guilt."

"But why, ma'am?" asked Cole stridently, lost in the horror of her story.

Lady Delacourt smiled grimly. "Although Kildermore was cruel enough to marry his only child to a man who was almost as wicked as himself, Jonet's loneliness and despair began to eat at him when death drew near."

"As well it should have," agreed Cole bitterly. "But in truth, ma'am, I cannot see what good such a confession could do anyone, unless it was a confession to God."

The old lady sighed softly. "Do you know, I daresay that it was the first and only time Kildermore considered his daughter's needs. But my son was left to suffer the consequences."

Cole drew in a sharp breath, but Lady Delacourt held up a staying hand. "Oh, do not mistake me, Captain. As shocking as it may seem, I am exceedingly fond of Jonet, and David loves her dearly. But he was still very young and impressionable when the letter from his father arrived, and it has left him bitter. My husband and I had hoped he would never know the truth."

Cole felt a sense of outrage on her behalf. "And what did Kildermore hope to gain by such callousness?"

"In his letter, he said that he felt badly for all that he had done, and that after his death, he wished for them to care for one another." For a moment, the old woman paused, as if deep in thought.

Despite the fact that he had come here for answers, Cole was still plagued by a nagging anxiety. He had learned everything, and yet, he knew nothing. While it was still possible that Delacourt could have murdered Mercer to silence his secret, Jonet had been right. There was no reason why he would wish Robert and Stuart, his own nephews, ill.

"I think, too," Lady Delacourt finally continued, "that Kildermore believed David would see to his sister's welfare, should Mercer mistreat her after his death. Though why he would have thought David more intrepid than Jonet, I cannot begin to imagine. I have never known a woman more capable of taking care of herself—which is something you'd best consider, sir, if you mean to marry her."

Cole stared at the floor, intently studying the pattern of Lady Delacourt's rug. "You are perfectly right, ma'am," he finally answered. "But I love her, and I believe that there is some hope that . . . well, that her *intrepidity* can be governed."

Her ladyship's thin brows arched elegantly. "Oh ho! Those are bold words, sir," she said appreciatively. "Yours will not be an easy life. But I daresay it will never be boring."

Just then, the door burst inward, and Lord Delacourt strode into the room, looking trim and elegant, and very, very angry. Tucked beneath his elbow, he held his hat, while with the opposite hand, he clenched a black leather crop. Clearly, he had been riding.

Without so much as greeting his mother, Delacourt turned on Cole. His polished arrogance was gone, his skin pinched and white across his mouth and cheeks. "Just what the devil is the meaning of this impertinence, Amherst?" he challenged, brandishing his crop in Cole's face. "By God, sir, if you have distressed my mother, then I must tell you that my patience with you is at an end."

In ironic amusement, Cole looked up at Delacourt's face, then down at his crop. How well he remembered his Uncle James's plight, cornered just so in Jonet's drawing room. How could he have failed to note the similarities between them? Not the least of which was that brash, irrepressible arrogance. Calmly, Cole rose from his chair. "Put down your whip, you impudent pup, before one of us gets an eye put out."

"Go to the devil, Amherst," retorted Delacourt. "I am not one of your pupils or parishioners. And I am damned sure not your foot soldier."

"David, please—!" interjected his mother, attempting to rise from her wheelchair unaided. Braced on one arm of the chair, she began to tip perilously. Quickly, Cole rushed to her side, leaving Delacourt standing in the middle of the room, looking rather foolish.

"Oh!" said Lady Delacourt as she was restored to her chair. "I thank you, Captain Amherst. Now, if the two of you would be so kind as to sit down and hush, I believe we may settle this." Then, jabbing purposefully with her gold-knobbed stick, she pointed them both toward chairs.

Her son scowled, but after a moment's hesitation, he laid down the crop and hurled himself into his chair, stubbornly crossing his arms over his chest. Lady Delacourt smiled faintly. "Now, David," she began imperiously, "you have come too late, and there is nothing else for it. I have told all. Captain Amherst means to marry your sister. He is family now."

Delacourt half rose from his chair as if he meant to argue the point, but his mother's steely gaze stayed him at once. "Marriage?" The viscount's tone was softly incredulous. "Do you mean to tell me that Jonet has agreed to this outrage?"

Cole opened his mouth, but Lady Delacourt cut him off. "*Agreed—?*" his mother retorted. "It was undoubtedly her idea. Now! Let us turn our attentions to more pressing matters." The old woman turned to look at Cole. "I take it, sir, that you did not travel away from, nor back to, London in such haste without a good cause?"

"I left London because I feared for the safety of Lady Mercer and her children," said Cole quietly.

"As well you might, sir," interjected Delacourt bitterly. "The risk to the children seems only to have increased since your move to Brook Street. But then, we must recollect at whose behest you came."

Cole fought down an angry retort as Lady Delacourt made a chiding noise in the back of her throat. "David! You will mind your manners, if you please!" Delacourt jerked from his chair and began to pace the room.

Cole willed himself to remain calm and struggled to remember that the viscount did seem to care deeply for his sister. *His sister—!* Cole could still barely grasp that reality, but grasp it he must. "I am not going to bandy words with you, Delacourt," he said quietly. "There is too much at stake. Tell me, do you truly believe that my uncle James is behind these attempts? Have you any evidence? If so, I would be almost relieved to hear it."

Lady Delacourt leaned forward in her chair as her son

continued to pace. "I do not know," he finally admitted, halting abruptly. "Certainly Jonet thinks James is behind it. For my part, I cannot see James doing such a thing."

"Nor I," agreed Cole dryly. "And I know him for the fool that he is."

Delacourt offered up a weak smile. "Yes, I think Edmund a more likely candidate, but I have had him followed night and day for weeks, to no avail. He has unsavory habits, and keeps very poor company, it is true. But by all accounts, he hasn't the nerve to do murder, nor the money to have it done."

Thoughtfully, Cole steepled together the tips of his fingers. He was almost relieved to realize that Delacourt's logic had been running parallel to his own. But they were still missing something—something very critical. "*Cui bono,*" he whispered, remembering his discussion with Colonel Lauderwood.

Lady Delacourt leaned forward in her wheelchair to wag a finger at him. "A very good question, Captain Amherst, so far as it goes."

Cole's chin jerked up from his fingertips. "What do you mean?"

"Come, Captain," she prodded. "Surely as a theologian, you are schooled in logic as well as Latin? *Who benefits* if *what?*"

Delacourt peered at her quizzically. "Yes, Mother? Go on."

Her ladyship looked at him in mild exasperation. "Do you not see, David? Here is yet another example of why you should not hide things from me! I vow, you men have no understanding of human nature. For example, if we rule out James and Edmund, who benefits if Mercer dies?" She looked back and forth between them, her palms turned up inquiringly. "Is it Stuart? He is the most obvious, but that is ridiculous, of course. He is a boy. Jonet? Again, ridiculous, for despite the gossip, we all know Jonet did not intend to marry David."

The old woman drew a deep breath and continued. "So was it David?" She gave a tight smile. "Perhaps I show my prejudice, but I fancy that had David wished Mercer dead, he would have been better pleased to call him out and run a sword through his heart, something which was not altogether out of the question. No, men rarely resort to poison when a more honorable means is available."

Lord Delacourt looked confused. "Well, who else is there, Mother? Are you saying that there is someone we have not yet considered?"

"Certainly there is some *thing* you have not yet considered," she answered. "I only wish I knew who or what."

Abruptly, Cole sat forward in his chair. "What if Mercer's death was an accident?"

Delacourt waved a dismissive hand. "That is ridiculous. Look at what has followed!"

Lady Delacourt drew in her breath sharply. "That assumes all these events are connected. But what if they are not? Or what if we are leaping to conclusions here? Let us begin at the beginning, always a good spot, yes? For example, what if the wine which killed Mercer was left in his bedchamber by mistake?"

"But Mother, that makes no sense," persisted Delacourt irritably. "Mercer took it there himself. We all know that."

Lady Delacourt seemed to fluff herself like an irate hen. "I know nothing of the sort!" she retorted. "I know that he drank it, and that it was thought to be poisonous. But I assumed it was brought to him by a servant."

Suddenly, Cole jerked from his chair and began to pace

the floor with Delacourt. "It was Jonet's," he said softly. "The decanter of wine—that was why the magistrate suspected her of having done the deed. The decanter was always kept in her sitting room. She drank from it every night—but she did not do so that night. Indeed, she went straight to bed, because the servants had kept her late after dinner."

Beneath his breath, Delacourt cursed violently. "Good God! Was Jonet the intended victim all along?" he asked sharply. "Could it have been Mrs. Lanier, hoping to marry Mercer? Or perhaps it was that lady's maid—I own, I never liked the look of her. But that gunshot in Scotland . . ."

"Yes, and the carriage bolt," murmured Cole. "But anyone might have hired a thug to do such things. Since the war, they run rampant, and can be employed quite cheaply by anyone vicious enough to do so." Suddenly, from the wheelchair, Lady Delacourt's walking stick clattered to the floor.

Cole's attention snapped toward her, taking in her deathly pallor and the tiny, clawlike hand that gripped her chair arm. Delacourt saw, too, and he rushed toward her. "Mother! What is it?" He shot a stricken look at Cole. "Amherst, get brandy! Over there—!"

Cole moved quickly toward the sideboard, dashed out a healthy measure, and took it to her. As Delacourt briskly rubbed his mother's hands, Cole put the glass to her lips and steadied her as she drank it.

Almost at once, the old woman choked, sputtered, and pushed the glass away. "Power," she rasped violently. "It is always about power, is it not? Or position or wealth—they are all very much the same. But we did not look! And so, we did not see."

Cole leaned over her. "Please, ma'am, what position? What power?"

The old woman's gaze was bleak. "The earldom of Kildermore," she said quietly. "Mercer may have possessed Jonet, but he could never possess her title. Only an heir of Cameron blood may do so. But remember what I said earlier—a female may inherit, but only *if no legitimate sons live!*"

The words, heavy, horrible, and certain, hung in the air for a long moment. "Delacourt," said Cole quietly, straightening from his position beside the chair, "you will fetch me, if you please, your fastest horse. I believe I have made a most dreadful misjudgement."

Over his mother's head, Delacourt returned Cole's stricken look, an expression of horrified comprehension dawning. "You certainly will not go without me," he said as he strode across the room and yanked hard on the bell.

Jonet was in the belvedere sewing and enjoying the afternoon sun when Stuart and Robert came in search of her. She was not surprised. Ellen and Nanna were still resting, and Cole was away, while Mr. Moseby had ridden to Huntingdon on estate business. That left Jonet as the last resort for bored young gentlemen, and these two looked particularly peevish.

"Mama," began Robert irritably, hands shoved deep into his coat pockets, "have you seen Mr. Moseby's cat? We have looked and looked and we cannot find her anywhere."

"We are a bit worried," confessed Stuart. "Nanna says she's to have kittens soon. Do you think she is all right?"

Jonet set aside her sewing, patiently smiling. "I am sure that she's just fine," she said reassuringly, patting the seat beside her. "Mother cats like to hide when the time comes for their kittens to arrive. It is only natural. We'll find them soon enough."

As Stuart plopped down beside his mother, Robert scuffed one toe in the grass stubbornly. "Well, I don't have anything to do," he said plaintively. "When is Cousin Cole coming back? Will it be today? It seems as if he's been gone forever."

"Yes, it does seem as if he's been gone forever," Jonet agreed, wrapping one arm around Robert's waist and settling him onto her knee. And it did, she inwardly admitted, resting her chin atop his head. Oh, it had been good to see Ellen and Nanna. And Charlie too. But she missed Cole dreadfully, and greatly regretted her part in the argument that had led to his swift departure. Now, absent the comforting influence of his presence, she was beginning to feel frightened again. And for no good reason. They were perfectly safe at Elmwood.

Stuart let his head fall limply back against the wooden bench. "I do wish he would come back," the boy sighed. "Really, I wish we could just stay here forever. Do you think we could do that, Mama?" He cut a suspicious glance at his brother. "Robin says that Cousin Cole is going to be our new father. Is that true? Will we get to stay here if he is?"

Jonet squeezed shut her eyes for a moment. Good Lord! She should have expected this. Undoubtedly, the few servants they had at Elmwood were gossiping madly. Perhaps the boys had even seen them kissing yesterday afternoon beneath the willow trees. And what was she to say? *Was* Cole going to be their new father? She all but stopped breathing as she considered it. Certainly, she hoped so. She prayed that her demands regarding David—or worse, something David himself might say or do—would not ruin her one chance for happiness.

To soothe herself, Jonet slid her hand back through Robert's dark hair. "Well, we have talked about it," she quietly admitted. "And of course, it would mean that Cousin

Cole and I would have to get married. And live here at Elmwood. But your father has not been . . . gone long enough for me to speak of such things. It would be rather like dishonoring his memory." She looked at the boys in turn, taking in their small, solemn faces. "Do you understand?"

As the boys' faces fell, Jonet caught sight of Ellen darting out the door and into the gardens. "Look!" said Jonet, relieved at the interruption and glad to see Ellen finally perking up. "I see someone who is eager to play with you!"

Girlishly, Ellen lifted her green muslin skirts and came tripping through the grass, rapidly closing the distance. "Now," she said breathlessly as she reached them, "what have you boys done about finding that mischievous mama cat? Must we organize a search party?"

As Cole had instructed, Delacourt's groom had swiftly brought forth a pair of edgy Arab geldings, perfect for the sort of journey Cole intended to make. With Lady Delacourt's assistance, it had taken but a few minutes to prepare. Cole sent word of his intentions around to the magistrate, Mr. Lyons, while Delacourt shoved bread, cheese, and a pistol into a saddlebag.

"What I do not understand," persisted Delacourt as they made their way out of London, "is why you came to town when Jonet and the children are in Cambridgeshire?"

Cole reined his horse to the right and spurred it past the last dray lumbering up the Shoreditch Road. "I came looking for you," he said grimly as they started the uphill grade. "I needed to know what you were about, Delacourt, and Jonet refused to explain. I had no alternative but to call upon you myself."

Across the width of the road, Delacourt eyed him narrowly. "You thought I'd killed Mercer, did you not? Well, if a man can be convicted for his intentions, then you were not far wrong, Amherst. I meant to kill him—but on the field of honor. Fate spared me the chore."

"You speak rather indifferently of life and death," responded Cole, staring blindly over his horse's head. "Tell me, have you ever watched a man die?"

Delacourt snorted disdainfully, sending his horse prancing sideways. "Oh, is this to be my first brotherly lecture?" the viscount snapped, reining in his mount. "No, I have never killed a man. Not yet. But I am sure you have vast experience in the subject."

"Yes," replied Cole, eyeing him gravely. "Vast experience, Delacourt. More than I should ever wish for you."

"Look here, Amherst—let us get one thing straight here and now," retorted Delacourt, reining his mount closer to Cole. "If you think you're man enough to manage my sister, call the parson tomorrow and have at it. But I bloody well won't have you patronizing me. Do we understand one another, sir? My father—whomever one considers him to have been—is dead and I do not require another."

Cole turned to stare at the younger man, struggling to suppress the twitch of humor that played at his mouth. Good God, but Delacourt was an arrogant devil. Inwardly, Cole shrugged in resignation. His life with Jonet—assuming she would not refuse him now—would be fraught with challenges. Clearly, the young viscount was to be one of them, a trial which would sorely tax his Christian charity. But he had no choice, did he? If he loved Jonet, he would strive to make peace with her brother.

"So noted," he snapped, and whipped up his horse.

The remainder of the long journey passed swiftly, although it did not seem so to the two men who pushed their horses north at a near-brutal pace. They stopped only when absolutely necessary for rest and water. For the most part, they did not speak but merely eyed one another with dark, sidelong glances. Had Cole not been nearly terrified, he would have undoubtedly found their behavior laughable. Yet he found himself strangely glad for Delacourt's companionship.

It was nearing dusk when Cole finally spied the brick gateposts of Elmwood coming into view. Wordlessly, he raised his hand to point them out, and they turned their horses into the long stretch of drive that ran beneath the sweeping rows of elms. Under the dense foliage, it seemed both darker and colder, and Cole was struck with a bone-deep sense of foreboding.

Delacourt sensed it, too. "What do you mean to say when we arrive, Amherst?" he asked, his voice suddenly unsteady. "Tell me what you wish for me to do."

"I am not sure." Wearily, Cole scrubbed a hand down his face. "I think that we should find Jonet and the children, and take them all into the library. Once we have them safely together, you occupy the children, and I will take Jonet aside and try to explain. Though how the devil I'm to do it, I do not know. She will be utterly devastated."

Delacourt crooked one brow. "I detest belaboring the obvious, Amherst, but we have no evidence. And there is always a possibility that Jonet will refuse to believe us. The truth is so heinous, I can scarce believe it. Indeed, I persuaded the magistrates to end their investigation, merely to save Jonet's feelings! Now I feel like a damned fool."

Sickly, Cole stared at the younger man. "You feel like a fool? How the bloody hell do you think I feel? I ran off to throttle *you*, leaving the people I am responsible for—my future wife and children—to be murdered in their sleep or worse, may God forgive me."

For once, Delacourt looked contrite, and not a little sympathetic. "You have done all that could be done, Amherst, and that is far more than anyone else had managed to do. In any event, we are here now. All will be well. Nothing can possibly have happened in such a short time. Besides, did you not say that they had all been ill?"

But just then, the house burst into view. Despite the late hour, Charlie Donaldson stood on the top step, a broom in one hand. With a soldier's instinct, the butler must have sensed their disquiet. Tossing down the broom, he hastened down the steps just as Delacourt dismounted. Donaldson's eyes widened at the sight of the man whom he had been ordered to bar from the house, but he said nothing. Cole let his horse's reins drop. "Where is Jonet?" he asked harshly.

Donaldson snapped to attention. "Out wi' the children, sir."

Suddenly, Cole froze. "Out where? With whom?" he asked sharply.

Suddenly, he realized that Delacourt was wrong—! Something had happened. Or was about to happen. He knew it with a cold, sickening certainty. All of his hard-fought control threatened to snap. Panic warred with anger. "Damn it, Donaldson—*where?* And where the hell is Miss Cameron?"

"I do na' know, sir," he responded, his face suddenly draining of all color. "Oh, my God," he said, his voice a weak, tremulous whisper. "You canna mean . . . oh, God! Come inside at once. Mrs. Birtwhistle may know where they've gone."

Cole burst into the entrance hall, Donaldson and Delacourt on his heels. He strode rapidly through the house, hoping for a few pathetic moments that the butler was mistaken. Perhaps Jonet had merely taken the boys into the gardens, and had since returned. But it was immediately clear that the drawing room and parlor were empty. The library and study were shut up, and instinctively, he sensed that the entire house was empty as well.

His heart leapt into his throat. *Where in God's name were they?* And what had he allowed to happen this time? Cole didn't give one whit for Delacourt's sympathy, because he *knew* how easy it was to fail to take care of one's family. And he had done it again. Cole's plan to remain calm went up in smoke as their heavy boots thundered down the corridor toward the back of the house. "Mrs. Birtwhistle!" he shouted, never breaking his stride until he pushed through the heavy kitchen door. "Mrs. Birtwhistle! Where the devil is Mrs. Rowland?"

The housekeeper and the new cook stood over the sturdy worktable, peering unhappily down at a pile of withered turnips. Terrified, the old woman jerked her head up, her hand flying to her heart. "Oh! At the st-stables, I b-believe," she managed to say. "Gone but five minutes, sir. Is ought amiss?"

At no time did it occur to Cole to introduce Delacourt, nor did the housekeeper seem to care. "With whom did she go?" he sharply returned.

Mrs. Birtwhistle's clawlike hand spasmed against her starched fichu. "Why, with that nice Miss Cameron, sir! She came in just beside herself, saying that she wanted the children to come with her to see some kittens, and she wanted Mrs. Rowland to go, too."

"God *damn* it all!" muttered Delacourt, bringing his fist down on top of the table. The housekeeper leapt back a pace as one of the turnips rolled off. "Which way are the bloody stables?"

The three of them exited the back of the house just as

Moseby brought their horses around. "Leave them and follow us, Moseby," said Cole.

Cole spoke softly as they walked, briefing Donaldson and Moseby. Together, the four of them approached until they were within a stone's throw of the building. Cole prayed to God that they were wrong, knowing all the while that he prayed in vain. Evil surrounded them, and the source of it was Ellen Cameron. It always had been. She had never seemed what she had appeared to be, and underneath, he had sensed it. How could he have failed to trust his instincts?

Through the falling dusk, Cole could see that the door stood open. Down the center aisle, in a stall near the end, a pale light shone, casting eerie, shifting shadows up the wall, as if someone working inside the stall carried a lantern. Silently, Cole motioned Moseby around back and Donaldson toward the loft. Together, he and Delacourt approached the open door. A strange, pungent odor assailed him. Delacourt's nostrils also flared wide, and he flicked Cole a worried glance. They stepped gingerly across the threshold just as a boyish giggle escaped the rear of the building.

"That one! The black one!" chortled Robert. "He's mine. I saw him first."

"I don't care," chimed Stuart. "I would rather have the yellow one. Mama? May I have the yellow one? Please? The one with the white ear?"

Oh, God! Sick, Cole stared into the gloom, watching the wicked shadows dance. *Jonet and the boys suspected nothing.* Unwittingly, trustingly, they had allowed themselves to be trapped in the back of a stable. There was no means of escape. And what now? What evil had Ellen planned? Did she have a knife? A gun?

But they could not blindly rush in! Ellen carried a flaming lantern, a far more deadly weapon in a dry, dusty stable. Stealth was their only weapon. Praying that one of his horses would not whicker in greeting, Cole jerked his head sharply, indicating that Delacourt should follow him. The smell grew thicker. What the devil was it? Turpentine? Oil? And something else. *Alcohol?*

"Mama," whined Robert, as if his mother were ignoring him. "Can I have the black one?"

"I—yes, I daresay you may if Mr. Moseby agrees," Jonet finally answered. Her sharp voice, edged with concern, carried easily over the stall. "Ellen! What, pray, is that smell?"

"*Hmm?* What?" The lamplight shifted erratically, and Ellen Cameron's pleasant voice could be heard. "Oh, the smell? Why, it is my own secret concoction, cousin. I sprinkled it on the straw to keep down the fleas. Poor kittens! Yes, yes . . . oh, are they not cute? Look, Jonet—blue eyes! I think this one must be yours."

Jonet ignored her explanation. "But Ellen, it smells like . . . like brandy and—*ugk*—something else," she responded fractiously.

Cole and Delacourt had neared the half-open door. Inside, something bumped against the wall. Through the opening, Cole saw a flash of green muslin. Ellen Cameron was backing out the door with the lantern in her hand. Cole leaned toward Delacourt. "The *lantern!*" he mouthed. "Take her down if you can but do not let the lantern fall! I shall try to seize it."

Even in the dim light, Delacourt looked pale. "This place is a tinderbox! Be careful!"

Cole nodded, and they took two steps forward. But they were still several feet away when Ellen darted into the walkway and shoved the heavy stall door shut behind her. From inside the box, Jonet's voice rang out, sharp and angry. "Ellen? Ellen! Open this door at once!"

As if she had not heard her cousin's demand, Ellen laughed softly, then whirled about. Aloft, she held the burning lantern by its handle, sending an eerie yellow light swinging up and down the walkway. The lantern was huge, and brimming with oil.

Ellen faltered when Cole stepped out of the shadows. From inside, Jonet's fist pounded on the wall. "Ellen! Open this door now!"

In the background, one of the boys began to sob. "Mama, I want out!" Robert wailed. "It's too dark in here!" Ellen stared at Cole, her lamp held high. High enough to send it hurling over the wall with one good swing. *Which was exactly what she meant to do!* Dear God! The door was secured from outside. The inside would ignite like dry kindling. A dreadful accident, Ellen would no doubt have claimed. Both the children were now beginning to wail.

"Jonet!" Cole shouted, willing away the fiery vision. "Jonet, I am here. There is no need to be frightened. But you must all be very still. Miss Cameron is playing a game."

"A—a *game?*" Jonet's voice was incredulous and unsteady.

"I don't want to play a game!" cried Stuart pitifully, beating on the door. "I want out!"

In the pale lamplight, Ellen Cameron's mouth curled up into an insane smile. "Ah, but play we shall," she whispered into the darkness. "And a *dangerous* game at that, Captain Amherst. I always knew you were too smart by half."

Delacourt shifted his weight as if to rush her. *"Tut, tut!"* Ellen sharply reproved, thrusting the lamp forward in a swinging *swoosh!* of light. "I shouldn't come closer, my lord, if I were you!" Her eyes were alight with an unholy gleam.

"Don't be a fool, Ellen!" responded Delacourt. "I'll shoot you where you stand."

Damn! Delacourt had drawn his pistol. Cole prayed he wouldn't shoot. If Ellen fell, the burning lantern would tumble into the hay. Oil would spill everywhere. Even on this side of the box stall, the blaze would likely be uncontrollable. There would be no getting them out alive.

Ellen lifted her chin and laughed, a sharp, wicked sound. "Never fear, my lord! I mean to play my game to the end this time. Come one step closer, and you'll smell burning flesh all the sooner!" She jerked her head toward the bolted door.

"*You heartless bitch!*" hissed Delacourt in a voice so low Cole barely heard it. The smile slowly slipped from Ellen's face.

"Why, you know nothing of *heartlessness*, my lord," she said softly, setting her head at an angle and studying him intently. "You with your lofty title and fine estates! You know nothing of what it is like to be *no one*. Just a woman, torn from the home she cherishes! Begging off relatives! Pushed to marry so she won't be in the way!" Her tone took on an edge of madness.

"*Ellen—!*" Pleadingly, Cole's voice cut her off, then dropped to a whisper. "Think of the children! For God's sake, put down that lamp and let us talk!"

"No!" Ellen's gaze began to shift anxiously back and forth between them. "No, we will not *talk!* I deserve to be the Countess of Kildermore! I love it better than anyone! And I know you're in love with Jonet—like every other man who crosses her path! Jonet, the beauty! Jonet, who has everything." Ellen's voice almost broke, and as if in response to her weakness, she forced the lantern higher, sending it swinging precariously from its bracket. "While all my life, I've been like a dog, something you might throw a bone to. Well, you'll not be so quick with your charity now, will you?"

"Ellen," said Cole harshly, "it is not too late. Please!" Desperately, Cole tried to maneuver toward a solution. If Delacourt grabbed Ellen, could Cole safely wrestle the lamp from her grip? Or would she be too quick for either of them? Clearly, Ellen was insane. She had little to lose now. Talking was futile. Stalling was increasingly dangerous.

Just then, a light dusting of hay drifted down through the lamp's glow, settling like snow over Ellen's hair and shoulders. For one brief moment, her gaze flicked upward into the darkness of the loft, and just as quickly, back down again.

The day had been hot, with nary a breeze to stir the air. That meant only one thing. *Donaldson!* The well-trained soldier had strategically positioned himself over the enemy. Suddenly, a huge cloud of hay cascaded from the loft. It was enough to send Ellen stumbling backward, coughing and flailing as the dust settled.

Cole had but a moment to decide. He darted forward. His fingers brushed the lantern just as Ellen regained her balance. She jerked hard against his grasp. Hot glass scorched the back of his hand. Twisting his knuckles away, Cole struggled to grip the handle.

Suddenly, Delacourt dived in low, trying to knock her off balance. Ramming his head into her chest, he tightened his arms and tried to squeeze the breath from her. Ellen grunted viciously. The lantern swung wild. From above, Donaldson dropped with a *thud,* landing in the darkness behind Cole.

Still, Ellen fought, cursing and biting as Delacourt tried to wrestle her under control. She had the strength of a madwoman. Cole shifted forward, leaning over her, fighting to keep the lamp upright.

With a last desperate snarl, Ellen sunk her teeth into

Delacourt's ear and jerked. Blood trickled off his earlobe as the viscount cursed, then shoved her roughly away from the door and into the depths of the stable. Cole followed the struggling pair, fighting to steady the lantern. Finally he got a solid grip.

Seizing the moment, Donaldson rushed in. He rammed back the door latch and rushed a white-faced Jonet and the sobbing boys to safety.

As they disappeared into the darkness, Ellen cried aloud, the low, keening wail of a mortally wounded animal. At last, she let go of the lamp, slumping awkwardly in Delacourt's arms, and striking her head against the corner of the last stall. Muttering a curse, she looked up at them, her expression glazed. Roughly, Cole jerked her to her feet as Moseby stepped out of the gloom, a length of thin rope at the ready. *It was over.*

It was almost midnight when Cole left the magistrate's office and began the short ride back to Elmwood, his emotions a maelstrom of sorrow and relief. Relief that the secret evil which had for so long threatened Jonet was now over, but sorrow for all that had happened, and for what he must now tell her. His hat in his hands, Cole stood for a long while in the driveway, quietly drinking in the sounds and smells of Elmwood at night, and finding himself strangely comforted by the light which shone in his parlor window.

At last, he went up the steps and pushed open the door, only to find Jonet waiting in the darkness of the hall. She came silently toward him, her expression perfectly mirroring his own emotions. Her arms came around him then, and for a long, silent moment, they simply held one another, her head tucked neatly beneath his chin. Cole let his hands slide up and down the black silk of her mourning gown, soothing as best he could the trembling which still vibrated deep within her.

"My darling, I am so sorry," he murmured into her hair, trying to infuse a lifetime of meaning into the inadequate words. Jonet was his everything. His hope. His dream. His future. And he had very nearly failed to protect her. Cole was very much afraid he would never get over that terror. But eventually, the soft sound of Delacourt deliberately clearing his throat interrupted them. Cole opened his eyes to see the viscount framed in the parlor door.

Nodding in acknowledgement, he set Jonet gently away and stared deep into her blue-black eyes. "I think we three need to talk, my dear," he said softly. "Are you up to it?"

"Yes," she answered hollowly, hardening her expression. Together, the three of them went in, Delacourt pausing long enough to pour out a tumbler of cognac. Without comment, he pressed it into Cole's hand.

Despite the summer evening, a small fire burned in the parlor hearth, no doubt for Jonet's benefit. The shock she had sustained had been profound. She had been betrayed by someone she held dear, and the worst was yet to come. Gently, Cole urged her into a chair by the fireplace and set his glass upon the mantel. Delacourt took the chair opposite, his eyes never leaving Jonet's face. Standing to one side, Cole rubbed pensively at one temple with his fingertips.

"I think," he said softly, "that we must all decide what we are to say to the children in the morning. But first, my dear, I am afraid I have some . . . grim news."

As if impelled by instinct, Jonet's hand went to her throat, as her gaze, flat and distant, turned to Cole. "Ellen is dead, is she not?"

Slowly, Cole nodded. "Yes. It was . . . yet another unforeseen tragedy."

Delacourt leaned urgently forward in his chair, but he did not look surprised. "She did herself in, is that what you mean to say?"

Again, Cole nodded, heartsick. Although Ellen Cameron had been tormented and evil, Jonet had loved her. "It happened at the King's Arms," he said quietly. "The constable secured her in an upstairs chamber to await the London magistrate, and while we talked in the taproom, she somehow . . ."

"Hung herself?" finished Jonet flatly as she stared into the fire.

"Yes."

"Oh, God," said Jonet softly. "And may God forgive her! But I am relieved. For it is better that than a lifetime in Bedlam or a public hanging."

"Bloody hell," whispered Delacourt, then he tossed off the rest of his cognac. "First murder, then suicide! Gad, who'd have guessed old Ellen was mad as a March hare? And yet, we should have put it together. No doubt her knowledge of plants and gardening gave her a passing familiarity with poisons. Yet no one ever suspected that she'd done in old Mercer."

"Because it was an accident," murmured Cole. "She never meant to kill Mercer. She had no claim to his title, only Jonet's. But after Mercer died, I daresay she took a secret pleasure in seeing Jonet vilified."

"Yes, by God, I think she reveled in it! She wanted us to think her a silly, simpering spinster. But it was nothing more than a carefully crafted role," said Delacourt softly. "But why now? After all these years?"

Cole shook his head. "Ellen once said that *heaven had no rage like love to hatred turn'd—*"

"*—nor hell a fury like a woman scorn'd,*" finished Jonet softly, her gaze distant and unseeing. Slowly she glanced from David to Cole. "But she referred to herself, did she not? She felt scorned by the world, even by fate itself. She always envied me. And slowly, she came to hate me, didn't she? She truly came to hate me." Her words were edged with pain.

"I daresay a lifetime of envy finally drove her mad," answered Cole softly, going down on one knee by Jonet's chair and taking her small, cold hands into his own.

Jonet stared down at their entwined fingers. "Yes, I think you are right. Ellen's aunt had become increasingly desperate to get her wed to someone. Not out of cruelty, mind you, but because she knew her own health was failing."

"Yes," interposed Delacourt. "But Ellen probably saw it as her last chance to seize what she wanted. Else she might be married off, and sent to live who knows where. And then, you and the children would have been beyond her grasp. The possibility of inheriting, of being able to live independently—and at Kildermore—must have tantalized her."

Jonet gave a little cry, a sharp, agonizing sound. "Oh, I knew Ellen loved Kildermore more than I ever did," she agreed, her voice tormented. "All my life, I have had to live with the fact that she envied my position as heir. A position I never even wanted! And so I tried . . . oh, I tried so hard. To give her *everything*—money, society, sisterhood! But it was not enough!"

"No," said Delacourt grimly. "Apparently not."

"Good God, she meant to kill my children," Jonet cried, her voice anguished. "She poisoned food, she hired thugs, and whispered her little insinuations. And then she stood in the wings and watched us all suffer! And for what? To inherit a title? A house? Oh, for that, I shall never forgive her!" Slowly, she lifted her eyes to Cole's. "Do not fear that I shall grieve over her, for I shan't. My children have been saved from a monster."

"Good," said Delacourt firmly. "And you need no longer worry about the opinion of the *ton*. After this, your position in society will be restored to you in full measure."

"Oh, David, I hardly think I care!" Her gaze turned to Cole, softening. "But I do care about protecting my boys. What shall we say to them?"

"The truth," Cole answered hollowly. "Or at least a carefully worded version of the truth. We will say that Ellen was . . . *not well*. Unfortunately, we cannot shelter our children from all the world's evil. Stuart and Robert have not only been left fatherless, they have been terrorized in a way no child should ever suffer. I'd gladly tarnish Ellen's memory to give them peace, if I must."

Jonet looked up at him then, her expression measurably calmer. "Yes. Yes, you are right," she said, her voice lifting. "This horrible nightmare is over, and we are safe. Now we must look to our future—one which will be bright and happy. I am sure of it."

"Well! That, I daresay, is my cue," answered Delacourt, jerking from his chair. "Having unintentionally flung myself upon your hospitality, Amherst, I am now for bed." Swiftly, he bent down to peck Jonet's cheek, and then, the viscount was gone.

Slowly, Jonet rose from her chair and closed the distance between them, taking Cole's hands in hers. "You are wrong about something, my darling," she said quietly. "My boys have suffered a great loss, yes. But I believe they have not been left entirely fatherless."

Roughly, Cole pulled her into his embrace and gazed into her eyes for a seemingly timeless moment. "Do you still mean to have me, then?" he asked softly.

Jonet looked at him in some surprise. "Oh, yes," she whispered. "I need you, Cole. And I most assuredly mean to have you. And I swear that I will do my best to be a good and obedient w—"

But Jonet never finished her sentence, because her husband-to-be was kissing the almost certain lie from her lips, worshiping her deeply and desperately with his mouth, and cradling her head between his big, capable hands.

And what did it matter, really? They both knew that Jonet would never be good. And probably never obedient—unless it suited her to do so. There were some burdens on this temporal earth which God simply expected a man to bear, Cole decided. And Jonet was his.

The fact that her mouth felt like his heavenly reward was not lost on him.

Epilogue

The very ecstasy of Love

The afternoon sun was setting, casting a warm, pink glow over the westerly sky. One hand set at his hip, Cole stood alone at his bedchamber window, drinking in the brisk spring air and gazing at the burgeoning swath of yellow that had recently brightened his garden. In his left hand, he held open a book, the phrases running absently through his head.

"*To everything there is a season—?*" he muttered, staring over his spectacles as Stuart went ripping through the bed of daffodils. Robert and the dogs followed on his heels, howling wildly.

"Ugh! That theme is overused!" Cole shook his head, then pensively, he pinched the bridge of his nose and tried again. "*Easter, a new beginning—?* No, no . . . too trite."

Suddenly, two very warm hands encircled his waist and ran up his waistcoat. "What is too trite, my darling?" asked Jonet lightly, pressing her cheek against his back.

Cole's attention snapped back to the present. With great care, he set aside the book and spectacles, turned gently in his wife's arms, and smiled down at her. "Never mind," he said, his eyes taking in the deep green silk of her dress. "My dear," he said, tucking a lock of her hair behind her ear, "you look the very image of springtime. That gown is most becoming."

Jonet looked coyly up at him from beneath a sweep of black eyelashes. "*Most* becoming?" she echoed, her voice suddenly dark and sultry, her busy fingers now massaging the back of his shoulders. Beyond the window, the boys' happy shouts filled the air.

Cole set his wife a little away from him. "Jonet?" he said, tilting his head to study her suspiciously. "What are you up to?"

In response, Jonet let her hands drift down to the small of his back and drew his hips into hers. With a sigh, Cole let his eyes drop shut as she skimmed her warm mouth up his throat and along the curve of his jaw. "*Umm,*" she moaned invitingly when her lips reached his earlobe. "Come with me, sir, and I will show you." Lending urgency to her request, Jonet's fingers brushed lower still.

Cole opened his eyes to look down at her, trying to maintain a sober expression. "Come with you where?" he asked warily, pulling back to study her. "Jonet, you are very wicked. I am trying to work, and you are tempting me to neglect my obligations."

Jonet's mouth formed a perfect pout. "Is marriage not an obligation?" she asked sulkily, one finger coming up to lightly brush his bottom lip. "Some men would say it is the worst sort of obligation, you know! And why is it wicked when a wife wishes a moment alone with her husband?"

It was on the tip of Cole's tongue to say that, after almost a year and a half of marriage to her, the word *obligation* had never once sprung to mind. But his retort melted in a rush of desire, because by then, Jonet had him by the hand and was leading him—not completely against his will—across the floor of his bedchamber and into the dressing room.

With the skill of a man who has had much practice, Cole easily kicked the door shut behind him, plunging them into utter darkness. And then, Jonet's mouth was on his, warm, eager, and infinitely comforting. Just as it always was. Instinctively, his arms banded her to his chest.

"My darling," she whispered, barely lifting her mouth

from his, "remember when you promised me that we would make love in every room at Elmwood?"

"Yes? . . ."

"Well, we missed one."

"Did we indeed?" he managed to murmur, finally certain he knew what she was up to, and knowing there was little point in arguing. Pausing long enough to ensure her door was also shut, Cole slid out of his coat and began returning her fervent kisses, his temperature quickly ratcheting up. Desperately, Jonet's hands tugged free his shirt, then slid beneath the fabric, making him moan her name into the sweet recesses of her mouth. He jerked her harder against him, and in one smooth motion, rucked up a fistful of green silk and let his palm slide beneath the soft swell of her buttocks, expecting to feel the fine lawn of her drawers. But Jonet had already taken them off!

He sighed with pleasure at the feel of her. Of course, it was sheer folly to be fondling one's wife in the middle of the day, but Cole had long ago given up trying to reason with Jonet. And after all, he had promised. Jonet pressed a little closer, until suddenly, a little alarm bell went off in the hazy recesses of his mind. He tried without success to push her away. "Jonet," he whispered urgently, "what about the baby?"

"Napping," she murmured desperately against the hot flesh of his throat.

Cole tried to shake his head. "Not *Arabella!*" he insisted, wedging one hand between them and smoothing it over her stomach. "*This* one."

Jonet had the audacity to giggle. "Oh, come here," she whispered urgently, ignoring his question and pulling him toward the chair in the corner. Halfway across the floor, Cole tripped over something—it felt like Jonet's riding boot—and muttered a soft curse.

He struggled to regain his balance, only to find himself being summarily shoved into the chair. In the darkness, Jonet's fingers worked feverishly at the close of his trousers. No longer able to maintain even the pretext of resistance, Cole groaned deeply when at last Jonet took him, hot and throbbing, into her strong, capable hands.

"Oh, have mercy, Jonet," he moaned, his hands going to her waist and dragging up her skirts. "I love you more than life itself, but if you mean to do this, *hurry up!*"

Without another word, she straddled his knees and laid her hands lightly atop his shoulders. Urgently, Cole guided himself toward the warm welcome he knew he would find, but Jonet, too, was impatient. She slid onto him hard and fast, drawing in her breath on a deep, hungry gasp. *"Oh, Cole—!"* she moaned appreciatively as he buried himself up to the hilt.

With his hands, Cole circled her waist, which was only now beginning to thicken with pregnancy. Gently, he lifted her, reveling in Jonet's soft sounds of pleasure. She moved against him, slowly at first, until eventually her motions took on a wild urgency.

With a mindless silence, Cole thrust inside her, the utter darkness of the room serving to heighten his sensual awareness, fanning the flames of his desperation to lose himself inside his wife. He thought he would die from the pleasure. With Jonet, he always did. But he hadn't—not yet, anyway. He thrust inside her again, feeling that sweet edge of release slide near them both.

The knock on the door came out of nowhere.

Cole froze in midmotion, grappling for reality. He glanced across the room to see a shadow darkening the shaft of light that shone beneath Jonet's door. On his lap, Jonet whimpered and shifted her weight. *"The boys?"* she asked witheringly.

"They're outside," Cole responded, his mouth pressed to her ear.

Beyond the door, heavy feet shuffled uneasily. "*My lady—?*" Donaldson's whisper was hesitant, yet urgent. "My lady? Are you in there? Verra sorry tae disturb you, but his lordship is below."

"Oh, God, what now?" muttered Jonet, in a tone loud enough to be heard beyond the door.

Donaldson shuffled again. "He's in quite a bad state, too, ma'am. A wee bit drunk."

In the darkness, Cole rolled his eyes, and Jonet's head fell forward to touch his. Her exasperation was understandable. During the first year of their marriage, Delacourt's escapades had become legendary, and Jonet's role as elder sister had been mightily taxed.

Of course, society—deprived of Jonet in the role of murderess—had cast her in the role of Delacourt's tragically lost love. That, combined with the utter humiliation of being bested by a quiet cavalry officer, was said to be the root of Delacourt's misbehavior. Cole suppressed a snort of amazement.

"My lady—?" Donaldson sounded pitiful.

"Oh, what does he *want—?*" repeated Jonet, her words ending on a frustrated wail.

Donaldson hesitated. "He says he has urgent business with *The Reverend Mr. Amherst*—his exact words, ma'am—and says I'm tae fetch him doon straightaway," he answered through the heavy oak. "Says he has need of a parson. And he's in a rare foul temper, that he is."

Nothing rare about his temper, thought Cole grimly. He was always in one. Worse, his visits inevitably heralded some impending disaster, but this time, the viscount's search for sympathy was particularly inconvenient. And this time, he had not asked for Jonet . . .

"Oh, all right, Charlie!" Jonet answered peevishly. On Cole's lap, she stirred ever so slightly, tightening on his shaft, then with a resigned sound, began to lift herself off.

Stubbornly, Cole tightened his grip around her waist and growled in the back of his throat. Delacourt could bloody well wait! Jonet sighed with pleasure and glided back down. And then up. Snug, silken heat flowed over him.

Beyond the door, Charlie waited.

Jonet rose up once more, and Cole could not restrain his hands from going to her bodice to tug downward on the green silk to expose the swell of her breasts spilling out of her stays. Jonet's head tipped back as a deep shudder coursed through her. "*Ahh*—" she softly breathed.

"M'lady?" whimpered Donaldson. "What am I tae do w' his lordship?"

Jonet snapped back to attention, her body jerking taut. "Oh, for pity's sake!" she screeched. "Tell him to go straight to—"

"—the drawing room," interjected Cole, swiftly clapping a hand over her mouth. "She wants you to send him straight to the drawing room," he repeated.

Jonet's tongue came out to tease at the palm of his hand. Very deliberately, she tightened on his shaft and slid partway up.

"Yes!" said Cole loudly. "Tell him that I . . . I will attend him there . . . *soon!*"

"Soon, did ye say?" asked Donaldson anxiously.

"*Very* soon!" confirmed Cole, falling deeper in love with Lord Delacourt's sister with every passing moment.

Turn the page for excerpts of
Liz Carlyle's latest trilogy:

One Little Sin

Two Little Lies

Three Little Secrets

One Little Sin

Upon returning home, Alasdair waved away his butler's questions about dinner, tossed his coat and cravat on a chair, and flung himself across the worn leather sofa in his billiards-room. Then he promptly slipped back into the alcohol-induced stupor which had served him so well on the carriage ride from Surrey.

For a time, he just dozed, too indolent to rise and go up to bed. But shortly before midnight, he was roused by a racket at his windows. He cracked one eye to see that the unseasonable heat had given way to a thunderstorm. Snug and dry on his sofa, Alasdair yawned, scratched, then rolled over and went back to sleep, secure in life as he knew it.

But his lassitude was soon disturbed again when he was jolted from a dream by a relentless pounding at his front door. He tried mightily to ignore it, and to cling to the remnants of his fantasy—something to do with Bliss, the beautiful Gypsy, and a bottle of champagne. But the pounding came again, just as the Gypsy was trailing her fingertips seductively along his backside.

Out of annoyance rather than concern, Alasdair crawled off the sofa, scratched again, and headed out into the passageway which overlooked the stairs. In the foyer below, Wellings had flung open the door. Alasdair looked down to see that someone—a female servant, he supposed—stood on his doorstep carrying, strangely enough, a basket of damp laundry.

Wellings's nose was elevated an inch, a clear indication

of his disdain. "As I have twice explained, madam," he was saying, "Sir Alasdair does not receive unescorted young females."

He moved as if to shut the door, but the woman gracelessly shoved first her foot, and then her entire leg, inside. "Now you'll whisht your blether and listen, sir!" said the woman in a brogue as tart as Granny McGregor's. "You'll be fetching your master down here, and making haste about it, for I'll not be taking *no* for an answer."

Alasdair knew, of course, that he was making a grievous error. But drawn by something he could not name—temporary insanity, perhaps—he began slowly to descend the stairs. His caller, he realized, was not a woman, but a girl. And the laundry was . . . well, not laundry. Halfway down the stairs, he cleared his throat.

At once, Wellings turned, and the girl looked up. It was then that Alasdair felt a disembodied blow to the gut. The girl's eyes were the clearest, purest shade of green he'd ever seen. Like the churning rush of an Alpine stream, the cool, clean gaze washed over him, leaving Alasdair breathless, as if he'd just been dashed with ice water. "You wished to see me, miss?" he managed.

Her gaze ran back up, and settled on his eyes. "Aye, if your name is MacLachlan, I do," she said. "And you look about as I expected."

Alasdair did not think the remark was meant to be a compliment. He wished to hell he was fully sober. He had the most dreadful feeling he ought to be on guard against this person, slight, pale, and damp though she might be.

"Miss Esmée Hamilton," she said crisply.

Alasdair managed a cordial smile. "A pleasure, Miss Hamilton," he lied. "Do I know you?"

"You do not," she said. "Nonetheless, I need a moment of your time. A *private* moment."

Alasdair looked pointedly down at her. "It is rather an odd hour, Miss Hamilton."

"Aye, well, I was given to understand you kept odd hours."

Alasdair's misgiving deepened. With a slight bow, and a flourish of his hand, he directed the girl into the parlor, then sent Wellings away for tea and dry towels. The girl bent over the sofa nearest the fire, and fussed over her bundle a moment.

Who the devil was she? A Scot, to be sure, for she made no pretense of glossing over her faint burr. And despite her damp, somewhat dowdy attire, she looked to be of genteel birth. Which meant the sooner he got her the hell out of his house, the safer it was for both of them. On that thought, he returned to the parlor door, and threw it open again.

She looked up from the sofa with a disapproving frown.

"I fear my butler may have mistaken your circumstances, Miss Hamilton," said Alasdair. "I think it unwise for a young lady of your tender years to be left alone with me."

Just then, the bundle twitched. Alasdair leapt out of his skin. "Good Lord!" he said, striding across the room to stare at it. A little leg had poked from beneath smothering heap of blankets. Miss Hamilton threw back the damp top layer, and at once, Alasdair's vision began to swim, but not before he noticed a tiny hand, two drowsy, long-lashed eyes, and a perfect little rosebud of a mouth.

"She is called Sorcha," whispered Miss Hamilton. "Unless, of course, you wish to change her name."

Alasdair leaped back as if the thing might explode. "Unless I wish—wish—to *what*?"

"To change her name," Miss Hamilton repeated, her cool gaze running over him again. "As much as it pains me, I must give her up."

Alasdair gave a cynical laugh. "Oh, no," he said, his tone implacable. "That horse won't trot, Miss Hamilton. If ever I had bedded you, I would most assuredly remember it."

Miss Hamilton drew herself up an inch. "Good God! What a revolting notion!"

"I beg your pardon," he said stiffly. "Perhaps I am confused. Pray tell me why you are here. And be warned, Miss Hamilton, that I'm nobody's fool."

The girl's mouth twitched at one corner. "Aye, well, I'm pleased to hear it, MacLachlan," she answered. "I'd begun to fear otherwise."

Alasdair was disinclined to tolerate an insult from a girl who resembled nothing so much as a wet house wren. Then he considered how he must look. He'd been sleeping in his clothes—the same clothes he'd put on at dawn to wear to the boxing match. He'd had rampant sex in a pile of straw, been shot at and chased by a madman, then drunk himself into a stupor during a three-hour carriage drive. And his hair was standing on end. Self-consciously, he dragged a hand through it.

She was looking at him with some strange mix of disdain and dread, and inexplicably, he wished he had put on his coat and cravat. "Now, see here, Miss Hamilton," he finally managed. "I really have no interest in being flayed by your tongue, particularly when—"

"Och, you'd be right, I know!" The disdain, if not the dread, disappeared. "But I've been on the road above a sen'night, and another two days trying to find you in this hellish, filthy city."

"*Alone*—?"

"Save for Sorcha, aye," she admitted. "My apologies."

Alasdair reined in his temper. "Sit down, please, and take off your wet coat and gloves," he commanded. "Now, tell me, Miss Hamilton. Who is the mother of this child, if you are not?"

At last, some color sprang to her cheeks. "My mother," she said quietly. "Lady Achanalt."

"Lady Acha-*who*?"

"Rosamund, wife of Lord Achanalt." The girl frowned. "You—you do not remember her?"

To his consternation, he did not, and admitted as much.

"Oh, dear." Her color deepened. "Poor Mamma! She fancied, I think, that you would take her memory to the grave, or some such romantic nonsense."

"To the grave?" he echoed, fighting down a sick feeling. "Where the devil is she?"

"Gone to hers, I'm sorry to say." Her hand went to the dainty but expensive-looking strand of pearls at her neck, and she began to fiddle with them nervously. "She passed just last month. My stepfather is not precisely grief-stricken."

"My sympathies, Miss Hamilton."

Miss Hamilton paled. "Save your sympathies for your daughter," she said. "She was conceived at Hogmanay, two years past. Does that jag your brain a wee bit?"

Alasdair felt slightly disoriented. "Well . . . no."

"But you must recall it," Miss Hamilton pressed. "There was a ball—a masquerade—in Edinburgh. A bacchanalian rout, I collect. You met her there. *Didn't* you?"

His blank face must have shaken her.

"Good Lord, she said you told her it was love at first sight!" Her voice was a little desperate now. "She said it was a grand passion!"

Alasdair searched his mind, and felt sicker still. He *had* been in Edinburgh some two years ago, because his Uncle Angus had returned from abroad for a brief visit. They had spent Hogmanay together. In Edinburgh. And there *had* been a ball. Alasdair remembered little, save for the roaring headache he'd suffered the following day.

"Oh, well!" Her voice was resigned. "Mamma was ever a fool for a pretty face."

A pretty face? The young woman was still sitting on the sofa beside the sleeping child, staring up at him. Her gaze was no longer so cool and clear, but instead weary and a little sad. Alasdair pressed his fingertips to his temple. "Dear God, what a mess!"

She looked at him sorrowfully. "'Tis rather too late for prayers," she said. "Look, MacLachlan, my mother is dead, and it falls to you."

Two Little Lies

Signorina Alessandri was ill. Again. With one hand restraining the flowing folds of her fine silk nightclothes, she lurched over the close-stool in her Covent Garden flat and prayed, in fluent and fervid Italian, for death to take her.

"Oh, please, miss, *do* speak English!" begged her maid, who had caught her heavy black hair, and drawn it back, too. "I can't make out a word. But I do think we'd best fetch a doctor."

"Nonsense," said the signorina, clenching the back of the close-stool in a white-knuckled fist. "It was the fish Lord Chesley served last night."

The maid pursed her lips. "Aye, and what was it yesterday, miss?" she asked. "Not fish, I'll wager."

With the other hand set at the small of her back, Viviana closed her eyes, and somehow straightened up. "*Silenzio*, Lucy," she said softly. "We talk of it no further. The worst is over now."

"Oh, I doubt that," said the maid.

Viviana ignored her, and went instead to the washbasin. "Where is the morning's post, *per favore*?" she asked, awkwardly slopping the bowl full of water.

With a sigh, Lucy went into the parlor and returned with a salver which held one letter covered in her father's infamous scrawl, and a folded note which bore no address. "Mr. Hewitt's footman brought it," she said offhandedly.

With hands that shook, Viviana finished her ablutions, then patted a towel across her damp face as her maid looked on in consternation. The girl had been both loyal and kind these many months. "Thank you, Lucy," she said. "Why do you not go have a cup of tea? I shall read my letter now."

Lucy hesitated. "But do you not wish your bathwater brought, miss?" she pressed. "'Tis already past noon. Mr. Hewitt will be here soon, won't he?"

Quin. Lucy was right, of course. Viviana laid aside the towel and took the note. Quin usually came to her in the early afternoon. And oh, how she longed for it—yet dreaded it in the same breath.

She tossed the note into the fire. She had not missed the furious looks he'd hurled her way in the theatre's reception room last night. Viviana had sung gloriously, hitting every high note in her last aria with a chilling, crystal-clear resonance, before collapsing onto the stage in a magnificent swoon. The theater had been full, the applause thunderous.

But all Quin had seemed to notice was what had come afterward. The compliments and congratulations of her admirers. The champagne toasts. The subtle, sexual invitations tossed her way by the lift of a brow or a tilt of the head—and refused just as subtly in turn. It had not been refusal enough for Quin. One could hardly have ignored his cocky stance and sulky sneer as he paced the worn green carpet, a glass of brandy clutched in his hand. His uncle, Lord Chesley, had even had the effrontery to tease him about it.

Quin had not taken that well. Nor had he been especially pleased to see Viviana leaving on Chesley's arm, as she so often did. And today, God help them, he would undoubtedly wish to quarrel over it. Viviana was not at all sure she was capable of mounting a spirited defense. But it almost didn't matter any more.

"Miss?" said the maid. "Your bathwater?"

Nausea roiled in her stomach again, and Viviana moved gingerly to a chair. "In ten minutes, Lucy," she answered. "I shall read *Papà's* letter whilst my stomach settles. If I am late, I shall receive Mr. Hewitt here."

Lucy pursed her lips again. "Aye, then," she finally answered. "But I'd be telling him straightaway, miss, about that bad fish if I was you."

Finally, Viviana laughed.

The water was wonderfully hot when it came, and remarkably restorative. Feeling perhaps a little more at peace, Viviana was still luxuriating in it when Quin came stalking into the room. He looked at once angry, and yet almost boyishly uncertain.

He stared down at her naked body and gave her a tight, feral smile. "Washing away the evidence, Vivie?"

It was a cynical remark, even for him.

For a moment, she let her black eyes burn into him. "*Silenzio*, Quinten," she returned. "I had quite enough of your jealous sulking last night. Be civil, or go away."

He knelt by the tub, and rested one arm along its edge. His eyes were bleak today, the lines about his mouth almost shockingly deep for one so young. He smelled of brandy and smoke and the scents of a long, hard-spent night. "Is that what you want, Viviana?" he whispered. "Are you trying to drive me away?"

She dropped her soap into the water. "How, Quin?" she demanded, throwing up her hands in frustration. "*Dio mio*, how am I doing this driving? I am not, and that is the truth of it, *si*?"

He cast his eyes away, as if he did not believe her. "They say Lord Lauton has promised you a house in Mayfair, and more money than I could ever dream of," he answered. "Not until I come into my title, at any rate. Is it true, Vivie?"

She shook her head. "Quin, what would it matter if it

were?" she returned. "I am no longer for sale—perhaps not even to you. Why must you be so jealous?"

"How can I help but be, Viviana?" he rasped, brushing one finger beneath her left nipple. It peaked and hardened, begging for his touch. "Men's eyes feast upon you everywhere you go. But at least you still desire me."

Viviana glowered at him, but she did not push his hand away. "My body desires you, *si*," she admitted. "But sometimes, *amore mio*, my mind does not."

He plucked the nipple teasingly between his thumb and forefinger. "And what of your heart, Viviana?" he whispered, looking up at her from beneath a sweep of inky lashes. "I have your body ensconced, ever so circumspectly, in this flat which I have paid for. Have I your heart as well?"

"I have no heart!" she snapped. "That is what you told me when we quarreled last week, if you will recall. And you need not remind me, Quin, of who has put this roof over my head. I have become mindful of it with every breath I draw."

Three Little Secrets

"I can *show* you the house at the top of the hill." Merrick extracted a key from his coat pocket. "The millwork, the joinery, the floors and ceilings, all that will be similar unless you wish otherwise."

The din of construction faded into the distance as they walked. Still, Merrick could hear a muffled banging noise from within the topmost house as they went up the steps. "Someone is inside," said Wynwood.

"They damned well oughtn't be," said Merrick. "The first coat of paint just went on."

The banging did not relent. Merrick twisted the key. Sun glared through the large, undraped windows, leaving the air stifling hot, and rendering the smell of paint almost intolerable. At once, he and Wynwood started toward the racket—a side parlor which opened halfway along the central corridor. A tall, slender woman with cornsilk colored hair stood with her back to them, banging at one of the window-frames with the heels of her hands.

Merrick looked at Wynwood. "Excuse me," he said tightly. "The buyer, I presume."

"I shall just wander upstairs," said Wynwood, starting up the staircase. "I wish to size up the bedchambers."

"Oh, bloody damned hell!" said the woman in the parlor.

Merrick strode into the room. "Good God, stop banging on the windows!"

The woman shrieked, and spun halfway around. "Oh!"

She pressed both hands to her chest. "Oh, God! You nearly gave me heart failure!"

"It would be a less painful end than bleeding to death, I daresay."

"I beg your pardon?" She turned to face him, and inexplicably, his breath hitched. Her cool blue eyes searched his face.

"The paint sticks the windows shut," he managed to explain. "They must be razored open, ma'am. And if you persist in pounding at the sash, you're apt to get a gashed wrist for your trouble."

"Indeed?" Her eyebrows went up a little haughtily as she studied him. For a moment, he could not get his lungs to work. Dear God in heaven.

No. No, it could not be.

Merrick's thoughts went skittering like marbles. There must be some mistake. That damned wedding yesterday—that trip to the church—it had disordered his mind.

"Well, I shall keep your brilliant advice in mind," she finally went on. "Now, this room was to be hung with yellow silk, not painted. Dare I hope that you are someone who can get that fixed?"

"Perhaps." Merrick stepped fully into the room to better see her. "I am the owner of this house."

The brows inched higher. "Oh, I think not," she said, her voice low and certain. "I contracted for its purchase on Wednesday last."

"Yes, from my solicitors, perhaps," said Merrick. *Good God, surely . . . surely he was wrong.* For the first time in a decade, he felt truly unnerved. "I—er, I employ Mr. Rosenberg's firm to handle such transactions," he managed to continue. "Pray look closely at your contract. You will see that the seller is MacGregor & Company."

But her look of haughty disdain had melted into one

of grave misgiving. "And—and you would be Mr. MacGregor, then?" There was more than a question in her words. There was a pleading; a wish to avoid the unavoidable. Her dark green eyes slid down the scar which curved the length of his face. *She was not sure.* But he was. Dear God, he was.

"You look somewhat familiar," she went on. "I am . . . I am Lady Bessett. Tell me, have—have we met?"

Dear God! Had they met? A sort of nausea was roiling in his stomach now. He could feel the perspiration breaking on his brow. He opened his mouth with no notion of what he was to say. Just then, Wynwood came thundering down the stairs.

"Eight bedchambers, old chap!" The earl's shouting echoed through the empty house. "So a double would have sixteen, am I right?" He strode into the room, then stopped abruptly. "Oh, I do beg your pardon," he said, his eyes running over the woman. "My new neighbor, I collect? Pray introduce me."

Merrick felt as if all his limbs had gone numb. "Yes. Yes, of course." He lifted one hand by way of introduction. "May I present to you, ma'am, the Earl of Wynwood. Wynwood, this is . . . this is . . . " The hand fell in resignation. "This is Madeleine, Quin. This is . . . my wife."

The woman's face had drained of all color. She made a strange little choking sound, and in a blind, desperate gesture, her hand lashed out as if to steady herself. She grasped at nothing but air. Then her knees gave, and she crumpled to the floor in a pool of dark green silk.

"Christ Jesus!" said Wynwood. He knelt, and began to pat at her cheek. "Ma'am, are you all right? Ma'am?"

"No, she is not all right," said Merrick tightly. "She can't get her breath. This air—the paint—it must be stifling her. Quick, get back. We must get her air."

As if she were weightless, Merrick slid an arm under

Madeleine's knees, then scooped her into his arms. A few short strides, and they were outside in the dazzling daylight.

"Put her in the grass," Wynwood advised. "Good God, Merrick! Your *wife*? I thought—thought she was dead! Or—or gone off to India! Or some damned thing!"

"Athens, I believe," said Merrick. "Apparently, she has come back."

Gently, he settled Madeleine in the small patch of newly-sprouted grass. She was coming round now. His heart was in his throat, his mind racing with questions. Wynwood held one of her hands, and was patting at it vigorously. On his knees in the grass, Merrick set one hand on his thigh, and dropped his head as if to pray.

But there was little to pray for now.

He had prayed never to see Madeleine again. God had obviously denied him that one small mercy. He pinched his nose between two fingers, as if the pain might force away the memories.

Madeleine had managed to struggle up onto her elbows.

"I say, ma'am." Wynwood was babbling now. "So sorry. Didn't mean to frighten you. Are you perfectly all right? Haven't seen old Merrick in a while, I collect? A shock, I'm sure."

"Shut up, Quin," said Merrick.

"Yes, yes, of course," he agreed. "I shan't say a word. Daresay you two have lots to catch up on. I—I should go, perhaps? Or stay? Or—no, I have it! Perhaps Mrs. MacLachlan would like me to fetch some brandy?"

On this, the lady gave a withering cry, and pressed the back of her hand to her forehead.

"Do *shut up*, Quin," said Merrick again.

His eyes widened. "Yes, yes, I meant to do."

Madeleine was struggling to her feet now. Her heavy blonde hair was tumbling from its arrangement. "Let me up," she insisted. "Stand aside, for God's sake!"

"Oh, I shouldn't get up," Wynwood warned. "Your head is apt to be swimming still."

But Madeleine had eyes only for Merrick—and they were blazing with hot green rage. "I do not know," she hissed, "what manner of ill-thought joke this is, sir. But you—you are *not* my husband."

"Now is hardly the time to discuss it, Madeleine," Merrick growled. "Let me summon my carriage and see you safely to your lodgings."

But Madeleine was already backing away, her face a mask of horror. "No," she choked. "Absolutely not. You—you are quite mad. And cruel, too. Very cruel. I came to see it, you know. I *did*. Now stay away from me! Stay away! Do you hear?"

It was the closest she came to acknowledging she even knew him. And then she turned, and hastened up the hill on legs which were unsteady. A gentleman would have followed her at a distance, just to be sure she was capable of walking. Merrick no longer felt like a gentleman. He felt . . . eviscerated. Gutted like a fish, and left to rot in the heat of his wife's hatred.

Wynwood watched her go. "You know, I don't think she much cares for you, old chap," he said when Madeleine's skirts had swished round the corner and out of sight.

"Aye, that would explain her thirteen-year absence, would it not?" said Merrick sourly.

"More or less," his friend agreed. "I hope you were not looking forward to a reconciliation."

"Just shut up, Quin," said Merrick again.